DEATH AND RELAXATION

ORDINARY MAGIC - BOOK ONE

ALSO BY DEVON MONK

DEATH AND RELAXATION

ORDINARY MAGIC - BOOK ONE

DEVON MONK

Death and Relaxation Copyright © 2016 by Devon Monk

eBook ISBN: 978-1-939853-01-1
Paperback ISBN: 978-1-939853-02-8

Published by: Odd House Press
Art by: Lou Harper
Interior Design by: Indigo Chick Designs

DEDICATION

*To the makers and dreamers and believers of everyday magic.
And to my family, with love.*

CHAPTER 1

"DELANEY," MY father whispered. "Wake up."

I reached for the gun under my pillow and pushed the quilt aside. My heart hammered as I searched the shadows of the room for my dad.

He wasn't there. And he shouldn't be. He'd been dead for a year now.

"Dad?" I asked anyway. No reply. I took a few steady breaths until the dual waves of hope and grief that had crashed down over me were gone.

The night of his death was still embedded in my mind. My sisters and me responding to the emergency call. His truck crumpled at the bottom of the cliff. Ben Rossi and Jame Wolfe in their fire-fighting gear, rappelling down the sea cliff to bring his body out of the cab.

It hadn't been raining. The moon was full and bright enough I had almost forgotten to turn on the headlights of my Jeep.

Dry pavement, familiar road. They still didn't know how it had happened. Still didn't know why a man who had grown up in this little town on this little stretch of Oregon beach, a man who knew the roads like the beat of his own heart, had driven right off the edge of a cliff.

That night had ended what I'd always thought of as a normal life. The very next day I'd stepped up as Dad's successor as both the chief of police and the eldest Reed in town: the confidant to gods and monsters.

I set the gun next to my badge on the wooden stepladder I used as a side table and sighed.

I'd need to be at the station in a couple hours to relieve my sister, Jean, from the night shift. By the time I fell back to sleep—if I fell back to sleep—it would be time to get up. I rubbed a hand over my face and scrubbed hot, dry eyes.

It was going to take a lot of caffeine to get me through the day.

I stood and tugged at the Grateful Dead T-shirt that had belonged to Dad. I hadn't had the heart to give it to the thrift shop when we went through his things. I thought both my sisters had kept something of his too, probably something of more value. But I liked the comfort of something he'd loved and lounged in.

I rolled my shoulders—a little stiff from yesterday's run—and bare-footed it through the small living room and into the kitchen.

"If you are going to haunt me, Dad, I could use some helpful poltergeist action around here. Fold the laundry. Start the coffee."

I knew Dad wasn't listening. It was probably just a dream that had brought me awake so fast. But now that I was living alone in the old family home—both sisters moved out, no boyfriend moved in, both Dad and Mom gone—I'd fallen into my childhood habit of talking to myself.

"They say talking to yourself is a sign of genius," I said around a yawn.

Or loneliness.

Yeah, that too.

I pressed the button on the coffee pot I'd pre-loaded only a few hours ago and pulled a Chewbacca mug out of the cupboard.

I bit back another yawn and scooped sugar into where Chewbacca's brains should be.

I felt like I hadn't slept in a year. Taking over as chief of police in Ordinary, Oregon, on the heels of Dad's death had been hard even with my sisters Myra and Jean right beside me. It might have been easier if Cooper, my oh-so-ex-boyfriend, hadn't also decided to run off to "find himself" a week after the funeral.

But then, maybe it was better to have my heart broken by both Dad's death and my boyfriend's restless urges in such a short span of time. Breaking, that hard that fast, made the rebuilding easier.

Right?

"Sweet-talking Cooper Clark, the heartbreak hit-and-run I should have seen coming a mile away, you did me a favor by leaving. Life is so much easier without love."

Liar, my heart said.

I ignored it, just like I'd been doing for the past year, throwing all my energy into my job as peacekeeper, guardian, and law for all the mortals, creatures, and deities who made Ordinary their home.

My job also included dealing with the Rhubarb Rally, Ordinary's biggest spring tourist draw.

The normally quiet, if abnormally quirky, town would be transformed into a bustling little city over the next week or so.

If I got more than three hours of sleep between now and Friday when the Rhubarb Regatta sailed to shore for the festival blessing, it'd be a miracle.

I believed in a lot of things. I had to. Not only to keep the peace between the mortals and creatures who lived here full time, but also to deal with the gods, goddesses, and deities who used the town as their official getaway vacation destination.

Growing up here, I had played spin the bottle with werewolves, crabbed the bay with Poseidon, and smoked my first (and last) cigar with Shiva.

But I had yet to see a true miracle.

I poured coffee and took it to the little kitchen table in the nook by the window that looked out over the Pacific Ocean. It was hours from dawn, the landscape bathed in ink. But sitting at this table with coffee was one of my favorite quiet places. And I'd need all the quiet I could get if I were going to survive this week.

A wash of ice prickled up the back of my T-shirt.

I held my breath, my body taut, instinct clamoring. Something was wrong. Something was very wrong.

A flash of orange cut through the darkness, burning my vision. Thunder blasted hard, close, loud, rattling the windows and setting off car alarms.

"Holy crap."

I ran to the bedroom, shoved on jeans, boots, and jacket, my mind spinning through possibilities.

It wasn't a god thing. Those powers were carefully locked away while the gods vacationed here. It wasn't a creature thing either. No creature in town could light up half the sky.

Gas main break? Bomb? Aliens?

I grabbed for my phone and keys. My cell rang.

"Delaney?" It was my sister, Jean. "Explosion. Southeast."

"Got it." I jogged out the door, not bothering to lock it. "Injuries?" I ran down the thirty steps to my Jeep at the bottom of the hill.

"Calls coming in. Hold on."

I ducked into the Jeep. Started the engine.

The house lights flashed on at the other three occupied houses tucked against the hill on this dead end overlooking the Pacific.

No one could have slept through that.

"Delaney?"

"Here." I thumbed on the speaker and dropped my phone in the coffee holder.

"It's Dan Perkin's place. Every neighbor within four blocks says the explosion went off in the field behind his shed."

"Fire? Anyone hurt?"

"Fire's on the way. Pearl said Dan is fine. Angry as a snake in a knot, but uninjured. No other injuries reported."

"Copy."

"Delaney? I have a bad feeling about this." Jean didn't bring it up much, but her gut instincts were usually dead-on. "Be careful."

"Copy that, sister." I flipped on the Jeep's light bar, followed the gravel road down to the cross street, and gunned it out to Highway 101, which cut the town into north/south.

"Just don't anyone be dead," I muttered as I sped down the mostly empty road. "Everybody stays breathing in my town, on my watch, in the middle of the night. Ordinary stays ordinary. No killer freak explosions."

I got to Perkin's place in under a minute and took half a second more to bind my long brown hair back in a ponytail as I stepped out of the Jeep. Not exactly the most professional look, since I was still wearing the Grateful Dead T-shirt and jeans, but it wasn't the clothes that made me an authority on this scene.

I crossed the gravel road to the small crowd of mortal neighbors gathered at the edge of Dan's front yard.

One of the Rossi boys was there, because one of the Rossi boys was always first to arrive at the scene of disasters. This time it was Sven, the very pale, very blond, blue-eyed poker cheat who didn't look a day over twenty-one in his light gray hoodie, jeans, and Converse.

"Chief Reed," Sven said with a nod. His arms were crossed, hands tucked under his armpits. He'd only been in town for a few years, arriving as the newest "cousin" of the Rossi clan, which was a wide and varied melting pot.

Old Rossi, the patriarch of the vampire clan, never turned away a new family member looking for a better life.

Not all of the Rossis stayed in town, of course. There were rules, strict rules, and those who broke them were never seen again.

Old Rossi made sure of that.

Sven was built like he might have been a fisherman, or maybe someone who worked a farm a hundred years ago. Here, he worked the night shift at Mom's Bar and Grill, which was more bar than it was grill.

He must have just gotten off work.

"Sven," I said. "You here when it happened?"

He squinted and tipped his head the way his sort did when they were scenting for blood, fear, and sometimes other things they hungered for.

"Nope. I got here right after the blast. Perkin's furious." His smile pulled up on one side, revealing a flash of his sharp canines. "Thinks someone wants him dead." His eyes widened. "Imagine that."

"Yeah, well, you let me know if you hear anything."

Dan Perkin's voice cut through the night air. "Throw him in jail! Throw that dirty, lying, cowardly, thieving scrap of garbage in jail!"

"Sounds like he's singing your song, chief," Sven said.

"I mean it. You hear anything…"

He nodded. "We'll bring it to you. Rossi word."

"Good."

Fire, but not ambulance—must have called them off—took the corner, lights flashing, sirens off.

I strode past Sven, across the yard, alongside the house to the backyard.

Looked like someone had used dynamite to start a bonfire. The fire wasn't spreading—early May was still too wet for anything to do much more than smolder—but the hole had blown the heck out of the burn pile and a couple nearby tire planters.

Dan Perkin stood in front of the fire, cussing. From the dirt on him, he'd either been standing right in front of it when it'd blown, or had fallen on his way to see what the commotion was about.

"Hello, chief," Pearl said from his porch at my right. "Everyone's all right here."

Pearl was in her early seventies—mortal—and a retired nurse out of Portland. She wore her hair back in a long braid and always carried her emergency kit backpack wherever she went.

Dan Perkin was lucky to have her as a neighbor.

"Thanks for coming over, Pearl."

"Couldn't sleep through this excitement, could I?" she said with a smile.

"Hey-up, chief," a male voice called out behind me.

I glanced over my shoulder. Ben Rossi, the angel-faced, pale-haired, slender but incredibly strong chief of the volunteer fire department grinned as he hauled a hose out across the lawn. A lot of the Rossis held jobs in the first-responder and emergency departments.

It might seem weird to have a fire department full of vampires, but they were cheerfully immune to human suffering, and their strength and un-aliveness made them solid allies in times of disaster.

Building burning down? Send in the guys who don't need to breathe and can't die by fire. Stuck in a ditch? A vampire was one of the fastest, surest climbers around. Kitten stuck in a tree? You've never seen a scary fanger go gooey and sweet so fast. Turns out vampires loved cats.

I wasn't sure if that was a Rossi thing or a fanger thing, but it was adorable.

Jame Wolfe, Ben's partner both at work and home, strode along behind him, the hose over his shoulder. Built like a wrestler, he had the Wolfe family dark good looks and swagger that pretty much made sure he never went to bed alone.

"Boys," I said.

"Chief Reed," Jame replied.

Jame wasn't a vampire—he was a werewolf. Big family of them owned the rock quarry south of town.

It had been quite the gossip—well, among those who knew about the supernatural inhabitants of the place—when Ben and Jame had moved in together. There had been more than a little speculation as to how the cross-species relationship would be handled. So far, they seemed to be dealing with it just fine: both the gossip and the relationship.

"About time you got here!" Dan Perkin yelled at the firefighters. "My whole house could have burned down by the time you showed up."

"He's not very happy," Pearl said.

Right about then, Dan zeroed in on me. "Chief!"

Dan Perkin was a small man—mortal—in his sixties, thin as a plucked feather. He was wearing a baseball hat, dirt-stained jeans, and John Deere jacket. He was also dusty, angry, and pacing the dirt in front of the burn pile.

He stopped pacing and stomped right up to me instead.

"Cuff him to the wreck at the bottom of the lake and throw away the keys!" he yelled.

"Mr. Perkin." I put one hand on his upper arm and guided him to the overhang of his back porch. I tried to get him to sit, but he was having none of it.

"Can you tell me what happened?"

"Canoe dummy wet napkin?" he yelled. "What are you talking about?"

"Blast blew his ears," Pearl said. "You'll need to speak up."

I raised my voice. "What happened?"

13

"I almost died is what happened! Heard something out here. Came to look. Then: boom! Worse than that, my patch, all of it is gone! Blown to bits."

"Patch?"

"My garden. My *rhubarb*." He pointed his finger at the sky. "As God is my witness, I'm telling you it was Chris Lagon."

I was pretty sure that the gods really couldn't be bothered to stand witness to most of anything Dan claimed to be true. He was always mad at someone, always convinced he'd been cheated, walked over, victimized.

Still, someone had just blown up his brush pile.

"Chris Lagon blew up your rhubarb?" I asked. "Did you see him?"

"No. But he knew I was going to enter the contest this year. Knew I was going to beat him in the drink category. Rhubarb root beer. It's gonna make me millions."

It was probably terrible, but I nodded and pulled out the notepad I kept in my pocket. I clicked the pen and jotted down Chris's name.

"He threatened me!"

"When? What exactly did he say?"

"Yesterday. At his place."

"House or business?"

"Brewery. Bum sleeps there in the boat. Did you know that? That must be a health violation."

I knew exactly where Chris slept, and why. Saltwater creatures always stayed near water.

"He threatened you at the brewery?" I said in an attempt to derail his next rant.

"Yes! He said, this is what he said. He said, 'Bring it on, old man.'" Dan stabbed a finger down with each word as if he'd just hammered the last nails into Chris Lagon's coffin. "He wants me out of the picture. He wants the rhubarb trophy."

I doubted Chris wanted anything other than to get Dan out of his hair.

"Can you tell me when this happened?"

He might be angry and bitter, but I was the chief of police. It was possible he had information that would lead me to who in town felt the need to interrupt my morning coffee with an explosion.

"Six o'clock."

"Were there witnesses?"

"Yes. Yes, there was. Ryder Bailey was there. You can ask him. He saw it all."

My heart skipped at the mention of his name.

I'd had a...what did one call a crush that started when one was eight and that one still hadn't been able to shake? Obsession? Longing? Sickness?

Love, my treacherous heart whispered.

I ignored it.

But whatever it was, I'd had that for Ryder for years.

It had just never worked out for me to ask him if he wanted to date. Either he'd be in the middle of a relationship, or I would. Or we were too busy with school, jobs, and family—or in my case: monsters, gods, and exploding rhubarb—to ever make a step forward.

It was probably better that way. Less complicated.

"Anyone else?" I asked, keeping it cool. Keeping it professional.

"No, but he was there. He knows Chris Lagon blew up my rhubarb in cold blood, and tried to kill me along the way. I demand you arrest him."

Following demands wasn't in my job description. Still, I gave him what I hoped was a reassuring smile.

"I'll stop by Ryder's place after I'm done here. Now, why don't you tell me where you were when the explosion went off?"

Ben and Jame had the fire under control and I was just about to call my sister, Myra, for some help with the crime scene when she showed up.

Myra always showed up when she was most needed. It was her thing.

"Hey there, chief," Myra said. "Brought you some coffee."

I gave her an appreciative nod and took the paper cup.

If someone lined up us three Reed sisters, one might think we all came from different parents. But if one paid

15

attention to our eyes, one would realize we were most definitely our father and mother's girls.

I took after Dad the most: straight brown hair, square cheekbones, athletic build, and a mostly easygoing, responsible nature over a temper I'd learned to mellow with humor. I was in shape from the job and jogging habit, and never went out of my way to wear makeup or heels. The one time Jean had forced me into a push-up bra, she'd whistled and told me I should wear it during interrogations because people would lose their minds faced with the dangerously sexy cleavage it gave me.

I'd slapped her phone away before she took blackmail pictures, and gave her back the damn bra.

Myra was the middle sister. Her hair was dark, almost black, and the blunt bangs over her eyebrows only accented the blue of her eyes. Her face had softer edges and a more generous mouth. Even without a push-up bra, her figure was curvy perfection that the square-cut uniform she was wearing couldn't hide.

She had also inherited a lot more of Mom's practical thinking, to the point that some people might say she was cool or clinical, though I never saw her that way.

Jean, the youngest, had deep blue eyes and was always dying her hair with colors not found in nature. She was the most petite of the three of us, had a wicked sense of humor, and an elbows-out attitude about life.

"Where do you need me?" Myra asked.

"Get some pictures of the scene and the blast area. I'm almost done with Dan's statement, then I'll talk to the neighbors."

"No problem." Myra pulled a camera out of the bag on her shoulder and got busy with that.

There probably wouldn't be any chance of finding actual footprints in the dirt. Dan and everyone else who had been out here before I showed up would have tromped right over them. Still, Myra had a hell of an eye with that camera. If there was something that could be seen, she'd see it.

It didn't take long to interview Pearl and the other neighbors. None of them had seen or heard anyone coming or going. They heard the blast, saw the light, and even the quickest to respond—Pearl—had only seen Dan out by the burn pile, spitting mad.

Ben and Jame both waved to me as they packed it up. They stopped at the back of the truck and argued over who got to drive. Ben flashed fang, Jame snarled and then they just stood there staring into each other's eyes, neither willing to back down.

I held my breath and watched them, wondering if I was going to have to break up what could be a very messy, very bloody fight, or a very hot make-out session.

The sexual tension rolling off those two could have scorched thin air.

At some unseen signal, they leaned away from each other just enough to make room for their clenched fists.

Rock, paper, scissors.

Ben threw paper, Jame rock. Ben jeered. Jame tossed his hands up in utter frustration and then growled and pointed at Ben like he was going to kick his ass, before he stomped to the passenger side.

Ben's head lifted and his gaze crossed the distance from the road to me. I could see a fire burning in him under that intense stare. Something more than lust.

Love, I thought. And a hollow need stretched out in me. Not a need for Ben or for a vampire like him. Just the very human need to see that light, that passion that he had for Jame, in someone's eyes for me alone.

Then he blinked, breaking our contact, and his cocky grin was back.

Jerk. He'd known I was looking at them, had probably felt my attraction to their fight, to their connection, and couldn't help but tease the new police chief. So he'd given me a little peek of my own desire, just for kicks.

Vampires had a strange sense of fun.

He swung up into the driver's seat, fluid and fast. I thought I saw a scuffle in the cab, then Ben ducked down and there was a moment of intense stillness. When he popped back into view he ran one thumb over his lower lip, wiping away a smile and maybe a drop of blood before he started the engine and sent the truck rumbling down the road.

CHAPTER 2

I LEFT Myra to finish up and deal with Dan, who wouldn't run out of righteous steam for a couple hours at least, and headed to Jump Off Jack Brewery. It was four a.m. straight up when I got there, but I knew Chris wouldn't mind me dropping in.

The brewery crouched on the edge of the working bay just south of city limits in what used to be a crab-packing plant. Chris had taken over the property fifty years ago. Half of it was still a packing plant, though it catered to tourists and locals now instead of international shipping.

What had started as a hobby—microbrewing—had landed Jump Off Jack's smack dab in the top-ten-rated beers in the Pacific Northwest, something that still seemed to surprise and amuse Chris.

I crossed the parking lot and knocked on the big red metal door of the warehouse. Waited. I knew Chris would hear that, even if he was in the far side of the building or upstairs. He had excellent hearing.

Sure enough, the latch turned and Chris pulled open the door.

"Chief Reed," he said in that lilt that always brought to mind New Orleans. His paperwork, filed back when my grandfather was in charge of such things, said he was from Louisiana but that his family originated from the Amazon. "What brings you out tonight?"

Chris was a creature. The polite term was gill-man, and if he had a few beers in him, he went to great lengths to explain the difference between his type and the other aquatics, such as mers and selkies.

Dark skin and hair, long, muscular build under jeans and tank top. When he was out of the water, the main physical difference between him and a human was his deeply set, heavily lidded brown eyes, which gave him a lazy smolder.

The scaling along his neck and back of his hands had been enhanced by a tattoo artist who knew how to keep his mouth shut. The scales looked like they were tattooed on, and Chris just looked like he was a man who was really into ink.

That Hollywood movie with the guy in the rubber creature suit had really sold Chris short in the looks department.

"There was an explosion," I said.

He nodded and stepped aside, letting me walk into the building. It was a working brewery and I inhaled the nutty yeast fragrance as I followed him down the roped-off pathway between huge metal tanks. "I heard. Up north of here?"

"Dan Perkin's place."

He chuckled. "Idiot. Always thought high blood pressure would be how he went out."

"He's not dead."

"Oh." Chris paused at the bottom of the narrow wooden stairs that led to the bar and restaurant on the second floor. "Well, good. Wouldn't want to lose such a valuable member of our community."

I snorted and took out the notebook, clicking the pen. "So where were you tonight? Exactly."

He clomped up the stairs and into the main room. Unfinished wood and timbers racked the ceiling and walls. Decoration was limited to giant chalkboards that listed the brew options, flags, and photos of the place when it was first being restored into a brewery. The rolling metal garage door at the far end was closed. I knew it just opened to the catwalk that let tours stare at the vats and machinery from above.

Large windows that looked over the fishing boats in the bay took up the length of the building and at the end opposite the garage door was the bar.

Chris glanced that way, toward the bar, and the little door in there that was easy to mistake as a cleaning closet. I knew that door contained a private set of stairs that led down to his boat.

"I was here tonight. In bed."

A little too much hesitation in that statement.

"All night?"

He caught the edge of my tone and gave me a very steady stare. "All night. Listen, Dan Perkin doesn't like me. Something about the Rhubarb Rally contest? But I don't care if I win—I'm brewing up that rhubarb cranberry lager as a marketing stunt. Speaking of which, how about an opinion on what to call it. Do you like the sound of Rhuberry Lager or Cranbarb Beer?"

"I like the sound of you getting on with telling me what happened between you and Dan."

He shook his head, each thumb slowly dragging across the back of his index knuckle. It was a nervous habit I rarely saw out of him.

"Nothing happened. I've won a lot of other awards—important awards. I don't care enough about a local festival to actually try to kill someone for it."

"Not even Dan Perkin?"

"Tempting." He flashed a smile. "But not even him. I know the rules. I listened the first time when your grandfather was chief of police. I would rather outlive Perkin than risk being thrown out of town."

"Things change. So do people."

"Maybe. But I'm not exactly people."

"Close enough. He mentioned Ryder was here when you talked to Dan."

"Earlier in the evening, yes. I saw him."

"When did he leave?"

Chris glanced up at the ceiling. "I think he left around one a.m. or so."

"Huh."

"Problem?"

"I didn't know he was closing out the place."

"He had some things on his mind."

"Did he happen to mention them?"

"We're friendly, but he didn't have much to say."

"Any of it pertain to a bunch of rhubarb getting massacred?"

"Not that I recall, no."

"All right. Well, I'm sorry to get you out of bed at this hour. If there's anything else that I need to know, I'll get in touch."

"Happy to help, chief." He glanced again at the door. There was something back there making him nervous. Something he didn't want me to ask him about.

"Oh, and one more thing?"

"Yes?"

"What's behind the door?"

"That door?" He pointed.

"No, the other door you keep looking at like a nervous schoolboy with a closet full of smuggled porn."

"Right. That door. Just my bed." He walked across the long room, his bare feet making no noise against the old timbers. He tugged on the latch and opened it.

I followed him. Glanced out at the railing and wooden balcony. The heavy scent of salt water and green things curled up around me. The floor was a hatch and it was shut. I bent, yanked it up on hinges that moved easily.

Stairs stepped downward into darkness. Water, wrinkled and black, rolled, lit by the thin yellow light from his boat anchored right beside the building.

"What don't you want me to see down there?"

"Nothing, I suppose."

"Or?"

"Well, I'm…entertaining tonight. Or I would be if you'd get out of here."

"Do I know this person?"

He shook his head. "We met up at the casino a few weeks ago."

"She have a name?"

"Margot Lapointe."

I frowned, searching my memory. "Blonde in a cowboy hat? Has those purple feather extensions woven in her hair?"

He nodded. "That's her."

I'd seen her around town, down with Lila Carson, who used to own an interior design store and here in the bar once or twice. "I need you to tell her to step out where I can see her."

He raised his eyebrows. "Now?"

"Yes."

"Really."

"Yes."

"Because you don't believe me?"

"Because I either hear her say you've been here all night with her, or I search the premises for signs of explosives, starting with the boat."

"Without a warrant?"

"If you've got nothing to hide, it's more of a friendly look about."

"They teach you that in cop school?"

"Nope. I learned to be a good friend in kindergarten." I gave him a winning smile.

He sighed. "I don't know how fast you think I can get across town to blow something up, but trust me—I'm not one of the beasts in Ordinary gifted with super speed."

"Not even in a rubber suit with flippers?"

He scowled. "Like I'd need one. And if I did, it'd at least be aerodynamic. Millicent might have been an artist, but that monster suit..." He just shook his head in disbelief.

"Price of living a secret life. You don't get to complain when you're portrayed incorrectly in a movie. You gonna call Margot out now so you can alibi out of this?"

"Since you asked so friendly-like." He pulled his phone out of his pocket, typed something into it, turned the screen.

It said: *Margot, could you come out on the deck? Have a friend who wants to say hi.*

"See? Friend," I said.

"Didn't want to tell her the cops are here. We aren't really at the tell-me-about-your-past-convictions stage of the relationship. Before you ask, she's been here since about eleven."

"Ryder saw her with you?"

"Yes."

The light swung wildly against the pilings, as someone walked out onto the aft of the boat. A face bobbed into view. Blonde, pretty, no cowboy hat. The lavender feathers in her hair shifted in the breeze. Margot had a beer in one hand, a lantern in the other, and no pants on under a large red Jump Off Jack T-shirt that reached her knees.

"Hello?" Margot called. "Chris?"

"Hey, Margot. This is my friend Delaney. She just wanted to make sure we weren't breaking the law."

Margot laughed. "I promise I'm over twenty-one, officer. Do you need to see my license?" She put down the lantern, and in so doing lit up the inside of her T-shirt so that every very naked curve of her was accentuated in shadow play against the thin cloth.

She had a good body.

Chris grunted like someone had punched him in the gut.

"Where's my purse? Hold on, let me get my hands free." She straddled the lantern now, and downed the beer in one long continuous pull before looking around for where to put the empty bottle. She was a little wobbly on her feet. I wondered how many beers she'd had.

"You done with the questions, chief?" Chris asked, his voice gone low.

"Margot, have you been here all night?"

"Up there in the taproom for drinks. Down here for dessert." She giggled. "Wait! My purse is next to the bed. Should I get it? I have a gun."

"What?" Chris and I said at the same time.

"Glock 19. A girl can't be too careful."

Chris's eyes went a little wide. Then he just grinned again. Apparently he liked a woman who knew how to look after herself.

"Are you licensed to carry?" I asked.

She nodded and gave me what she probably hoped passed for a serious look. "Gun range every month. Safety first. But I'm a little tipsy. Don't wanna take it out of the holster."

"Is it loaded?" Chris asked, taking the words out of my mouth.

She chuckled. "Not much use to me if it isn't."

"Do you have anything else with you, Margot?" I asked. "Explosives, maybe?" Yeah, I knew she couldn't have gotten out to Dan's house and back here in the amount of time it took to set off the explosion, but I figured it wouldn't hurt to see if she had another line of defense in her Louis Vuitton.

"Uh…explosives? No. One gun. That's it, I swear." She blinked hard and looked up at Chris, clearly confused.

"She's joking," he said.

I wasn't, but Margot smiled, then laughed, snorting. Okay, maybe she was a little more than tipsy.

Chris grinned down at her, then gave me the side eye. "Anything else?"

I decided to give the poor guy a break. "I've seen enough."

"Good. Because I haven't. Lock the door on the way out." Chris slipped past me and flowed down the stairs like a professional trapeze artist.

He jumped the short distance between the last step and the boat, landing with just enough momentum for him to wrap his arms around Margot, lift her off her feet, and carry her off in one smooth motion.

Margot squealed, giggled, and then both of them were gone from view.

I stood there staring into the darkness, listening to the rhythmic lap of waves, and suddenly felt more alone than I had in years.

I dropped the hatch and dusted my hands.

"At least someone's having a good night." I left the warehouse the way I'd come in, and locked the door behind me.

CHAPTER 3

I SAT outside the brewery, finished up my notes about the conversation with Chris and Margot, and debated driving to Ryder's house. It was almost five o'clock on a Monday morning. He might be up already. Might be at work already. I could wait a bit and meet him at his office.

Or he might be at home sleeping off his night at the bar.

I flipped down my visor and stared at myself in the lighted mirror. Clear blue eyes with tiny flecks of green stared back at me from out of the smudges of too many sleepless nights. There was a little too much shadow under my cheekbones.

"Dad wouldn't have worried about waking up someone he needed to question. It doesn't matter that he's… It doesn't matter that he's Ryder. He's a witness, so he gets treated the same as any other witness."

Mirror me looked as unconvinced as I felt. So I kept staring at her until she looked like the professional cop she was.

Myra, Jean, and I had been training under our dad since we were eighteen. Which for me meant I'd been at this job in one form or another for eight years. I knew how to interview a witness.

Pep talk over, I was soon parked in front of Ryder's house, a nice two-story log cabin on the shore of Lake Easy, just east of town.

Ryder had built the house, with its deck overlooking the lake, with his father before he was out of high school. His dad had moved to Florida just after that and given the house to Ryder as a graduation gift. Ryder rented out the prime bit of real estate for the six years he'd been in college, then for the two he'd lived in Chicago, working for an architectural firm.

Ryder had a way with details, taking a big picture and a pile of random pieces and somehow making them all fit together like it was never a puzzle to solve in the first place. That quality and an artistic eye had landed him a job with one of the top architecture firms in Chicago.

He'd come back to Ordinary a year ago with a client list of his own. I knew he had people wanting his work all over the Pacific Northwest, but he seemed to be trying to spend most of his time here, in his hometown, doing work for easily a third of what he could get paid elsewhere.

I didn't know why.

He'd come back to town with a duffel bag, a career, and even though I had never admitted it to anyone, my heart.

Ryder fit right back in to the small town pace and life, setting up shop out of a building on Main Street next to the town's quilt shop and dinosaur museum. Not that Ordinary was on the edge of a building boom or likely ever would be. Vacationing gods liked to keep the town from growing too large.

But that meant Ryder was out of town fairly often at other projects in the state. When our local paper had asked him why he hadn't set up shop in Portland or Seattle, he'd just smiled and said he needed some time away from the big-city rat race and where better to get away from it all than Ordinary?

The neighborhood was quiet at this hour. A few small windows lit up and birdsong began to stir the air. The scent of salt was fresher here, lake air swallowing it down to a sweetness that spoke of forest and shade and deep, clear water.

I resisted the urge to check my hair in the rearview mirror.

I hadn't been sleeping well lately and a pot of coffee had replaced two of my three square meals.

Dad would be disappointed in my lack of self-care. Maybe it was time to make some changes.

I made a mental note to pick up some pastries on the way into the station. Pastries were always a step in the right direction.

"All right, stop stalling," I said to the thin air. "Let's see if Ryder can corroborate Chris's story."

I strolled up the concrete path to the porch. I hadn't even put on deodorant or brushed my teeth this morning. I dug in my pocket for a mint then rang the doorbell.

I bet I was just a vision.

It took a second press of the doorbell before the door finally opened.

"What?"

Ryder Bailey was a fine-looking man. His dark hair, mussed from sleep and a five o'clock shadow did not take away from the well-defined muscles of his chest and arms. He had hard six-pack abs with a dusting of dark hair that led downward toward lean hips over bulging thigh muscles. His eyes were that peculiar mossy hazel that leaned gold, his dark eyebrows heaviest just to the middle of his eyes. His nose was straight and his hard jaw was balanced by lips that were thicker on the bottom than the top.

So this is what he looked like when he woke up. Rumpled and sexy. His naturally tanned body was marked only by a few freckles, dark hair, and the tattoos. At twenty-eight, he was lean, muscled in a way that spoke of a very active life, or a lot of training, and absolutely gorgeous.

What were his ex-girlfriends thinking, dumping him? If I ever touched him, if he ever even thought of me that way, I wouldn't let him out of bed for weeks.

I savored the details of him, the sepia tattoo of Leonardo da Vinci's hand proportion sketch that capped his shoulder with the words NATURE NEVER BREAKS HER OWN LAWS scrawling an arc beneath it. The other tattoo: a drawing tool called a compass spread out in a V against his hipbone, one point pinned on a star of a constellation that licked across the lowest cut of muscle of his stomach.

I looked a little lower and got more than I bargained for.

Wow.

"Laney?" he asked in sleep-dogged confusion.

"Hey, Ryder," I said, dragging my gaze up and trying not to grin. He was rubbing at one eye with the heel of his palm. "You're buck naked."

His smile was slow, sleepy, and didn't quite clear the glassiness out of his slightly unfocused eyes. Still, his gaze lit a fire that started somewhere down at my knees and stroked all the way up to my collarbones.

"And you're wearing too damn many clothes, Delaney."

Whoa, what? We were friends. Weren't we just friends?

"What did you just say to me, Ryder Bailey?"

"That you…" His dog, a mutt named Spud that looked like a cross between a Chow and a Border collie, came barreling through the living room and licked his feet happily.

Ryder's eyes widened. Maybe in surprise. Maybe in horror.

"I'm not asleep, am I?" Spud nosed up to lick one knee, making Ryder wince before the mutt ran over to lick my bootlaces.

"Nope," I informed him gravely. "You are all the way awake."

Now *that* was definitely surprise in his eyes. Before it could turn into embarrassment, it settled into a grin that was not nearly as abashed as it should be.

"Well," he said, not bothering to cover himself. "That's awkward."

It took everything I had to keep my eyes up on his face, only his face. I bit the inside of my cheek and sang the alphabet song.

I think he noticed my struggle. Fine laugh lines at the corner of his eyes deepened with his smile. "Sorry 'bout all this."

"It's all fine," I assured him, not bothering to elaborate on what I thought was fine.

L-m-n-o-p.

"So." He bit his bottom lip.

My eyes zeroed in on that motion, liking the look of his moistened lips curled at the edges in a smile.

Q-r-s-t-are you just messing with me-v.

I gave him a bland police chief stare, as if him being naked in front of me was just another boring part of the day job.

I could tell from the lift of amusement in his eyebrows that he wasn't buying it.

W-x-y-and-z.

"Give me a minute to drag on my dignity," he said. "And my pants."

"I could come back later."

"Naw, you're already here. Come on in. Do you want coffee?" He turned and walked off toward his room.

No tattoos on his back, or at least none that I noticed. Too busy staring at that fine ass, thank you.

"Laney?" he asked.

Right. What had he been talking about? Coffee.

"No thanks," I said. "This won't take long."

Spud couldn't decide which human he wanted to lick the most. He gave my boot a last once-over, then barked and took off after Ryder, who shut the door in his face.

Spud barked again, then lay down, licking the underside of the door, his curled tail thumping furiously on the floor.

I clamped my palm over my mouth to smother my heavy exhale of laughter. Wow. For a day that had started out bad, it had just totally turned around.

My chest fluttered as the images of Ryder, naked, played over and over in my mind.

I took a deep breath. No laughing. No swooning either. Time to pull myself together and act like a cop.

I studied the interior of the place.

While the outside of the house was rustic logs, sturdy and just a little rugged, the inside was all sleek and modern. Black leather couch and wingback chairs took the center of the living room and adjoining sitting area that overlooked the big windows facing the lake. A gas fireplace took the corner of the far wall and clean white-shaded lamps strung across the high vaulted ceiling.

Art on the walls was original oils and watercolors in stark black against white with single, bold brushes of color. I stepped a little closer to a piece that looked like a ship going down in a dark sea, the lighthouse a blind, useless eye in the storm. Ryder's blocky initials linked together to create a small signature in the corner.

There was a lot of power in that painting. A lot of pain.

The house was a study of clean lines that anchored the negative space, furniture set to allow for a clear path to the deck and front and back doors, the open kitchen offering a clear view of most of the living area.

A blueprint spread across the immaculate glass coffee table, round black stones from the beach pinning the corners.

This wasn't what I'd expect from a small-town bachelor. This was sleek, refined, and undoubtedly masculine.

For just a moment I pondered how much of his life I'd missed. How much he'd changed since I'd known him. The high school boy with dreams in his eyes had come back a man with goals. I just didn't know what those goals were.

"So—" he called out from his room, "move it, Spud—what brings you by, Laney?"

"I responded to a call this morning."

Spud rocketed out of the hall, claws clicking on the wooden floor as he hit the living room, carved a tight circle then skidded into my legs. He lifted his head so I could pet it without bending, and raced over to the fireplace, where he pounced onto a basket of toys.

"So it's work?" Ryder had changed into a long-sleeved Henley and jeans, but was still barefoot.

"It's work."

He dropped down on the couch, pushed one of the pillows out of the way, and extended one hand.

"Have a seat."

When he smiled like that it was hard to remember work. Ryder might have been gone for a long time, but my fantasies of him seemed to have no expiration date.

"I won't be long, thanks." I remained standing and pulled the notebook out of my pocket.

"Where were you yesterday evening around six o'clock?"

He frowned. "I'm a suspect for something?"

"You might be."

"Pretty sure I haven't broken any laws, unless indecency counts." There was that smile again, tugging all the needs in me like unknotted strings.

Okay, maybe he hadn't changed all that much from the high school boy I had fallen for.

Spud bombed back over, a stuffed moose in his mouth. He stopped at my feet, dropped it, and sat, tail wagging.

I patted his head again and that seemed to be the signal he'd been waiting for. He bolted back to his toy box.

"It's not against the law to be naked on your own property," I said. "As long as your neighbors don't complain you're in the clear. So where were you last night?"

"Around six? Jump Off's. Had dinner. Burger: double cheese, double onion, and a couple beers."

"No fries?"

He shrugged.

"Do you have something against fries?"

"Does this crime involve fries?" He was still smiling. I was trying not to.

"Answer the question, Mr. Bailey."

"I wouldn't accuse them of murder, but it's rather suspicious how many heart attacks they leave in their wake." He raised one eyebrow.

I nodded slightly. Well played.

"Were you with a date?"

"As in fruit?"

"As in person."

Spud was back. Dropped a stuffed fish this time. I petted his head, and he was off.

"Steve—a guy who wants me to convert a space in Tillamook—sat with me for a bit."

"How long did Steve stay?"

"He left around eight, I think."

"And how long did you stay?"

"One o'clock or so."

"Pretty late on a Sunday night."

"I didn't have anywhere to be in the morning. What's this about, Laney? What happened?"

Spud arrived at a trot and dropped a cow at my feet. I knew the routine. I scratched behind his ears and Spud dashed off again.

"Did you see Dan Perkin there?"

He frowned and settled back a bit, his body relaxing into the couch, one arm out across the back of it, the other with his hand loose at the side of his leg. People who wore guns tended to do that: keep their hands clear so they could get to weapons in short order. Maybe the city boy did it to keep his cell phone hand free.

"I saw him. He came in right after me. Yelled at Chris for a while."

"Did you hear what they were talking about?"

"The same thing everyone is talking about—the Rhubarb Rally. You are starting to freak me out, Delaney. What happened?"

"Let me finish and I'll tell you."

"Is everyone okay?" Gone was the easy smile and easy body language, though he hadn't moved. He was taut, alert, coiled to spring into action and fix whatever was wrong. I didn't know how he did it. He hadn't moved, and yet in the span of a breath he'd gone from easygoing to dangerous.

It was sexy as hell.

"Everyone's okay," I assured him. "No one's hurt. Can you tell me anything specific you heard Dan and Chris say?"

He ran one hand over his tousled hair and tipped his head to one side, finally bending his elbow and resting his head on his fingertips. "I wasn't really paying attention. I tend to tune Dan out. He was angry. Demanded to see Chris. Chris didn't seem upset—you know how he is."

I nodded.

"He offered Dan a free beer. That made Dan angrier. I think Dan told Chris he was a liar, a cheater, and was trying to put him out of the running in the drink category by bribing judges." He shook his head. "Why did they add so many new categories to the rhubarb contests?"

"To spark more community involvement. Which appears to have been wildly successful," I said dryly.

"I hate rhubarb," he muttered.

"So do I. But it draws people together to argue over family recipes and triples the business in town. That's the foundation of a civilized world. Was that all you heard?"

"There was some sort of dramatic accusation at the end of it all. Dan yelling that as God is his witness he would do whatever it took to keep Chris from winning the prize."

"And how did Chris handle that?"

"He smiled and told him something like 'good luck with that.' No—he told him, 'Bring it on.'"

"Anything else?"

"Like what? It would help if I had an idea what you think I might have heard."

I didn't answer yet. "One last thing: did you see a woman having drinks with Chris?"

"Blonde, mid-twenties, French accent? Wore a silk western shirt mostly unbuttoned and a lacy sort of thing under it. Um...wet designer jeans?"

It was always interesting to see what details a person noticed. Apparently Ryder noticed underwear and designer labels.

"Wet? Is that a brand?"

"Wet as in water. I think I heard her say she got caught by a sneak wave along the jetty."

Well, that would explain why she was wearing Chris's T-shirt on his boat.

"You are a very observant man, Ryder Bailey."

"Habit of an artist. I like to people-watch. I saw her at the bar. I don't know when she came in—eleven, maybe? But she was still there when I left. From the way she was flirting with Chris, I didn't think she had plans to leave."

Spud made a whining sound. He was headed my way, but a lot slower than before. That was because he was trying to carry a stuffed whale the size of a couch.

"And who's a big ol' show-off?" Ryder said to the dog.

"That's a...uh...big whale. Is he supposed to have that thing?"

"Look at who took down the biggest whale in the sea for his new friend." Rider sat forward and scratched at Spud's head as he passed. Spud tried to bend in half so both his butt and head were available for Ryder's strong scratches, but the whale sort of got jammed between the chair and couch and Spud had to straighten out and back up to get in the clear.

"Where did you even find that silly thing?"

"Craigslist."

"They sell whales?"

Ryder barked out a laugh. "I thought you meant Spud. The whale I picked up in Seattle. He only drags it out when he wants to really impress a girl with his hunting skills. So what is this about?"

"The whale?"

"The third degree. What happened?"

"There was an explosion."

He was no longer sitting. He flowed up onto his feet and stepped out so neither the coffee table nor the whale-hauling dog were in his way. "Explosion?"

"You didn't hear it?"

"I was sleeping really hard. Might have been a little drunk. What exploded? Where? When?"

I wanted to ask him why he had been drinking. Maybe he had just wanted to blow off some steam and have some fun. But I'd heard through the grapevine—namely my youngest sister, Jean—that Ryder's last ex-girlfriend, Char, had tried to hook up with him. She had made a messy scene in his office that ended with her crying and flipping him off before she drove away.

"Rhubarb exploded," I said, answering his first question.

"You don't often see that in the heritage strains," he said.

I fought back a smile. "At Dan Perkin's place. Early this morning."

"Oh. Hell. Is he okay?"

"He's fine. So are his neighbors and his house. It looked like a small blast. Intended to wipe out his rhubarb."

"You really think Chris is the kind of guy who would blow up another man's garden patch?"

"I really think I'm going to consider all the angles and get to the bottom of it before something worse happens."

Spud shook his head and successfully dropped the whale on my boots. His tail was pounding a million miles a minute and his mouth was open in a happy dog smile.

I gave him an extra-long rub on the head and he flopped down, content to prop his head on the tail fin.

"I wouldn't expect anything less of you, Delaney," Ryder said. "But you should know that if I'm asked to be a character witness for Chris or for Dan, I'm throwing in with Chris."

"You and everyone else in Ordinary," I said. "But I'll note your bias in my official write-up."

I gave Spud one last scratch behind his ear and then pocketed my notebook.

"Sure you won't stay for a cup of coffee?" Ryder had crossed the space to stand right in front of me. He'd done it silently on a hardwood floor. Nice trick, that. "Won't take but a minute to brew."

"No, thanks."

Why was my heart pounding so hard? Why was he standing so close? I took a step back in the hope my brain would have room to join me again. "I need to get to the station. It's about time I relieve Jean. We're still short-handed. Haven't found anyone to hire yet and no one's dumb enough to volunteer."

He made a humming sound. "You look like you haven't gotten any sleep for a while."

"I've slept." *Not well. Not often.*

"Maybe another time?" he suggested. His eyebrows were knitted, like maybe he was worried about us seeing each other.

It was a small town. There was no way we could avoid seeing each other.

"Sure," I said. He still didn't look convinced.

"Are you sure you're okay?"

"I just... It's been a year. Since Dad..." I shut my mouth. Why was I talking to Ryder Bailey about the anniversary of my dad's death? It wasn't like Ryder and I were in elementary school. I'd shared everything with him when I was little. Even my ridiculously pink marshmallow Sno Ball desserts.

But not now. I was the one who kept the secrets of this town secret. And that meant I'd never really be able to share my life—my real life—with anyone like Ryder.

On bad days, I was pretty sure that was a big part of why Cooper had left me. There were too many things in my life I couldn't tell him about, too much of me I couldn't share.

"Hey," he said softly, the word formed out of gentle acceptance and comfort.

I forgot how tall he was. At six-two, he was a good five inches taller than me. And even though he'd just rolled out of bed, he smelled nice: warm with a deep honey note—maybe the fabric softener or laundry soap from his clothes.

Images of him—naked him—flashed through my mind again in high-definition detail, and everything in me stirred.

"It's only been a year," he said. "If you ever need to talk about it. About your dad...about anything..." He reached over.

For a moment, from the way he was looking at me, I wondered if he was going to tip my face so he could kiss me. But instead, he pushed a strand of my hair that had escaped the hastily tied ponytail away from the edge of my cheek. The back of his fingers grazed my skin and my heart started beating harder.

His gaze followed his fingers in my hair, like it was some kind of rarity, to touch a simple lock of hair, then his eyes shifted back to me.

"…I'm right here," he finished.

He waited, his hand warm, cupping my shoulder while still putting very little weight on it, his other hand in his back pocket, as if he was unsure he should even be touching. He was stepping over that invisible line of friendship between us, reaching over it for something more.

He was trying to help me, just like he always helped people.

I looked away from his eyes—looked anywhere but his eyes. He was just concerned for me, like he was concerned for anyone he thought was struggling.

But I wasn't struggling. If he knew what I handled on a daily basis, not just the police work, but everything else that came along with keeping tabs on creatures and deities, he wouldn't be giving me that look of concern. He'd be giving me a look of respect.

And I needed that much more than sympathy.

We were friends. I didn't want to mess up our friendship just because I'd had a couple hard days—weeks, the whole last year—and he felt sorry for me.

I leaned back, my shoulder slipping out from under his hand, breaking the connection.

He put his hand in his other back pocket so that both his elbows jutted out. Looked a little curious at my reaction.

"Thanks," I said. "I appreciate that, Ryder. I haven't really had…" I inhaled, exhaled. He was right about one thing: I was bone-tired. "I haven't really had time to think about it too much lately. Think about Dad. Sorry, it just sort of fell out of my mouth. I need to—"

"Have dinner with me tonight."

"What?" That was so not the subject I thought we were on.

"Let's have dinner tonight. I'd like to take you out."

"For dinner?"

DEVON MONK

"Yes." A smile heated all the way up into his gold-green eyes. "It's the meal that happens after lunch, which is the meal after you buy something out of the vending machine because you forgot to pick up donuts at the bakery before it closed again."

"I assume Jean has been talking to you?"

"You've defaulted on three pastry promises last week. She thinks you're not sleeping enough. I'm beginning to wonder if you're trying to set her up with Hogan at the shop."

"Hogan? Why would I— Hold on. She *likes* Hogan?"

"I don't think she doesn't like Hogan."

"And she tells you this, not me? Not her sister?"

His eyebrows went up and he took a step back, one hand twitching upward. "She didn't tell me directly."

"Then how do you know she likes him?"

"I, uh, ran into her at the grocery store. We chatted, one thing led to another, Hogan walked by with a fifty-pound bag of flour on his shoulder and her gaze glued to his ass until he was out of sight."

"She was that obvious?"

"I have amazing observation skills when it comes to women."

"Oh?"

"It's true. Family curse."

"You have a family curse."

"Doesn't everyone in town?"

He was joking, fighting back a grin. He didn't have a curse. He didn't even know about the creatures and deities in town. Rule #5 of my job: no spilling the beans to the mortals about the supernatural contingency.

"Sure," I said. "Everyone in town is cursed or worse."

He tipped his head for a second, the smile still not lifting, but the laughter in his eyes turning to that sharp curiosity again. "All right," he said, "go out with me. Take an evening off. I'll buy you one of Chris's rhubarb beers."

"If you promise to not buy me one of Chris's rhubarb beers, I'll think about it."

"Can I upgrade that to a yes if I throw in burgers and fries?"

"I don't know. How's the new cook he hired?"

38

"She's amazing. If Chris gets tired of brewing, her cooking would keep him afloat for years."

Yes, it would. Chris's cook happened to be a goddess—Nortia, the Etruscan goddess who nailed down fate for people once a year. And like most deities on vacation in this town, she had settled into a mundane job that had nothing to do with her actual power.

She cooked.

At least she was good at what she'd chosen. Unlike most of the other deities, who disastrously overestimated their mundane skill set.

"I can't. Tonight's not good. With all the prep for the Rhubarb Rally, and no extra hands, I'm pulling some crazy hours."

His shoulders relaxed, even if his eyes didn't. "Right. Bad time of year."

"Maybe later?" I suggested. "After?"

"Sure," he said. "After. When things aren't so busy." He gave me a small smile. "Or if you hire someone."

I chuckled quietly. "Between now and the Rhubarb Rally? That would be a miracle."

"Miracles happen."

"Not to me."

"Then it's long overdue, don't you think?"

"Optimist."

"Oh, so not. Realist on my best days."

"This must be a great day."

"It started out pretty good so far. Naked. With a beautiful woman."

"Only one of us was naked."

"Statement stands." The intense look he gave me was going to make me blush, so I reached down and patted Spud's head one more time. He nosed at my hand and opened his mouth in a big doggy smile.

"I should head out now." I glanced back up. Ryder was still smiling, like he knew what that smile did to me. "Bye, Ryder."

"Bye, Laney. Don't forget the donuts."

"I'm not going to forget the donuts." I already had, but I wasn't about to tell him that.

CHAPTER 4

I STOPPED by the Puffin Muffin Bakery on the south end of town. Hogan wasn't manning the counter, which meant he was somewhere in the back working the ovens in a cloud of flour and heat and rock and roll.

The girl handling the breakfast rush was young, chipper, and the daughter of the high school principal.

I ordered a dozen donuts, a couple popovers, and a loaf of rosemary sourdough. My mouth watered as I inhaled the sweet, buttery smells of the shop, and my stomach grumbled.

When had I last eaten? Dinner? Lunch? Vending machine?

I made a mental note to catch at least one solid meal a day. The rally would keep me running, but that was no excuse not to eat.

I devoured an apple fritter and a cinnamon cruller on the way to the station and was in a much better mood. If I could land a hot cup of coffee, I'd count this day as a win.

Dawn crept over the Coastal Range, the heavy wing shadow of the hills pulling slowly away from the ocean and shoreline like a curtain revealing the stage.

The station was still in shadow, a one-story building on the south side of Easy River, tucked back off the main road and surrounded on two sides by an empty lot that had gone to forest.

Three cars were in the parking lot, one of them Jean's truck, but Myra's cruiser wasn't among them. I wondered if she was getting photos of the crime scene, or more likely, still trying to get Dan Perkin to cool down.

I strolled through the front door and dropped the two boxes of pastries on Jean's desk, right between her Snape bobblehead doll and Dr. Orpheus figurine.

"Donuts," I announced. "Stop telling everyone in town I don't feed you."

Jean was the youngest of the Reed girls, and arguably the most cheerful.

While my hair was brown, and Myra kept her hair black, Jean's hair was whatever color she wanted that morning. Current preference? Purple and blue with a streak of red in the front, all of it braided down behind both ears. She'd somehow inherited our grandmother's blonde hair naturally—which, according to her, made it perfect for dying—and her blue eyes were deep and dark, like Mom's.

"Holy crap! You finally brought me donuts!"

"Among other things."

Jean stood and opened the box lids, grinning. "Aw...you remembered the maple cayenne sea-salt bars. You're my hero."

"Oh?" I stopped by the table with the coffee pot and poured a cup of overcooked coffee. "I heard Hogan was your hero."

I watched her out of the corner of my eye.

She was stuffing the maple cayenne abomination in her mouth and paused, her thin body still as she stared at me.

The only thing that could freeze my sister like that was the truth.

Wow. So she did like him.

I turned, stirring the sugar cubes with a plastic spoon.

Jean was all grin around a mouthful of pastry. She swallowed and dropped back into her chair, waving her hand in front of her lips. Those bars were spicy. "Do not know what you're talking about. He has a great ass though, and the arms on him? Big, thick. Rock solid. Sexy. Gives a girl unclean thoughts."

"Ryder said you drooled when baker boy sauntered by you."

"Damn right I did. Have you seen that man?"

"Once or twice."

"Then you know I'm not the only girl in town who drools over him." She shoved the rest of the pastry in her mouth and chewed, watching me. "So, Ryder, huh? I thought you were avoiding him."

I stifled a groan. Why had I even brought him into the conversation? "Not avoiding. Just giving him space."

"He's been in town a year, Delaney. That's plenty of space."

I walked over to my desk, around the corner in a recess where I was out of direct line of sight but could still see the front door and most of the rest of the small office.

Unlike Jean's desk, mine was clean and spare, with a computer, a document filer, and two phones taking up the surface. One phone was part of the switchboard and emergency call system. The other—old-style black brick of a thing with a rotary dial—was a direct line from a special room at the casino.

"And now we're going to forget I mentioned him," I said.

"Why would we do that?" Jean followed me to my desk. "Anything you're avoiding that hard is like catnip to me. You know that."

I did know that. I leaned forward, rubbed one hand over my eyes.

"What did Ryder have to do with Dan's rhubarb? Please tell me Ryder was naked during at least part of your thorough examination."

I held very still and took a deep breath. I was glad most of my face was covered by my hand, otherwise she'd see my expression and know that, yes, Ryder had been naked.

"Ryder was one of Chris Lagon's alibis. That's all."

"That is so not all."

"It really is. All. Any luck finding a new hire?"

She made a rude noise. "Changing the subject won't work."

"If that won't, then maybe you should."

"Should what?"

"Work."

"I am working. Getting details on this alibi situation. What did Ryder say?"

"He saw Chris and Dan talking. Was there late enough to see Chris close the place."

"All right. He's an alibi. He didn't...say anything about anything?"

I dropped my hand and studied her. "What are you getting at?"

"He told you I was staring at Hogan. How did that come up in the alibi conversation?"

"It was mentioned in passing."

"Ask him out."

I paused with my coffee cup halfway to my mouth. Ryder had said he'd run into Jean at the store. I was beginning to wonder if she'd orchestrated that chance meeting. She'd wanted Ryder and I to date since middle school. Had some sort of fairytale idea of a happily ever after between us. Plus, my little sister was sneaky. "How long have you been talking to Ryder behind my back?"

She ignored me. "If he's not going to ask you, ask him. He likes you."

"I know he likes me. I like him too. We're friends. Friendly."

"Be more than friends," she said. "Take a chance. I know he's been gone awhile, but he's great. It will be great."

"How about you stay out of my personal business?"

"Oh, like that will ever happen." She leaned on the edge of my desk and polished off the rest of her donut. "You know he's not dating," she said around a mouthful.

"Not talking about this." I put down my coffee and logged in to the computer.

She snagged my cup, took a gulp. "Ow. Hot." She pressed her lips together and her eyes watered.

I just shook my head. Officer of the law couldn't figure out that hot coffee wasn't a good idea with spicy food. Brilliant.

"He's not dating," she continued, "ever since he's gotten back. He's had a few ex-girlfriends try. Remember Char?"

Char had been a gymnast in high school. Tiny, bendy. Popular and rich. She'd just missed out on qualifying for the Olympic team. She and I hadn't ever been in the same circles. I was more of a softball, swim team, and volleyball girl.

She was more the kind of girl all the boys wanted to date. Including Ryder.

Jean kept talking as if I'd answered her. "Well, she tried to get back with him. He wouldn't even give her the time of day. And you haven't dated since Mr. Find-Myself—what an ass— bailed town."

"So?"

"So why not go out with Ryder?"

"Because I'm the one deciding what to do with my life, not my little sister. And that…" I pulled my coffee out of her hand before she finished it. She was such a glutton for punishment. "...is the end of the conversation."

Jean opened her mouth.

Just as the old black phone rang.

We both stared at it.

She shook her head. "I'm clocking out in fifteen minutes. This is all you."

I sighed. "Where's Myra?"

"Responding to a call. Someone stole Mrs. Yates' penguin and tied it up a tree."

Mrs. Yates' penguin was a concrete yard ornament that someone in town couldn't get enough pleasure harassing.

The black phone kept ringing like a windup alarm clock. That phone only rang for one reason. There was a god on the line.

I squared my shoulders and picked up the heavy receiver. "This is Police Chief Delaney Reed of Ordinary speaking."

"Reed Daughter," the cool voice said from the other side. It was always a little disconcerting talking to a deity under full power. But I had had plenty of practice with it growing up. The Reed family were basically immune to such things.

Yet another reason why we made such good lawmen in this town.

"Yes," I said. "May I ask to whom I am speaking?"

"I am the god Thanatos. And I wish to recreate in your small mortal town."

Thanatos. God of death. I couldn't remember Thanatos ever vacationing in Ordinary, Oregon. It wasn't like every god in the universe had spent time here. Plenty of deities had given Ordinary a try and decided they didn't like living a powerless mortal life—not even for a short vacation. Other gods just never seemed drawn to the place.

I had a good memory. I could recite all of the deities who had ever stopped by for long as a Reed had been in town— and a Reed had always been in town, if not this one, then in some other town in the world.

Why would Thanatos suddenly decide he wanted to feel the sand between his bony toes?

"Hello, Thanatos." I caught Jean's eye and made a hurry-up motion when she just stood there in surprise at the mention of his name.

Jean jogged off to the locked and hidden record vault behind the false wall where we kept the family files.

I went on in a pleasant but firm tone. "There is some paperwork you must fill out and sign with a binding oath before you can stay in the town."

"I understand the procedure, Reed Daughter."

"Good. I'll swing by tomorrow and bring you the paperwork."

"I would prefer that you meet with me today. It is the terms of service upon which your family agreed."

Crap.

It was in the original oath. The Reeds were bound to answer the call of the deities as quickly as we could.

The casino, where I made a once-a-week mail run for the deities and met with out-of-town gods to go over terms before they entered Ordinary as mortal, was a half-hour drive northeast from here. I'd lose an hour on the round trip, more for the inevitable conversation with Death, and I hadn't even filed my report on the explosion yet.

Myra walked through the door, just in time, as she always was. She raised one dark, sculpted eyebrow in question.

"Yes, of course, Thanatos," I said, watching Myra's surprised blink. "I can be there in just under an hour, if that works for you."

"It will suit me, Reed Daughter. Do not be late," he intoned. Then Death hung up on me, the phone clicking once before it went silent and dead.

"Death?" Myra asked.

"Death." I dropped the receiver in the cradle and scowled at the phone. "He wants a vacation."

"Doesn't everyone?" Myra said. "New here, right?"

"As far as I know."

"Okay, got it," Jean said as she came around the corner. "Hi, Myra."

Myra nodded.

Jean was carrying the large leather-bound book with fine vellum pages over both her palms. She had it opened to about a quarter of the way through.

"Anything in there on him?" I asked.

"Never taken a vacation. Hasn't been forbidden. No warnings. No notes. Nothing. He has a clean record."

"So there's nothing stopping him from being here," I said.

"Nothing in the book," she agreed.

"Myra?" I said. "I'll need to go. Haven't had a chance to file my report."

"It can wait. I'll hold down the fort."

"We so need another officer," I muttered.

"Or a strapping volunteer," Jean said.

"Anything new on the rhubarb attack?" I asked.

"Got the pictures." Myra shrugged out of her jacket and placed it on the back of the chair behind her desk, which was across from Jean's. "I'll look through them while you're gone."

I glanced at the clock. It was almost seven. Roy should be in soon to help out with emergency dispatch.

"Did you have any luck with Dan's neighbors?" I asked.

"Nothing about the blast. No one saw or heard anyone come or go, and Tibs was out walking his cat. Said the only one he saw out there was Dan. Thought I'd do a rundown of where the explosive might have come from."

"Dynamite?" I asked.

"Thinking it might be."

"Check in with the quarry?"

"Planning on it."

"Good." I snagged a buttermilk donut on my way to the door. "I'll check in when I get a chance."

Myra was already on the computer and waved one hand in acknowledgment. Jean walked with me out of the station.

"The contract." She handed me a yellow envelope.

"Thanks. Get some sleep. No staying up all day gaming."

"I am not twelve."

"You weren't into MMORPGs when you were twelve."

"Worse, I was into boys."

"Yeah, but now you're into massively multi-player online role playing games *and* boys."

She rolled her eyes. "Fine. I won't stay up all day. Laney?"

"Yes?" I opened the Jeep and tossed my coat and the envelope inside.

She didn't say anything, so I looked over at her. Jean had that look on her face. The one she'd worn when Mom had died. The one she'd worn when Dad had died. The one that I always wanted to hug away.

"Remember that bad feeling I mentioned this morning?" Her gaze searched my face for understanding. "It's gotten worse."

Jean didn't like talking about her bad feelings, so I knew how much it must be bothering her to bring it up.

"Do you have any clue as to what it might be? Who it might involve?"

She shook her head, purple, blue, and red glowing in the bright of the morning. "It involves you. Or you're involved with it. Death, maybe?"

"Death certainly," I said. "Thanatos is my lunch date."

"I mean dying death, not the god of death." She looked away and crossed her arms over her chest. "Shit, I don't know."

"That's okay." I pressed my hand on her arm. "Thanks for the warning. I'll be cautious and careful."

"Drive safe, too. And don't gamble with Death. There's that whole challenge Death to a game thing in the myths."

"I promise I won't play with death. I'm not twelve either." And because that barely got a smile out of her, I leaned in and gave her a hug. "I'll be fine. Stay safe yourself, okay, and let me know if that feeling changes at all."

"I will," she whispered.

"Good woman. See you in a few hours." I swung up into the Jeep and started the engine.

Instead of walking to her truck, Jean just stood there, inches away from the Jeep as I backed away, staring at me like it might be the last time she saw me.

With a quick wave and a smile I did not feel, I headed to the highway and a date with Death.

CHAPTER 5

THE CASINO was impossible to miss. Nestled in a valley and built over what used to be a roadside fruit stand with a wheat field behind it, the local native tribe had installed an inviting collection of buildings. The casino was nicely faced, with deep orange and white brickwork, and each of the connecting buildings spread like a small city just east of twisty Highway 18, which was the main road between the capital city of Oregon and the coast.

Used to be tourists only came in from the Willamette Valley to get to the beach and ocean. Now more people stopped here at the casino than made it over to the coastal towns.

Dad had grouched about it, and didn't much like it when the casino became the meeting place for the gods. But I liked it. I liked the noise and lights, the excitement of people making those big and little wins.

Everyone deserved a few lucky breaks in their life. Why not here?

The fact that it had also attracted the attention of the gods was fine with me. It was nicer to deal with beings of universal power here, than in the old gas station and bait shop we used to meet up in.

I parked on the far side of the lot and left my jacket and badge in the Jeep. I didn't like bringing attention to my profession when I was meeting with deities.

Since I'd rolled straight out of bed and hit the ground running, I hadn't had time to pull together my casual professional look.

What was I wearing anyway?

I glanced down: jeans, boots, and Dad's Grateful Dead T-shirt.

Great. Of all the T-shirts to be wearing when meeting Death for the first time, it had to be this one.

"Hopefully Death has a sense of humor," I muttered. "Or an appreciation for classic rock."

I dragged the rubber band out of my hair and combed fingers through it, trying to smooth a few tangles.

"You got this, Delaney," I said as I slicked back my hair and tucked the rubber band in my front pocket. "Reed family hasn't met a deity we can't handle." Although we'd never, apparently, met Death.

The casino was cool and well lit, little pockets of shadow strategically placed to let the lights from the machines shine out invitingly like stars twinkling in a dusky sky.

I made my way past the main game room, a gift shop, and to the coffee shop at the far end of the building.

Since it was still early, there were only three people in the café. A gray-haired woman in a bright pink sweater and a younger woman wearing a yellow pantsuit chatted at a table in the front.

There, at the back of the place, sat a man in black.

Death, I presumed.

He stared out the window at the forested hills that drew off into ever-rising blues of the distance, his face in profile to me.

If I didn't know what he was, if I couldn't sense the power he carried, I would immediately know he wasn't from around here.

He was very thin, very pale, and sat very stiffly. Only the fingertips of his long hands rested on the edge of the table, like a piano player paused mid-song. His hair was black and meticulously trimmed. There wasn't a wrinkle on a face that seemed to be so much older than it appeared.

When he turned his eyes to me, they were gravestone black and devoid of humanity.

It was like staring into an empty gallon bucket of ice cream: both sad and disconcerting.

His gaze lowered to my shirt, and one eyebrow twitched ever so slightly.

I crossed the room toward him.

"Reed Daughter." He spoke in a cultured accent. I swore the temperature in the room dipped by five degrees. "Join me."

I did so, settling down into the chair opposite him. Most gods didn't like idle chitchat, so I got right down to brass tacks. "Thanatos. I am here because you have requested to vacation in Ordinary, Oregon."

It was formality, but words were a binding thing among deities, so words needed to be said.

"That is correct."

"You understand that my family is the law in the town, and our word is the final justice."

"I understand."

I placed the envelope on the table. "You will fill out the paperwork with all true intent and honesty. If you agree to all that is written and required of you, you and I will both sign on the final page."

I slid it across to him.

Only one finger moved. He stretched it out to press against the envelope and better position it. His eyes, those cold, cold eyes, remained on mine for an uncomfortably long time.

"Do you enjoy telling the powerful what to do?" he asked coolly.

His beautiful accent did that god-echo in my brain. Power was a noisy thing for me. My Dad had said it was too bright, like a fire burning. But to me, power was loud.

"I am honored to uphold my family's agreement with all those of power," I replied. I smiled extra brightly, because we both knew I hadn't really answered him. "Coffee sure smells good. Would you like me to get you a cup?"

"I do not require it."

"That's all right," I said. "My treat. It will give you time to read."

I slid out of the booth and strolled over to the barista, who was restocking the refrigerator with quarts of heavy cream.

The girl turned and gave me a quick smile. "What can I get for you?"

"I'll take your dark roast, sixteen-ounce hot." I glanced over at Thanatos, thinking about what kind of coffee I should bring him. "And how about a twenty-four-ounce double-double mocha caramel raspberry blended."

"You want whip on that?"

Thanatos had slipped the papers out of the envelope and held them pinched between just his forefinger and thumb as if they were made of dirt and shame. He was so not a frou-frou drink kind of guy.

"Oh, I definitely think I do need whip. All it can hold."

I paid and lingered while she fulfilled the order. Then I strolled back over to the booth with both coffees.

"Here you go." I plunked the frosty cup of sugar-high whipped-cream overkill in front of him. The barista had really outdone herself and added shaved chocolate curls, a ruby-red cherry, and a bright pink straw.

Thanatos paused. His gaze flicked to the caffeinated monstrosity, flicked to my humble cup of plain black coffee, then up to my face.

"This is a beverage?"

"I am assured it is." I sat down again and took a sip of my coffee.

He seemed to consider the situation and make a decision.

Thanatos drew the straw to his lips with one finger, and, still staring me in the eye as if this were a game of Drink-the-Poison, took a sip.

Okay. I had to admit it was all kinds of satisfying to watch Death suck on a whipped cream and coffee milkshake through a pink straw. Totally ruined that dangerous vibe he'd been throwing.

He straightened and went back to reading through the contract without comment.

"Well?" I asked after a second or two.

He raised one dark eyebrow. "Yes?"

"Do you like it? The coffee?"

He still wasn't looking at me. "Not at all."

Still, at least he had tried it. It was a good sign that he might actually want to give the whole vacation thing—the actually being a mortal thing—a try.

Because vacationing for a god wasn't quite the same as vacationing for a mortal or creature. For one thing, the god had to give up his or her power for the entire time they were in Ordinary. For another thing, while any god was vacationing and powerless, he or she would be mostly human, and therefore could be injured, and even worse: killed.

"Where will my...personal effects be stored?" he asked archly.

"Personal effects?"

"Power, Reed Daughter. Where will the power of Death be stored?" He looked over at me as if he were peering down over glasses, even though he wasn't wearing any.

"That changes each year. One god in town has the right to keep the powers under lock for one year, then that responsibility changes to a different god."

"And who currently is responsible for storing powers?"

I shook my head. "You either agree or disagree to the terms. I will tell you more when we've both signed the contract."

I took another sip of coffee, which was throwing off a lot more steam than it should. Thanatos's personal space was a cold one. But I refused to rub my hands over my arms even though I had goose bumps. He could give me the stink eye for as long as he wanted. I wasn't intimidated by him or his power.

Much.

Even though a power was locked away while a deity vacationed, it didn't mean the power wasn't still in operation.

I'd gone fishing with Chronos when I was about eleven and asked him why the clocks didn't stop while he stayed in Ordinary. He'd chuckled, offered up some philosophical doublespeak about time not being a linear concept, and threw in some mathematical equations that had soared right over my head.

And then, when he realized I wasn't following his line of reason, he told me the powers of the gods continued to exist, even when the god wasn't actively wielding the power. There wasn't a way to turn it off. Instead, power ran on a sort of autopilot while the gods vacationed.

Sometimes that autopilot was easy and everything went as it should. Sometimes, a power left alone without god supervision caused disasters, floods, earthquakes, war, and worse.

I hoped Death had a really good autopilot set on his power.

That way, even though Thanatos might stay in Ordinary for a while, it didn't mean the world would be death-free, or suddenly suffer from massive deaths.

"This clause," Thanatos said, breaking my reverie. "I don't believe it will apply to me."

"Which clause?" I knew which clause. It was the same one every god thought didn't apply to them.

"Section six, subsection six, paragraph six."

He didn't read it out loud. He didn't have to. I had it memorized.

"Yes," I said. "In the unlikely event that you die while vacationing in Ordinary, your power will be transferred, within seven days, to one mortal who will go on to become the god of death."

"Me, dead." His mouth almost lifted toward a smile.

For the first time, I glimpsed a spark of something that might actually be humor kindling in his eyes.

"Wouldn't that be something?" he mused.

"For you, maybe," I said. "For me, it would just be a ton of paperwork, and a lot of legwork to find a mortal suitable and willing to take on your power."

"Must they be willing?"

"One hundred percent."

He nodded with what he might have intended to be sympathy but which only looked like gallows glee. "I am sure I will not need to inconvenience you with such a thing, Reed Daughter."

"Delaney," I said. "If you're coming to town you'll need to follow human conventions in language too. I prefer to be addressed by my given name."

"I am aware of that. I read section twelve. But I believe those rules only apply once I have signed and am residing in your town, is that correct?"

I stifled a sigh. He was going to be a stickler for details. Of course. But outwardly, I gave him the old Reed family smile. "That's how it works."

"Shall we sign?"

Well. That was quick.

I fished a ballpoint pen from Joe-Boy's mechanic shop out of my pocket and handed it to him.

He took it, careful not to let his fingers so much as brush mine, which was good. This near, his fingers gave off a chill as if they were made of dry ice.

He clicked the end of the pen with his thumb, stacked the pages so that the last was on top, and pressed the edges cleanly together.

Then he signed on the line with a flourish. As soon as he lifted the pen there was a sort of shift in the air. The temperature rose ever so slightly, the lights seemed to burn brighter.

He clicked the pen again, placed it precisely in the center of the contract, and pushed the pages across the table toward me.

Cold black eyes watched me with the silence of all the world's graves.

I picked up the pen—which, surprisingly, wasn't cold—and glanced at his signature. Amazing, scrolling piece of art. Beautiful, really.

I set my own name—clean, no-nonsense, and easily legible—beneath his.

The temperature rose just a bit more and I could hear the music over the shop speakers I hadn't realized had faded. Being around Thanatos had a heck of an insulating effect on the world.

"That's it," I said. "Let me be the first to welcome you to Ordinary, Oregon. I do hope you'll enjoy your vacation stay. Remember, you'll need to choose a name you wish people to address you by. Using one that is more common among mortals makes it easier on all of us."

"I should prefer Than," he said.

"Good," I said. "That'll work. I'll drive back to town. You can come at any time you wish, but need to stop directly at the police station so I can take care of your personal effects."

"My power?"

"Your power. And as a quick reminder, you will follow the three basic laws: Get a job or otherwise be a contributing member of the community. Don't kill anyone or harm through intent or neglect. And most importantly: do not procreate."

The corner of his mouth twitched. Not a smile, but compared to any other sign of amusement he'd shown, it was practically a belly laugh.

"I understand each of these requirements, Reed Daughter."

"Delaney. Do you have any other questions?"

"Endless. But I do enjoy a good surprise."

I wasn't sure how it was that everything he said came out so sinister and threatening. Any other mortal would probably cower from this kind of direct contact, but I had family blood to thank for my cool head and fortitude.

I gave him a smile. "I'm sure the residents of Ordinary and the unique experience of spending a little time as a mortal will more than satisfy your need for surprises."

"I quite look forward to it."

"I like your attitude." I stood with cup in one hand and envelope in the other.

"Reed Daughter?"

"Delaney," I corrected again.

"Now perhaps you will tell me which god will be guarding over my…personal effects while I am in town."

"Sure: Raven."

One perfectly manicured eyebrow lifted. "The trickster?"

"The glassblower. You should stop in his shop sometime. He holds glass-float-making classes on Saturday afternoons. Calls it: 'Blow Your Own Balls'."

A slight frown tucked lines between his eyebrows. "Humor?"

"He thinks it is." I grinned. It was going to be fun to see how this very serious, very dark god managed life once he was more or less just another ordinary human like the rest of us.

"See you around, Than."

"Farewell, Reed Daughter."

I raised one hand over my shoulder and waved with two fingers.

Just because god power didn't affect me like other mortals didn't mean that I liked to be in the company of it for long. And not for the reason most people thought. God power didn't repel me, it made me yearn a bit. Made me itch.

My father had said it was a sort of a tuning fork reaction. When I got around god power, it resonated through me like a perfect pitch. There was a reason for that.

There was only one Reed family member at a time who could act as the bridge for god power. Only one Reed who could transfer it into safekeeping, whether that meant in storage when the gods vacationed in town, or giving it to a mortal when an original god somehow got themselves killed.

That second reason—death of a god—was something I hoped I'd never have to deal with.

I headed toward the cashier counter to check for mail.

It was something Great-Great-Grandma had set into place before telephones were invented. The family story was that it all happened during a time when Mercury—messenger to the gods—wanted to stay in Ordinary. Unlike some other gods, Mercury's power didn't really have an autopilot and didn't operate if he wasn't wielding it.

The gods were more than a little upset when they'd found out their messenger boy was going to take a few years off. Typical of powerful deities, they started a war over it.

Great-Great-Grandma came up with a solution that allowed the war to be resolved peacefully.

A message drop was established outside Ordinary so that the deities outside town could send notes to the deities inside town. That drop was now here in the casino.

I drove up once a week and gathered the notes, then delivered them to the vacationing deities. I'd been here last Friday and didn't really expect anything new to be waiting now, since it was only Monday.

I handed the cashier a key that would open the contents in a safe they kept in the back.

She glanced at it and pressed a button under the counter. A young man strolled through the door behind the cashier, took the key, and slipped back through the door again.

I stepped to one side and waited. The casino traffic was starting to pick up.

The young man came back and handed me a single white business envelope.

"Thanks," I said.

He nodded and I turned to leave.

I checked the name on the envelope and nearly stopped cold. One name was typed across the front of it: DELANEY.

There was no one else in town named Delaney. This had to be for me.

This was highly unusual. Gods didn't send me notes. They called, I answered, they signed contracts—or didn't—and that was that.

Why would someone send me a note here?

I thought about opening it, but didn't want to mess with something godly near mortals who were just out to play a game of bingo or two.

Better to put some distance between me and those who could be harmed or affected by it.

I walked out of the building like nothing was bothering me. Kept an eye out for trouble. Didn't see anything but mortals walking into the place, flat gray sky above, and cars rolling past on the highway.

As soon as I got in the Jeep, I took a closer look at the envelope. White, unremarkable. It was the kind that business letters were mailed in. The seal at the back was pointed and not self-moistening.

There was no stamp, not that I would expect one, and no other indentation or mark on it. I tipped it up to the light, shined my flashlight behind it.

It was security lined, but I could tell that it held a piece of folded paper. My name wasn't computer printed. Each letter left a small indent in the envelope.

So an actual typewriter had been used to address it. That might narrow down who the sender was a bit, but not by much.

I flipped open my pocket Leatherman, sliced the side edge, and drew out the paper. It was folded in thirds.

In the center of the sheet of paper was one line:

Tonight. One will fall.

"What the actual hell," I breathed. Dread and fear clenched my stomach and my heartbeat picked up the pace. Was this a warning? A threat? Was this the bad feeling Jean had been sensing?

What did it even mean? One what would fall tonight?

I searched the parking lot again to see if anyone was watching me, but it was empty of people, creatures, and deities.

There was no date on the envelope or the paper, but someone inside would know when the mail had been delivered, and how. If this had come to the casino via some unusual way, I wanted to know the details.

I tucked Thanatos's contract into the glove compartment and locked it, then walked back into the casino, my nerves tight, even though I didn't let it show.

Myra had the gift of always being where she needed to be at the right time. Jean could tell when something bad was going to happen and usually had an idea as to what it was.

My family gift was a little different.

What I hadn't told Thanatos, because it wasn't his concern, was that the only way a god power could be given to a mortal was through me. I was the bridge between mortality and the immortal, a wire through which power could travel and connect to its new host.

That was a family thing too, handed down through the generations. It didn't always show up in the firstborn—there was a great-great grand uncle Otis, who was the sixth-born, and he had been one of the best bridges for power transfer.

Dad had been the most recent bridge. He'd made me stand with him one time when I was fourteen to watch him endure that pain. Endure that power.

I'd had nightmares of it for years afterward.

So far, I hadn't had to bridge a god power. Not a single god had died while on vacation in the last year. Not even Poseidon, who was a chronic idiot when it came to staying alive as a mortal.

If I had any say in it, no god ever would.

I strode back into the casino to do my due diligence. I'd check in with the cashier and anyone else who had seen the envelope delivered. Find out who had dropped it off. Then I'd head back to town before Death got there.

CHAPTER 6

I PULLED into the station. Six cars filled the parking lot—one was Myra's squad car. One was Roy's sleek convertible. Two had tow tags on them, and one was Jean's truck. The other was a sedan—Washington plates. Out-of-towner.

I dragged my hair back into the rubber band and swung into my official jacket, the white envelope in my pocket. I dug Thanatos's contract out of the glove box and strolled in.

Roy sat behind the counter and switchboard. He was a big, amiable man in his seventies. His wide, dark face supported a thick white mustache and a shock of white hair trimmed tight to his skull, making his bright brown eyes stand out. He worked LAPD dispatch back in the day, retired up here to Ordinary, and was one of the few mortals who knew the town's secrets.

"Afternoon, chief," he said.

"Afternoon, Roy. How's the day?"

"Smooth sailing."

He always said it was smooth sailing. If a sinkhole swallowed up the station and dropped us all into a volcano, he'd say it was smooth sailing until the last sizzle.

Myra stood at her desk talking to the out-of-towner—a businessman who was waving a parking ticket in her face. She glanced up at me over his shoulder, her light blue eyes narrowing a moment. I gave her a *later* nod, and she went back to not changing her mind for the guy.

I strolled to the record room, which was just a little storage space with shelves for cleaning supplies on one wall and files on the others. I stashed Thanatos's contract in the hidden safe we used for temporary keeping until it could be stored back home in our family vault.

I didn't lock up the white envelope. I wanted to show it to Myra.

By the time I walked back out, the parking ticket guy was out the door.

"So did you give him the small-town rent-a-cop break?" I asked Myra, using the insult he'd last thrown at her.

"I gave him the small-town hospitality of not throwing him in jail for being an ass."

Roy chuckled. He was working on his newest Rubik's Cube, which looked tiny in his hands. He had a collection of them. I had no idea why.

"How'd it go?" she asked.

"He signed. So I expect him to swing by for his welcome packet in the next day or so." I dropped my jacket across my chair and sat.

"What does he look like?"

"Thin. Meticulous. Pale. Black suit and eyes. Elegant undertaker sort. I think he'd be hard to miss." I dug the envelope out and handed it to her.

She scanned the name. "Typewriter?"

"Yep."

"Did he give this to you?"

"No. It was left at the drop. Delivered by normal means. The cashier said it arrived like all the others: in a sealed, prepaid postal box."

"Weren't you just out there Friday?"

"This showed up today. Same route driver."

Myra pinched it so that the envelope yawned open. She tugged out the paper and read it.

"What in the hell does that mean?"

"I have no idea. Thoughts?"

"Thanatos?"

I shook my head. "He doesn't strike me as the type who would go through the mystery of whatever this is. I think he's the kind who would enjoy telling bad news to someone face to face."

She scanned the back of the envelope and held it up to the light. "Could it have something to do with the explosion?"

"I don't know. Did you find anything?"

She replaced the letter in the envelope and handed it back to me. I dropped it into my In box.

"It was dynamite. About a half a stick."

I nodded. That wasn't going to do us a lot of good for narrowing down who the suspect might be. Plenty of people in this area had dynamite. Especially anyone with land that needed clearing.

"I've gone through the photos. Can't see any evidence of who might have snuck into his backyard to blow up the garden patch, but it was a direct hit. Only his rhubarb was destroyed."

"And his burn pile," I added.

She nodded. "That was a favor, if you ask me."

"So who in town doesn't like Dan Perkin?"

"I think the shorter list is who in town doesn't hate Dan Perkin."

I nodded and scrubbed at my forehead. The lack of sleep was starting to catch up with me. "Pearl likes Dan."

"Pearl has a soft heart for everyone," Roy said, finally joining the conversation.

I walked over so I could see him better. Also to make coffee, because I hadn't had nearly enough pots of it yet today. "You have insight on this one, Roy?"

"Not really, no. But I think if someone had been out to kill Dan, or to do him any real harm, they wouldn't have blown up his burn pile. Just as easy to stick dynamite under his house. Or his car."

I agreed with him. This was sounding more like a case of criminal mischief with the intent to harass. Certainly damage of property too, but not something intended for a lethal outcome.

"Did you check the hardware and feed store?" I asked Myra.

"Yes. They're going through their books and will be sending me a list of people they've sold dynamite to in the last few months."

I scooped coffee into the filter and added a second helping.

"Hitting the hard stuff a little heavy today, aren't you, chief?" Roy set the cube down. All the same colored squares were lined up on their respective sides, except for the corner square of each, which had the colors out of place.

"Not hard enough," I said.

Myra gave me that look that said maybe I should knock off the coffee and take a nap instead.

"Maybe you should knock off the coffee and take a nap."

Mind reader.

"Too much to do. Haven't even started the report from this morning. Still need to hire someone to help out around here. Did either of you know Chris Lagon was seeing Margot from out of town?"

"Cowboy hat, feather-hair Margot?" Roy asked.

I nodded. The grumble of coffee filling the carafe soothed my nerves with the sweet promise of un-soothing them.

"They've been off and on for the last week or two." Myra plunked a tea bag in her mug, then poured hot water out of the electric kettle into it.

Roy made a "hm" sound. He didn't miss the things going on in town, but he wasn't a gossip.

"Do you want to let us in on that?" I asked.

"She's Lila Carson's sister, you know."

"I did not know." I poured coffee into my mug even though the pot wasn't done brewing. "Thought her name was Lapointe?"

"Divorced. Maiden name."

"Has Lila been in town with her too?"

Myra swished the tea bag, then looped it around the handle of her mug. "I saw Lila and Margot at their old place last week."

"The antique shop?"

Their parents had opened a curiosity and antique shop that could not be missed, since they'd painted it cotton-candy pink with turquoise trim. It had drawn tourists and turned a good profit under their care for years. But when they'd retired to Arizona, Lila had inherited it.

She'd reluctantly returned from Paris, cleaned out the place, and changed the old candy-colored antique shop into a fussy importer of Parisian art and decor.

It hadn't turned a profit since.

"I thought she was done with this town," I said.

"She didn't leave because the business was failing," Myra said quietly.

I knew exactly why she'd left. She'd been dating a god—Heimdall, to be exact. She hadn't known he was a god. That was another unbreakable rule deities had to follow—no sharing the secret. She thought he was a fisherman who took people out on whale-watching trips in the spring.

And yes, he was a fisherman. Nice, quiet-spoken man for the god who was supposed to alert all the gods in Valhalla that Ragnarok was upon them.

It never ceased to amaze me that the gods worked jobs during their mortal vacation that had nothing to do with their god powers.

The quiet of the sea had been Heimdall's chosen profession.

Still, he had a little of that light that gods, even unpowered gods, carried. Some mortals were more susceptible to it. Moths to eternal flames.

Lila Carson had fallen fast and hard for the quiet fisherman.

It had lasted two years, then Heimdall—or Heim, as he preferred to be called—had broken up with her.

Heim might be a quiet fisherman, but Lila Carson and her broken heart did not leave that relationship quietly. Furiously would be a better term.

Vengefully.

Great. Just what I needed in my town. A jilted ex-lover to a god.

"So we're keeping eye on Margot and Lila," I said.

"I'll make sure Chris knows that Margot and Lila are sisters," Myra said.

"Better go out now and tell him," I said. "The easiest disaster to deal with is the one we can prevent."

"Sure." Myra shrugged into her jacket. "Oh, and Jean got a line on someone for temporary help. You okay with us hiring without your input?"

"Able body, listens to orders, not Dan Perkin, and it's fine by me."

I thought I caught an all-too-satisfied smile before she started toward the door. "Good. We'll do paperwork, then introductions tonight at Jump Off's around seven."

"Why are we conducting a hire in a brewery?"

"Because you need to eat a decent meal, and the casual setting will make getting to know our new team member more pleasant."

"Who put you in charge of office decisions?"

"You did. Just now." She paused at the door. "As soon as you get that report done, go home and get some sleep."

"Not my boss."

She snorted. "Call it a strong suggestion from a coworker. Take a long lunch break, okay? Roy will call if something else blows up."

Roy gave a quick two-finger salute, then went back to clicking the Rubik's Cube.

I shook my head and watched her stroll out the door. Death, destruction, and a pile of paperwork. What a way to start the day. I took a drink of the coffee.

It went down bitter and thick, and I chuckled. If Myra and Jean really had roped someone into helping us out, I'd make them do my paperwork.

"Any idea who they have on the hook to hire?" I asked Roy as I settled in at my desk again.

"Nope."

I was pretty sure he was lying.

"Any reason why you're lying to your boss?"

This time he smiled, though he didn't take his eyes away from the cube. "Yep."

The phone rang, and he answered it. By the time he was done taking down the information about a car that had been sitting in the community garden parking lot for the last six days, a car that was either filled with brown clothes or clown clothes—I couldn't quite catch the details—the coffee had done its trick and I was deep into my report, making headway.

I PARKED below my house. It was evening, just a little after six, and already getting dark.

Even in the warm enclosure of my car, I could hear the ocean, could hear the rain on the roof, the wind smoothing the tough, twisted coastal pines.

The day had just never let up, and I was utterly beat. I'd pulled together my report on the explosion and all the people I'd talked to, then had followed up on Odin's complaint that Zeus had purposely trashed his favorite chainsaw when he'd borrowed it. After that, it was six phone calls from Dan Perkin, who wanted to know when I was arresting Chris Lagon. He'd called three more times since then, but I'd let them all go to voice mail.

Jean stumbled in late to take over the switchboard from Roy—wouldn't game all day, my ass—and Roy cut out early because he had grandchildren coming to visit. It had been nonstop fires to put out all day.

I had an interview to conduct in less than an hour. In a bar.

How had I let Myra talk me into that?

I think it was the promise of a decent meal I didn't have to cook.

What I wanted to do was sleep for about a day. But I needed to shower, change. Maybe do something with my hair.

At least Thanatos hadn't shown up yet. Maybe he would tomorrow. Or better yet, maybe he'd come to town tonight while Jean was on duty. Good. Let her handle our newest vacationing deity.

All I had to handle was one new hire. And since Myra and Jean had already picked him or her out, I could just eat my burger and fries and pull the friendly-but-stern boss act.

Piece of cake.

I picked up Thanatos's contract and got out of the Jeep. My very steep concrete stairway built into the hill might as well have been carved into the side of Mt. Everest. I slogged up the stairs.

The problem with being tired and distracted was that I didn't notice that something was wrong with my house, something was different, until I was on my front step under the tiny porch roof that sheltered the worst of the rain.

I pulled my gun, suddenly very, very awake and alert.

One will fall echoed through my head. I thought about calling my sisters for backup. But this was my home, my family home. There hadn't ever been anything that had happened here that I couldn't deal with.

Plus, I had a gun, a badge, and any number of monsters and gods at my call, if needed.

I opened the door—unlocked—and stepped into the dark living room.

No lights on in the house. No streetlight below on the little gravel cul-de-sac.

A few steps into the living room and I spotted the backpack thrown on the floor next to the couch.

Robber? Why would a robber leave a backpack in the living room?

Transient? All the way up at the top of a hill several streets away from the main roads? Not likely.

I made a quick search of the living room, office area, kitchen. The faint light from under my bedroom door caught my eye.

Whoever it was, they were casing my bedroom. And they were being quiet about it.

I took a quick breath, set myself, and opened the door with one hand, my gun steady.

"Don't move," I shouted, "Police."

"Whoa, hold on, hold on!"

There was a man in my bed. For a wild, happy second, I thought it was Ryder. But that lasted only a second.

Because I knew who was under my sheets.

"Cooper?" I said, my voice still loud from the adrenalin.

Cooper Clark, my ex-boyfriend, had let his blond hair grow out and wore it tied up in a knot at the top of his head. He was the epitome of surfer good looks, clean-shaven with a lean swimmer's body that he'd decorated with a couple new tattoos bracing his ribs.

He was shirtless, just the edge of his boxer briefs visible under my blanket, which he had thrown over his hips, both legs sticking out from underneath.

He was in my bed. Mostly naked.

My ex-hit-and-run heartache was stretched out in my bed. Smiling at me.

Would this train wreck of a day never end?

He held up both hands in mock surrender. "Hey, officer," he said, his eyes slipping to the gun I was still pointing at him, then back to me, to my mouth. He always used to stare at my mouth instead of my eyes. I'd forgotten that. "Did you miss me, Delaney?"

I lowered the gun and holstered it before I was tempted to squeeze the trigger. A minor injury would be hell on my record, but sure would make me feel better.

"Cooper," I said with exaggerated patience. "Why are you here? In my house. In my bed."

That charming smile quickly swapped out with an expression of chagrin.

"The door was open. You never lock it, you know. I thought you were at work, and I wanted to surprise you. Make you dinner. Double garlic chicken lasagna. You'll love it. You still weren't home and, well, our bed looked so comfortable."

"My bed," I corrected.

He shifted his wide shoulders, pushed up to sitting so he could lean against my headboard. "Right. That's what I meant. Your bed looked so comfortable. Are you mad? Don't be mad. I just wanted to make you smile. Surprise?" He lifted his hands and grinned.

Then he shifted off the bed and stood, walking toward me, his eyes on my mouth.

"I wanted to surprise you." His smile lit up his soft brown eyes. "I'm back, Del. And this time I'm staying right here. Right where I belong."

He stopped in front of me. His strong, long fingers rested on my shoulders. Talented fingers that pressed gently. His touch was familiar, as was the spice of his cologne.

He'd been a musician—could play any instrument he put those long fingers on. It was a failed application to Juilliard that had sent him into a spiral of self-pity and alcohol in high school. He'd dug himself up out of that and worked for the cable company, making his way up to manager.

When I thought back on it—and I'd had a year to do just that—he'd never seemed at peace or content with his life even then. He'd rolled through a dozen failed hobbies, two failed business attempts, and had decided it wasn't his lost chance at Juilliard that was holding him back. It was this town and all the things here—me included—holding him back from his true potential. From happiness.

He'd told me that. Right to my face. He'd said I was ruining his life.

And then he'd left, ruining mine.

"Not with me," I said, surprised it had taken me several seconds to find my voice. Surprised at how vulnerable him being here made me feel.

"What do you mean?" he asked.

"You can stay in town, but you can't stay with me." That came out stronger. Good.

I stepped away from his touch and crossed my arms over my chest. "You need to find somewhere else to sleep."

His hands dropped to his side like a puppet whose strings had been cut. He suddenly looked lost and sad.

"I screwed this up, didn't I?" He sat on the foot of the bed, shaking his head. "I shouldn't have just walked in here and thought you'd want to see me. It's been months since I went away."

"A year," I said. "That's twelve months."

He nodded, his brow furrowed. "Yeah. A year. A lot can change in a year. People can change." He looked up at me, at my mouth. "I've changed, Del. I've… I'm not that mixed-up mess I was. But you haven't changed. Still as beautiful as ever."

"Listen," I said, feeling bad for him despite my desire to shoot him. A little. In a non-dominant limb. "I'm glad you're back in town, Cooper. But you and me? That's not happening."

His face lit up with a smile. "You're glad I'm back?"

"You heard the rest of the 'not happening' thing, right?"

"Sure," he said. "Right. I know. We need time. New person"—he pointed at his chest—"new relationship. We'll start with dinner. One of my roommates was a professional chef, and I can make a mean pasta."

"Same old person." I pointed at my face. "We're not having dinner tonight."

He gave me a kicked-puppy look. "Why?"

"I have a thing I need to get to."

"A thing?"

"An appointment. It's work."

The corners of his eyes tightened and his hand curled into a loose fist. "Of course it's work. Always work."

"What?"

"Still the number one thing in your life. I would have thought you'd give it a rest. After your dad…"

One look at my expression and he had the good sense to shut up.

"I think Hal has a room open." I pushed past him to the bathroom. Hal was Hades, god of the underworld. He ran a sweet little bed and breakfast on the north side of town. All frills and doilies and old-lady knickknacks. "He might give you a homecoming discount, but don't hold your breath."

"Hal? I thought… Look. Sorry about the work comment. Really. Can I sleep on your couch? For one night? I'll find a place to crash tomorrow if you want me to go."

"I want you to go find a place to crash tonight."

He followed me to the bathroom and leaned in the open doorway.

Cooper was a little on the thin side, his long, lean muscles well defined. The tattoo across his left ribs was a stylized ram charging into fire. Down his right were words to a poem I didn't recognize.

No track marks on his arms. Yes, I looked. He had no impulse control, and high school had seen him through some pretty bad habits. He didn't smell like old alcohol. When my gaze finally finished wandering up and met his eyes, it set off that slow electric tingle somewhere deep inside of me.

It wasn't love. But I'd known Cooper for years. Dated him. Thought I loved him. Thought I was building a life with him.

The tingle was familiarity. Even though I was still angry at him for breaking up with me, I was surprised to find that I didn't have it in me to hold on to the anger. What we'd had was gone. And now that he stood right there, half-naked in my bathroom doorway, wanting to patch things up, wanting to try to rebuild the card house he'd knocked down, I knew it wouldn't happen.

I'd fallen out of love with him. My heart had broken, but it was well on its way to healing, without Cooper in it. It was…unexpected. I'd spent a year wanting to yell at him for what he'd done to us, for giving up, for leaving. And now I wanted him to get dressed and get a room. Was it normal to get over a year of heartache in an instant?

"Huh."

69

He must have taken that surprised huff of air as some kind of invitation to grovel. "I know I left at the worst possible time," he said.

"Not at all. Well, yes, you did. But you know. Things. They work out."

"I was just mixed up. Looking for something"—he lifted his hand and waved absently—"more."

"Looking to find yourself, away from this one-road sinkhole of a town, I believe you said."

His mouth twisted down ruefully at that. "I was a jackass for saying that."

I couldn't help but smile a little. "Any luck? Finding?"

His eyes narrowed slightly. Probably trying to figure out why I was being so nice about all this. I smiled enigmatically. Just because I wasn't angry anymore didn't mean I couldn't enjoy watching him squirm.

"Yeah. No. Maybe." He exhaled a hard breath. "I thought, I *know* I want big things. To make a mark. To be *someone*."

"You are someone," I said softly.

"Someone better." His words were so quiet, I almost didn't hear them.

"Start by being better than sleeping uninvited on your ex-girlfriend's couch."

"Ouch." He nodded. "I needed to see you. To talk."

"We can talk. Not tonight. I have work."

This time he didn't give me attitude for it. He pushed off the doorframe, all those lean muscles and ink sliding away from me.

This was right. I knew it was. My heart skipped for a doubtful moment, second-guessing my decision, but I knew Cooper and I were done.

"Give 'em hell, chief," he said with the playboy grin that had started us dating in the first place. That twinge of electricity hummed over my skin again, a reminder of what we weren't anymore. Maybe a clue to what we could be eventually: friends.

"Always do," I said. "Pick up your backpack on the way out."

"So I'll see you? Around?"

Those brown eyes were soft with hope, with need. There were shadows in his face, in his eyes I hadn't seen before. The time he'd been away hadn't been easy on him.

He was asking me for a second chance.

I was good at that. At giving people second chances. In some ways, it was my job to do so. It was also in my nature.

"In this one-road sinkhole of a town? Count on it."

He chuckled and I shut the bathroom door. I listened for the sound of him walking away. Finally heard the creak of footsteps.

I leaned on the sink and stared at myself in the mirror.

My eyes, which had a habit of shifting from gray-blue to cloudy green, were stark against my pale skin, my pupils dilated. I looked like I'd just seen a ghost.

"Ghost of an old relationship." I pulled off my T-shirt and sat on the edge of the bathtub to untie my boots. "I'm over him." It sounded weird on my lips, but it also sounded true. "When the hell did that happen?"

An image of Ryder came to my mind unbidden. Ryder at the Fourth of July beach bonfire, shirtless while he played tackle volleyball with a bunch of the Wolfes and Rossis. Ryder showing Roy's little grandson how to skip rocks on the flat wash of shallow waves. Ryder, dripping wet and muddy, strong arms and muscled back flexing as he tirelessly filled and hauled sandbags, working through the night with half the town to save the Murphy's place from the flood.

Ryder. Ryder had happened. Ryder had happened to me, and I hadn't noticed. Hadn't wanted to notice.

I paused and rubbed at my face, trying to scrub away the images and the realization. I was falling for Ryder. No. I had fallen for him. Cooper coming back had just flipped the switch on the neon sign in my head that spelled "Ryder" in swirly, lovesick loops, a giant cartoon-y arrow pointing down at my heart.

Great. I didn't have time in my life for sleep, much less for a relationship.

Whatever was between Ryder and me would have to wait. Until we had an extra hand at the station. Until I'd figured out who was blowing up garden patches in the middle of the night.

And it would absolutely have to wait until after the Rhubarb Rally. Adding Ryder into my life before then—if he even wanted to be added—would be madness.

There was enough crazy in this town without me adding more to my life.

CHAPTER 7

WHEN I looked out into my living room after my shower, I was relieved to see that Cooper had taken his backpack and left my house. I spent five minutes I didn't have tucking away Thanatos's contract in the family vault in the basement, because we never left contracts at the station, then standing in front of my closet trying to decide what to wear.

I had a dress. Three, actually. Well, two, if you didn't count the one I wore to funerals.

Of the two other dresses, one was a spring sort of number, soft yellow with a splash of watercolor petals falling from shoulder to hem. The other was black, short, and tight.

I bit my bottom lip. Was this a dress sort of thing, or should I wear my uniform? I stared at my uncomfortable dress shirt, slacks, and badge. Too formal? I didn't want to scare off my new employee. We needed the help. And as long as this person was able and willing (and not Dan Perkin), I wasn't about to say no to hiring him or her.

"Burgers and fries at a brewery is jeans all the way."

I pulled on my favorite jeans, added a brown leather belt, and a red tank top. Jump Off Jack's tended to get hot when it was at full tilt, brick ovens rolling and the big fireplace lit. I scurried to the bathroom to do something with my wet hair.

"Yikes."

By the time I'd dried and brushed my hair and applied a little mascara to try to distract from the circles under my eyes, I was already five minutes late.

I threw phone, badge, wallet, and gun into my purse, grabbed the first socks in the drawer—black and red striped—stuffed my feet into my boots, and took off out the door.

Rain drizzled down, a sort of misty fog that soaked a person to the bone in under five minutes. I'd forgotten my jacket, but didn't turn back. I jogged the stairs and was in the Jeep in less than a minute.

Jump Off Jack's was busy tonight, even though it was Monday, and it looked like there were more locals than tourists. The word must be getting out about the new cook Ryder had said was so good.

Ryder. My heart picked up the beat just thinking of him.

I checked my reflection in the rearview mirror. "This isn't about Ryder. This is about work. Also, let's hear it for waterproof mascara. Not a smudge."

I pushed out of the car, noting a figure in a stocking cap walking down the fishing pier, ships tucked into their slips for the night casting yellow ripples of light into the bay. I strode through the drizzle across the parking lot then into the old warehouse between huge vats and past the tiny gift shop and register. The hostess at the register was with customers. She pointed me up the stairs with a nod, and I gave her a quick wave and took the stairs to the bar and restaurant above.

Heat and music and the stomach-growling smell of burgers, fries, and garlic wrapped me up so tight and nice, I closed my eyes for a second and just inhaled, enjoying the moment.

Then I strolled into the main room. What a difference a few hours made.

When I'd come by to talk to Chris, the warehouse had felt cavernous, empty. But now the knotty pine booths and rustic tables and chairs, bare wood floors between walls decorated in the Jump Off Jack's logo, were filled with happy people. The bar that took up the left half of the room, with its truly impressive offerings of brews, had every stool and table filled, and people leaning against the walls in small clumps.

A group of Rossi boys—not all of them pale, but all of them that certain kind of vampire graceful—milled around the pool tables that took up some middle space between the bar and restaurant. Half a dozen of the Wolfe family were there too, the shades of dark hair and solid builds giving them away as relations.

Ben Rossi wore slacks and a deep blue button-down dress shirt, and Jame Wolfe, wearing a black T-shirt and faded jeans, stood shoulder to shoulder with him by a pool table, putting up a united front against both groups, whom they good-naturedly harassed.

There had always been a lot of tension between the weres and vamps in town. But Old Rossi and Granny Wolfe had made it a point that an all-out war between the two families would not be tolerated.

That didn't mean there weren't scuffles, fights, and the occasional permanent relocation that caused a lot of animosity and the occasional vendetta between the families. But Old Rossi and Granny Wolfe ran tight ships and kept a lid on what could be utter chaos.

Which just made Ben and Jame's relationship that much more fraught with disaster. I'd heard there were bets on how long it would last, and who would end up being the first one killed. The two of them seemed to be taking their impending doom with cool indifference. There was a reason they were two of the best firefighters in town. They only got stronger under pressure.

Both Ben and Jame must have felt my eyes on them. They turned a look my way, Ben curious, Jame more wary. I lifted an eyebrow, asking without words if I needed to throw some weight around with their relatives, who were arguing over whose turn it was to break.

They both smiled and gave me a nod. They weren't worried. The argument hadn't escalated into trouble yet.

Ben glided over to Sven Rossi and shoved his shoulder. Sven shut his mouth and stepped away from Jame's brother, Tonner Wolfe. Tonner's lip pulled up in a snarl, but Jame, who stood so close to Ben their shoulders touched, stared down his brother.

Tonner finally looked away and Ben smirked, then took a drink of his beer. That alpha situation apparently settled, Tonner threw both hands in the air and took a step back from the table, giving Sven room. The vampire made the break and the game was on.

I scanned the rest of the faces in both halves of the room.

There were several deities in the place. Odin, who refused to go by any other name, sat at the back of the room. With his eye patch and wild gray hair, he looked every inch the eccentric

75

chainsaw artist that he was. In the same booth, her back toward me, was the goddess Athena, or just Thena, as she chose to be called. Her hair curled long and sleek, dark as midnight against a white T-shirt that brought out the brown of her skin.

She ran the surf shop, giving lessons and renting out wetsuits, boards, and other gear year round. Surfing was just starting to pick up around here, even though the Pacific was brutally cold. To supplement that building business, she also owned a specialty tea and candle shop.

Raven, who thought it was hilarious to go by the name Crow, flirted outrageously with a pretty redhead back at the bar. He was medium built, a good-looking full-blood Siletz, with spiky, short hair and a wicked grin that got him all the women, or men, he wanted.

Lots of mortals in the room too. Many of them from around here, but a good half or so were tourists. Proof that Jump Off Jack's was doing healthy business. Good.

I finally spotted Myra in the restaurant area, sitting sideways to me and looking my way. Jean sat across from her, giving me a huge grin, blue and red hair glowing in the light. A man sat at the table, his back to me.

This must be our hire.

I walked their way, studying what I could see of him. Tall. Probably six foot or more. Good shoulders. He shifted forward to lean elbows on the table, muscles straining the material of the Henley he wore. Change that: *great* shoulders. Dark, short hair, tanned neck, hands he liked to talk with.

I knew him.

No. They wouldn't hire him. Even my sisters weren't that cruel.

I shot a look at Myra, who simply blinked like a satisfied cat. Jean snorted a laugh, then covered her mouth.

And that was when the man turned.

Ryder. Ryder Bailey was sitting at that table. Ryder Bailey was our new hire.

My heart pounded double time. He watched me, his expression a heat that pulsed all the way down to my toes.

Something about him had changed in the time he had been gone. Or maybe it wasn't a change. Maybe it was just that the years he had been away had concentrated him into something undeniably sexy. Something that made my mouth water and knees weak.

I took an involuntary breath as he raised his hand and slowly pinched his bottom lip between the side of his index finger and thumb, hiding a smile.

His eyes glittered with humor.

Great. Everyone was in on the new-hire joke. Fine. I was determined not to let it bother me.

"Evening," I said as I strolled around the table to the empty chair and sat directly opposite Ryder. I kicked Myra in the shin as I scooted the chair forward. I said I wouldn't let it bother me, I didn't say I wouldn't be petty.

She winced and tried to step on my foot, but I knew her tricks and quickly wrapped my boot out of the way around the lower rung of the chair.

"Evening, Laney," Ryder said.

"Sorry I'm late."

"Everything okay?" Myra asked.

I nodded and picked up my menu. "Terrific. Just terrific," I said through a false smile.

She wasn't buying it.

"So, Ryder," I started, "I didn't know you had an interest in law enforcement."

"Food before business," Jean said, cutting off his reply. "We were waiting on you to order. Except for beer. Got you a Haystack. Your favorite."

"Thank you." I glanced over the menu edge, with a look that said one beer would not make me forgive her for choosing Ryder as our new employee.

She opened her heavily outlined eyes even wider, feigning innocence.

"What's good here now?" I went back to actually reading the menu offerings, surprised by how varied the selection was. Just a few months ago Jump Off Jack's offered basic bar food: chips, bread appetizers, burgers, and sandwiches. Now there were some impressive options.

"Crab cakes with chili hollandaise, yellow curry rockfish over peanut rice, whiskey honey sauce sirloin, wild shrimp in smoked tomato glaze," I recited. "Wow."

"Mmm-hmm," Ryder said. "The joint's gone classy. Might have to up our game."

"It all sounds good," Myra added.

"New cook, new experiences," Jean said. "We should all try something we've never done before. It might make us much less bitchy."

I kicked her.

"Had," she corrected. "Try something we've never had before. The bitchy comment stands," she muttered.

I checked out Ryder's reaction through my lowered lashes. Other than a crooked smile, he was studiously ignoring my stupid sister, poring over the selections.

"I know what I'm getting," he said.

"Something fancy?" Jean asked.

"No." He placed the menu down in front of him, and when I glanced up, he tipped his head just a bit to hold my gaze. "Burger, double cheese, double onion, side of fries."

The same thing he said he'd had last night.

"I thought you were an adventurous man, Mr. Bailey," I said.

"Naw. A small-town boy like me? I know when to savor a good thing that's right in front of me before it slips away."

My lungs stopped working.

He was flirting with me. He was really, right here, in public and everything, flirting with me.

What happened to the friend thing we had going?

Was he just acting? Was this a joke to him? Something Myra and Jean had talked him into? If he saw me tongue-tied and flustered, would he laugh because I had mistakenly thought he was really flirting?

We were just friends. We both knew that.

Or did we?

"Burgers and fries are great," I said, my voice too high. Stupid. Nervous. Jean covered her laugh with a cough.

Ryder might be messing with my concentration, but Jean was an easy, clear target. "What are you having, Jean?" I swung a boot her way, but she shifted sideways, easily avoiding the under-table war.

"Well, I hear the burgers are great. But you know I always go for the hot, dark, and delicious."

Ryder's eyebrows tucked down, but just the corner of his mouth slid up as he glanced over at her.

"Dark?"

"Chocolate," she said with an innocence she hadn't had a right to claim since she was sixteen. "Unlike Delaney, who is compelled to plan out every little thing in her life and then boss us around about doing the same, I'm more of a jump-in-all-the-way, dessert-first person."

"I boss you around because I'm your boss. Order food that isn't sugar," I bossed.

Myra sighed and placed her menu down, her eyes scanning the room for the waitress just as a mortal named Molly walked over with our drinks.

Molly was a college student staying with her grandmother this term and saving up money for next term by working at Jump Off Jack's.

"Hi, officers. Hi, Ryder," she said with a quick smile as she set out our drinks. "Everyone ready to order?"

"Hey, Molly," Myra said. "I'll take the chef salad, blue cheese on the side."

Jean pointed to the back of her menu. "Can I get the chocolate lava cake with a side of vanilla ice cream?"

I scowled at her. She rolled her eyes.

"And carrots?"

"Uh...steamed carrots?" Molly asked.

Jean made a face. "Do you have raw?"

"Sure. Do you want those on the side?"

"Yes, please." Jean handed her menu over and took a nice long drink of her beer, daring me with her eyes to nag her about her food choices.

"Chief?" Molly asked.

"How's the fish?"

"We're out tonight. We've been having some trouble getting shipments in."

Getting fresh fish around here didn't seem like much of a challenge. We lived next to the ocean, the brewery abutted the bay, and there was more than one fisherman who would be happy to supply a restaurant that did this much business on an off night.

"Sorry to hear that," I said. "I'll go with the blue cheese maple bacon burger, fries."

"Excellent," she said. "Ryder?"

"Burger, double cheese, double onion with fries," Ryder said.

She nodded and tucked all the menus under her arm. "Anyone want to try the Barberry Butte beer? On the house."

"Is that Chris's rhubarb-cranberry beer?" Jean asked.

"Yep."

"No thanks," Ryder and I said at the same time Jean and Myra said, "Sure."

"Two yes, two no, got it." Molly was off at a quick clip.

"I didn't know you liked cranberries," I said to Jean.

"You know I like free beer."

Ryder chuckled.

I took a drink of my beer, watched Ryder drink his, spending a little too much attention to how his lips moved against his glass. Maybe our wait would be best spent going over business, not my fantasies of his lips on my skin.

"Which of my sisters conned you into volunteering for the department?" I asked. Jean might think I planned everything out before jumping in, but she was wrong. Look at me— spontaneous.

He shook his head. "Neither. I volunteered."

"When?"

"This morning, after you came by and mentioned you were short-handed."

"I didn't bring that up so you would offer your time."

"Why not offer my time? This is my town too. My home. I don't mind pitching in. I'm a quick study. Took some law classes in college. Keep up at the gun range, know self-defense. Plus, I'm charming and capable of talking people into seeing things my way, which should come in handy during the crowd detail at the Rhubarb Rally. I know I'm not a trained police officer—I understand the rigors it takes to become one. But I'd make a decent security detail, or handyman, or janitor, or whatever you need around the place." That last he offered up with a shy smile. It added a dose of humility to his assurances.

Confident in his abilities, but not an overbearing jerk about them. Damn him. Could he get any sexier?

"You already have a job."

"I set my own schedule. I'm sure I could take a week out to help with the rally, then maybe we can talk about how many hours a week you'd need me after that."

"You think this is permanent?"

"I'm hoping it might be." The way he said it, with a low purr in his voice, made me wonder if he was talking about the job or if he was asking how many hours a week I, personally, would need him.

Both ideas made my pulse race.

Okay, the me-needing-him-personally made my heart race a little more than the other thing.

"And I suppose you're both on board with this?" I asked my sisters.

Jean rubbed her thumb down the condensation of her glass and gave me the most serious look she'd had all night. "Ryder's smart, went to college, owns his own business. Other than coming back to this Podunk town, he seems to have good decision-making skills. He plays well with others, isn't a gossip, and—not to make your head swell, Bailey—he's hardcore physically fit. Plus, he shoots a gun. The perfect man..."

Ryder choked on his beer but got himself quickly under control.

"...for our department," she finished. "Jeez, Bailey. Did you think I was hitting on you in front of my boss?"

He grinned down at the table, and the laugh lines that spread from the corners of his eyes made him look younger somehow. "No, Jean. I'm sure you'd never think of such a thing."

Myra tapped her fingers on the tabletop. "We need extra hands. We do. You know that, Delaney. We've been short since..." The slight pause was an ocean wave of silence crashing over us. *Since Dad died.* It echoed in the silence, it washed

81

between my sisters and me. But Myra continued smoothly: "...a year or so. We've needed the help. No one wants to take a post in this town. There's no upward mobility, for one thing, the benefits and pay aren't that great, and honestly, we only need the extra help when the festivals are in town. Ryder is the perfect choice. We know him. He knows us. Knows the town and people here." *Mostly*, her shrug seemed to say.

"You have bedazzled my sisters," I said.

Ryder held my gaze. "Have I bedazzled their boss?"

Yes. "No."

"Enough to land me a job?"

I wanted to say no. Working with Ryder was going to be distracting and difficult and distracting, and had I mentioned distracting? But Myra and Jean were right. He was the perfect choice for the position. If I didn't have a raging crush on him, I wouldn't even hesitate to hire him.

We needed the help. He was offering. I would be stupid to turn him away. All I had to do was manage my heart, manage my feelings for him. Put him on opposite shifts from me, partner him to Myra. It could work. It would work. I'd done harder things in my life. Plenty of them.

I could do this.

"Your qualifications and our desperation landed you the job," I said. "Welcome aboard, Reserve Officer Bailey." I lifted my glass in toast and tried to calm my heartbeat as Ryder gave me a smile that made me tingle with heat.

Or maybe that was just the beer. I took a sip.

Nope. It was all Ryder.

I could do this. I could ignore our attraction. My attraction.

Jean slapped Ryder happily on the shoulder and he chuckled. The sound of his laughter stirred deep down inside me and I found myself staring at him. Wanting him.

I could do this.

He slid a glance my way. Laughter. Heat. And desire.

I caught my breath. Oh, gods. What had I done?

I was saved from that thought by Molly showing up with our meal.

CHAPTER 8

THE ROSSI and Wolfe crowd got a little rowdy, voices raised in argument.

We all glanced over to see if we'd have to muscle them apart.

Jame Wolfe stared down his brother, Tonner, doing that silent were-dominance thing again. Ben Rossi smoothly and firmly pulled Sven—who looked like he'd had several too many drinks—off to one side to have a private conversation with him.

"Not good," Jean said, popping the last bit of a carrot she'd dipped in chocolate into her mouth.

I pushed back to stand.

"We got it." Myra's hand landed on my shoulder.

I let Jean and Myra stride over to check out the argument before it escalated into a fight.

The Wolfes and Rossis closed ranks on opposite sides of the table and glared at each other in silence. This silence, filled with the ever-present tension between the families, was somehow much more worrisome than the quick shouting match.

Myra walked over to talk to the Rossi clan while Jean approached the Wolfe family.

"Still surprises me about Jame and Ben," Ryder said.

"Because they're gay?" I said without looking away from the vamps and weres.

Out of the corner of my eye, I saw him shake his head. "Everyone knew that."

"I didn't know it."

"You didn't get hit on by Ben in high school." He sounded like he was smiling.

Finally, Ben and Jame brought Tonner and Sven back together. Ben's hand was planted on Sven's shoulder, and Jame had his arm around Tonner's back.

Tonner and Sven didn't look like they were in a forgiving mood, but after a quick talk with Myra and Jean, money was exchanged between the two creatures and no blood was spilled.

Jame and Ben both patted their stubborn relations on the back, and everyone went back to playing pool.

Jean, I noted, had been invited to the Wolfe side of the game, so Myra lifted one eyebrow and gave her a challenging smile as she casually joined in with the vampires.

The universal schoolroom you're-in-trouble taunt of "Oooooooh" rose from both teams.

Sometimes being a cop meant remembering you were just a regular person like anyone else in town. Even the irregular ones.

"So why are you surprised Ben and Jame are together?" I said, picking up the conversation again. "Don't think workplace romances are a good idea?"

"Their families don't exactly get along. Never have. I can't imagine what major holidays are going to look like for them."

I lifted my chin toward the pool game. Sven and Tonner were laughing loudly as Ben flipped them both off with a flash of fang and then took his shot. Jame leaned against the wall next to his pack, watching his partner. After Ben's shot and groan, Jame rolled his eyes and slapped a few bills into his brother's palm.

Someone, or maybe two someones, had just lost a bet. But in doing so, it looked like they'd restored harmony between the groups.

"If anyone can make it work, it's those two stubborn men," I said.

Jean was up, leaning over the pool table and shifting her butt just a little as she did so. As one, every Wolfe head tipped to the side, watching her butt like puppies watch a stick.

I turned back to the table and picked at the remaining French fries on my plate. I was stuffed. I felt amazing. Full, grounded, satisfied.

"Why haven't I been eating lately? Eating is wonderful."

"That's a good question," Ryder said. "Why haven't you been eating lately?"

Terrific. I'd said that out loud. Another reminder that I'd been home, alone, talking to myself far too much lately.

"No time?" I suggested.

"No sleep?" he countered.

I dragged my fingers back through my hair, and let it fall. He watched me, savoring every move, as if there was something about me worth savoring.

I made a face at him, which broke the intensity in his eyes. He grinned and went back to pushing his remaining fries through a puddle of ketchup and Tabasco sauce.

Thank gods. If he'd kept looking at me like that, I would have crawled over the table just to find out what Tabasco sauce and ketchup tasted like on his mouth.

"Maybe you haven't been eating because something else has been on your mind. Your dad?"

Yeah, that. He wasn't wrong. There wasn't a day that went by that I didn't wish he were still here with me. With us. His death had been so sudden.

I loved him. I always would. But it was more than just his death that had disrupted my life. It was also this job, this family responsibility that I still wondered if I was handling as well as I should.

"You want to talk about that?" Ryder asked gently. "You went pretty quiet."

I didn't want to talk about what was really bothering me—the crazy secrets of gods and monsters in this town. My job to look after them all, and to be there when god power needed to change hands.

But maybe I could talk about Dad.

"I think about him every day. Think about what he'd do when I'm responding to a call. Keep expecting him to stop by and see me and my sisters. But I'm getting...well, better isn't really the right word, but maybe I'm getting used to the way things are now?"

"Grief is a terrible houseguest," he said. "It shows up when we least expect it and leaves long after it's overstayed its welcome." His eyes darkened, and he stared into his empty beer glass.

"Something wrong?"

"No." He was lying. Then he looked back up, some of the darkness gone from his eyes. "This is nice. Why don't we do this more often?"

"Because we are hardworking people who forget to put ourselves first every once in a while."

"About that." He leaned forward, took my hand, and rubbed his thumb gently, maddeningly, across the back of it, soft, slow strokes. My breath bunny-hopped and I worked to pull it back under control. "I've been thinking. Maybe it's time we put ourselves first."

"You mean burgers and fries every once in a while?"

"I mean go out. Date. I'm asking you if you'd like to date me, Laney. Just to see...just to see where things could be between us."

Everything in me wanted to say yes. I'd been waiting to hear those words out of Ryder's mouth since I was in elementary school and thought dating meant sharing the green M&M's.

But I paused. Ryder's hazel eyes were filled with patience, softened by compassion and maybe something more.

He licked his lower lip, biting it just a bit as he watched me.

That look was filled with a lot more than compassion. It was filled with a heat and fire I wanted to lose myself to, wanted to be devoured by.

"I thought you didn't like workplace romances."

"I never said that."

My heart whispered with need. I'd never know if Ryder was the man I dreamed he was, if being with him how I'd always wanted to would live up to my imagination if I didn't try it. Dating was a good start. All I had to say was yes.

I opened my mouth to say yes.

"Delaney." Myra strode across the room. "We need to talk. Now."

She was scowling. Pale. Jean was already jogging toward the door, her phone at her ear.

Something was wrong.

"What's wrong?" Ryder asked.

"Police business," she said. "Not for you."

I stood, reached for the back of my chair, and only then remembered I hadn't brought my jacket. "Sorry. I need to go. Report to the station tomorrow morning."

He stood too. "I can come along."

"No," Myra and I both said. "We'll get you sworn in tomorrow, officially," I added. "Then you can come along. Tomorrow. Don't be late."

I had to jog a little to catch up to Myra, who was already hauling it across the room and out the door.

"Talk to me," I said.

"I'll tell you in the car." She wrapped her arm around my waist, which seemed like a strange thing for her to do as we stepped outside.

"What?"

Ryder jogged out the door. "You forgot your purse. Delaney?"

Myra swore quietly.

And that was when it hit me.

God power.

I'd never felt it before, not like this, not so strong. But I knew exactly what it was. God power, uncontrolled, wild. It slammed into me, trying to reshape me. Trying to change me.

A wave of sensations swallowed me whole, pulled me down with electric fingers and explosions of color. I felt my knees give out, heard my moan as I fell. Ryder's voice, Myra's voice, were faint echoes behind a chorus of sound raised in raw power.

The world shuddered under that song, then rebuilt itself to meet the call of this mighty, unstoppable, exquisite force.

A universe of sensation—beautiful sensations, terrifying sensations—filled me.

And then silence and blackness closed it all down.

CHAPTER 9

RAIN. A soft patter of it against a metal roof. The smell of gardenias—Myra's perfume. I heard her voice too, building slowly, like someone turning up the volume in increments.

"Right here with you. Just come back, Delaney. Just come back, right here."

"I'm awake." Had to clear my throat a little and push hard to get my eyes open. I was lying in the back seat of Myra's cruiser, the engine running, heater blowing full-blast, police radio on in the background.

"I'm awake," I said again. "What happened?"

She glanced over her shoulder at me as she drove. "It knocked you out. I was worried that it might."

"What knocked me out?" I sat. It was warm in the car, but I shivered and pulled the throw blanket she'd covered me with over my shoulders. The tank top felt like a poor decision at this point. "Do you have a spare jacket?"

"God power," she said. "Jacket in the trunk."

God power. That meant that one of the gods, in their mortal form, had died.

Oh, shit.

"Who? When?"

"Can't you tell?" She parked the car, flipped off the windshield wipers, and turned back toward me. "You're still white as a bone, Delaney. Let's just sit here for a second."

I nodded, but was thinking about her first question. Couldn't I tell what power had just hit me like a freight train?

"Heimdall. Norse God. Herald of Ragnarok. Oh," I said, putting it together with a terrible sinking feeling. "It's Heim, isn't it?"

"Tourists found his body washed up on the shore about an hour ago. We don't know how long he's been dead yet."

"How long have I been out?"

"About twenty minutes."

"So maybe he's only been dead that long?"

"I don't think so. This is the first time a god has died since you became the bridge for power. I remember Dad saying it took some time for powers to focus on him until it had happened a few times. Each power left a bit of a mark, he said. So the next powers could more easily find him."

He had never told me that.

"You talked to Dad about being a bridge?"

Her profile was outlined by the faint streetlight filtering in through the rain-spotted windshield. In this light, the lines of her were softened into the kind of femme fatale I'd expect in a noir mystery, her straight, dark bangs the perfect counterbalance to the round edges of her eyes and cheeks.

"I talked to Dad about a lot of things. Each of our gifts, yours in particular. I wanted to be prepared."

"Why mine in particular?"

"Because I knew this wasn't going to be easy. And I knew it would be me and Jean who made sure you got through it."

It was sweet. And a little annoying that she thought I couldn't handle it.

"I can handle this. It just caught me off guard."

The lights of a pickup truck swung past us, and the truck parked on the side of the road behind us.

"Company?" I tried to get a good look through the rain-stained window.

"Boyfriend."

"You have a boyfriend?"

"No. You do."

And sure enough, that was Ryder's truck. He got out and, with a drink carrier balanced in one hand, walked around the back of the cruiser to rap his knuckles on Myra's window.

She rolled down the window.

"Didn't I make myself clear, Mr. Bailey?" She was in full cop-mode. "This is a police matter. I need you to evacuate the area."

"Since I'm not sworn in yet, I'm bringing coffee in a non-official capacity." He smiled and lifted the cups. "I thought you and Delaney could use it. Is she okay?"

I opened the door and stepped out. "I'm fine." My teeth chattered as cold rain hit my bare skin.

He held out one of the coffees and jiggled it.

I couldn't help but smile.

"Thanks." I wrapped my fingers around the paper cup and took a gulp. "This is police business, Ryder. You're not on the clock."

"I'm here as a concerned citizen, nothing more. I heard it's about Heim? Is he okay?"

Myra got out of the car and snagged up the other coffee on her way to the trunk.

"Who have you been talking to?" I asked. Myra handed me a jacket and I practically crawled into it. It was too big for me, but the flannel interior felt wonderful on my bare arms and shoulders.

"I've got a scanner," he said. "Heard Jean talking to the EMTs she sent out here. Also heard the bay master. They're bringing in the *Gulltoppr*."

The *Gulltoppr* was Heimdall's boat.

"When we need an amateur detective," Myra said, "we'll call you."

"I wouldn't say no to that," he said amiably. "If it comes with a cool hat and magnifying glass. Although a badge and gun sounds like a lot more fun."

Myra squared off to him. "If you get in my way, Ryder Bailey, I will lock you up for obstruction."

He held up both hands and took three steps back. "I'll stay at a distance. I'll even keep other people at a distance if they show up. I know how to stay out of the way."

"Really?" she asked.

He tucked his hands into his coat pockets. "Most of the time, yes. Although, now that you mention it, I wouldn't say it's a strength of mine."

I snorted a chuckle into my coffee cup.

His eyes flicked over to me, laughter and worry filled them in equal measures.

I sighed. "Once again—I'm fine. And you aren't fooling anyone, Ryder."

"Wasn't trying to. Just concerned about you. That's not a crime, is it?"

No, my heart said. Caring about someone—me—enough that he'd go through the trouble to track down the call, and meet us here with coffee, wasn't a crime at all.

It was really nice.

"Not yet," Myra said.

"Good, then. We're good."

Myra looped her arm through mine and we started down the trail that cut through the tough sea grass, the rise of the shore hunched up on either side of us.

"Sorry," I said. "I don't know why he's suddenly so worried about me."

"I do."

I waited.

"I've never seen you go so cold and unresponsive, Delaney. When you passed out in front of Jump Off Jack's, I thought you'd stopped breathing."

She said it in a matter-of-fact tone, but I knew her. She had, maybe only for a moment, thought I'd died. It could happen to someone who bridged god power, though usually the deadliest part of that transfer was when a new mortal had to pick up the power. If the mortal panicked, changed their mind at all, the bridge was left holding the power.

Which was usually fatal.

Dear gods, she thought I'd died.

"Never like that." I squeezed her arm still draped through mine. "Never going out that easy, that quick."

"Good." She squeezed back for a second, then we both let go.

"How far out did they find him?" I asked.

"Just down the beach about a quarter mile." She pointed.

I pulled up the hood on the jacket and we started off that way. The wind was steady, strong, and sent rain and sand spattering across the back of my jacket and jeans. I was glad I'd decided on boots tonight. There was no way I'd be tromping through the sand in strappy sandals.

Even in the rain and wind and darkness, it didn't take us all that long to reach the body.

The EMTs were already on the scene. They'd set up portable lights and had driven the ambulance down from the beach access just north of here.

The tide was on its way out. It hissed and crashed a good thirty feet from the ambulance.

Five people were at the scene, two tourists texting on their phones, and three responders—all of them vampires. Mykal, a short, dark-haired Rossi, drove the ambulance. He finished pounding a stake rather effortlessly into the sand so he could string bright orange webbing in a ring to close off the area. The other two Rossis were the twins, Page and Senta. Though not identical, both were ice-blonde beauties. Page wore her hair long and Senta kept hers trimmed in a short swing.

Senta was photographing the sand outside the fence, looking for footprints or evidence that would tell us if there had been any foul play. Page was inside the fence, photographing the body.

"Hey-a, chief," Mykal called out. "Myra. Cold night for it."

Since he was a vampire and couldn't feel the cold, it was nice of him to sympathize with us mortals.

"Are these our witnesses?" I asked Page.

She glanced up, her eyes doing that bio-luminous glitter of her kind when they were in the dark and around fresh blood. "Couple from Eugene in for the Rhubarb Rally," she said. "They're staying at the Sand Garden and were out for a late walk."

"I'll go talk to them," Myra said.

I watched her approach them. Their body language changed to one of relief. I was sure they would be happy to give statements so they could get out of the rain.

Another movement caught my eye.

Ryder stopped near the ambulance, hands tucked in coat pockets, knit beanie on his head. He stared down at Heim, his face lined with something sharp and dark. Concern. Maybe anger.

I tried to remember how well they'd known each other. Not extremely well, I thought.

He looked up, but not at me. Instead, his eyes scanned the cliffs and the hint of road weaving along it as if he were putting together a puzzle of his own.

I took another gulp of coffee, then set my cup in the sand, twisting it to dig in a little. I ducked under the fencing and paused before moving farther. "We got shots of all this?"

"In triplicate," Page said.

I crossed the short distance to where Heim lay on his back, one arm thrown up over his head, the other by his side. He wore a flannel shirt, thermal under it, Carhartts, and waders.

In the harsh glare of the lights, I could make out no blood. His face was peaceful and relaxed into something that was almost relief. Not what I expected from a corpse.

"Head trauma?" I asked as I knelt.

Sage nodded and crouched on the other side of the body. "A couple hours old, I think."

"Think? I thought Rossis were better pinning down these kinds of things."

She flashed me a grin with a little fang. "We are. But I don't think it was the head wound that killed him."

"No?"

"I think he drowned."

I took a moment to study her face. She was not lying.

"Yeah?"

"We'll run labs, of course."

"Good. Any other wounds?"

"A few nicks on his hands—hooks, wood slivers, that kind of thing."

"His only large injury is the head wound?"

"Yes. And water in his lungs. The scrapes on his hands are common for a fisherman."

"Have you heard anything about the *Gulltoppr*?"

"It was adrift, all in one piece, unmanned, just north of here."

"Distress signal?"

She shook her head, moonlight hair swinging.

"Who found it?"

"Coast guard. They brought it in. Not sure where it is right now—in the bay, I'd guess. I heard Jean tell them to close it off

93

DEVON MONK

and to not allow anyone to touch it until we determine the cause of death."

"All right. Do you have a flashlight on you?"

"Hold on." She stood. Without saying anything or making any kind of signal that I could see, she caught the flashlight Senta tossed to her.

Vampires and their intra-species mind-reading tricks.

Never play Pictionary with them.

She handed me the light. I blocked out the rain, the cold, the wind. I blocked out the sound of the ocean, the rumble of the ambulance engine and generator running the lights.

I opened my senses—eyes, ears, nose, touch—to the dead man in front of me, trying to understand his story. Trying to understand how his life had ended.

Shirt wasn't torn; still had on the boots he always wore on the deck. No rope burns on his palms, no deep gouges to indicate he got caught in a winch line, dragged. The scratches and nicks Page mentioned really were just that.

I didn't move his hair to inspect the wound, since I didn't have gloves in this borrowed jacket, but I took the time to pass the flashlight slowly over every inch of his body, trusting that if there was a detail the Rossis had missed, I'd see it.

Nothing.

If I had to file my final report right now, I'd say he hit his head, fell overboard, and drowned.

"Can you smell alcohol on him?"

Page leaned in, holding her satiny white hair out of the way. Sniffed.

"I don't think so. But other things are in the way of knowing. His heritage is bright." Her eyes flashed blue with light again.

By heritage, she meant god power.

Yeah, that was the wild card in this. God power leaving a body could do all sorts of things to mess up the evidence and cause of death.

I'd need to handle that—handle my part in dealing with the god power that no longer had a mortal vessel to inhabit.

"Take him in," I said. "Let me know what labs say as soon as we know. I want a full autopsy."

"Will do, chief. If there's anything I can do. To help with...you"—she nodded—"say the word."

This was the first time I would have to bridge a god power. And since uncontrolled, unclaimed god power was more than happy to kill mortals and creatures alike—even the undead, like vampires—it was as much her unlife resting in my very inexperienced hands as it was the life of the mortals in the town.

"I got this."

She patted my shoulder. "If you need the Rossis, we're here for you."

"You might want to check with Old Rossi before you go promising a pact between me and your entire clan."

"He likes you."

"That's not what he said last month when I told him jogging nude wasn't allowed in the neighborhood.

"I didn't say he always likes you."

"How does he do that, by the way? All of you? The skin-in-sunlight thing?"

It was a well-kept secret even my dad hadn't gotten out of the local vamps. Sunlight didn't seem to give them much trouble.

"Ask Old Rossi."

Myra ducked under the orange fence webbing.

"Anything?" she asked.

"Head wound. Page suspects drowning."

"We'll want to run full labs," she said.

"Yep." I straightened into the gusting wind to face my sister. "What did the city folk say?"

"Nothing new. Out walking. Thought he was sleeping at first. The woman has a flashlight app on her phone. She was worried he wasn't breathing. The man checked for a pulse while she called it in."

"Did he find one?"

"No. Cold to the touch."

"Okay." The wind chopped across the sand, cold and biting. My gaze wandered over Myra's shoulder to where Ryder stood, one hip leaned against the front bumper of the ambulance.

He wasn't watching the cliffs any more. He was watching me.

A warmth that had nothing to do with the thick jacket, wrapped around me.

"Delaney," Myra said, "I think you should go home for the night. Take a nice hot bath. Get some sleep."

Honestly, nothing sounded better right now. I hadn't slept in a day, and the blast of god power had made me much too alert, and jittery tired.

But I was the chief of police and there was a dead god to deal with.

"I'll come into the station," I said. "Write up my report."

"You're beat."

"Nothing a dozen cups of coffee won't fix."

She pressed her lips together and twisted to glance at Ryder.

"Nope," I said. "Do not drag him into this. I'll do my job, then go home after." I picked up my coffee, which had gone cold. Swallowed some along with the grit of sand caught on the edge of the lid.

"Dad told me the power was exhausting," she said. "That the first time nearly knocked him out for days."

"Good thing I'm not Dad," I said with false cheer. I tugged her arm as I walked past her. "You coming?"

It took a minute, but she finally caught up to me.

"What's it like?" she asked.

I kept my head down against the wind, my boots sinking in the soft, wet sand. How could I put this in words? "It's like a sound, a lot of sounds, all clashing together in my head. Voices, string, drum banging around under my skin. It's loud and...uncomfortable. Like a crappy apartment neighbor who won't keep the stereo down."

She huffed, not quite a laugh, then was silent as we walked. I wondered how hard it was for her to resist checking my forehead for a fever and maybe shining one of those little stick lights in my eyes. She tried to keep a cool exterior, but Myra was more maternal than any of us Reed girls.

"What did Dad tell you it was like?" I asked.

"Hell."

Great. Thanks, Dad.

By the time we made it back to the car, I was breathing too hard and shaking from the cold and sweat. I was also considering the benefits of throwing up.

Still debating that with my stomach, I leaned against the side of the cruiser and closed my eyes. I worked on breathing—in through the nose, out through the mouth—and tipped my face up, hoping the wind and dampness of the night would clear my head and ease my gut. I was used to pushing my body hard. I stayed in shape for just this sort of thing, but the impact of god power had taken more out of me than I'd expected.

Arms wrapped behind my back and under my knees. My eyes snapped open.

Ryder.

The man was quiet when he wanted to be.

"What do you think you're doing?" I asked, searching his eyes. Was he going to kiss me? Because that might be a terrible idea, considering the state of my stomach.

He lifted me off my feet. "Following orders."

"Wha— Put me down. This is not a good idea."

"This is not a bad idea."

"I'll barf on you."

"I'm washable."

"I can make you put me down."

He had been walking toward his truck this entire time, and despite myself, all my muscles were relaxing into him. The scent of his cologne—something with coconut in it—wrapped around me, and all I wanted to do was put my head on his shoulder and sleep for a year.

"I know you can make me," he said calmly. Then he lowered his voice to a conspiratorial whisper. "Out of the two of you right now, I'm more afraid of your sister."

"Don't argue with him," Myra called out as she opened the cruiser door. "He'll take you home."

"He's not even our employee," I said.

"Yet," he added.

"See you in the morning, Delaney," she said. "If you show up before nine, I'll duct-tape you to the cot."

"I think she's serious," he said, stopping at the passenger side of the truck.

Myra got in the cruiser and started the engine.

"She is." I sighed. "Put me down. There's nothing wrong with my legs."

"True." He somehow got the passenger door open without dropping me. "You have very nice legs. But your sister was clear with her instructions."

"Which were?"

"Not to let your feet touch ground until you're at your house."

"Oh, for Pete's sake."

He gave me a grin. Then, with far too much ease, he tossed me gently into the front seat of his truck.

"Almost like you've done that before."

He shrugged. "I am a man of many talents. At your service." He gave me a slight bow then shut the door in my face.

I watched him saunter around the front of the truck, the rain-shattered light catching at the hard edge of his profile and wide shoulders. He looked good in his skin. Confident in who he was, confident in his place in the world. In his goals. It was sexy the way he moved, shoulders and hips shifting with controlled power. Very male. It made me wonder how he would move on a dance floor. Or in bed.

"So, Officer Reed." He settled in the front seat and started the engine. "My place or yours?"

"Mine?"

He glanced over at me, the cool light of the street lamp doing amazing things to his eyes, his mouth. And when he bit his bottom lip, tugging before he smiled, something that felt like butterflies fluttered across my stomach. I shivered.

"You don't sound too sure of that. And there are a million steps up to your place. There's nothing but an easy path to mine."

"You know what they say about taking the path of least resistance."

"Leads to temptation?" He wiggled his eyebrows. "I have hot cocoa."

I closed my eyes and pressed cold fingertips over my lids. "I totally set myself up for that, didn't I?"

He chuckled. "You totally did."

"That's it. I am officially too tired to operate my mouth and brain."

"Does that mean you're too tired for stairs?"

I turned my head and gave him a small smile. "I'm not too tired to operate my feet. I should go home."

"Then home it is." He eased the truck out onto the road and turned on the heater. Classic rock wafted through the speakers, turned down so low, it was almost a lullaby. I leaned my head against the side window and closed my eyes.

"Hey, Lane," Ryder said softly. "We're here."

I opened my eyes with a start and tried to get my bearings. We were parked at the bottom of my stairs, the engine turned off, rain clattering across the truck's roof.

Lane. He hadn't called me that since we were in school. I had forgotten how much I liked his nickname for me. "Tell me this isn't the worst date you've ever been on," I said.

"Not even in the top ten worst."

"Top twenty?"

He rocked his hand back and forth. "The dead body definitely puts it in the top twenty-five."

"Well, good. Wouldn't want the night to be a total loss." I tucked my hair back behind my ears and narrowed my eyes at him. "Thanks for the ride, traitor."

"Whoa. Traitor?"

"You sided with my sister back there."

"You didn't see your sister's face when you passed out in front of Jump Off's. She looked like a valkyrie."

"Valkyrie?" Chills ran down my arms. I knew the town's only valkyrie: Bertie. Did he know? Did he know about the creatures in this town?

"Norse myth. Warrior women who gather up the fallen heroes and take them to their final party place in Valhalla."

"Right. Sure. Norse thing. It's been a while since I took that mythology class in high school."

He dipped his head to catch my eyes. Waiting until I met his gaze. "Myra's worried about you. Since she's your sister, and a cop, and isn't the kind of person who overreacts, I'm worried about you. Are you really okay, Lane?"

"It was just a fluke. Passing out. Must have had too much to drink."

"Two beers?"

"I'm out of practice, apparently."

He frowned, his gaze searching my face. He didn't believe me. Or he didn't want to.

I didn't want him to find the truth—that I was tired, a little scared, and full of really noisy power. I pulled on the door handle and turned away. "Anyway. Thanks for the ride. Congrats on getting conned into helping out at the station, you foolish man. See you in the morning."

I got out of the truck before he could say anything and sucked in a hard breath at the temperature change. Cold, blustery, wet. Springtime in the Pacific Northwest.

I crunched over gravel to the bottom of the stairs, put one hand on the railing, and started up. Halfway to my goal, I heard the truck door close and then the *shuck-shuck* of boots jogging up the stairs behind me.

Jogging.

Seriously.

"You don't have to follow me." I didn't bother looking back at him.

"I promised Myra I'd make sure you were home." He slowed to move in rhythm with me as I trudged up the stairs. His boots, my boots *shuck-shucking* as one.

"I'm here. I'm home. You've fulfilled your contract with my pushy sister. You can go."

"I'm to give her a full report, and it is to include you taking off your boots and either getting into a hot bath or crawling into bed."

"For the love of Pete," I said. "She told you that?"

"I'm just a law-abiding citizen doing what the local law tells me to do. You don't want me to break the law, do you, Laney?"

"Brown-noser," I mumbled.

"What?"

"Come on in, citizen," I said with all the sarcasm I could shovel. "And watch the amazing Delaney Reed take off her shoes."

I opened my front door, strolled in to my living room. I was pretty sure he was laughing at me.

"You should really lock your door. All sorts of people could just walk in to the place."

"Don't I know it." I turned around, held my arms out to either side. "Ta-da! I am here. I am home. And..." I held up one finger then toed off my boots and kicked them to one side. "I am de-booted." I grinned. "Now you and my sister can get out of my hair, okay?"

"Almost."

"Almost?"

"There's one more thing."

I tipped my head back and groaned. "It's illegal to shoot siblings, right?"

"Only inside state lines." He crossed the distance between us in three easy strides.

And then his arm was around my back, his other hand slowly rising to the side of my face, fingers tucking back in my hair to curl at the nape of my neck.

"Just in case a workplace romance doesn't work out, I thought we could start here." His gaze held mine. I couldn't move. Didn't want to move. All the sound inside me went silent, still.

Ryder was warm—hot, his jacket open so I could feel the heat of his body even through the coat I wore.

When I didn't resist, he lowered his mouth, softly, gently.

His lips, warm with the taste of rain, found mine.

Everything in me went upside down and the world somersaulted into deep water.

I was suspended there, drowning there. My only lifeline: the man who had swept the world out from beneath me.

Friends.

Who was I kidding?

This was not a friendly kiss. This was passion.

This was Ryder.

DEVON MONK

Before I could understand it, before I could sort the truths of him from the fantasies, he quietly pulled away.

Hands still holding me, gaze locked on my eyes. On me.

"That goodnight kiss was my idea. Not your sister's. Just in case you weren't sure."

I nodded. Had to swallow to remember how to make words come out of my mouth. "Good. Great. Good to know."

The corner of his mouth slid up into a smile.

"So I'm going to leave now," he said. "And you are going to…?"

Oh. He wanted me to say something? To put a cohesive thought together with my brain and mouth? That was impossible while he was standing this close to me.

I went with the first thing that popped into my head. "Bed?"

"Perfect."

But before I could do—or not do—anything, he stepped back.

And just like that, the world snapped into place: solid land formed beneath my feet, gravity clicked back on.

"Sleep well, Delaney." He paused at my front door and turned the lock. He stepped through the doorway. "Let's do this again. With fewer dead people."

I couldn't even find the words to answer that. Lifted my hand in a lame wave.

He grinned and then shut the door firmly enough that I knew he had locked it behind him.

Air whooshed out of my lungs. My head went light from the air I was suddenly gulping down.

"Well," I said with a shaky laugh. "Well, how about that?" I smiled and bare-footed it into the bathroom for a nice, long soak before bed.

CHAPTER 10

DEATH CAME to our little beach town on a Tuesday morning. It was one of those rare, clear spring days after a night of rain that hinted at better days right around the corner.

Death looked similarly optimistic in his bright Hawaiian shirt over a T-shirt with the words 100% ORDINARY across the chest.

I was on my fourth cup of coffee and the last page of my report when Death walked into the station.

"Can I help you, sir?" Roy asked.

"You may inform Delaney Reed that Than is here to see her about a private matter."

"Chief?" Roy called.

I strolled around the divider that separated my desk from the rest of the station. To Death's apparent amusement and my own satisfaction, Roy wasn't the least bit concerned that the grim reaper was in our waiting area. He instead went back to fiddling with his newest Rubik's Cube.

"Hey, Than. It's very good to see you. When did you get into town?"

I noticed the temperature in the station had dropped by a few degrees.

"Moments ago."

"Nice duds."

He peered down at his shirt and brushed long, thin fingers over the riot of colors and palm fronds. "Appropriate vacation apparel, I believe?"

"Absolutely," I said with a straight face. "Really goes with your expensive black wool slacks and shiny shoes."

Roy chuckled.

"One must keep a sense of elegance even when one is in repose," Death said, airily. "I believe you and I have personal business to attend, Police Officer Delaney Reed?"

"Just Delaney or chief works fine," I said, shrugging into my jacket. "Roy? You got the shop for an hour or so? Ryder should be back from the ride-along with Myra soon."

"Take your time. Can't imagine we'll have much excitement today."

Death, ever the gentleman, opened the door for me.

We walked out to the parking lot. "How do you like the place so far?" I asked.

"It is...quaint."

"Quaint is what we aim for." I stopped by my Jeep and nodded toward the passenger door. "Get in. I'll take you to Raven and we'll get your power secured."

I opened my door and watched him cross to the other side. He walked with a fluid poise, back straight, head high. I thought if I stacked a tower of full wineglasses on his head and told him to walk a mile, he wouldn't spill a drop of it.

I settled into the driver's seat and he eased himself into the passenger seat.

"I need to ask you a question." I drove to the main road. Turned on my blinker, waiting for a break in traffic.

"Many do."

He sat with his hands folded in his lap, his eyes taking in the scene of the town moving past us with rapt attention. I couldn't tell if he was amused or fascinated by the people and traffic.

"Heimdall died last night."

"Heimdall remains," he said.

"If you mean in a body bag, then yes."

"Heimdall represents the power of that name. That power still exists. In you, Reed Daughter. Do you not hear it? Heimdall remains."

"Delaney," I reminded him. "Yes, I understand his power is still around. And that it's...inside me."

Heimdall's power had done more than knock me out last night. It had taken up residency in me. It was a weight of sound, a constant crash and shrill occupying a weird space in me I didn't even know I possessed.

I had one week to find it a new home. I knew I wouldn't take on the traits of the power—that was the Reed gift: we were completely immune to god power. But I'd watched Dad when he carried Poseidon's power for almost the full seven days before finding a mortal to give it to.

Carrying the power that long had exhausted him. He hadn't really recovered for a month afterward.

"The red of pain," Than said.

"What?"

He pointed at the traffic light. Red.

"Crap." I stomped on the brake and brought the Jeep to a hard stop. I threw my arm in front of Than to keep him from hitting the dashboard.

Than looked down at my arm, looked over at me, one eyebrow raised. "Is this customary?"

"I was just worried you'd get hurt. And it's just a red light, by the way. Not red of pain."

"I shall note it. That, then, is not the green of life?"

"Just green light. We mortals keep it simple. You'll get the hang of it."

"So too will you, Reed Daughter."

What did he mean by that?

When I glanced over at him, he was back to staring at the town like it held mysteries he'd never seen.

I smiled. New gods were so cute. "Thanks. I intend to be good at my jobs. All of them."

"It has always been the way with the Reeds."

I could ask him why he had taken my father. Could ask him if he knew the details of his death. Ask him if he knew why Dad drove off the cliff on a road he'd been driving since he was fourteen.

It had happened so suddenly.

But that wasn't the question I most needed to know. That wasn't the death I had to solve today.

"Do you know how Heimdall died?"

He was silent for long enough, I wondered if he was just ignoring me. But finally, just as I was turning into Raven—or Crow's—glassblowing shop, he spoke.

"I am Death, Reed Daughter. I know each light that enters the darkness."

"Useful. But what I'm asking is how Heimdall—his mortal body—how he died."

"Quietly."

I parked the Jeep. "Are you being vague just to tease me, Than?"

"That doesn't appear to be my way, does it, Reed Daughter?"

"Oh, I don't know. I think you've got a wit."

His mouth twitched. Not a smile, but as close to one as I'd seen today.

"He was peaceful. Content. That I know." His voice took on a sonorous tone while the air in the car dropped five degrees. "He did not struggle into the darkness, but welcomed it, his soul at rest."

I waited, hoping he'd have something more specific for me. "Uh...right. That's nice to know. But I was really asking if it was an accident, and where the head wound came from."

"I am the god of death, Reed Daughter, not an enthusiast of murder."

"Murder? You think this is murder?"

He regarded me with gravestone-black eyes.

"I need you to be very, very clear with me, Thanatos. Do you think Heimdall was murdered?"

"Yes."

I waited for more. But trying to wait out Death was sort of a dumb tactic. "Would you care to tell me who did it?"

"As I said, Reed Daughter, I am not a prognosticator of murder, nor do my ambitions include dime-store divination. I believe I have signed a binding contract which states I will only be allowed to remain in Ordinary if, upon entry, I immediately relinquish my power onto a resting state.

"I have been within these borders twenty-eight minutes. If I remain much longer, I shall be in breach of contract. You would find the results of breaking a contract with Death most regrettable."

"I liked you better when you were vague."

That got another not-smile out of him.

"I shall strive to acquiesce to your wishes, Reed Daughter."

"Good. Start by calling me Delaney. Let's stow that power." I got out of the Jeep, and Than followed suit.

Crow's shop used to be a Mexican restaurant. He'd hired Ryder to redesign it. Between the two of them, they'd turned it into something that looked more like a piece of art than a restaurant.

Dark brick was scattered by marble stones of red, white, and deep turquoise. Set on top of, under, over, and between the bricks were the glasswork that Crow was so good at creating. The side of the building facing the main road was decorated by an ocean of sea creatures from starfish to gray whales, and of course the famous float orbs, all hand blown out of glass.

On the side facing north, the glass pieces became whimsical. Some sea life, yes. But intertwined with that were fantastical birds, reptiles, and little fey creatures that didn't exist in nature (except maybe in Ordinary) and a truly stunning waterfall and river that looked like real water when traffic headlights or the afternoon sun caught it just right.

The nature-scape of glass was strategically placed so that darker brick around it created the very clear impression of dark wings and a raven's head above it, the black door its center.

Clever, that. His building looked like a raven with the world in its wings.

We walked through the raven's heart and into the shop.

It was a lot warmer inside, and the display shelves that lined the room were filled with glass that glittered and beckoned.

Crow hunched on a stool behind the counter, sketching on a pad of paper. "Welcome to the Crow's Nest," he said without looking up.

"Hey, Crow."

He glanced up, his eyes widening just a moment when he saw Than.

"Hello, Delaney." Crow set the sketchpad aside. "What trouble have you gotten yourself into?"

"Nothing much. Do you have any customers today?"

He shook his head. "It's early. Most show up after noon."

"Good. We need to make a deposit."

Crow stuck his fingers in his front pocket and studied Thanatos. "Been a while, old bones."

Thanatos raised one eyebrow. "I intend to vacation here, Trickster. I have signed the contracts necessary."

"You understand that your power remains with me, locked up until you leave town? You understand you will have no access to it during that time?"

"I do so understand."

"Have you positioned the power so that it will rest?"

"Yes."

Crow studied him. Thanatos looked immensely unconcerned. If there was one god in the known universe who didn't scare easily, I supposed it would be Death.

"He telling the truth, Delaney?" Crow asked.

Thanatos didn't scowl, but his countenance darkened. He did not like his word being called into doubt.

"He's agreed, signed, and followed through. All you have to do is take us back to the storage area so we can settle the power, and he can start his vacation."

"Huh." Crow clapped his hands together once and rubbed them. "All right. Let's do this, then. C'mon back."

We followed him to the furnace where he did a lot of his glassblowing for the tourists, and where he taught his classes. Then we moved back to the furnace set in the farthest corner of the building.

A worktable filled with all his glassblowing tools was situated in close proximity to the oven, and other, older-looking tools were hung on the wall beside it.

The tourist furnace was hot, and so was this furnace. But I could tell that the older one had more than just heat in it. I could hear the god powers singing.

"That's where you're keeping them?" I asked. "Really, Crow? I thought you had them in a safe or something secure."

"Do you see any deities accessing their power?" he asked. "Do you see power escaping and running loose in town? No, you do not. Do you see any trouble with the powers held here?" He opened the oven door so I could look inside at the hot coals.

To my eyes, those coals burned with more than fire. The flames were filled with wild, indescribable colors, scents, and music. God powers curled and flexed in that crucible. Each power contained in its own space, quiet and passive, and unlike the noisy, angry power inside of me, these powers seemed happy.

Yes, that sounded silly. But I could sense the calm radiating off them. Pretty amazing, considering the mix of powers in there.

"If you don't like my oven, you can give them to another god for safekeeping."

"That's not the way it works and you know it. It's your turn. You watch them for the rest of the year. And that's that."

He sighed. "I know. But it's so *boring*. You know I haven't had a vacation in months?"

"Cry me a new river. Living here *is* your vacation, remember?"

He grinned. "No need to resort to the truth. You've had your look," he said to Thanatos. "Hand over your sparkly bits to Uncle Raven."

"My bits," Than said icily, "never sparkle."

"That's what they all say." Crow held out his hand. "Give over."

Thanatos stretched out his right hand, and after a moment's hesitation when I thought I'd have to break them out of an alpha stare-down, he shook with Crow. I'd seen this before. I'd been there when Dad stood witness to a dozen or so deities who relinquished their power.

He said he saw the power as living light and color. I didn't see it like that. To me, the actual power transfer was nearly invisible, but wholly audible. To me, there were just two men, very different men who were also very the same—standing, hands clasped, gazes locked, a slight glow building between their hands.

What my father saw as wildfire, I vaguely perceived as a low light.

But what my eyes could not see, my ears heard. The transfer of power was a sub-audible thrumming, like a tornado growing louder, closer, as celestial voices howled a rising, clashing chorus of war and joy.

Dad told me he never heard power. Not even a whisper. I didn't know how he could miss it. It was song that resonated in my bones and haunted my dreams.

Raven and Death drew their hands away, and Crow turned to shut the oven door.

Before it closed, I could see the new color in that fire. Death burning cold.

Crow turned. "Got you covered. You need it back, you let Delaney know first. She says it's okay, then it's all yours."

"I am aware of my responsibilities," Than said. "I did read the contract thoroughly."

Than hadn't changed, really. Even without his power, he was every inch the aloof, dark undertaker in a Hawaiian shirt.

Maybe there was a little less shadowed edge to his face. Maybe his eyes carried something less hollow, less of the grave. But no matter what he resembled on the outside—god or mortal—he was all mortal now.

And since he was Death, I felt the need to remind him of some of the ground rules.

"Thanks, Crow. See you around."

"Come by anytime, Delaney. I heard about Heim."

"What did you hear?"

"That he washed up dead last night."

"You hear anything else?"

"Myra said you have it under control. His power," he added, as if I didn't know what he was talking about.

"I do."

"Do you?"

"I said I do. So I do."

He narrowed his eyes. "If you say so."

"I say so. We have a problem, Crow?"

"Not today we don't." He smiled again to take the threat out of those words. "You know I love you, girl."

"I know." And I did. Crow had been in town my entire life. He was like an uncle to me. But that didn't mean he wasn't still a trickster god.

No matter how mortal, how "normal" the god became, they were still, and always, colored by and connected to the power they carried.

"If you know something about Heim's death," I said, "I want to hear about it."

"I have no idea how he died. But you could probably ask your friend Chuckles here."

"I already did."

"And?"

"He was sort of vague."

Crow snickered. "He always has been."

Thanatos, who had gotten bored with our conversation, was looking at the tools on the worktable, his hands folded behind his back, fingers of his left hand wrapped around the bony wrist of his right as if he were perusing artifacts in a museum.

He sniffed once at Crow's accusation, but had no further comment.

"If you hear something," I said again. "Tell me."

"I will."

"Good. Thank you." I strolled over to Than. "Can I have one word with you?"

He slipped his gaze away from something that looked like a gaffing hook. "Yes."

I walked back out into the main shop. The front door opened and two women and a young girl stepped into the shop. I caught the door and smiled as we stepped past them and out into the parking lot.

I walked over to my Jeep, and Than followed.

"You worry, Reed Daughter?"

"Today seems to be a good day for it. I just wanted to remind you that now that you are here, in Ordinary, and your powers are stored there." I pointed back to the shop. "You are vulnerable. You are mortal. You can be killed."

"I know." His eyes gleamed. "Wouldn't that be a most interesting thing?"

"No. It's not interesting. It's just a permanent thing that will take loads of my time and effort and even more paperwork. I already have one power to deal with. I don't want to have to hold two and find new owners for both, understand?"

"I understand your concern."

I didn't think he was taking me seriously. Maybe the direct approach would work. "Please, don't do anything to get yourself killed."

"I shall strive to become an upstanding and long-lived mortal, Delaney."

I nodded. "Using my name? That's a good start. Thank you, Than."

He tipped his head to the side and gave me the kind of half bow that I would expect out of a butler.

"Do you have a place to stay? Would you like me to drop you off anywhere? Hades runs a cute little bed and breakfast."

"Hades," he said with some distaste. Then he looked up at the sky and down at the street, the cars, the people walking into the city library, all with the same sense of quiet wonder.

"I believe I shall take a constitutional and acquaint myself with the possibilities. Good day, Delaney."

"Good day, Than."

With that, he started off north. His smooth, even gait, head held high, was an odd contrast with his crazy-bright shirt and sleek black slacks. I wondered if his shoes were going to give him blisters, but decided that might be another mortal experience he would find interesting.

CHAPTER 11

MYRA AND Jean were both at their desks, pretending to work. Roy was over at the coffee station stirring a paper cup. They all threw me glances filled with relief.

Trillium Ruiz, a graceful, poised woman with deep brown skin and eyes that leaned hazel-gold sat on the small couch in our lobby. She wore a cascade of earrings, slacks, and a tailored jacket over a white shirt. She ran the *Ordinary Post*, our local newspaper, and didn't know about the creatures or deities in town.

"Chief Reed." She stood, her pad and pen already in her hands.

"Hello, Trillium. Here on personal business?"

"No. Just need a statement for the paper."

"Sure. What do you want to know?"

"Is it true that Heim Dalton was found dead last night?"

"Yes."

"Do you know the cause of death?"

"The cause of death is still under investigation. We suspect drowning."

"When did this drowning happen?"

"Late last night."

"Were there any witnesses?"

"No comment."

She raised one eyebrow. "Really, chief? That's not exactly a make-or-break question for investigating a drowning."

"My statement stands. And I'll finish it off for you. We at the department are very sorry for the loss of one of the members of our community. We are doing everything we can to confirm the cause of his death and to alert his next of kin. I think that about covers it."

"Do you suspect foul play?"

"No comment. This is an ongoing investigation, Trillium. We're not going to give our final report until we have one."

"All right," she said. "All right." She clicked the pen and flipped the cover on the notepad.

"Why hasn't this death hit the news?"

I leaned against Jean's desk. "I have no idea. It's not my job to babysit the local stations."

"So you're telling me you're not trying to keep this death out of the media?"

I sighed. "That's correct. Look, we're small potatoes among small potatoes. News of a fisherman falling off his boat and drowning gets a ten-second mention on the news stations in Portland only if it's a slow news day. There's no sizzle in it. He wasn't lost as sea, he's not a minor, he wasn't on vacation or battling cancer, or drunk, or saving a puppy.

"It's not surprising that our story, his story—no matter how tragic it was—didn't make the evening news. Believe me, I am very, very sorry he has passed. This kind of thing shouldn't happen to anyone. But I don't expect most people outside this town to take note of it."

What I wasn't about to tell her was that a few of the supernaturals in town kept tabs on how our news was delivered to the larger cities. We basically had friends in low places outside town who either took the shine off any news that might give away our secrets, or found ways to bury it in more important, more urgent stories.

"It just seems like someone should care," she said.

"Someone does. We do. You do."

"Does he have any next of kin?" She sounded a lot less reporter, and a lot more person concerned about how this loss was going to affect others.

I liked her for that.

"As far as we know, no. Parents passed away, no siblings. Last of his family line. We're doing our due diligence."

That was a lie. Heimdall was not the first Heimdall. But he was several hundred years old by my calculations. Any relatives he might have—and he might actually have some great-great-greats descended from his bloodline—would never have met him, and certainly wouldn't have known of him.

Gods were darned private people.

"Here you go," Roy said, handing Trillium the coffee.

She smiled, instantly more at ease with Roy than with me. I didn't know how he did that—and there was nothing magic about it. Roy was as mortal as I was. Maybe more.

Definitely more.

But whenever he was around, people felt more relaxed, more at ease.

It wasn't the only reason I was grateful he had decided to work with us, but it was a reason I had come to appreciate.

"Thanks." She took the cup. "One more thing."

"Sure," I said.

"Do you know who's going to replace him on the Rhubarb Rally judging committee?"

"On the what now?"

"Heim was a judge for the Rhubarb Rally."

I glanced at Myra and Jean, who both shrugged. "When did that happen?"

"I think Chris talked him into it three or four months ago."

"Chris Lagon."

She nodded. "Since Heim has passed, the committee is looking for a replacement."

He had just passed hours ago. It was amazing how quickly word got around this town. I was seriously impressed we could keep anything secret.

"Those contest coordinators are on the ball. Who's heading that up?"

"Bertie."

Bertie was a sweet old lady with so much energy that she left the rest of us in the dust. She was also a valkyrie, which meant if she wanted you to do something, you were going to do it, even if she had to drag you over your own dead body.

"I'd check with her, then. I'm sure she'll have a new judge nailed down by the end of the day."

"All right. If I need clarification on anything, I'll call. Thanks for the coffee."

"Come on back anytime."

She walked out of the lobby.

"Nicely done, sis," Jean said.

"Just doing my job. Which I do every day. All the time. Why are you all looking at me like that?"

"We're not looking at you like anything," Myra said. "We're just watching out for you. Now that you've taken on that part-time job."

She meant the god power.

"How are you doing with it?" she asked.

You mean that thing that's yelling and thrashing around in my head?

"Fine," I said. "Still fine."

"How did it go?" Jean grinned. "Did they throw punches? Break any bones?"

"Who?" I walked to my desk and dug through my drawer for some painkillers. The yelling and thrashing were edging toward headache land.

"Death and Crow. Crow made him angry, didn't he? Crow makes everyone angry."

"They got along fine, you big ol' gossip. And even if Crow did make him angry"—I lifted a finger and pointed it at Roy, who gave me wide, innocent eyes—"none of you should be betting money on these things."

"It wasn't money," Jean said. "It was just a bet."

"Do I want to know?" I sat, took the pills with the cold coffee left over in my mug, and logged on to my computer.

"If Death would punch Crow in the face," Jean said. "From all the stories Crow tells, Death has been after him for years. Since they are both mortal, I thought a little payback might be on the menu."

"Crow's always telling a story about something," I said. "Only some of it is true, and the true stuff isn't usually the part you'd think it is."

Jean walked over to my desk and messed with the pencil cup. "That's so disappointing."

"Peacefulness is disappointing?"

She shrugged. "I like it when things get a little stirred up. Speaking of stirred up: how was your night?"

"Well, someone died, and I got knocked out by a god power. So pretty terrific, thanks."

"Not that part of your night. The before part with Ryder, and the after part. With Ryder."

"It was fine."

"No. Nope." She sat on my desk. "I need to hear a lot more than 'fine' when Ryder Bailey is involved."

I looked away from my computer, sat back. "Where is he?"

"Lunch run." She waggled her eyebrows. "Spill."

"Death thinks someone murdered Heim."

That wiped the gleeful look off her face.

"What?" Myra said. She walked over to stand by my desk too. Roy rolled his chair out into the aisle so he could watch us and the switchboard at the same time.

"I asked him if he knew how Heim died. He said he wasn't a dime-store prognosticator nor a big fan of murder."

"Huh," Jean breathed, surprised. "Whatdoyouknow."

Myra rubbed a thumb over the inside of her finger. It was a habit she'd had for as long as I could remember. Some kind of fake luck gesture Abban, the tallest leprechaun I'd ever met, taught her when we were in elementary school. "He said it was murder?"

"I asked him point blank if he thought Heim had been murdered, he said yes."

"Wellshit," Jean said, running her words together like she did when she was dealing with something over her head. "Fuckhell."

"All right." Myra's voice was calm, professional. "We can work with that. Who would want Heim dead?"

"None of the deities come to mind immediately," I said.

There were squabbles and grudges between deities that couldn't be erased just because they were on vacation. But we kept an eye on those sorts of things. Heimdall didn't seem to have enemies among the gods here. Not enemies who would be willing to kill another deity and risk losing vacation rights permanently.

"Maybe Hera?" Jean suggested, getting some space between her words. "I heard Heim was taking his best fish to Chris's place for his new cook, and giving the seconds to Hera's bar and grill."

I tapped her name into the suspect list. "We can check. Did she seem upset about it?"

"I overheard her calling him a lot of bad names," Jean said.

"Okay, have we seen any other deit upset?"

She shook her head, and so did Myra.

"Creatures?" I asked.

"Chris?" Myra suggested.

"Because he's getting the best fish Heim could catch? How does that warrant murder?"

"According to Dan Perkin, Chris is dead-set on winning the drink category in the rally. Heim was a judge. Maybe Heim told him he wasn't going to vote for Chris's beer."

"Chris told me he doesn't care about the award."

"Still," Myra said. "We should follow up."

Jean unwrapped a square piece of pink gum and stuck it in her mouth. "Labs came back." Her words smelled like blueberry. "Blunt trauma to the back of the head, salt water in the lungs."

"So another water creature? Nymphs? Mers? Any other creats upset with Heim?"

We all looked over at Roy. He shook his head. "Not that I can think of."

"We'll check the waters people anyway. Which brings us to mortals." I placed my fingers on my keyboard. "Go."

Myra started. "We'll want to talk to his ex Lila, and her sister Margot. See if there is any hostility there. Maybe Pete Bell? He was always trying to steal Heim's whale-watching customers."

It wasn't much to go on. We all knew that. Heim had been easygoing and not the type to make enemies, which, while admirable while he was alive, made our jobs a lot harder now that he was dead.

"Maybe we should check in with Bertie," Myra said. "She talked him into judging for the festival. Maybe he edged out someone else who got mad about it. She'd know who else was in the running."

I nodded and put her in as an information source to follow up on.

"I'd like to take a look at his finances too," I said. "Make sure he was on the up and up with what he was catching and shipping."

"He was," Roy said. "Clean as a whistle. Barbara's firm does his accounts."

Barbara was Roy's wife. She owned the accounting firm in town. If she said he was clean, I believed it.

"Maybe we should add Dan Perkin to the list," Jean said. "He's made an enemy of everyone."

It was sort of the office joke, although it was also true. Dan really didn't have many friends. Any investigation from criminal mischief, lost newspaper deliveries, or missing socks always pointed to Dan.

Dan was never the actual perpetrator, though we had once caught him throwing rocks at tourist cars parked illegally in disabled parking zones.

Since Jean sympathized with his stance on that, if not his action, she let him off with a warning.

But since Dan had also been a target of explosives and he was tied into the Rhubarb Rally, I added his name as an avenue we should explore.

"I can't believe you put him on it," Jean said. "No-goes." She touched her nose. Myra quickly did the same.

"Are you two kidding me? What are you? Five?"

"No," Jean said, her finger still on her nose. "We are smart. Because we don't have to interview Dan."

I rolled my eyes. "Fine. I'll talk to Dan, you big babies. Is this it for the start?"

Jean and Myra dropped their fingers off their noses.

"All I can think of," Roy said. "Well, we could check with his deck hand."

"Heim had a deck hand? I thought he let Rufus go."

"He did." Roy looked up at the ceiling a moment. "I think the man's name was Walter. Came hitching into town on his way to California. Fresno. Heim picked him up for a couple whale-watching runs."

"Did he go out with him last night?" I asked.

Myra walked to her desk and plucked up a file folder. She flipped through a few pages. "Coast guard didn't find anyone else on the boat. No missing persons report."

I typed him onto the list. "Not that a hitcher working day jobs is really going to be noticed as missing."

She frowned at the file and nodded.

We all knew we didn't have much to go on. I found myself wishing we had a dime-store prognosticator on call.

"This is a good start," I said, trying to bring up the mood. "Let's divvy it up and cover ground, ladies. Roy, you got the fort?"

"I'll keep the coffee on."

"What about Ryder?" Jean asked.

Oh. I'd forgotten our fifth wheel. We all raised our fingers at the same time and jabbed our noses. Roy sighed like a veteran kindergarten teacher.

I glared at my sisters through my fingers.

"I already did ride-along," Myra said around her palm.

"My shift's almost over." Jean had chosen to use her middle finger on her nose, of course.

"I am not going to drag him around behind me all day," I said.

And then the door opened and a man walked into the lobby.

CHAPTER 12

MYRA DROPPED her finger a split second before the rest of us and squared off toward our visitor. Not Ryder. It was Cooper, my ex-boyfriend.

"Can I help you?" If Myra's words could invoke weather, Cooper would be buried under a snow pack.

Cooper wore a dark blue T-shirt that was tight enough to show his muscles, and jeans that belted low on his hips. His light hair was pulled back into a band at the base of his neck. Daylight did good things to the angles of his face and lit up his deep brown eyes. He gave Myra an embarrassed smile. "Hi, Myra. How have you been?"

"Busy. As a matter of fact, we're all busy." Not snow pack. Glacier.

"Right, sure," he said. "I just…" He glanced over at Jean, who shook her head like she couldn't believe he was dumb enough to be here.

Cut your losses, turn around, don't look at me, I thought.

When his eyes turned to me, he had that gonna-hurl look of a man begging for a second chance. His gaze strayed to my lips.

"What's up, Cooper?" Yes, I took pity on him. Yes, I heard both my sisters' disgruntled sighs. No, this wasn't a second chance. This was me being polite and doing my job. He'd come to the station. Maybe there was a problem.

"I thought maybe you'd have time for lunch?" He finally looked back up and met my gaze. His eyes were amazingly deep, and warm as an endless summer.

An electric zing rattled through me so hard and fast, I felt like someone had punched me in the sternum. I held my breath as the buzz grew and grew into something bigger, louder, intense.

Holy crap.

One look at him and I couldn't think. Everything in me either went dead still, or was vibrating so fast it felt like stillness.

And there was Cooper. Right in front of me, brown eyes burning. He was everything I wanted. Everything I desired.

What? That couldn't be right. I didn't want Cooper.

I couldn't get those words out. I couldn't move, talk, or do anything more than stare at him in hyper-stillness. Something was wrong. Something was very wrong.

"Hey." His voice dropped low and husky. He was standing in front of me.

Had he moved? Had I blinked? When had he moved?

"Hey, gorgeous." He wrapped his arm around my waist and dragged the other hand down my back, pulling at my shirt.

I was on fire, buzzing, but I couldn't feel my heartbeat, didn't know if I was breathing. Was this a dream? A hallucination?

"Delaney," he breathed.

I watched my hand lift and brush across the back of his neck even though I couldn't feel it. *Creepy.* I watched my hand draw his face down to mine.

Weird, weird, weird, weird.

His breath hitched. He kissed me. Full, hot.

That, I felt.

Everything in me sang—a chorus of emotions avalanched through me. I was lost to it, buried under it, fighting to surface through a tumble of sensations so sharp and clear they blended into pain.

I think I groaned. Not in pleasure.

A hand clamped my shoulder and another gripped my arm, squeezed, and jerked.

The world stuttered. Time snapped and skittered into its normal flow. Things I didn't realize I'd been missing: color, sound, smells, notched into overdrive, and I stumbled backward, reeling. My knees felt like overstretched rubber bands, and I think I would have crumpled to the floor if Jean hadn't wrapped her arm around my ribs and held me tight.

Someone was in front of me. Shorter than me. Dark hair cut in a swing. Police uniform.

My brain tried to put two and two together. Finally got it on the fourth or fifth try.

Myra stood in front of me. Between me and Cooper.

And suddenly, I could think again.

Holy shit. Cooper had kissed me. In the middle of the police station. In front of my sisters and Roy.

"Problem?" a male voice asked.

The prickly hot sweat of fear and embarrassment washed over me. I turned my gaze woodenly to the door.

Ryder Bailey stood there holding a takeout bag in one hand and a drink carrier with five drinks in the other.

Cooper had kissed me. In the middle of the police station. In front of my sisters and Roy and *Ryder.*

There had been times in my life when I'd wished I was a more religious person. But since gods spend their sand-and-sunburn days in my backyard complaining about things like cell reception and plugged storm drains, I decided at a young age that they were too busy to answer my prayers.

Still, if I thought there was a chance someone up there could hear me, I'd pray that the ring-of-fire volcanoes might choose this moment to blow so the resulting earthquake would swallow me whole.

"Uh…" I said, but it came out a little high and panicky.

Myra waded into the verbal fray. "Cooper, I'd like you to step outside. Ryder, you can put the food next to the coffee there." She pointed with one hand while she started toward Cooper, ready to corral him toward the door.

"Delaney?" Cooper didn't move.

"She said to move to the door, Clark." Ryder's tone of voice rang with the low, quiet authority of a man who was used to holding a gun at someone while insisting they calm down.

It was that, the change in Ryder's voice, that brought me back to the situation at hand.

Fact: Cooper had just kissed me.

Fact: I'd been frozen in place. Caught by something in him.

Fact: I should probably double-check our database and make sure he wasn't a long-lost descendant of some kind of creature with kissing powers.

Fact: Did I mention he'd kissed me?

"Let's all calm down." I pulled away from Jean's hold and took a couple steps toward Myra so I could grab her before she decided to swing Cooper around and frog-march him to the street.

And wonder of wonders, everyone calmly stared at me.

Well. No pressure or anything.

"Cooper, I don't know why that just happened, but it's not happening again." Ryder wasn't the only one who could use a put-the-gun-down tone of voice. "Sorry if you thought that might be something more—"

"Don't tell me you didn't feel that," Cooper said with a scowl. "There was something there. Something between us. You know it. You felt it."

Oh, yeah, I'd felt it. But I hadn't liked it. One look into his eyes had me frozen, unable to control my own body, and throwing myself into his arms.

"Cooper…" I said.

"You think you can ignore me? Think you can jerk me around?" He took a step forward. Two things happened in quick succession:

One, Myra reached out and smacked a hard palm into his shoulder.

Two, Ryder crossed the room so quickly, it didn't register he'd done it until he'd grabbed Cooper's other arm and twisted it up behind his back and shoved his palm flat against the back of his neck. Ryder's stance was squared with a foot inside Cooper's stance. One twist, and Cooper would be kissing linoleum.

Jean tugged me back and slid around in front of me, her hand on her sidearm holstered at her hip.

Okay, that was three things, but it all happened so fast, a couple of them together.

"Steady," I said in a voice that was exactly that. "Cooper, we'll talk later. Myra, please make sure he gets to his car. Ryder, you need to release him."

Ryder was watching me over Cooper's shoulder. A flash of hot anger clouded Ryder's hammered-gold eyes. Then he smiled, all the anger stowed as if it had never been there.

"Sure," Ryder said with an easy chuckle. He released Cooper's arm and stepped back, sliding his hands into his back pockets. "Sorry about that, Cooper. Didn't mean to go all self-defense on you. When I first moved to the big city, I took a couple classes, and I guess they kicked in."

Cooper shifted to the side so he could glare at Ryder. "Keep your hands off me."

Ryder held both hands, palms out. "Sorry. Didn't mean to jump in the middle of this...whatever this is."

"Let's go, Mr. Clark." Myra pointed Cooper toward the door. She wasn't holding on to him yet, but her body language said if he tried anything, she'd have him in cuffs.

Ryder just stepped to one side so they'd have a clear path to the door. I noticed that he'd also left the takeout and drinks on the floor, neither bag nor drinks disturbed.

"Let me get that." Ryder scooped lunch back into his hands.

Did his eyes linger a moment over Cooper as if he were looking for a weapon? Did his gaze flicker to the door, to Myra's Glock, to the distance, her reach, Cooper's height and level of animosity?

Did Ryder just do cop things?

Before I could settle on an answer to that, Myra had Cooper out the door, and Ryder was standing there with the lunch bag in one hand, drinks in the other. "By the coffee pot?"

"Right over there," Roy, who had been quiet this whole time, said. The sheer normalness of his voice did a lot to settle the tension in the room. Or maybe just the tension in me.

Ryder walked around the front counter and back to where the coffee was set up.

I put my hands over my face for a moment.

Breathe in. Breathe out.

Even behind my hands, I could feel Jean lean toward my ear. "So Cooper's back in town. Are you okay?" Her breath still smelled like fake fruit.

I dropped my hands. Ryder was at the coffee table, his back toward us as he pulled Chinese food boxes out of the bag.

"I am now," I whispered, even though I still felt a little feverish. "That was weird."

"How weird?"

"Ordinary weird. Track Cooper's blood heritage. Make sure we're not missing something."

That was all the whispering we had time for. She patted my shoulder, letting me know she would.

Roy shifted in his chair and it made a crunchy metal-on-metal noise. "You get me my salt and pepper squid?"

Ryder still hadn't turned around from sorting containers. He held up a little white box and jiggled it.

I swallowed down my revulsion to all things tentacled and tried not to imagine Roy chewing through the deep-fried wriggly things.

"They threw in an order of pork fried rice." Ryder turned.

"Well, don't hold out on me, rookie." Roy held up a hand and Ryder tossed the box, which Roy easily caught.

"No throwing food in the station." Wow. Could I sound any more like a mother? Boss. I sounded like a boss.

Ryder gave me an apologetic new-guy-at-the-job shrug along with a small smile that about melted me into my boots. "Do you have time for lunch, Delaney?"

It was almost exactly what Cooper had asked me.

I eyed the boxes he'd opened in neat rows. "The last guy who asked me out for lunch almost left in handcuffs."

"Then it's a good thing I brought lunch in." He looked relaxed, though his eyes still flickered with low-burning anger. Cooper Clark had made no friends today.

"I need to talk to Dan Perkin. So I'll just take one to go."

"I'll go with you," Jean said.

"You have other leads to check into," I reminded her.

"I can come along," Ryder said.

Jean and I exchanged a look. We couldn't ditch Ryder. There wasn't enough pre-rally stuff to throw at him yet today, and if we left him here, he'd probably end up listening to some god complaining about their cell phone roaming bill. Seriously. Get a data plan, Momus.

Temperamental gods were something I'd rather leave to Roy.

"Or," he said casually, "I could do some filing. Familiarize myself with the records room, that sort of thing."

I didn't know why he willingly volunteered for the scut work, but it seemed mean to make him file all day.

"You brought me on to help," he said. "Let me help. I can go talk to Dan if you want. But I'm just as happy to stay here and categorize the evidence room. Familiarize myself with things."

It was tempting to send him out to get a statement from Dan. So tempting. Jean's eyes lit up, practically begging me to say yes.

But no matter how observant Ryder was, or how quickly he could put someone in a headlock, he wasn't a cop. We needed to find out if Dan saw anything at Jump Off Jack's that might help us find out who murdered Heim.

Evidence that would be admissible in court. Which meant an officer of the law had to be there.

"You might as well come along and see how we do this," I said. "Leave the filing for later."

I thought I saw a flash of disappointment in his eyes that he quickly covered up. Wondered if he had a filing fetish. A sexy Mr. Librarian fantasy, staring Ryder Bailey, a tweed sweater, and a thick pair of glasses rolled through my mind.

I turned to the door so he couldn't see me blush. "We'll eat in the car."

CHAPTER 13

IT TOOK one full order of orange chicken and a side of fried noodles to find Dan Perkin. He wasn't at his house, though his laundry—a heavy flannel shirt, waterproof jacket, knee-high rubber boots, and a pair of waterproof pants— were draped over the railing of his front porch to dry. They had that starched look of material that had seen salt water and sunlight.

We checked in with Pearl, who told us she thought he was down at the community center talking to Bertie about the Rhubarb Rally.

Jean and I were in her old, crappy truck, Jean driving, and Ryder was following behind in his newer, less-crappy truck. The two-vehicle split had been Jean's idea. I wasn't sure if she wanted privacy to talk or to give me a breather from the craziness of the morning.

Either way, I appreciated it. Even though the morning wasn't the weirdest thing that had ever happened in Ordinary, it was up there. I spent the drive time with my hands in my pockets, thumbs tucked between my middle and ring finger, which was an old, comforting habit I hated anyone else to see, sorting through my feelings and reactions to the whole thing. I finally gave up and just stuck the event in a corner of my mind marked: Supernatural Crap To Check Into Later.

Thumbs out. Thumbs all the way out.

"Ready?" Jean asked as she parked outside the community center—a two-story brick elementary school that had been abandoned when the new middle school and high schools were built fifteen years ago.

There had been some wrangling over what to do with the old building, and while it had served as an art center for a couple months, and a storage room for a few more, Bertie had finally convinced all the people necessary that it should become a community center—the heart of our town.

And she'd officially set herself up there like a bird in a big brick nest.

I pulled my hair back into a loose braid and finished tying it. "It's just Dan."

"Right. But if you feel the need to slip him the tongue, give me a signal, okay?"

"Like this?" I flipped up my middle finger and she laughed. "I promise I won't make a habit of randomly kissing men."

She chewed her gum into little snaps. "I don't know. There's a few boys in town I wouldn't mind kissing, randomly or not."

"I thought you had your eye on Hogan."

"I'd like to have more than my eye on him."

"Yeah, you talk big. When was the last time you went on a date?"

"Two weeks ago."

I looked over at her. She was staring at Ryder's truck, which was coming up behind us.

"Who?" I asked.

"None of your business."

I wanted to ask her why she didn't want me to know things about her personal life. A small part of me wondered if she and I were drifting apart. How long had it been since we'd watched crappy monster movies together?

Since Dad died? Before that?

Becoming the eldest Reed had taken over my life. This town, these people and creatures and deities, consumed my free time. I didn't want to lose what I had with Jean because I was working all the time.

"What?" she asked as Ryder got out of his truck and stood next to it, waiting for us. "Seriously. What?"

"Have I been a terrible sister over the last year?"

"Just the last year?"

I made a face at her. "We need to go see a movie."

"Right now?"

"No. Soon. Yes?"

"Sure."

We both spoke at the same time: "I pick the movie."

"Eldest picks," I said.

She opened her door and I followed. "You picked last time. That sob-fest teen romance." She stuck her finger in her mouth and flicked her thumb down like firing a gun.

"Movie?" Ryder asked as we walked to the front of the community center together, Ryder falling into step behind Jean and me.

"It was pretty terrible." I pushed open the door and stepped in. We walked down the empty main hallway, our feet and voices echoing off the painted ceiling and wooden walls. "You'll make me watch a space movie, won't you?"

"Maybe," she said. "With one hundred percent more explosions than the last thing you made me watch."

The door to the main office was ajar. Dan Perkin was behind that door, his voice raised in mid-tirade.

Speaking of explosions. I took a deep breath, then strolled into the room. "Afternoon, everyone."

Dan Perkin had his back to us, one hand raised, finger pointing at the sky, his other hand on the bill of his baseball hat. He was right in the middle of his patented God-is-my-witness move.

Bertie sat behind a desk with two vases of flowers on the corners and a laptop to one side. She had placed a tea towel in front of her and was slicing an apple in her palm over it. The knife in her deceptively frail hands slid through the meat of the apple with a razor's ease.

Bertie was a sparrow of a woman who appeared to be in her eighties: petite, short shock-white hair with a jag of bangs over her sharp green eyes. Her skin was pale as the moon, the golden polish on her nails sparking with each stab of the knife.

Great. Dan Perkin had pissed off the valkyrie.

I didn't know how this man wasn't dead yet.

"Good afternoon, Delaney, Jean, Mr. Bailey." Bertie gave the kind of look that said she was glad we'd stopped in because she was just about to stab Dan in the jugular with that little apple knife.

Dan Perkin turned so he could glare at us. His eyes narrowed at Ryder then ticked back to me.

"Maybe you can make something decent come out of this mess," he said. "I've been trying to make her listen to me for an hour."

"Is there a problem?" I asked. Those four words were like Perkin's own catnip. He loved hearing them.

Next lecture in three…two…one: "There has been a death in this town, Officer Reed. I demand to know who is going to replace Heim on the judging panel immediately."

Dan Perkin. A lover of his fellow man.

"That decision falls to Bertie," I said. "I assume she needs time to choose who would be most suited for the job. Is that correct?"

"Yes." She placed her apple on the towel. She hesitated, then placed the knife next to it, staring at it with longing in her eyes. "As I told Mr. Perkin, the list of candidates is narrow and vetted. Whomever I choose will be unbiased."

"It better be someone who won't favor big business in this town." He stabbed a finger into the top of her desk, hard enough to make the flowers tremble. "It better be someone who judges entries on their merits, not on marketing razzle-dazzle. Someone who won't cave in when some rich guy slips them a few dollars."

Bertie was not amused. "Are you accusing me of taking bribes, Mr. Perkin? If so, I will see to it that the rhubarb contest is cancelled. Today."

"No," he said. "Wait! No. Don't do that."

"I wouldn't want to tarnish the good name of our town," she went on. "If you and other contestants doubt that our contest judges are anything but impartial, it throws the entire event into question, doesn't it, Officer Reed?"

It took everything I had to keep the smile off my face. When Bertie wanted to draw blood, she didn't need a knife.

"Yes," I said grimly. "I believe it does."

"But—but no!" Dan was on full defense now. "I don't want the rally cancelled. I never said I wanted the rally cancelled. I just want a fair judge. An honest judge. I know you can find one."

Bertie was hardcore genius getting him to turn around like that.

"I happen to have a judge in mind," she said. "Someone who will absolutely follow the rules and laws of the contest."

She had him on her hook. Dan shifted the brim of his baseball hat, nervous as a worm. "All right. I trust you, Bertie. Always have. Who is it?"

"Delaney Reed," she said, "would you please do Ordinary the great honor of becoming a judge for the Rhubarb Rally?"

Jean snorted. She knew I hated rhubarb. Ryder coughed, and I suspected he was covering a laugh—not coming down with sudden hay fever. Dan wasn't the only worm on her hook.

I opened my mouth to say no, but the slight twitch of Bertie's eyebrow stopped me.

I was wrong. She didn't resemble a sparrow, she resembled a hawk. If I refused to judge, I was pretty sure she'd stab me with her apple knife.

Maybe I could talk her into letting me judge the art or textiles. Something non-edible.

"Sure," I said. "I'd be happy to help out."

"Well, I don't know…" Dan muttered.

Seriously, nothing satisfied this man.

"We could always ask Molly if she'd judge," Ryder suggested. "She's got a culinary school background."

Molly was Chris's waitress. Nice girl. I was sure Dan had hassled her when he'd been at Jump Off Jack's, just like he hassled everyone else. She'd probably be happy to throw him under the rhubarb bus.

I resisted the urge to look over my shoulder at Ryder to see if he was making up the culinary school thing. I hadn't known she'd studied.

"Culinary school training is a very nice credential," Bertie said.

"But she works for Chris Lagon!" Dan said.

"That's right," Ryder said, as if he'd forgotten. "Isn't Grace Nordell a sommelier? She's one of your neighbors, Dan."

"Grace?" he said with even more disdain. "That busybody and snoop?"

"How about—" Ryder started.

"No," Dan said. "I supposed Officer Reed is as good a choice as any."

Jean took a breath that shook with suppressed laughter. I could see her shoulders trembling out of the corner of my eye, but her face was still and neutral.

"Excellent!" Bertie's voice was a cheerful gavel nailing down the silence. She stood, walked around the desk, and plucked at Dan's arm as if he were escorting her to a dance.

"I'm sure our very own police chief will be the most impartial of judges," she said.

"I suppose," he said. "But—"

She guided him out into the hallway and toward the door. "You don't have any family entering into the contest, do you, Delaney dear?" she called over her shoulder. They were almost out of earshot.

"Nope." I followed them. "Jean and Myra will be working crowd control and emergency response. Don't have time to do anything more."

"I'll be sure to contact you with the judging schedule. I'm sure we can make it work with your other duties."

"I'm sure we can," I agreed, wishing there were a way out of this. I glanced back at Jean, who was still in the office. Her finger was pressed to the tip of her nose.

Brat.

Bertie tugged open the outer door and disengaged from Dan with the grace of a dancer. "Thank you for coming by, Mr. Perkin. See you in a few days at the rally!"

She shut the door in his face. "There." She dusted her palms together. "That should keep him for a while. Can I help you with something?"

"No, I needed to talk to Dan."

"Oh." She stared at the door distastefully. "Do you want me to invite him back in?"

"No need. I can talk to him outside." I reached over for the door, and she placed the golden tips of her fingers on the back of my hand. Her fingers were warm and soft.

"You hired Ryder?"

I wondered how she'd heard about that already. Small town, big ears, I supposed.

"Temporarily. He doesn't know about…everything."

"If I can be of any help with what you've recently picked up, do let me know." She was talking about the god power I'd need to offload onto some poor mortal in the next six days. Something I still hadn't even started working on.

It was on my to-do list. Right up there in the top ten.

"I will."

"Mr. Bailey," Bertie chirped.

Ryder had sauntered up behind us, quiet and casual as a cat.

"Want me to come along while you talk to Dan?" he asked.

Jean lingered inside the office, a big grin on her face. She wasn't going to help with Dan. "I don't think—" I started.

"Mr. Bailey." Bertie swooped down on Ryder's arm with a bit more relish than she had Dan's. "Could I have a brief word with you?"

Ryder threw me a questioning look, and I nodded.

"It will only take a moment," Bertie cooed, taking him back to the office.

Valkyries. Couldn't keep their hands off a hero. Ryder taking her side and shutting Dan up scored up there with Prometheus bringing the fire, though Prometheus insisted it had all been a big mistake, since he'd been drunk at the time and took a wrong turn.

I slipped outside. I wasn't going to ask Dan any questions Ryder couldn't hear. But in case I needed to press the supernatural angle, I didn't want to worry about what Ryder would think.

Dan sat in his car, windows up, looking furious and talking to himself.

Which was to say: normal.

I walked around the front of his car and knocked on the driver's-side window.

He jerked and glared.

"Can we talk?" I asked through the glass.

His eyes darted to the right and left. He looked so nervous, I was about to stand back up and double-check that I didn't have an axe murderer looming behind me. My eyes strayed to the handgun he had holstered under his console.

Finally, he rolled down the window. "I have a license to carry," he said.

"I know that, Dan."

"It's not loaded."

"Good, but that's not what I wanted to talk to you about."

"Well then, I don't know what you want from me. I'm doing everyone a favor coming here to demand justice. Demand we get what we deserve. A panel of fair judges. A fair contest."

"I didn't come to talk about the contest either, Mr. Perkin. I want to talk to you about Heim."

He pressed his thin lips together. He was sweating a little too heavily for this cool weather. But then, he was always sweating, always worked up. So that was normal too.

"I don't have anything to say about him." His gaze jittered. That would be a first.

"I'm just wondering where you were last night."

"Why? Do you think I have something to do with... You think I killed him?"

"I'm just wondering where you were last night," I repeated calmly.

"I won't sit here while you prosecute me. I have rights, you know. I don't have to tell you anything without a lawyer present."

"Dan," I said. "Settle down. Of course you have rights. And if you want your lawyer present, I'll give him a call and have him meet us down at the station so we can do this all formally and on the record. But we can do this friendly too. All I'm asking—all I'm asking—is where you spent your evening. That shouldn't be a hard thing to remember."

"Of course I remember," he said. "I was...I was at Jump Off Jack's. I went in to talk to Chris, but he wasn't there. If you ask me, he's the one you should be talking to. He had plenty of reasons to kill Heim. There was the fish Heim kept shorting him. That's hard on a place as busy as Chris's, though why people think his rundown shack is any better than the other bars in town is beyond me. Tourists are half idiot, half stupid."

"Tourists are the seasonal lifeblood of our town, Dan," I said. "And it's those tourists who are going to be trying out all the food and drink at the rally. It's the tourists who are going to buy the souvenirs and whatnots, fill the hotels, buy the gas. When did you go to Jump Off's? When did you leave?"

"I don't have to tell you that. I already answered your question."

"This is still friendly," I said. "Answer a few more details and we can keep it friendly. Push me hard, and I will take you on in, lawyer and all."

He fiddled with the bill of his hat again. I checked his knuckles for signs of a struggle. No blood. No scratches.

But he was more aggravated than usual. Could be the fact that he'd recently had his garden explode on him. Could be he wasn't coming clean with me.

"You went to talk to Chris around what time?"

"Five," he said shortly.

"And left?"

"I don't know. Five thirty."

"Did you drive?"

"Of course I drove."

"Did you talk with anyone else when you were there?"

"That do-nothing waitress of his."

Molly. No love lost there. Ryder had certainly played that card right.

"Where did you go after that?"

"Home."

"Did anyone see you there?

"Probably all my neighbors. They spy on me, you know. Grace is the worst. Pearl's always stopping in to visit. They're jealous of my property—I have the largest lot on the block, and they never let me forget I've got more than them. Well, I say damn them all. And damn Chris Lagon while He's at it. You are talking to the wrong man, officer. It's Chris that's behind all this."

"How do you figure that?"

"He wanted me out of the picture, so he blows up my rhubarb. He wanted Heim out of the picture because Heim was a judge. Chris cozied up to him, treated him like a friend. And all the while, it was just to buy off Heim. To make him give that piss-poor beer of his the prize. Have you even tasted that swill?"

"No."

"Terrible! Worst thing you'll ever taste in your life. He thinks he's so above us. High and mighty. Entitled hipster is what he is. Smug bastard, thinks his beer is something special. Well, I'm telling you it's not."

"You think Chris wants the prize enough to have Heim killed?"

"I think he went out there—got on Heim's boat all friendly. You know how he is, always on the water. Gets on his boat. Maybe they drink some beer. Maybe they talk, maybe it's all nice and chummy. Then Chris tells him he doesn't like the good catch going to Mom's, doesn't like competition. No, no. He can't stand someone competing with him. It's why he blew up my rhubarb. Afraid my rhutbeer would win the blue ribbon. So he sweet-talks Heim into giving his piss-poor beer a high score. Maybe tries to bribe him. But Heim—we all know he was a reasonable man, decent reputation, even though he slept with that Frenchwoman and drinks too much—Heim won't take the sweet talk. Heim won't take the money. Chris gets fed up, and…"

He paused, looked at me, his eyes a little wide. "How did he die? Did Chris shoot him? Slit his throat? Stab him in the chest?"

His heart was beating so hard, I could see the throb of his pulse at his neck.

"I'm not convinced Chris killed anyone, Mr. Perkin. This is a very…thorough picture you're painting. How do you suppose it all ended?"

"Bang!" He pointed his finger at me, and I resisted the urge to reach out and break it.

"Chris is a low-life coward and shoots Heim right in the back. Then he…he swims back to shore—you know how he's always swimming. Says it's good for the heart. Like he has one. I swear he's part fish, the freak."

The freak was, actually, kind of part fish. I decided to steer the conversation away from that truth.

"He's a good swimmer. A skill that would have saved Heim."

"Is that…is that how he died?" His eyes darted to everything but my eyes. "Drowned?" He sounded worried. It was the first time I'd heard him worry about someone else. I tried out the idea of Heim and Dan having a friendship.

Nope. Couldn't picture it.

"I don't have the report back yet." It wasn't a lie.

He rubbed his fingers over the bill of his hat three times, and then three times again. "Well, if it was drowning, you'd think a captain of a boat would know how to swim. Wouldn't you? Anyone who spends their life on a boat should swim. Hell, I swim, and it's been years since I've been on a boat. Back in my Navy days. When a man's word meant something."

"All right," I said. "That's all an interesting story. But last I'd heard, he and Heim were pretty close friends."

"Friends," he spat. "That doesn't mean anything when there's an award on the line."

"An award in a small festival in a small town? I don't think anyone deserves to die for a blue ribbon, do you, Mr. Perkin?"

"It's not the blue ribbon. It's the pride." He jutted out his chin. "Chris Lagon is prideful as sin."

I heard footsteps approaching and glanced at the sidewalk. Ryder.

My stomach filled with butterflies. There was something about the way he walked that drew my gaze. Hands tucked into his coat, stride fluid and easy, eyes flashing with a kind of intensity that set flecks of gold to glitter. Maybe it was his mouth, turned always at the corner as if barely containing a wry smile. Maybe it was the width of his shoulders, the thickness of his chest, all tapered down to lean hips and long legs.

Maybe it was everything, and me wanting to know it all better.

I only took a second to size Ryder up before I turned my gaze back to Dan.

I could feel Ryder's eyes on me, and had a moment to wonder what he saw. I was bent forward, my butt sticking out, my hips shifted on one bent knee, so I could lean far enough down to talk to Dan through the car window.

I'd traded my jeans for my uniform slacks today, though my plaid button-down shirt tucked into my slacks wasn't regulation. The slacks weren't much for figure flattery, and frankly, neither was my shirt.

"Did you hear Chris and Heim argue?"

Dan frowned. Looked angry that nothing came to mind. "Lots of people hate each other quietly. For years. Plan their revenge. Quiet is best for revenge. Lots of people know that."

That wasn't creepy.

"One last thing, Mr. Perkin. I'd like you to put together a list of people who you think would want you harmed. People who would want to blow up your property."

"It's a short list. Chris Lagon."

"No one else? No one at all?"

"Nope. That's it. He's your man. Find him, and you'll find your killer and your bomber. I promise you that, officer."

"Okay," I said. "Thank you for your time."

"Bring Chris Lagon to justice," Dan said. "For the good of Ordinary."

"I'll do my job, Mr. Perkin. Don't you worry about that."

I patted the doorframe and moved back. He started his car and drove away. He checked the rearview mirror an awful lot, his hand reaching up to stroke the bill of the hat again. Nervous about what I was going to do with that information, or maybe he had just developed a new paranoia since the explosion.

Not that I would blame him.

My gut said something was going on with him. Although he'd done nothing but talk, there was more he wasn't saying. More he didn't want me to know.

Who did Dan Perkin have to protect in this? Who did he even care about enough to protect? What wouldn't he want me to know?

"Any breakthroughs?" Ryder asked.

"Dan doesn't like Chris. Newsflash."

He grinned, and I smiled right back. The world just took on a lot more sunshine when he smiled.

"So about last night," he said.

I raised my eyebrows.

"I was thinking maybe we could try that again tonight. The dinner part. My place?"

There was no reason for me not to—other than a killer I needed to track down and a power I needed to give to some poor, unsuspecting mortal. Somewhere in the middle of all that I should have time for a life—my life—right?

139

Not really. If I failed to give the power over to someone, the power would kill me, injure my sisters, then turn on the town. Flirting over breadsticks while trying to outrun a ticking time bomb wasn't the kind of multitasking I was made for.

Or was it? Dad had loved Mom through the years of carrying the bridge responsibility. He'd handled several power handovers and never missed one of our dance lessons or volleyball games. When he'd remarried, he'd had the time to love Kirali too.

How did you make it all look so easy, Dad?

"Or we could break up a fight," he suggested. "See a sappy teen movie without explosions, go on a stakeout."

"What?" That was when I realized I'd been standing there silent, probably scowling at him like a hemorrhoidal lunch lady.

No wonder I never got any dates. I had zero moves.

"Tomorrow?" I blurted. There. That felt better. Also a little embarrassing.

He tipped his head. It felt like forever before he answered. "I could do something, maybe."

"Dinner?"

He shook his head. "Meeting with a client."

Right. He did have a business to run.

"After dinner?" he suggested.

"Dessert. My favorite meal. Where?"

"Who's open after nine now?"

We'd lost the Sweet Dreams restaurant that opened late and closed early. It had been surprisingly successful selling specialty desserts and drinks. But when Ganesha had decided he was done with his vacation last year, he'd shut the business down.

The loss of our all-night dessert shop had been mourned by everyone in the town, and nothing had taken its place yet.

"Besides the bars and grocery store?" I thought of canned pudding and stale donuts.

"Curly's?" he suggested.

Curly's. I hadn't thought about the homemade ice cream and dessert parlor for years. It was almost an hour's drive to Netarts, where the little shop lorded over the tiny town's boat launch next to the bay.

"I haven't been there in ages," I said with longing. "It's too far, though. Maybe the casino? The dessert bar there is decadent."

"You go out there a lot, don't you?"

Every week to pick up god mail. "Off and on."

"What I think you meant to say was every Friday."

It was true, but it was also, actually, a weird thing to say.

"Are you stalking me, Ryder Bailey?"

"Just paying attention. You like to gamble?"

"I like to get out of town every once in a while." It was the excuse I thought up when I'd become the courier for the gods. "They have good food."

"And a nice hotel."

I paused before answering that, wondering if he'd just accused me of what I thought he'd accused me of. "What does that have to do with anything?"

"Nothing." He ran his hand back through his hair, mussing up the dark waves. "I shouldn't have. I didn't mean anything by it." The tension was back in his heavy shoulders, and if I didn't know better, I'd think he was embarrassed.

What could embarrass the easygoing, big-city, own-my-own-business, open-the-door-naked Ryder Bailey?

Hotel room.

It clicked, and I had to swallow down a burst of laughter. "You think I'm going up there to sleep with someone?"

"I did not say that." His eyes flashed in warning. I was not intimidated in the least. I had the upper hand here.

"But that's what you meant, isn't it? You think I have a weekly booty call." I grinned. "My, my, Mr. Bailey. How quickly your mind slips to the gutter."

Ryder grew more uncomfortable, hazel-gold eyes squinting like it was suddenly too bright out. "Delaney. I didn't—"

"I *am* single. I don't see why I *shouldn't* have myself a little weekly dessert on the side."

"Are you done? It was a stupid thing to assume. And none of my damn business." He still looked uncomfortable, but his body language was loosening, and that shadow of a smile was back. Good. I liked a man who could laugh at himself.

"I don't know. Is there anything else you've been dying to ask me?"

"How about what that kiss this morning with Cooper was all about."

He would have to bring up the one thing that would make *me* blush.

"That was a miscommunication. A mistake." *Is it suddenly hot out here?* 'He thought there was something to salvage from our relationship. There isn't. I'm not seeing anyone. Not in town, not out of town, and certainly not Cooper Clark. My trips to the casino are a chance to get a cup of coffee where I'm not Delaney Reed, the chief of police who couldn't figure a way not to get roped into taste-testing rhubarb, a fruit that is an affront to all things decent."

"Vegetable," he said. "It's a vegetable."

"That's what you got out of the conversation?"

He shrugged one shoulder and the smile was back, along with the light in his eyes. "Everyone knows it's a vegetable."

"New York ruled rhubarb was a fruit in 1947. Lower tariff fees."

He pursed his lips, hiding the smile. But not for long.

"I did not know that," he said.

"So what about you?"

"I like the coffee in town."

"Are you seeing anyone?"

"I'm trying to, but she works really long hours and has no concept of the food groups."

Oh. That was sweet.

"Are you going to keep trying? To see her?"

"Dessert is a strong possibility."

"Good."

He stood there. I stood there. We stood there. One of us was going to have to do something. The ever-present wind tossed his dark hair, sunlight highlighting the stubble along his jaw. I wondered what his scruff would feel like against my lips.

"We lost Jean." He waved vaguely at the door, his gaze on me. He hadn't moved. Hadn't looked away.

"She knows her way around." He was wearing that nice cologne again. Just strong enough that, standing this near to him, I could catch a hint of it on the breeze.

I wanted to kiss him, taste him. Wanted to run my fingers over the curve of his lip and bite at the soft skin near his ear. A knot of ache, of desire filled my chest. This felt right. The idea of Ryder being mine, even if it was only for a short time, felt really right.

"Ryder, do you think—" I started, then shut up as a door slammed.

Jean jogged over to us. "Hey, Ryder," she singsonged. "Hey, Delaney. How's it going?"

Better before you butted in. "Swell," I said.

Ryder exhaled, then rubbed his palm over his hair to smooth it. He looked off to the horizon for a moment, and I thought his breathing was a little faster than it should be. I thought mine was too.

"Did I interrupt something?" Jean asked. "I sure hope I didn't interrupt anything."

"Were you going to ask me something, chief?" Ryder met my gaze again.

I nodded. "Do you think it's stupid to work with your siblings, or do you think it's super stupid?"

"No comment," he deadpanned.

"Good answer." I walked toward Jean's truck. "Ryder, head on back to the station and see if Roy or Myra need a hand with anything. Jean and I will be back in a bit."

"Roger that." He strode over to his truck and swung up inside.

I got into Jean's truck and slid on the seatbelt. She hopped up into the driver's seat, but immediately turned to me. "You two were standing in the middle of the sidewalk mooning over each other."

"We weren't mooning."

"You were mooning." She glanced at the rearview mirror, watching Ryder as he pulled out of the parking lot. "Tell me you kissed him."

"I did not kiss him."

She groaned. "Why won't you just *do* something? Can't you see that you two were meant to be together? Seriously, Delaney, glaciers move faster than you."

"We have a date."

She whooped. "About time!" She held up her palm. "High five, sister! C'mon. Don't leave me hanging."

I shook my head. "It's just a date. You and I still have work to do."

She grabbed my wrist and smacked my palm into hers. "You can't have fun for two seconds in a row."

"You can't stay serious for one."

"That's because my two older sisters are serious enough for the entire town. Did Dan pan out?"

"I don't know yet. I think we need to go find us a gill-man."

CHAPTER 14

THE VAMPIRE was waiting for us outside the bar. Ben Rossi wore a canvas jacket, dark red beanie, tight jeans, and boots. He looked more like a dockworker just out of college than a hundred-year-old firefighter. The shadow from the roof overhang kept him out of the spotty sunlight as he leaned against the warehouse and tipped two fingers to his forehead in greeting.

"Good day, officers."

"Ben," I said. "What's down?"

He pushed off the wall, hands still in his pockets. "Old Rossi heard you hired Ryder Bailey on to the force. That right?"

Was there anyone in town who hadn't heard that news? And why was everyone making such a big deal out of it?

"That's right."

Ben bit at his bottom lip and raised his eyebrows. "You might want to rethink that."

"I don't think I do."

"All right. Old Rossi would like you to rethink that."

"Why?"

Ben shrugged. "He was cleansing his chakras or fluffing his aura or some such bull. Didn't go into details. Just told me to tell you: fire Ryder."

"I don't allow vampires to dictate my human resource decisions."

Ben flashed a bit of fang in his smile. "I figured you'd say that. You know I'm just the messenger."

"I know. Do me a favor? Tell Old Rossi that if he has a problem with Ryder, he can come talk to me himself."

"I'll let him know, chief. Say...come on by our place next Saturday. Jame and I are having a housewarming party."

"Do you want me there as a friend or in an official capacity?"

"Yes. I figure we're gonna have a lot of family stop in." He grinned again, then pushed off the wall. "See you around, chief. Jean."

"Bye, Ben," Jean said. "Think we should be worried?"

I didn't know if she meant about Old Rossi's warning, the housewarming invite, or us hiring Ryder.

"Probably," I said, just to cover the bases.

We found Chris right where I expected him to be: upstairs at the bar.

We found him in a state I didn't expect him to be: drunk.

Even more interestingly, we found him in the company of both Lila Carson and her sister Margot Lapointe.

They sat in the corner booth, mostly out of sight of the rest of the diners, though I noted the bartender, Nick, a mortal, was keeping a close eye on them.

I gave Nick a nod as Jean and I walked over to Chris and company.

"Delaney Reed," Chris said, drawing out my name with more Louisiana than I'd heard out of him in a while. "Have yourself a seat. Have yourself a drink."

Chris wore a black shirt with a black band tied around his upper arm. A petrified shark's tooth centered his chest, hanging from a chain I knew was very old, and pure gold. It was an ancient talisman. I knew he wore it whenever a god died.

He'd once told me it was a symbol for life and death, a reminder that there was always something out there bigger than you that could, and likely would, kill you and eat you.

"I need to talk to you, Chris. Business."

"Do you need us to go?" Margot asked.

Margot and Lila looked like sisters if you compared their pointed chins, petite noses, and the shape of their eyes. But while Margot was blonde with loopy curls held that way by lots of product, Lila's hair was brunette and worn straight. They must have had a girls' day out and both gotten multicolored feather extensions scattered in their hair.

Chris's arm was draped over the back of the booth seat behind Margot, his hand absently stroking her curls and feathers. Lila sat just out of his reach, head down.

Lila was the elder sister, I decided. Any makeup she might have been wearing had been scrubbed off hard enough to leave her eyes and cheeks spotty and pink. When she looked up from the nearly disintegrated wadded napkin in her hands, her eyes were bloodshot and red-lined, her nose pink. She hadn't scrubbed off her makeup. She'd cried it off.

"I'm so sorry about Heim, Lila," I began, gently.

Her eyes filled with a wrenching mix of emotions, as if her heart strained for a shred of hope, even though her mind knew he was dead.

"There's nothing to be sorry about," Margot snapped. She looked...angry. Annoyed. Probably mad that her sister's ex-boyfriend had made Lila cry again. "Heim was a selfish, cheating bastard. He deserved what he got."

"No," Lila said quietly, her voice softened by tears. "He didn't deserve that. He didn't. He was...he was so young."

Several hundred years old, but I couldn't tell her that. She'd loved the man he'd been when they dated for two years. I knew that man was most often kind and good, even if he did love the ocean and his ship more than he loved Lila Carson.

Gods and mortals never lasted.

Margot was still scowling at us, but she wrapped her arm over her sister's shoulders and pulled her tight. "It's okay. It's going to be okay. Is there something you wanted?" she asked.

"Just some basic information about the last time you saw Heim," Jean said evenly. "Would you ladies mind if I sat with you for a bit?" Apparently, she was going to take the sisters, which meant I was on gill-man duty.

"Chris?" I said. "Can we talk in private?"

"Sure." He lifted his arm and slid out of the booth.

Margot looked a little startled that he was leaving her. "It will be fine." He leaned down and placed a kiss on her temple. "I'll be right back. You're in good hands with Jean."

Margot nodded and Lila wiped the tattered napkin over her nose as Jean sat next to her.

"This way, then." Chris walked with a little less of his distinctive grace. Not that he was unsteady on his feet, but he had been drinking, and it showed in his almost overly loose joint movements. I was pretty sure he had a skeleton of bone, but right now he appeared to be held together by sinew and cartilage.

I followed him to the other side of the room, and up a flight of stairs to a door that opened on his office.

The two large windows ate up the back wall behind the desk and looked out over the ships, the bay, and the opposite shore, with lights from houses twinkling in the low haze that covered the hill. The office was smothered in label designs, awards, and certificates of excellence, along with a few signed photos of Chris posing with celebrities, musicians, and a smattering of other famous people.

He walked straight to a dented mini-fridge that looked like it might have once been painted red, and pulled out two beers. He popped them open, offered me one.

"Can't. This really is business."

"I know." Chris took a drink of his beer, and still held the other bottle out at arm's length for me. "It's about Heim. He was Asgardian. He would have wanted you to at least take one drink in his memory."

I sighed. "I know." I took the beer, glanced at the label. It was a dark porter Twin Rocks, one of the ones that had made Chris, and Jump Off Jack's, so famous. I lifted it a little, and Chris lifted his.

"To Heimdall," Chris said. "Long may he live."

"To Heimdall." I took a gulp, holding a memory of Heim in my mind. A time when he and I and Chris took the chairs out on the dock to cast lines for rockfish. Heim and Chris sang a song I thought had been incredibly raunchy. I'd been twelve, and by the end of the afternoon, I'd learned every word and been sworn never to tell my father where I'd heard it.

Good times.

The rich, deep flavor filled my mouth and ran a cool heat down to the bottom of my belly. "You know what I'm going to ask you, Chris."

He sat on the edge of his desk, stretching his long legs out in front of him, one ankle crossed over the other. He was wearing slippers. "If I know who killed him?"

"Yes. But first, I need to know if you killed him."

He took another drink of beer, watching me as he did so. "Let me get this right. You're here, in my office, asking me if I killed one of my closest friends?"

"It's what a police officer does. Asks all the hard questions. Of everyone."

"All right, I'll say it here, and I'll say it anywhere else you need me to. I didn't kill Heim. I loved him, as a friend. He was a good man. He understood the sea, understood life and the pace of it in a way I could only share with a few others. He was my friend, Delaney. If I knew who wanted him dead, you'd have to throw me behind bars, because I would find them and beat the life out of them."

His eyes, usually a smoky brown, glinted with red for a moment.

He was angry. Very angry.

"I know," I said. "I'm sorry. I liked Heim too. I'm going to miss him." I sat down in the chair next to the mini-fridge and took another drink of beer, then pressed the bottle against my forehead. "We don't think his death was an accident."

"I gathered that when you accused me of killing him."

"Do you know who was angry at him?"

He tipped the beer up and then set the empty bottle on his desk. "There's always someone upset about something."

"Names, Chris. Any you can think of. I want to know who did this. I'm not going to let them get away with it."

He shook his head and folded arms over his chest. "No one stands out. Hera was upset that he slipped us a few prime catches over the last month or so, but you know her. Liked to make us think she was angry about it, when she had Pete supplying her plenty of prime catch on the side. She wouldn't stoop so low as to kill Heim and risk being thrown out of Ordinary over fish."

I nodded. "I know."

"He had his arguments with a few other people, a few other gods and creatures. Odin once or twice, but Odin yells at everyone. Bertie, over judging the contest. Tried to withdraw when he found out I had entered. But I can't...I just can't see why any of them would kill him."

"Not even for the Rhubarb Rally?"

Chris stared at me for a long moment. "Is that a serious question?"

"Dan Perkin seems to think it would be enough motivation for murder."

"Dan Perkin is an ass. I'm looking forward to the day he's the one we're burying."

"That's what he says about you."

"At least something about this week is normal." He reached into the fridge for another beer and flipped the cap off with his thumb.

"This is Ordinary," I said, lifting my nearly full beer. "Nothing about it has ever been normal."

CHAPTER 15

CHRIS HAD an alibi for the time period wherein Heim had been harmed. He had been spending that time with Lila. Mostly, he admitted to me, trying to talk Lila out of enacting petty revenge against Heim. He assured me her plans involved egging his house, or putting sugar in his gas tank, or welding his crab traps shut, not clubbing him over the head and kicking him into the sea.

She had certainly looked torn up about his death. I just hoped she wasn't faking it.

"She's not faking it," Jean said as she and I took a seat at a table close to the front door of Jump Off Jack's. Jean had ordered us iced tea and cheese bread.

"Late lunch or early dinner?" I asked.

"Both. You're too thin. We're on our break." She tore off a piece of bread and took a big bite.

I pulled a piece of bread my way and dug in. It was delicious, the cheese from local farms in Hebo, the bread fresh, with just a bite of heat in it. Jalapeno, I thought.

"Get anything useful from the sisters?"

Jean didn't look over at Margot and Lila, who stood at the table, saying their goodbyes to Chris.

"Not really. Lila's reeling from his death. She had plans, things she wanted to do to him to make him pay for breaking up with her. She *wanted* a chance at making his life miserable. She didn't want him dead. I think she's truly sorry that he is."

It was a backward kind of logic, but I could understand it. The heart, even the jilted heart—maybe especially the jilted heart—wanted what it wanted.

"You think she's upset she didn't get a chance at revenge?"

"No. I think…" She popped another bite of bread in her mouth. "If he were still alive, she'd be buying rotten potatoes to hide in the walls of his house. Now that he's gone, she's mourning him. Thinking of all the great times they'd had together. She's sad."

"She was never really over him, was she?"

Jean tipped her head a bit. "He was a god. There's a certain...I don't know, tingle about them, you know? Even though they're temporarily mortal, there's something really attractive about them. When I was little I had the biggest crush on Shiva, remember?"

I smiled. "I'd forgotten about that. Dad thought it was cute."

"Dad did. Mom didn't. She sat me down and made me promise I wouldn't run away to go live with him in the junkyard."

"You wouldn't have run away."

"Oh, yes, I would. I had my suitcase packed. But she explained it was the god stuff that drew me, like a magnet to a refrigerator. And then she made Dad take me out to Gaia's place so I could see all the god powers she was keeping that year."

"When did this happen?" I asked. "Where was I?"

"Worrying about if Ryder would like your hair in braids or in a ponytail."

I grimaced. "Middle school?" I'd worn a braid on one side and a ponytail on the other for a week, to try and figure out which one he liked more. He was more interested in Sheila Guberman's rainbow braces.

I gave up and wore my hair long, tucked behind my ears.

Jean took half the remaining bread and pushed the plate my way with one finger.

"Did seeing the powers make a difference?" I asked.

"I was hypnotized by it. I think I cried, out of joy or wonder, or...I don't know. It was a lot for a nine-year-old to see all that power, that magic right there in a hollowed old log."

"Is that where she kept it?"

Jean nodded. "It was absolutely wonderful. And then when I looked at Shiva, he seemed less wonderful. Still...intriguing, but I could tell that the thing about him that I'd found so amazing was the echo of his power."

"And then what happened?"

"I went back to playing video games, happily ever after. Haven't you ever felt it? That draw to the deities?"

I shook my head. "I'm immune to it, I guess. I can tell when they're being god-ish, even when they aren't carrying power, but it's not hypnotizing, doesn't draw me in."

"Not even now?"

I shook my head again. "That... Okay, I'm not going to lie. It's weird to have a power stuck in my head. It's loud and...thrashy. But it doesn't make me feel any differently. Does the power in me make me look like a god?"

Yeah, it was a weird question. But this was Ordinary, after all. Weird was our second cousin.

"I don't see it in you at all. If it's in there, it's behind a lead blanket."

"What did you just call me?"

She grinned. "You look normal. Be happy about that. Any idea who you're going to offload that crazy shit onto?"

"No."

"Are you worried?"

"Should I be?"

She took a drink of her iced tea and tipped her head a little. "I don't get...that feeling of imminent doom about it."

"The one you had yesterday?"

"Gone as soon as I heard Heim's body had washed ashore."

I studied her a second. "You think you were picking up on his death?"

"Either that, or the fact that it wasn't accidental. Like maybe I was picking up on someone wanting him dead?"

Since Jean didn't usually talk about these things, I wasn't sure how much experimenting she'd done to see if she could control her talent.

"I don't suppose you picked up any clue as to who that might be?"

"Would I be driving around with you questioning suspects if I did?"

"Point taken. I don't think Chris did it. They were friends. He has Lila as an alibi. Plus, he said a couple of his crew saw him in and out of the restaurant last night. We can check with them."

153

"Lila mentioned she and Chris talked last night too."

"What about Margot?"

"She said she was out at the casino."

"Do we have any corroboration on that?"

"Nope, but we can look into it tomorrow. Do you know why Chris is getting all the mortals out of here?" she asked.

I glanced around the restaurant. A few of the tables that had been full minutes ago were empty, dishes removed. The remaining people in the restaurant besides the wait staff, who Chris was even now sending out the door with a wave, were gods.

Not all of the gods in town, but a good dozen or more filled the booths and a few of the tables. They were all, of course, drinking beer.

"Do you know what's going on?" I asked.

"Nope."

I wished Myra was here.

And then, of course, she walked in through the front door, Death gliding in behind her.

Chris moved behind Myra, locked the door, and turned off the neon sign in the window.

She frowned at him, then scanned the room and walked over to Jean and me.

"What's going on?" she asked.

"Have no idea," I said.

Chris strolled to the center of the room, positioning himself between the bar and the restaurant. "I've locked the doors for the night," he announced. All the voices in the room silenced.

"Let this be the beginning of celebrating our fallen," he said in that lilt that carried soft melancholy. "Let this be the beginning of recognizing the long and good life of our friend, Heimdall, who was once the mortal Ephram Dalton. May he drink deeply in the great halls of Valhalla while we drink deeply in this humble hall in his honor. First round is on me."

A low hum rose to a shout that ended with "Heimdall!" chanted in a cascade of voices reaching the peak at different times. It was beautiful. Moving. A kind of vocal fireworks.

Chris strode around behind the bar and began filling glasses with beer, whiskey, and wine as if this night would never end.

CHAPTER 16

ONE CANNOT conduct a murder investigation when one is drinking with gods.

One can be coerced into singing, judging an arm-wrestling contest, and breaking up a bar brawl before friendly back pats become less friendly fists to the face.

Thor, who went by the name Thorne, was in the corner with a microphone and his guitar singing—sadly and badly—about the total eclipse of his heart. I was alone at a table, nursing a glass of water and wondering who Thorne had been dating to cause him the case of the mopes.

"Delaney." Odin pulled up a chair and sat down heavily at the table next to me.

"Odin," I said.

"So." Hera, who preferred to be called Herri, owned Mom's Bar and Grill—and was Chris's direct business competitor and friend. She plunked down on my other side. "We should talk." She appeared to be in her mid-thirties, beautiful, heart-shaped face with long, dark hair streaked with candy red. Her skin was a shade darker than mine, her light brown eyes smoldered.

The other chairs were dragged across the wooden floor and quickly taken by Crow and then Ares, who went by the name Aaron and looked like a computer programmer who wasn't old enough to drink. The god of war's hair was yellow-brown over a softly angled face, green-gray eyes behind glasses in a blocky, stylish frame. He had darker skin than me, but also freckles.

Zeus and Frigg were the next to claim seats, Zeus making it a point to sit as far as possible from Odin. Whereas Odin looked a bit as expected for the Norse wandering god, from wild gray hair to burly build and eye patch, Zeus, who went by the name Zeus, looked like he should own a fashion boutique for only the very rich and very famous.

And he did. He was tall, thin, elegant, and impeccably dressed in deep blue slacks, business shirt, and a jacket that probably cost more than my year's salary. His dark hair and goatee were trimmed tight, his face long and tanned. Even though he sent a sneer Odin's way, he was handsome.

Frigg, tall, pale, her golden hair pulled back in a ponytail, went by her name too, though she told people it was a nickname. She reached across the table and patted my hand before sitting. She wore jeans and a tank top with the logo of her towing company, Frigg's Rigs, across the front of it. The tank was tight enough to accent her curvy figure and showed off the tattoos of a goose in flight, with a spindle in its beak across her muscular arm.

Well, lucky me. Half a dozen gods, all in a row.

"Is this an intervention? Because it feels like an intervention." I leaned back in my chair and thumbed off my phone.

"It's not an intervention," Herri said.

"Do you want an intervention?" Crow interrupted.

"It's just," Herri said before I could answer, "we want to talk about that power you're holding."

Oh. Well, that made sense. Of course they'd be worried. My dad had been an old pro at this, but this was my first time dealing out a power.

"You let a new god into town today," Crow said.

"Crow," Zeus said, rubbing the bridge of his nose. "Shut up."

"Thanatos?" I looked them each in the eye. "He signed the contract. As long as he follows the rules of Ordinary, he's just as welcome here as any of you."

"We're not worried that he's here," Aaron said. "We just think it's interesting that hours before he arrived, one of ours falls."

A chill rolled over my skin. That quote was almost exactly what the anonymous note had said. "What?"

"Hours before Thanatos shows up," Aaron repeated slowly, as if I needed time to hear each word, "Heimdall dies. Anyone else find that suspicious?"

Crow shot his hand up.

Great. The god of war and the trickster god thought something fishy was going on. Or, more likely, the god of war and the trickster god were trying to stir up trouble.

"I don't see how they're connected," I said.

"Thanatos is death," Aaron said.

"Exactly!" Crow said.

"Don't humor them, Delaney," Zeus said. "Children, find another pot to stir."

"He's death," I said to Aaron, "and you're war. No one's blaming you for the Kressler/Wallery garbage can feud."

He rolled his eyes. "Amateurs! If I were running that feud, one of them would be dead by trash compactor by now."

He might look like a mild-mannered gardener, but Aaron had always been a cheerleader for blood and mayhem.

"I don't see why we should blame Thanatos for Heimdall's death," I said. "Just because he is Death doesn't mean people randomly die around him."

Crow chuckled and even Odin smiled. Okay, it was a dumb thing to say, but it wasn't wrong.

Odin leaned forward, resting two beefy arms on the table. He had several scars and nicks on his arms and the backs of his hands. Being a chainsaw artist hadn't come naturally to him, but he was too pigheaded to give up his preferred mortal occupation.

Just like most of the gods.

"Don't you find the timing convenient?" he said. "That death was no accident. Someone was behind it. Likely a trickster." He leaned back as if that were that, and the case was closed.

Crow grinned at Odin. "Screw you, old man. I didn't kill Heimdall."

"You think you're the only trickster?" Odin asked, unperturbed.

He was right. Between the creatures, deities, and heck, even the mortals in town, we had plenty of people who were jokers.

"Do any of you know who wanted him dead?" I asked. "Who he might have been fighting with?" I glanced at Herri expectantly.

This is a safe place. You're with people who care about you, Herri. Tell us you killed him.

Huh. Maybe it did feel like an intervention.

She pulled her hair back from her temples with her thumbs and let it fall. "He and I argued. But I have never disliked Heimdall. As a mortal, he was companionable. Even-tempered. Despite screwing me out of a few choice catches, he was fair to me."

"As a mortal, you got along with him," I said. "What about as a god?"

"We leave that outside this town, outside these lives," she said.

"Do you?" I asked.

"Yes," Zeus said in his cultured accent. "We all do."

Herri rolled her eyes at him, and Aaron adjusted his glasses and snorted.

"You have an opinion, Ares?" Zeus asked.

"I'll believe gods leave petty squabbles behind the day you and Odin kiss and make up."

"Ass saddle," Odin muttered.

"What's that?" Aaron cupped his hand to his ear. "What did you call me?"

"Boys," Herri warned.

Crow shook his head. "And you thought the tricksters cause trouble."

"I thought," Odin said, his deep voice loud enough to silence both of them, "that we were telling Delaney that we're worried about her."

"Wait," I said. "We're what now?"

"Worried about you," Odin said, still glaring at Aaron and Crow in turn. "Isn't that right, boys?"

Crow slid me a small smile. "I think that was actually the point."

"Worried? That I can't do my job?" Okay, maybe I said that a little louder than I'd intended.

I could feel all the gazes in the room turn to me.

Terrific. Now all the gods were interested in the subject of my inexperience.

"It's just that your father..." Zeus began.

"My father what?" I demanded. "He taught me how to do his job. I've known for years that I would take it on. Just because he and I don't sense power in the same manner doesn't mean I'm not living up to the Reed blood and word. I will not fail this town nor the gods, creatures, or mortals within it."

"...asked us to look out for you," Zeus finished quietly.

Oh.

Well, I'd just been getting all worked up over the wrong thing.

"I can take care of myself."

Frigg reached over and patted my arm. "We know. You're a Reed. We know you're strong. Your family always has been. But you're new to this, Delaney."

"And"—Zeus held up one finger to keep me quiet—"you not only have a new god in town, but you also need to rehouse your first power. It is a lot to take on at once."

"Not to mention the murder," Aaron said.

"And the murder," Zeus agreed.

I hadn't told any of them I thought Heimdall was murdered. "Who told you he was murdered?"

"He fell off his boat and drowned," Odin said. "We're on vacation, we're not idiots."

Thor stood up on a table and wobbled like a surfer trying to catch a wave. "Let's swim the sea naked! In Heimdall's honor! Who's with me?"

Death, who was sitting primly in a corner booth sipping a fruity drink with umbrellas in it, glanced around the room, keenly interested in the answers.

"Well, some of us aren't idiots," Zeus said. "Some of us just raise them."

Odin stood. "At least some of us aren't cheap."

"Cheap?"

"You broke my chainsaw."

"It was dull."

"Not before you used it on concrete."

"I paid you to replace the blade."

"You gave me store coupons. To your store!"

"Of which you should make immediate use. Your decor is hideous."

"I make all my decor!"

Zeus gave him one slow blink. "I know. Destroying that chainsaw was a service."

"Screw you and your damn service." Odin curled his massive, scarred fists. "I'll take my payment out of your face."

"Finally!" Aaron cheered.

"No." I stood, grabbed Odin's arm. "You touch him and I'm dragging you to jail."

"Worth it," he growled.

Zeus was slouching a bit in his chair, relaxed, like he had no care in the world. "Let him go, Delaney. He couldn't hit me if I carved a target on my forehead with a dull chainsaw."

"I'll carve you a target, right up your—"

"Bargain." I pointed a finger at Odin and turned it on Zeus. They watched me. All the gods watched me. Nothing interested a god more than a juicy bargain. "In exchange for the excessive wear and tear on Odin's chainsaw..."

Zeus made a short, offended sound.

"...which I am sure was unintended," I amended. Odin growled. "Zeus will carry five pieces of Odin's art in his shop on a sixty/forty commission until they sell."

"Ten," Odin said, his single gray eye lit almost silver. "Ninety/ten. And the owl statue is one of them."

"Owl? That hacksawed lump of pine on your porch? That, dear sir, is not art," Zeus insisted, offended.

I gave him the look. The one that said I could throw the book at him if I wanted to.

"One piece." He sniffed. "Eighty/twenty. No owl."

"Eight," Odin said. "Eighty/twenty. Owl stays."

I let go of Odin's arm like a parent letting go of a child's first ride without training wheels. Quibbling over numbers should keep these two on the up-and-up, but I wasn't going to leave anything to chance.

"Too much like your father," Crow said quietly. I glanced his way and thought I saw pride. "Peacekeeper."

I shrugged and took stock of the gods around the table. Aaron stared raptly at the argument, like a starving man watching bacon sizzle. Frigg and Herri seemed uninterested in the argument.

Once the terms had been settled—three pieces, fifty-nine/forty-one, owl included—the two gods shook on it. And that was that.

Aaron sighed and leaned back in his chair as if he'd just consumed an amazing meal. "Marvelous."

"Don't get used to it," Odin said. He patted my shoulder, then went off to raise a toast at the bar with Thor, Chris, and Death.

"Thank you," I said to Zeus.

He plucked imaginary lint off his suit. "We all know who would have won if it had come to blows."

"Odin," I said. "He could have taken you to small claims court over the chainsaw."

"That is beside the point," he said.

"What we were trying to say," Herri said, "is that we are here and will help you if you need us, Delaney. With the power, or anything else."

"Thank you," I said. "Can you tell me that you didn't kill Heimdall? Complete truth, Herri."

She looked me straight in the eyes. "I did not kill him. Nor was I involved in his death. On my word, honor, and power, Delaney Reed. The complete truth."

I believed her. That kind of a statement, with that kind of oath, was binding.

Words had power. Even the gods knew that.

"That's really good to hear," I said.

She stood up and patted my shoulder. "Come on over to my bar sometime when you're off duty. We'll talk, just us girls. It isn't just the town fish who can pour a decent brew."

"I will."

"Good. Then I'm out. See you all at the rally."

She sauntered over to the bar, maybe to look for Chris, who, come to think of it, I hadn't seen for a while. She leaned over the bar to look at the floor behind it. She shook her head then walked around the bar and bent.

Myra walked over and helped her with whatever was back there.

Correction: whomever. The two of them half dragged, half carried an unconscious Chris out from behind the bar and lugged him over to a pool table, where they laid him out more or less in a comfortable position.

Herri also placed a pitcher of water on the table for him, and patted the side of his face. He made a lazy swipe at her hand, rolled over, and snored.

"So," Crow said, "you got what we're saying?"

"That you all promised my dad you'd help me?"

"That. Keep us in mind. For anything."

"Anything? Want to judge the Rhubarb Rally instead of me?"

His eyes widened in shock. "Oh, hell no. Anything *but* that."

"Chicken."

"Maybe, but at least I won't have to live in a town full of people angry at me for voting down their nana's secret recipe."

"You know they wrote legends about how brave and clever you are," I said. "Schoolchildren read them."

"All true. I am clever. And brave. Which is why I would never get roped into judging a rhubarb contest in Ordinary, Oregon. What were you thinking?"

"To serve, protect, and keep Bertie from going to jail for hitting Dan Perkin over the head with her desk."

"And that," he said as he stood and planted a quick kiss on my cheek, "is why you are the police chief. I always feel safer knowing you're on duty."

"Suck-up."

He waggled his eyebrows. "Good night, Delaney. Don't get into too much trouble."

He started toward the door, and so did Aaron and Frigg. Zeus got up and wandered over to talk to Thanatos, or maybe to pick another fight with Odin. It didn't matter.

It looked like the party was over and everyone was leaving.

Myra walked my way. "Everything okay?" she asked.

"I think so. Is Chris?"

"He had several too many. He'll be fine in the morning. You know his constitution. Jean's waiting for us in the car."

We walked to the door.

"What did the deities have to say?" she asked.

"They don't think Heimdall's death was accidental either."
I pushed out into the cool, salty breeze. Took a nice deep breath.
Smelled rain on the air.

"Is that all?"

"They made a deal with Dad that they'd help me through
my first power transfer."

"That's…nice?" she said.

"And a little condescending. But yes. Mostly it's nice."

Jean perched on the hood of the car, drinking a beer and
staring at the sky. "Finally. I thought you two would never come
out. I am not the desig-ig…desig-nated driver tonight."

Myra looked at me.

"I'm good. One beer two hours ago."

She nodded and tugged on Jean's leg, sliding her down the
hood a bit.

"Yo-ho-ho," Jean sang, "where's my bottle of rum?"

"We're leaving," I said.

"Shotgun," Myra said.

"Shotgun," Jean said too late. Then: "Crap. Fine. I'll sit in
the back seat. Who's covering my shift tonight?"

"You," I said. "Roy's already over his hours for the day.
Ryder should be gone." I started the engine. "Finish the beer.
I'll stay at the station, do some paperwork until you sober up,
then it's all yours."

"Killjoy," she said.

I glanced in the rearview. She stuck out her tongue at me.

"Want me to drop you at your place?" I asked Myra.

"No. I'll go to the station too."

"It's not your shift." I turned onto the main street. "You
should get some sleep."

"I can nap on the cot."

"Are you that worried?"

"I just think we should all stick together tonight."

And since it was such a nice thought, I didn't argue.

CHAPTER 17

"CANNON LUBE?" I suggested, looking over the situation with a critical eye.

The groundskeeper's daughter, Treana, who was sixteen now, snickered.

The groundskeeper was a woman named Stella with #6.5R Nice-n-Easy auburn hair pulled back in a tight bun and a badge and uniform that looked more official than mine. She speared me with a hard glare.

"If I kept that much lube on hand, I would have used it, wouldn't I?" she asked.

That got another snicker out of her daughter, and I huffed a laugh.

Just because Stella was made of the same stuff as the cannon—hardened iron—didn't mean she didn't have a sense of humor. As a matter of fact, as the one and only keeper of the historic significance of Ordinary, I thought she had to have a roaring sense of humor to remain serious about her work.

Ordinary lived up to its name as far as mortal history was concerned, although this one ridge was once a bunker put in place during the Civil War. Unluckily for Stella, the only attack to reach this side of America's coast was a lone submarine that lobbed a few shells at Fort Stevens up north of us a bit. It knocked out a telephone line then turned and went home.

And while our mortal history wasn't exactly teeming with excitement, Stella was the caretaker of it, and she took that job seriously.

Which was why the concrete penguin with the little red Superman cape jammed into the barrel of the cannon was no laughing matter.

Well, no laughing matter to her.

"How long has this been going on?" Stella asked.

"What? Mrs. Yates' penguin harassment?"

She nodded.

"I don't know. I guess a year or so."

"And you still haven't found the person doing it?"

"No."

"Seems to me a year is an awfully long time to let something like this go on."

I nodded as I crouched at the front of the stuffed cannon barrel, unconcerned that she'd accused me of not doing my job.

"Well, we figure it started with a kid. Maybe a graduating senior at the high school. We figure he or she moved on, but the tradition was passed on to someone else in the school."

I sent a look to Treana, who shifted her eyes and suddenly found her shoes more interesting to look at.

"What I'd like," I said, "is for whoever is behind this to knock it off. It's eating up my time, and Mrs. Yates no longer thinks it's funny."

Treana still wasn't looking at me.

"What I'd also like is for the class to give me a heads-up on what they'd like to do for senior trick day. I'm fine with non-damaging mischief, but the penguin escapades are bordering on harassment. Harassment comes with a large fine and can land a person in jail. And if I knew someone who knew about this, I'd kindly ask them to inform the lawbreakers to knock it off with the penguin before I decide this is something serious enough for me to shake down the entire school."

Treana lifted her head, guilt clearly written across her face.

"What about Mrs. Yates?" Treana asked. "If she doesn't like it, why doesn't she just put the penguin inside her house?"

I shifted on the balls of my feet and looked up at her and the heavy gray clouds behind her. We'd get rain within the hour, I was sure of it. "She said penguins can only thrive in the wild. And I'm hoping to make Ordinary a safe habitat. Understand?"

She nodded.

"So." I stood. "I'll get my rope and my Jeep and see if we can pry Super Penguin here free. Can you swivel the cannon?"

"Or fire it," Treana suggested. I was sure that had been the hope of all the kids involved in stuffing the poor thing in the cannon.

Stella raised one eyebrow, but a smile played across her lips. "We do not use historical artifacts to shoot penguins."

Treana shrugged, but over her mother's shoulder, her eyes glittered with hope.

I dusted my hands. "Well, it won't be the *first* thing we try."

Treana burst into a grin, and I turned toward my Jeep to get out from under her mother's stern gaze.

IT HADEN'T taken much to pull Super Penguin to safety. Mrs. Yates had accepted the little caped waterfowl with a disapproving *humpt* and placed him firmly back in the flowerbed below her window. I noted she left the cape on him.

It was early still, and I yawned hugely as I got back in my Jeep and headed at a leisurely pace through the quiet neighborhood.

Once Jean had sobered up, she had sent me home with a firm order to get some damn sleep. I had not gotten any sleep, damned or otherwise.

Ever since Heim had died, his power had been railing and shouting in my head. At first, I could ignore it, but it seemed to be growing louder with each passing day. After two glasses of warm milk and a white-noise machine cranked up loud enough to overpower a jet engine, I'd been hit with a new, slightly terrifying realization.

If I didn't give the power over to someone really soon, by midnight Monday, as a matter of fact, I might not have the strength left to do it at all. It wasn't a comforting thought. So for comfort, I decided I needed copious amounts of coffee and several donuts.

The Puffin Muffin was more crowded than I'd expected, but it was Thursday, and the festival would officially begin tomorrow morning. Tourists were already in town, filling up the hotels and apparently indulging in their love of baked goods.

I walked into the bakery and only made it three steps toward the counter. It was so crowded in here, even the fruit flies looked claustrophobic.

The line was twelve people deep, the two out-of-towner women ahead of me wearing coats that were too heavy for the weather and perfume that was too strong for the heat of the bakery. I scanned the people seated at the six small tables that took up all the space beyond the counter. No faces I recognized. Maybe I'd just grab my order and eat it in the Jeep. I rubbed at my temple and the power song thrummed louder.

Not helping.

"Grande mocha and a bear claw," a familiar low voice said in my ear, close enough I could feel his breath on my cheek. "I'll hold down that table for us."

My pulse raced for two reasons. One, I wasn't used to someone coming up behind me without me knowing it, and two, it was Cooper.

Terrific.

I twisted to look over my shoulder, but he was already moving, his hand briefly on my arm as he slid past me and wove between the tables to the little booth in the corner where a mother and teen daughter stood, preparing to leave.

He gave them a smile they both fell for, and they gave him the booth.

He could certainly charm a person when he wanted to.

I'd followed the line closer to the counter and tried to breathe through my mouth to filter out the overwhelming stink of perfume. The line moved along faster than I expected, but by the time I reached the counter, the roaring song in my ears had turned into a full-blown headache. I rubbed at both temples and scowled at the pastries behind glass.

"...help you, chief?"

Hogan stood behind the counter, a smile on his wide, expressive lips. The light blue Velvet Underground T-shirt clung to his muscular chest and thick shoulders and complemented his dark skin and surprisingly blue eyes.

"Long night?" he asked.

"Yes."

"Isn't Jean supposed to be pulling the night shift?"

I nodded. "It's been busy with the rally coming up. All-hands-on-deck kind of thing. Can I have a double-shot café breve, and a mocha, both grande. And I'll take a bear claw and one of your strawberry cream crullers."

"You got it." He rang up my total. I paid in cash while he wrote on a couple cups and passed them to Billy, who was pulling coffee for the rush. Billy was ninety if she was a day, with thick glasses and short, curly hair dyed traffic-cone orange. An unlit cigarette hung out of the corner of her mouth. "Anything else?"

I shook my head. "Just make sure that coffee's strong."

He smiled, and it did amazing things to his eyes, making the cut of his high cheekbones even more pronounced. I could see why Jean stared at him. "Extra shot for the chief, Billy."

I took the receipt he handed me, dropped enough to cover the extra shot and more in the tip jar, and moved down to wait while Billy made our drinks.

Cooper was watching me. I didn't look over at him, but I could feel his gaze on me like a hand between my shoulder blades. Something in me jumped knowing he was here back in town. I was happy about it, though I didn't know why.

Maybe it was just that it was so very clear that I had moved on. Gotten over him. Cooper had broken my heart, but I had healed. I was stronger without him.

There was something satisfying in knowing he knew that.

Billy set the coffees and the white bag of pastries down for me.

"Thanks," I said.

She flashed me a quick smile and a wink, already turning for the heavy cream to use on her next order.

I made my way over to Cooper.

He lounged in the booth, both arms out across the back of the bench seat, watching me, his eyes on my mouth.

The song in my head kicked up a notch and my headache tightened. I hooked my boot around the leg of the chair and pulled it out, scraping it noisily across the tile floor. I tossed the bag on the table.

"You owe me seven bucks," I said.

"Sorry about making you get the food." His eyes were on my eyes. "I had to jump on the table while we had a chance."

I placed the mocha in front of him and gulped three throat-scorching swallows of my coffee, ignoring him, my headache, the power song, and everything else in the building.

Sweet, sweet caffeine.

"Delaney?"

"Shhhh." I held up a finger and swallowed fortitude.

Bliss.

He claimed the bear claw. I spun the bag and lifted out my cruller. There was a maple bar in the bag. Had Hogan screwed up our order?

I shot a questioning look over my shoulder at Hogan and held up the bag so he could see. He grinned and gave me a thumbs-up, then smoothly went back to the next order.

I couldn't help but smile. Maple bar was Jean's favorite. He knew I'd see her at her shift change and give it to her.

I wondered just how serious it was between Hogan and my youngest sister. Serious enough that he was making me a de facto pastry cupid. He worked early mornings and she worked night shift. I guessed love, and the people in it, always found a way.

"Problem?" Cooper asked around a mouthful of bear claw.

"Not at all."

"What about us, Delaney?" His voice was softer than I expected, as if he'd already given up hope, but didn't know it yet. "We were good together. Think we can give it a go?"

"We already gave it a go, Cooper. This is our stop. We're done."

He nodded, his eyes flicking away as he drank coffee.

I rubbed at my temple again, wishing the headache would let up. But it only got worse the longer I sat here with him. "So what did you do when you left town?"

He winced. "I, uh, joined a band."

"Of course you did. Why didn't you stay with the band?"

His gaze slid to the window, where he stared out at the cloudy day. "I don't know. I thought... It sounds weird, but I thought maybe I left something here. Maybe I took off when I should have just stayed. So I came home to see if I'd lost...if I'd left something behind."

"Did you?"

He took a drink of coffee, thinking that over. "Maybe not." He put his coffee down. "I don't know. When I'm around you...it feels...right."

"Cooper..."

"You kissed me," he said.

"You kissed me," I corrected. "That was a mistake."

"It didn't feel like a mistake." His eyes were on my lips again, soft and needful.

"Look—"

"Mind if I join you two lovebirds?"

I jerked.

Ryder stood next to the table, a buttermilk twist in one hand, coffee in the other. He wasn't looking at Cooper, his gaze riveted to mine. And he was smiling.

The look in his eyes was inscrutable. Humor? Curiosity? Mockery? I couldn't tell. Ryder Bailey knew how to keep his true feelings tucked behind his glowing eyes when he wanted to.

I waved at the booth next to Cooper. "Have a seat."

"No room," Cooper said. He didn't budge, using up bench space that would seat at least two people.

Ryder glanced around the room looking for a spare chair, but the place was full. "It'll work." He dropped down so close to the other man that Cooper grunted and moved to one side to keep from getting pinned.

Ryder bit into his twist, still not looking at the man next to him. Which might be because they were sitting so close, they'd have to lean away from each other to actually make eye contact. That could not be a comfortable arrangement.

Cooper pulled one shoulder forward, leaning his elbow on the table.

Ryder sat there, unconcerned, drinking coffee.

"When did you say you were leaving?" Ryder asked.

"I just got here," Cooper said. "Might never leave."

"He got a reason to stay, Delaney?" Ryder chewed with nonchalance.

"In the bakery or in Ordinary?"

"I find myself curious to both answers."

Cooper snorted. "Jackass."

"Freeloader," Ryder shot back.

I watched them. Wondered what history between them that I'd missed. Wondered if I'd have to break them up like Odin and Zeus. Seriously, could I not go a day without two men having it out?

"When are you skipping town again?" Ryder asked, still not looking over at him. "I'd like to throw a parade."

171

"Get off my back, Bailey. You play Boy Scout, but you're a liar. Where the hell have you been all these years? College and some fancy job in a big city doesn't lead a man back to this low-rent shack town. You came back for a reason, and it isn't a good one."

Ryder didn't show any reaction to that except for his eyes. For the first time since he'd sat, he looked down, looked sideways.

If I were trained to read body language, to interrogate, to read people, I'd say Cooper had hit too close to secrets Ryder didn't want to tell. I might even think Ryder was sizing up how many times he could sucker-punch Cooper before I stopped him.

"Take it outside, Reserve Officer Bailey," I said calmly. "You might not be on the clock, but that won't keep me from arresting you for disturbing the peace."

Ryder's gaze flicked up. Eyes filled with heat, mouth curved at one corner into a wicked smile, he did not look like someone willing to apologize for his behavior, nor worried about arrest. His tongue tip slipped at the bottom of his lip, which he then bit.

My own mouth went dry. The brief touch of teeth on the soft swell of his lower lip, the heat in his eyes telling me he liked the idea of being on the wrong side of the law—or maybe just liked the idea of me manhandling him.

An entirely different kind of heat shot through me, leaving an electric hum deep in my belly.

Maybe Cooper was right about one thing: Ryder Bailey was no Boy Scout.

Ryder shifted, the heat, the wicked smile, stowed away. "Sorry, chief. I'm not here to cause trouble." The sparkle in his eyes said differently.

You, Mr. Bailey, are trouble.

He popped the last of his donut in his mouth and leaned back. "I like this town, Cooper. Low rent or not, it has always been good to me. If you don't like it, I hear the casino's looking for talent. They need a guitarist."

And this was helpful Ryder. The guy I'd always known to offer a hand even before someone asked for it. Even if that person was someone Ryder didn't particularly like.

Like Cooper Clark.

"I don't need your help," Cooper said.

The song of power throbbed behind my temples, and the coffee wasn't settling well in my stomach. I took a couple deep breaths to try to settle both, but the hot, damp air wasn't doing me any good.

"Delaney?" Ryder said.

I stood up. "I need some air."

"Let me—" he started.

"See you at the station," I said.

I wove through the patrons and out the door, the bag with Jean's maple bar clenched in my left hand, the song of power rolling like a drunken choir going through tune-up with a rusty band in my head.

The cool air hit my face, and I swallowed it down until the noise leveled off and my stomach evened out. I'd forgotten my coffee on the table, but I was not about to go back for it.

I rubbed at my eyes and the foggy creep of fatigue that was dogging my thoughts. I'd have to sleep soon. But not yet. Today I had to try to make headway on suspects for Heim's death, and time was slipping away for finding a mortal to hand this power over to.

I had no idea who in this town might be the new Heimdall.

It wasn't like every mortal was made for taking on a god power.

That much I knew. Dad had said there must be a fire in the person. Not necessarily one of anger or aggression, but something he described as sharp—a clarity that the power was drawn to. He said the mortal who was made for the god power was tempered like hard metal. Driven. They knew who they were, and remained true to their nature no matter what life threw at them.

That made sense. I'd seen five Poseidons over the years. All of them were cocksure about their ability to control the sea even before they'd taken on the power. And all of them had

173

done something stupid on vacation here in Ordinary and gotten themselves drowned.

So, yes. There was a similarity in the mortals before they had taken the power, even though one of the Poseidons had been a woman.

Maybe that meant I was looking for someone who carried the same traits as Heim.

I started the Jeep and rolled out into traffic.

What did I know about Heim? He shied away from commitment, off on his boat for weeks at a time, sometimes leaving whale watchers without a ride out, which Pete, one of the other boat captains, always seemed willing to pick up the slack for.

He'd fallen in love with Lila. And he'd broken her heart, saying he needed something different in his life, as if he were looking for a new horizon.

I knew she'd never picked up the pieces of her life in town or her business here. She'd left, and hadn't returned until now.

I supposed Heim was a loyal friend. He and Chris got along great. When he wasn't wandering toward the edges of the horizon, Heim seemed happy enough doing his job—fishing and guiding tourists.

Somehow Bertie had railroaded him into judging the Rhubarb Rally, so he had the ability to give to his community. I supposed most people would see him as an easygoing charmer. A bit of a mooch, a drifter.

Who in the town had similar traits?

Too damn many people.

It was a start, though. I'd make a list of things that seemed consistent with Heim's personality, ask Jean and Roy and Myra to add in anything that came to mind. Then I'd start sorting possible candidates, even if that meant going through all of Ordinary from A to Z.

I sighed and rubbed at my eyes again. I was not looking forward to crunching these numbers and wading through this paperwork. But I'd do it.

No matter how long it took. As long as it didn't take longer than four days.

CHAPTER 18

"Took you long enough." Jean sat in my chair at my desk, eyes closed, arms crossed over her Venture Bros. T-shirt. The uncomfortable position meant she was trying to get a little shuteye without sinking into a deep sleep. I'd seen her do that ever since she took over the graveyard shift.

"I bring a peace offering." I dropped the white bag with the maple bar on her lap.

Her mouth curved, but she hadn't opened her eyes. "You brought me donuts as an apology?"

"One, I don't owe you an apology. Two, that donut's not from me."

She cracked one eye open. "I'll get to one in a second. Talk to me about two."

"Your boyfriend gave it to me, on the house, with a wink and a smile."

"My boyfriend?" She frowned, and finally put it together. "Hogan?" she exclaimed delightedly.

"You have some other guy working in some other bakery who likes you? Where else would I be going for pastries? Get out of my chair."

"I'm not slow, I'm tired." She dug out the maple bar and stared at it like it was a diamond ring. "Oh." Her voice wavered. "He remembers."

"So how long has this been going on between you two?"
"What?"

"Maple bar love-o-grams with hunky Hogan." I pushed at her until she got out of the chair, and perched on the edge of my desk instead.

"Today." She stared at the donut with a sort of dreamy sparkle in her eye. "Just. Now."

I smiled and shook my head. The first, early moments of falling in love were always so sweet. Honest, true. And I knew my sister. When she liked someone she fell fast and all the way, regardless of the consequences.

I just hoped he didn't break her heart, because he'd have a hard time doing his job after I'd broken both his arms.

"He's still there now." I booted up my computer.

"I'll go by later. When he gets off."

I pulled up email, clicking on the rally itinerary from Bertie.

I groaned. I would be needed for judging tonight at nine. My stomach, which I'd just gotten settled, roiled at the thought of having to eat rhubarb. Maybe she'd grant me mercy and let me judge non-edible entries.

I committed the list to memory, then moved on to the next email.

Nine o'clock meant I'd have to cancel the dessert with Ryder.

Hell.

"And now we go back to number one," Jean said. She still hadn't bitten into the pastry, but was eyeing it fondly, like she wanted to frame it or something.

"Take a picture. Number one who?"

"Number one what," she corrected. "You do owe me an apology. I've been waiting for you all morning."

She dug out her phone and held it for a selfie, angling the maple bar against her slightly parted lips. She smiled, opened her eyes with feigned innocence, and somehow made the whole thing look dirty.

I wondered if Hogan knew what he was in for.

"I didn't sleep well. Wanted some strong coffee."

"You look exhausted. Did you sleep at all?"

"No. I was sort of...distracted."

"By the murder or by Ryder?"

"Both, I guess. And the power." Truth all the way, especially with my sister. "I don't suppose you might get any...hints or feelings about who might be the right person to give the power over to?"

She shook her head. "It doesn't work like that. I think...I think I felt that Heim was going to be killed. That was the bad feeling I'd had. But since then, nothing."

"Do you think if you got close to someone who might be a candidate for power you might pick up on something?"

"I'm a disaster warning system. How is gaining god power a disaster?"

"Poseidon."

She tipped her head side to side. "Okay, yes. That's always a disaster. But I can't narrow down why I get those bad feelings until after the bad thing has happened. I know bad is on the way, but only recognize it after it hits. It's a useless gift." She laughed, but it didn't cover just how uncomfortable and disappointed she was.

"It's not useless," I said. "You just need more practice to figure it out. I still don't have a handle on how I'm supposed to deal with the power transfer."

"Yeah, but you've only had that job for the last year and this is your first time. I've lived with this all my life. Plenty of time to practice." She finally bit into the maple bar, chewing slowly, her eyes unfocused, though from the pleasure of the donut or displeasure at her abilities, I wasn't sure.

"Don't get some idea in your head that you can ignore it," I said. "I'm relying on you to let me know when you get those gut feelings."

"All the help it will do. But yes. I'll let you know if I get the doom twinges."

I chuckled. "Is that what you're calling it?"

She smiled, and this time I could tell she meant it. "Dunno. Sounds ominous, right? So let's hear it. Apologize."

"Oh, for Pete's sake. Fine. Sorry it took me so long to get to work today."

"Forgiven. Why so late?"

I picked up my coffee cup. Stared at it. Empty. Right, I hadn't brought my coffee. I stood, ambled over to the coffee pot.

"There was a penguin about to get blown out of a cannon, and by the time we jimmied it free and restored it to its natural habitat, I wanted coffee and deep-fried sugar. Just my luck, half of Ordinary had the same idea. I would have been here sooner if Cooper and Ryder hadn't shown up."

DEVON MONK

I poured the last of the coffee into my mug and shoveled sugar into it without measuring. I added flavored cream, figuring a double blast of sugar would count for breakfast and lunch and might keep me awake for an hour or two.

"Cooper *and* Ryder?" she asked. "Where? When?"

I took a drink. My molars hurt.

Ryder strode through the door. He hesitated a second, then strode across the waiting room. He still had that wicked light in his eyes, that one-corner smile, like he was up to no good and wanted me to know it. Broad shoulders were square in the jacket he wore over flannel, and his heavy boots came down with audible thuds.

He was sexy as hell. My heart raced. My breath caught in my throat. I felt stretched taut, against the power of him, of his gaze.

He pushed past the front counter and stopped right in front of me, so close, I could feel the heat rolling off him, could smell the soap and spice of cologne on his skin mixed deliciously with the cold salt air he'd pulled into the station.

"You wanted to see me, chief?"

Forget coffee. Ryder Bailey was what I craved.

For all my life, my heart said. I opened my mouth to say that and caught myself. How stupid would I sound? He was just here reporting for work. That was all.

"Uh," I replied, brilliantly.

He exhaled and smiled, and everything in him went loose and relaxed. A dimple appeared by his mouth and I wanted to draw my fingertips over it, over his lips, over the dark stubble on his jaw, down the hard planes of his chest and stomach, and anywhere else that would make him kiss me.

He was just standing too close to me. I couldn't think.

I took a step back. "Why do you smell like fir trees?"

Okay. Maybe I still couldn't think.

He rolled his shoulders in a shrug. "I helped Mr. Tippin stack a cord of wood he had delivered yesterday."

Mr. Tippin lived a few houses down from Ryder. He was also a jinn with a slight case of pyromania.

"Good," I said. "That was good."

178

"Just being neighborly," he said. "Did you have anything you wanted me to take care of for you today?"

Wild images of him kissing me, tumbling me down onto my bed so I could tear his clothes off, flew through my mind.

"If not," he went on, "I thought I'd take care of the filing in the record room."

"Filing," I repeated, heat creeping up my face as the memory of him standing naked in his living room chose just that moment to come back to me.

Why did he have to be such a good-looking man? And kind? And funny? And the love that I'd never dared ask for?

Jean cleared her throat. Or maybe she was just trying not to laugh at me.

"Filing," I said. "Sure. Yes. That would be good."

"Good." His eyes crinkled in the corners. He was holding back laughter too.

Don't bite your bottom lip, don't bite your bottom lip, don't bite—

He bit his bottom lip, tugged, let it go.

All my bones went a little rubbery.

"Maybe Ryder should go on a ride-along with Myra again," Jean suggested.

"No." I walked back to my desk, needing the space between me and that man and his smile and his eyes and his bottom lip. "Filing needs to be done. That's a good job for the morning."

"And tonight?" he said.

"Tonight?"

"We're still on for dessert?"

"Oh. Uh...no. I can't make it."

The pleasant man in a pleasant mood disappeared. "Really."

"Bertie just sent my itinerary. I have to judge tonight."

"Right," he said. "Judging. I forgot."

"Another time?" I suggested.

"Sure." He didn't look happy about it. "I'll get to those files now. Holler if you need anything." He walked back to our file and evidence room.

I rubbed at my eyes and groaned.

"That was some serious public display of affection you had in your eyes," Jean said.

"Aren't you supposed to be going home now?"

"And miss all the fireworks? The scintillating conversation? Good," she mimicked. "That was good."

I groaned again. "Did I sound like that much of an idiot?"

"Maybe a little more."

I dropped my hands in my lap. Jean sat at her desk, looking smug.

"Fine. Ryder makes an idiot out of me."

"I know. You let him in the records room."

Huh. I tried to remember if there was anything in there that would betray the secrets of Ordinary. Maybe not right out in the open, but if he went digging far enough.

"Well, hell," I said quietly.

"You stay here," Jean said. "My brain works fine when I'm around him. I'll give him something else to do. Check in with Bertie to see if she needs extra help with the rally, maybe."

I rested my elbows on the desk and lowered my face into my palms. "God," I said through the muffle of my hands. I was such an idiot.

I didn't know how long I sat there listening to the screech and bang of the song in my head. Long enough that eventually I heard Jean and Ryder's footsteps as they walked through the office, Jean keeping up a conversation that I pretended not to hear.

Long enough for them both to leave and shut the door behind them.

"Reed Daughter," a soft voice said from right next to me.

I jerked, looked up.

Death stood next to my desk. He wore a novelty T-shirt that said ORDINARY TOWN, EXTRAORDINARY FUN, over which he had thrown a Hawaiian shirt featuring palm tree fronds and tiki heads. He was also wearing a slick pair of dark gray slacks and shiny black shoes.

His dark hair was cropped short, making his deep eyes seem even wider, his heavy lids languid. Even though he wasn't smiling, I got the distinct impression he was laughing at me.

"Hey," I said, straightening. I glanced around the station. No one else was here.

"How is your health?" he asked.

"My what?" I didn't like the idea of Death asking me if I was sick.

"Ah, I may not have stated that clearly. How are you?" His eyes glinted with something I was pretty sure was humor.

"Very funny. I'm good. What can I do for you?"

"I am here to inquire on the methods for acquiring a license to do business."

"All right. You want to see Bertie over at City Hall for that. She'll have the forms you need to fill out. I'm glad you've chosen a job so soon."

"Is it not in the contract that I must do so?"

"Sure, but sometimes it takes time for a deity to decide on an occupation."

He raised one eyebrow. "I am not a creature of doubt or indecision, Reed Daughter."

"Delaney," I corrected absently.

"Of course." He paused. For a creature who didn't doubt, it looked like he was weighing a decision.

"He wasn't frightened," he finally said.

"Who?" I belatedly realized he must be talking about Heim.

"Your father."

His words hit me like a falling building. He must have taken my silence as a tacit invitation to continue.

"I waited for him, gathered his soul. He had questions. Several."

I swallowed and nodded, a hundred questions of my own crowding out my words.

"What did he ask?"

"That I look after you."

Okay, forget the shock over him talking about my dad's death. This was a bigger shock.

"Why? Why would he ask you to do that? Is that why you're here? Did you agree to do it? Why me? He has two other daughters, you know. Wasn't he worried about them? Was he worried about us?"

He waited a moment longer, probably to see if I had anything else to say. I did, but I needed a few answers before I tore off into a pile of new questions.

"I assumed it was out of love."

I waited. He didn't say anything more. "Which question were you answering?"

"The first."

"Okay." I sighed. I hadn't slept in almost twenty-four hours. I was tired. "Is that why you came to Ordinary?"

"I came for a vacation, Reed Daughter." He pointed one finger at his T-shirt, as if that made it obvious.

"Which is why you're telling me about my father's death?"

He frowned, looking confused. "Is that not what you wished to ask me?"

I opened my mouth to tell him no, but that was a lie. "I did. But I didn't expect you to talk about it. Not really."

"Ah, then." He gave me a stiff nod. "I must be away to secure my business license."

I had a hundred other questions besides the half a dozen I'd already asked that he hadn't answered. But he was already walking back to the door, gliding silently in his shiny shoes. "Is he a ghost?" I asked.

Death paused, his hand on the door latch. "Perhaps you should ask him if you see him again."

And then he pushed out into the daylight, a colorful, unexpected shadow.

CHAPTER 19

"Don't be such a baby." Myra shoved my shoulder as we walked to the building, rain spattering us with tiny, halfhearted drops. "It won't kill you."

"I hate rhubarb."

"Which should make judging even easier. If you can stand it, it's a good recipe."

"Or it's a terrible recipe because it tastes the least like rhubarb in a rhubarb recipe contest."

"Just give your honest opinion."

"I honestly don't want to do this."

"A little less honest than that."

She opened the door to the great hall, which was in truth the only hall on our festival ground, great or not. Built of brick and shingled with cedar, it was plenty big enough for the exhibits that couldn't stand the mercurial moods of coastal weather.

Quilts started at the right and lined two walls, all of them having something to do with rhubarb. The art was on that side of the building too, hung on pegboard stands that created aisles.

Food things such as canning, dried herbs, smoked meats, and drinks took up the left side of the building. The middle space carried an odd variety of art, from chainsaw statues and dream catchers to a ten-foot beast welded out of spare parts and gears that looked like a caveman in a porcupine hat carrying a battle-axe and a Colt .45.

"That's…"

"Rhu-ban the Barb-barian," Myra said with a straight face.

I laughed. "You are kidding me."

"Nope."

"Who made that big hunk of metal pun?"

"Ben and Jame, and the rest of the fire department."

"I want to see it." I started toward the thing, but before I got more than six steps a hand landed on my arm, sharp fingers squeezing.

"Delaney," Bertie chirped happily. "I am so pleased you've made it. Come with me."

There was no arguing with a valkyrie when she had it in her mind to get a person somewhere. So I let her pull me along, and took in the rest of the show as best I could.

A lot of entries this year. Maybe almost double from last year. The outreach of adding in more judging categories had really helped boost participation.

About halfway across the building I realized there were a lot more people at this end of the room than needed to be there for judging.

A crowd of about sixty people milled around the metal chairs set in straight rows in front of a long table with white table cloth and a skirt of blue. The long table was for the judges, twelve empty chairs behind it so that the judges were facing the audience.

"Why are there so many people here?" I asked Bertie. "The rally hasn't even started."

"People like to watch judges when they're eating."

"Watch judges?" I repeated. "Watch us eat?" I bit back a groan. I was going to have to clench my teeth in my best courtroom smile to keep from sticking my tongue out and gagging in front of these people.

"Maybe I should be an art judge. I could judge art." I tried to keep the panic out of my voice. "I'm good at art. Just ask Mrs. Heather."

"Your first-grade teacher?"

"Best thumbprint turkey artist of the class right here." I lifted the thumb on my free hand.

"Nonsense," Bertie said. "All these people are here before the rally even begins because of *your* schedule, Delaney. I knew you'd be working crowd control and being very busy over the next three days with your police work, so I decided to move up the judging date of the edibles. Luckily, everyone was able to modify their schedules to be here. I do love a town that pulls together in times of crisis."

"Crisis? How many edibles?" I was totally panicking. "Which categories am I judging? How many categories?"

"Two. Drinks, dear. And savories."

"No pies?"

"Not the sweet pies."

I didn't know why that made me feel better, but taking on a wet pink mess of pies eye to eye without a convenient dog under the table to feed it to seemed like the highest level of insanity.

"I need a dog."

"What?" she asked.

"Nothing." I squared my shoulders and tugged my hand, but she was not letting go. Valkyries were also smart. "How bad can it be?"

"Oh." She frowned. "I forgot this is your first time."

"What? What was the 'oh'? It's going to be bad? How bad? Bertie, how bad?"

"It's going to be lovely," she lied through her pretty, straight, sharp white teeth, her short white hair puffed up like a halo atop her head. "Just sit here at the end of the table. I'll gather the other judges and your assistant."

"I get an assistant? To feed me?"

"Delaney," she said with one eyebrow raised. Ah. I had finally hit the end of Bertie's patience. "I'm not dragging you to your grave. You would know."

"Is it an option?"

"Oh, it could be arranged, dear." She shoved me down into the chair with a firm finality that made me wish for another explosion, or maybe a friendly class-five hurricane.

"Now, much like death," Bertie said through her smile, "this will be much more pleasant than you think. Food, drink, and all the men you could desire."

I angled a glare up at her. "Are you selling me a castle in the sky, Bertie?"

"I am comforting you and promising you glory for your bravery on this battlefield," she said quietly, and with the tone most people would associate with someone complimenting a six-year-old who had made a gold-star thumbprint turkey painting.

Deities and creatures always showed their true nature, right in front of us all, even if most of us didn't know to look for it.

Still, it had been a while since Bertie had threatened me with my own grave.

"What's the assistant for? Really?" I asked.

"Didn't you read the information I sent you today?"

"Some of it?"

"Delaney. You're an officer of the law. I expect you to take this seriously and pay attention to details."

"I will. I was just"—*staring at Ryder*—"distracted by work."

"Don't worry. I've put you in very good hands."

And then she was off, swooping down on some other poor, unsuspecting soul in the crowd.

Valkyries made amazing party planners.

Bertie gathered the judges, who all took their places at the table with a lot less complaining than me.

I was surprised to see Fawn Wolfe, one of Jame's sisters, at the end of the table, but decided maybe it was a bit of brilliance to have a werewolf among the judges. They had amazing sense of taste and smell.

Frigg took the chair next to her and gave me a big wink, while she waved to the audience. Next to her sat our postmaster Chester, a mortal, and his niece Aluvia, the lead chef from the The Kraken, our one high-end restaurant.

The last chair was taken by big, tall, dark-haired, bearded Tomas, who was our local Leshy. A guardian and creature of trees and forest in his native land, here Tomas spent most his time as the second-in-command at the public library.

So we had two creatures, one deity, two mortals, and me. Pretty nice showing. I scanned the crowd, waiting for the starting gun, or whatever would be used to kick off this event. I was also taking note of the nearest trash cans in case I had to barf.

The audience settled into their seats. Mortals I knew, tourists I didn't, and a smattering of creatures. I even caught sight of Herri in the back, her arm around Chris Lagon, who looked exhausted and sad. It looked like Herri was there to keep Chris on his feet, or maybe had been the one to talk him into attending the judging event.

He wasn't taking the death of Heim very well, not that there was an easy or correct way to grieve the loss of a friend.

Herri caught my gaze and gave me a small smile and nod. She was there in support of Chris, which was really nice of her.

I looked through the crowd for Margot, Chris's girlfriend, and didn't see her. Not that I expected Margot to be there. She and Chris hadn't been seeing each other for all that long. I couldn't blame her if she wasn't into rhubarb.

Dan Perkin had been sitting and twitching in the front row since I first walked in, his baseball hat shoved down hard on his head, his eyes flicking around the room, and then coming back to focus on me like I was the only light in the place.

I made eye contact, gave him a polite half-smile, and ignored him.

How many other people in the audience were competitors and how many just liked to watch people eat? And who was my assistant?

Bertie plucked assistants out of the crowd and ushered them up to the table, introducing them to the judges, and then moving quickly away to snatch up the next person.

She was obviously having the time of her life.

The buzz and thrum of conversation had a friendly, excited tone to it.

Well, that was what we wanted, after all. These festivals were about getting people together to share their passions, hobbies, and ideas. Yes, it brought money into the town, but in many ways the biggest strength of it was drawing people together.

I saw him before he saw me—tall, dark, walking easy in his work boots and jeans, he moved like a man who had spent his life in deep forests, head tilted just a bit, eyes bright, movement fluid and graceful for a guy in flannel and boots.

Ryder Bailey.

My heart raced faster. My skin warmed. I liked watching him when he didn't know he was being watched. Took my time to soak in his details.

He hadn't shaved, and his thick, dark hair was tossed by the wind. He looked like he'd been working, and might have changed his dark gray T-shirt, but not the brown and green flannel shirt he had rucked up to his elbows. His hands were long-fingered and strong, his forearms muscled and nicked with a couple of old scars.

He was a man who worked with his hands for a living, a man who worked with his body for a living, a man who strolled through a crowded room and caught the eye of every person without knowing it.

He reached the edge of the seating area and tipped his head up to meet my gaze.

That direct stare stoked the heat under my skin, and I held my breath so I could savor the fire roaring across my nerves.

How could a man I'd known all my life make me forget what I was doing, forget my job, this town, and everyone in it?

I was here to judge the contest, to keep the peace, to find a murderer, to change someone's life by making them a god. That to-do list was enough to satisfy anyone.

But all I wanted, all I could think of, was what it would be like to stand up, walk over to that man, and devour him with my mouth.

He blinked once slowly, but it didn't break the spell. And that soft, almost intimate, and certainly hungry curve of his lips didn't do anything to put out the fire smoldering in me.

The connection that I could practically feel thrumming gently over my skin like a fingertip slipping up and down my spine was amazing. Addictive.

I wanted more.

I wanted Ryder.

Bertie suddenly appeared in front of Ryder, smiling and talking quickly as she took his hand to lead him to where ever she wanted him to be.

I inhaled, exhaled shakily. I'd been staring. And if anyone was watching me, they'd caught me at it.

Mooning.

Great.

I kept my gaze somewhere safely toward the back of the hall, my face neutral. Bertie walked down to the far side of the stage again just as footsteps on stage approached me.

"Evening, officer," Ryder said, his voice much too low, too full, too throaty for a concrete community hall in the middle of an old cow field.

"Reserve officer. You might want to take your seat. I think Satan's about to start the torture."

He pulled out the empty chair next to me and settled in it, his wide shoulders brushing mine before he shifted slightly to make room.

"What are you doing?"

He rested his forearms on the table and smiled at the audience. "I'm your assistant."

"No."

"Yes."

"Why?"

He wasn't looking at me. "Have you found any way to refuse Bertie when she's on the warpath to acquire volunteers?"

I groaned.

He agreed with a nod.

"When did she get you?"

"This afternoon when Jean sent me out of the file room. I would have been much happier doing menial paperwork."

"So noted. At least you don't have to eat this crap." I mimicked him, smiling out at the crowd.

See? I could do this. Be a happy person helping out her community one plate of gooey pink fruit at a time.

"Honor and duty, officer," he said.

"Stuff it, Bailey."

He chuckled then cleared his throat. "Here we go. Smile for the cameras, darlin'."

His voice, low and intimate, rolled through me, and I laced my fingers together on top of the table to keep from reaching for him. He was so close that our hips and legs were almost touching.

But there would be no touching here. This was serious business.

Bertie took the stage with the strut of a professional ringleader, and then gave a short speech on the history of the Rhubarb Rally that ended with her thanking the community for being so flexible with their hours and allowing for a change of judges under such terrible circumstances.

She asked for a moment of silence for the passing of Heim, a good man and judge who had served on the rhubarb panel for the last two years.

The crowd complied. While I bent my head, I also watched the reactions in the audience. If our guilty party really was connected in some way to the rally, they would be here.

Everyone lowered their heads, except for a couple parents who were busy trying to keep their children quiet.

Dan Perkin didn't lower his head. He scowled and messed with the brim of his hat, as if even this slight delay of him winning first prize was an indignity he refused to endure.

Then Bertie thanked everyone and, in an arresting, uplifting voice, introduced the judges and announced we would begin with the savories, of which there were twenty-three entries.

I groaned quietly through my teeth, and Ryder chuckled.

He pulled a pen out of his pocket and clicked the top of it. "Don't worry. I've got your back."

"You might want to get a barf bucket instead." One of the food handlers set a small plate with a wedge of necrotic pink cheese in front of me, along with a clean plastic fork and napkin.

"Thank you," I said with fake enthusiasm. "How exciting."

She left a glass of water within reach.

"Round one." Ryder produced a white sheet of paper.

I picked up the fork. I quickly decided there was no way I'd be able to fake a smile through the whole thing, but keeping a straight face was something I had long practice with.

"Something wrong?" Ryder asked.

"Nope. I plan to deal with that cheese like I would any other perpetrator under interrogation."

"Cheese interrogation. That a special course they teach you in the academy?"

"Maintaining professionalism in unfriendly environments."

"You think this is unfriendly? People have gathered just to cheer you on as you eat. You couldn't have stronger support."

"It's a hostile work environment. Hostile cheese too."

"You don't know that. You haven't tasted it yet."

"Yeah." I had been staring at the cheese the entire time, the fork poised in my hand. I couldn't bring myself to actually make my arm and hand move down to touch the gelatinous mass. The air shifted a bit and I got a strong whiff of cooked rhubarb.

And goat cheese.

"You might want to get on with stabbing it," he suggested. "You're falling behind."

I glanced down the table. All the judges had already moved on to new plates. One that looked suspiciously like macaroni and cheese. Pink macaroni and cheese.

I fought back my gag reflex. "Switch places?"

"I think they'd notice. Take a bite."

"It's rhubarb."

"Only some of it is rhubarb. Some of it is cheese."

"Don't be reasonable with me."

"Wouldn't dream of it."

His hand under the table pressed down on my knee and rubbed a gentle circle, fingertips dragging softly down the inside. Even through the heavy denim of my jeans, I could feel the heat, the pressure of his hand.

"One bite and I'll make it worth it," he murmured.

I might have been holding my breath. I didn't look over at him, but from the corner of my eye, I could see his polite and interested expression as he stared down at the plate, and my fork hovering over it.

He was surprisingly good at hiding the truth behind that polite expression. Now where had he learned to do that?

"That's a dirty move," I said.

"Not yet it isn't."

He gently stroked my knee again, slowly letting his fingers drift upward along the inside of my thigh. It was only a couple of inches, but his hand drew my attention away from this room, these people, and that insult to the dairy aisle in front of me.

"You think that's going to help?"

"I'm enjoying myself."

"Delaney?" Bertie called out.

I swallowed a yelp of surprise. She stood in front of the stage, her back to the crowd.

"Problem?" I asked.

"Not with me, dear." Her words were sharp as knives. "Is there something wrong with the entry?"

"No. I was just…admiring the…"

"Presentation," Ryder provided. "High scores for presentation on this one."

"Love the mangled chunks of rhubarb that doesn't resemble raw hamburger mixed with curdled milk at all," I said. "High points for that."

"Delaney," Bertie said through her teeth. "I hope you're not thinking of disappointing me and all the good people of Ordinary with complete disregard to Heim's memory by making light of your duties."

I raised my eyebrows. Impressive. Bertie knew how to lay on the guilt trip.

"Not at all." I forked up the tip of the cheese and popped it in my mouth.

"Mmm." I tried to make it sound good while an explosion of soft, salty but slightly sweet cheese held battle with tart, bitter, disgusting rhubarb.

Bertie was all smiles.

I held in my gag reflex.

"Well done." She moved along.

Ryder stroked my knee again, then gave me a gentle pat. "So. On a scale of swill to crap, where does this rate?"

I choked back a laugh and pressed my fingers over my mouth, then took a drink of water.

"Um…seven?"

"We'll go with that." He was busy writing on the small white card.

"Doesn't take that long to write seven." The cheese plate was lifted away and the next was placed on my table with a clean fork and napkin.

Bread the color of a flamingo.

"I'm allowed to note your comments. The contestants like a personal touch. Did you mean raw hamburger and curdled milk, or would you say rotten hamburger and cottage cheese more accurately describes the dish?"

"Do. Not." I leaned toward him and peered down over the card.

His handwriting was bold, clear, and neat, each letter squared.

"A festive confetti of colors and textures?"

He grinned. "Too much?"

I smiled back. "Oh, I think it's just exactly enough."

"Good. Now eat your crayon bread."

CHAPTER 20

I CHOKED my way through twenty-three entries. Two entries were tied for first place. One: a rhubarb-pineapple salsa had made me gasp in surprise because it was actually good, and the other, a rhubarb-chicken salad wrap that Ryder teased me about when I went back for a third bite.

To solve the tie, the judges all gathered behind a standing curtain to re-taste the top entries and decide which was the best.

To my delight, and maybe because I made a lot of loud noises and reminded people I had a gun, the rhubarb-pineapple salsa took first place.

"You look pleased with yourself," Ryder said as we waited on the sidelines for Bertie to announce the first, second, and third prize winners.

I took another swig out of my water bottle, scanning the crowd. Everyone seemed happy enough. Maybe a few nervous faces—probably contestants waiting for the verdict. No one looked like they would shoot the winners. "I just survived the seven-layer dips from hell. I am beyond pleased."

He stuffed both his hands in his front pockets. "Then you should be downright giddy after the drink round."

I groaned. I'd forgotten about the drink round.

"I hate my life."

Ryder grinned. "Some of them are alcoholic."

"Let's get to those first so I can forget this night."

"My offer still stands," he said as Bertie took the stage.

"Offer?"

"Get through this, and I'll make this worth your while."

"Did Bertie pay you to say that?"

"She's good. But not that good."

"Well, well, Mr. Bailey. I do believe you're coming on to me."

"Is that going to get me arrested this time, officer?"

"Play your cards right and it just might get you something."

"It's not too late for dessert," he murmured.

Bertie made a grand show of announcing the winners from fifth to first. The salsa took first, and in a surprise that got the entire room applauding louder, the salsa recipe had been entered by fourteen-year-old Jimmy Stanton.

"Ready?" Ryder asked as the crowd shifted and milled, some people leaving while others were still arriving. The drink round would start in five minutes.

"Can't wait."

A phone rang, and Ryder frowned as he pulled his out of his pocket. He glanced at the screen and I saw surprise, then anger fly quickly across his eyes before he pushed those both away and turned to take the call.

I strolled to the front of the room, and several people stopped me to shake my hand or offer up a little idle chat. Jimmy waved his blue ribbon over his head at me like he'd just stolen the flag from the top of the world, and I gave him a thumbs-up and a nod.

Trillium from the newspaper was walking his way, her phone cupped in her palm as she spoke into it. Looked like Jimmy was going to get a picture in the paper.

I gathered with the other judges and assistants who hadn't just ducked out on their duties, at one side of the stage.

The judges and assistants were all in a good mood. Gazes flicked over the crowd and lingered a little longer on Jimmy. He hadn't won the prize because of his age, but there was something wonderful in rewarding someone who was practically vibrating with excitement over a blue ribbon.

It gave the entire event a buoyant sort of lift, and my mood couldn't help but rise right along with it.

Frigg cracked her knuckles one at a time and frowned. "Where's Ryder?"

"Deserted me."

"Couldn't hack it, huh?"

"Phone call."

"Will he be back?"

"I have no idea."

I took a little more time studying the faces in the room. Chris and Herri were still in the back. They'd found two chairs and had placed them near the quilts, about midway across the hall. Close enough they could hear and see what was going on, but still be separate from the audience.

I thought they must have done that out of deference to Chris, who was still reeling from the death of his friend.

The rest of the crowd were already in their seats, about forty people scattered across the chairs, most of them staring at their phones or sending messages. In this modern day, the newspaper would not be the first place to break the news on the winners. Probably half of Ordinary already knew how the savory round had gone down.

I noted the newlyweds Hallie and Joe Wolfe were there. Joe was full werewolf, whereas Hallie was a shifter who took feline form. Funny how the two of them, cat and dog, were more easily accepted in the Wolfe family than Ben and Jame.

But then, the Rossi and Wolfe truce was an uneasy one.

Other creatures in the audience included the linebacker Nash, who was big for a man, but small for an ispolin, and the three black-clad, perpetually moody Dryads: Basil, Coleson, and Delta.

Dan Perkin perched once again in the front row. Two empty seats were open beside him. Since the only person I could think of who spoke moderately kindly of Dan was his neighbor Pearl, and she spoke kindly of everyone, I wasn't surprised that he was sitting there in his own little bubble.

He was fidgety and angry. So: normal.

Ryder was still nowhere to be seen.

Bertie took up the microphone again, introduced us as judges, and we all took our previous places.

After a smattering of applause, the handlers stepped up with small, clear plastic cups and placed one in front of each of us.

A stack of new white scoring cards were positioned in front of Ryder's noticeably empty chair. If he didn't show up soon, I'd have to do this solo.

I pulled one card and the pen closer just as a figure folded down into the empty chair next to me.

"Delaney Reed," a soft baritone drawled. "What have you done to your assistant?"

I turned to my companion.

Old Rossi, patriarch, ruler, lord of the vampires in Ordinary, looked to be about fifty years of age, with a short shock of black hair that tended to curl above ears that stuck out just a bit. One curl over his right eye was a thick streak of silver and a salting of silver touched both temples. His face was long, lips very full beneath a thin black mustache and goatee that only drew attention to his hard cheekbones and the crook in his strong nose.

But it was his eyes, a shocking ice blue, that seemed to have the power to peel their observer right down to the bone and, once caught, refuse to release.

Luckily, those eyes were bright with humor. A lazy smile without any teeth pulled at his full lips.

I knew he had a good body—everyone in town knew he had a good body, since he also had a streaking habit.

"I didn't do anything to my assistant. Why are you here?"

"Replacing him." He picked up the pen and tapped it on the edge of the table while he slouched back and stared at the ceiling. I noticed he was wearing a string of beads centered with a peace symbol over his tie-dyed T-shirt and another string of what looked like crystals of various sizes and colors wrapped in hemp circling his wrist three times. This close, I could smell the slight sour-sweet of marijuana on his clothes.

Was he stoned?

"I am here to assist with the judging. That"—he tapped the table with the pen—"is tea. Rhubarb raspberry."

I picked up the plastic cup and took a tentative sniff.

"What did you do to Ryder?" I lifted the cup. Held my breath.

He rolled his head sideways, still tapping the pen, blue eyes bright beneath his close, dark eyebrows. "I haven't done a thing to our new reserve officer. Bertie asked for volunteers. When I realized he was gone, I volunteered. For karma. Balance. Peace." His voice slipped into a sonorous drone. "You will drink the tea..."

"Oh, please. I'm immune."

He smiled again—still no teeth, but plenty of glee. "Reeds have always been particularly resistant to such things. I find it…refreshing. Have I ever told you of the time your great-great-aunt begged me to have my way with her?"

"Graygray Gertie? Begged?" The image of my great-great-aunt, a tiny ninety-three-year-old white-haired dry-apple of a woman, flashed through my mind. And so did an image of naked Rossi and Graygray in bed.

I so didn't need to be imagining that.

"Beautiful young thing at the time. Ripe with that Reed bravado. That incredible *fairness* and empathy that even the gods can't deny. Reminds me of you."

"I'd never want you to have your way with me."

He chuckled and settled his shoulders against the back of the chair. "Not that I would. Our auras are not at all compatible. Drink the tea. People are watching."

"Don't tell me what to do."

"Free will is my groove."

I swallowed the drink. I wanted to tell him to go away. But he basically had me pinned down in front of all these eyes.

I had one job to do, and that was to sit here and drink my way through the next hour or so with a smile on my face. I could do that even with the bloodsucking Woodstock dropout over there.

"Four," I said, tapping the plastic cup. "Too bitter. Too much pulp."

He straightened and wrote on the card, then flipped it over with his long, almost delicate fingers.

The cup was withdrawn and a new cup was set in its place. I sniffed the frighteningly pink milky liquid, hoping it might be a cocktail, but got a nose full of bitter rhubarb. I stifled a groan.

"Since you have brought up the subject of Ryder Bailey," he said, "I'd like to know why you hired him."

The casual tone layered on top of something that sounded like anger stopped me. I looked over at him. "Why I hired him?"

The air around us thickened in that wavy way I knew meant he was exerting his powers. The sounds of the room around us quieted, as if someone had just closed a window between us and the rest of the people in the building.

We would not be overheard. We might not even be remembered, if Rossi was going full out and making people avert their eyes, but since I was a judge and most of the town knew it, I assumed he was just keeping our public conversation private.

"Were you bribed, coerced, threatened?"

"Threatened? By Ryder?"

"Be calm. Take a drink." His smile was in place but held no warmth. "It's strawberry rhubarb milk."

"Why would he threaten me?" I said through teeth clenched in a smile.

"Not what I asked. Not what you need to know. I'd like to know *if* you were threatened."

I sipped the pink milk. "Seven." I picked up the glass of water and took a drink, swishing away the thick coating on my tongue. "It's like a popover in milk form. Kids would like it."

"Huh." Rossi dutifully jotted that down, his handwriting small and slanted with curly bits at the top and bottom. "It looks disgusting. What you people enjoy." He shook his head.

"I wasn't threatened. Now you're going to tell me why you think I might have been."

The next drink was dark and carbonated. I could hear it popping in the cup before I even got my hands on it. Soda of some kind. I swigged down a gulp without sniffing it first or really knowing what it was.

"I do not trust Ryder Bailey."

It went down wrong, and I choked, sputtered, and coughed against my palm. Every eye in the audience turned to me. Including Dan Perkin, who had gone lava red.

Old Rossi had dropped the dampening barrier around us and patted my back gently.

"Rhubarb root beer," he informed me.

I could tell. I wasn't going to get that smell out of my sinuses for days.

I got my coughing fit under control and wiped the tears away from my eyes. "Sorry," I said to the audience, probably breaking protocol. "User malfunction. The entry is fine, I just forgot how to swallow for a second."

I raised the glass in a toast and took another sip of bitter, bubbling rhubarb swimming in the caramel-sweet wetness. I suppressed a shudder and nodded and smiled for the crowd.

"One," I said quietly. "No, let's do two. It's terrible. But don't write that. Um…say something like: robust flavor. And what is your problem with Ryder?"

"I wouldn't say it's a problem. I don't trust him."

"Why?"

"He's been out of town on weekends."

Last time I looked, that wasn't against the law. "Why are you paying attention to his schedule?"

"Peach rhubarb apple smoothie," he said.

I decided caution was going to be a strength if I was going to get through all the entries, and picked up the cup. I sniffed the fruity drink before taking a small mouthful. "You're avoiding answering me." I took a second sip.

"We are in the middle of something very public here," he said.

"You started this while we were right in the middle of this very public something. It must be important if it's dragged you away from your ice yoga or Tibetan throat-clearing or whatever it is you do on Thursday nights. What's going on? Nine, by the way. Milkshake goodness. Sweet and tart."

"You've answered my question. There's no more for me to say."

"Travail."

He raised his eyebrows at my use of his first name. No one used his first name.

"If you know something about Ryder or this town, I need you to tell me. We had a man murdered on Monday. I do not need any other grim surprises."

"Why do you think it's murder? Hot lemon rhubarb tea. Sweetened with organic blackberry honey."

I sniffed, sipped. "Four. Honey's too powerful. I can't taste the rhubarb. I can't believe I'm complaining about that. Heim didn't hit himself in the back of the head and throw himself into the ocean. The gods agree."

"Gods." He shook his head, as if they were of no consequence.

"And?"

"Hot chocolate rhubarb with strawberry marshmallow."

I stared at the pink marshmallow dissolving into pink slime that coated the top of the slurry of pinkish-brown liquid. "Well, this one isn't going to win on presentation. Do you know who killed Heim? Do you suspect Ryder?"

"Do you?"

A chill washed down my spine. I took a drink of the cocoa, trying to remain objective about the beverage and my almost-boyfriend as I weighed the information that the man I thought I was falling for might be involved in illegal activities. Could Ryder be a killer?

"Two. Too heavy on the dark cocoa. Needs more pink slime. I don't...I don't think so."

"Is that your head or your heart speaking, Delaney Reed? Rum rhubarb screwdriver."

Alcohol. Finally.

"You came up here telling me someone might threaten me over hiring Ryder. You led me to believe he could be a murderer. Is there another conclusion you'd like me to jump to?"

I sniffed the cocktail and hoped they'd gone generous on the rum. Tipped the cup and took a long swallow.

The air was thick again, the sounds muted.

"Why did you hire him?"

"We needed help. Myra and Jean thought he could help. He said yes."

"Is that all?"

"That is all. Do I need to fire him? Watch him?"

Arrest him? Search his house? Fall out of love with him?

"No," he said quietly. "This is a matter of my own. It will not affect the town, or the people within it. It's all good. If it changes, I'll let you know. How's the screwdriver?"

"A solid six. Rhubarb is a refreshing, if slightly disgusting twist. Don't write down the disgusting part. How long have you been watching him?"

"Rhubarb strawberry lime daiquiri. Leave it. I'm an old man. Sometimes I am too curious for my own good. It's why I meditate. You should try it."

"No."

"I hold a session every Tuesday morning."

"No."

"Clothing optional."

I knocked back a gulp of daiquiri and almost set off on another coughing fit.

Hello, tequila.

"Strong. Um…seven? Hold on, let me try to actually taste it." I took a smaller sip, moving the icy liquid around on the tip of my tongue. "Change that to a four. It's all tequila, no flavor. Good tequila, though."

I looked over the crowd. Mostly happy faces. A few people were bored, others still staring at their phones. And of course there was Dan Perkin, the eternally simmering ball of anger seething in the front row.

If he didn't die of a rage-induced stroke, I'd be amazed.

"Rhubarb wine," Rossi said. "That sounds intriguing."

I lifted the cup, gave it a swirl, and downed the single-ounce serving in one go.

"Okay. That was unexpectedly sweet. Nice dessert wine. Let's give it a nine, and move on to the next."

"Barberry Beer."

I wasn't supposed to know who had entered which drink into the contest. But it was a small town and people and creatures and deities liked to talk. A lot.

It was nearly impossible to create a blind tasting event. Bertie had done a fine job, as far as I was concerned. I hadn't known any of the entrants' items for the savory round, and I only knew two for sure in this round: Dan Perkin's root beer and Chris Lagon's barberry beer.

I made a point of not looking at Dan or Chris as I lifted the cup, glanced inside at a deep amber beer with just a hint of an almost fuchsia tint that was actually pretty. It smelled a little like blackberry or raspberry tones over the light scent of hops.

There was a reason Chris was such a respected brewer. He was good at it. I just hoped this beer held up.

I took a drink and quickly stuffed my smile under a neutral expression as I leaned toward Rossi. "Ten. I don't know why I didn't trust him. How does he make a vegetable as evil as rhubarb taste good?"

"It's a fruit," Travail said absently.

"Yes, it is. An evil fruit."

"Except when it's in beer, apparently," he said with an easy smile.

"Apparently," I agreed.

"Whiskey sour," he said. "Guess what the sour is."

"After this, probably not my mood." I lifted another glass to my lips.

CHAPTER 21

"ARE YOU sure you can make it all the way to the top of the stairs?" Myra asked, parking the cruiser below my house.

"I'm not drunk." I waved a hand at her before unbuckling my seatbelt. It took me two tries to get the button thingy right.

"Uh-huh. Maybe you should stay with me tonight."

I sighed. "Okay, I'm a little tipsy, but not drunk. I am also a little sick to my stomach from all that rhubarb. I plan to drink half a bottle of Maalox, take a bath, and sleep."

"You sure? I'm…" She chewed on the inside of her cheek and glanced up at the house. "I'm feeling like maybe I should go up there with you."

"Nope. No. You are officially relieved from duty. I can bathe myself."

"I—"

"No. Good night, Myra." I tugged open the door and stepped out into the cold air, shivering as it whipped over my bare skin.

"Good night, Delaney. I'm watching you until you lock the door behind you."

"Fine. Good. Night." I tromped to the steps and took them at a steady pace, one hand sliding along the metal railing, wind chopping in wet and salty from the west.

I didn't have to find my keys because I didn't lock the front door. So I pushed the door open, waved at Myra, then stepped in and shut it behind me.

Someone was in the room. I could feel it like a pressure between my shoulders.

I didn't have my gun on me, and the one I kept in the house was tucked away in my bedroom.

I pulled off my coat and tossed it in the little chair by the door, acting as if I didn't know I had company. I casually pulled my phone up into my palm.

"Long night?" a voice asked from the darkness near my kitchen.

I knew that voice.

"Hey, Ryder." I hadn't turned my phone off, but hadn't dialed for backup yet. "Why are you in the dark, in my kitchen?"

Are you a murderer?

There was a snap and a flare of light as a match flickered to life. "I made a promise." He bent and lit a candle on the bookshelf outside the kitchen, then moved to light three more. "And I am a man of my word."

"Do those words include 'breaking' and 'entering'?"

Why does Rossi think you're so dangerous?

His smile in the soft yellow light carved deep hollows of shadows beneath his jaw and under his cheekbones.

"I know those words," he admitted. "But only one of them might be on the agenda tonight."

I tucked my phone in my front pocket. "What are you playing at here, Ry?"

He looked up at me, eyes deep as still waters in this light, soft and needful. "Who says I'm playing?"

I swallowed hard. "Then what are you doing?"

"I'm lighting candles." He touched another match to more candles set on the little side tables near the couch. "What are you doing, Delaney?"

I realized I had taken a couple steps inside the door and had rooted in place. "I'm...uh...standing."

Trying to decide if I can trust you.

He inhaled, holding back a laugh.

"Shut up," I said. "I've had a long day and never want to see another rhubarb in my life." I got moving toward the bedroom, pausing in the doorway there. "I'm taking a bath. I don't know what you're here for, Ryder, but if it's dessert, don't bother. I'm not good for anything except sleeping. So you and your matches should go."

He shook out the match pinched between his fingers and walked toward me. "All right." He stopped right in front of me. We stood there, facing each other. My breathing was a little fast, and I couldn't seem to look away from the candlelight caressing his skin. Couldn't stop myself from wondering what he would

205

look like naked in it. What he would feel like naked. In my bed right over there.

The vampire doesn't like you. Doesn't trust you. Why?

"Can I kiss you good night, Delaney?" I liked the sound of my name on his tongue. Liked it a lot. Maybe the vampire didn't know what he was talking about.

I hadn't slept in over twenty-four hours. And that, along with the day, the song of power that still felt like a knuckle pressing out from behind my eyes, and the mix of alcohols I'd downed in a short span of time all made me feel like maybe it would be fine to sink here to the floor and get a little shuteye.

But then, there was a perfectly soft, comfortable bed just a few steps away. It might be worth the effort to walk over there. Just.

Except there was a man in front of me. Waiting for an answer.

Yes. Kiss me. Make me forget about the power, the vampire, the murder, and this town.

"Ryder." I didn't know what I was going to follow that up with. I lifted my hands, as if somehow he would understand the words I couldn't even find.

His gaze flicked across my face and he bit his bottom lip briefly. "Mmm." His shoulders squared and he nodded as if he'd made a decision. "Bed, I think." He took my wrist in one hand and guided me off toward the bed.

"I don't—"

"I know," he said. "You're exhausted. We'll take a rain check on dessert." He walked me to the head of my bed and tugged at my hand so I'd sit.

I yawned and pushed at the toe of my boot with my other foot, trying to pop them off without unlacing. "Yeah," I said. "Probably best. I couldn't eat another bite. And I think I got a contact high from sitting next to Old Rossi for two hours."

"Rossi?"

Did he sound worried? Startled? Did he sound like someone dangerous who had something to hide?

"Hippy who inherited that big house on the hill and runs yoga classes or crystal detox seminars and all that other woo-woo kind of thing."

"I know him. Why were you sitting with him?" His voice was even, carefully casual.

Too casual?

"Well, my assistant got a phone call and dumped me. What was the call about?"

"Work." He shifted his weight a bit, and I watched his body language out of the corner of my eye as I continued to kick at my boot heel to no effect.

"Dammit," I whispered.

"Need some help?" He knelt and set the box of matches on the little wooden stepladder I used as a nightstand.

"I thought you were busy setting my house on fire."

"That was one of the things I wanted to set on fire."

A thrill of heat licked lazily across my skin. I stared down at his bent head, hair tousled from the wind, wide shoulders and back bent to the task of untying my boots.

His strong, steady fingers tugged at the laces on my boots. Why couldn't we have this? Why couldn't we have each other? Just because one vampire thought a person was dangerous didn't mean he was.

Or did it?

"What kind of work?" I asked. "Problems?"

"I'm in the construction business." His fingers loosened, pulled. "There's always problems. They always happen during off-hours, and they are always mine to deal with."

"Oh. Sorry. Angry client?"

He lifted one shoulder in a shrug. "I might have to go out of town for a while. I think it can wait until after the rally—so don't worry about that." He tipped off first my left boot by grabbing at the heel and tugging smoothly, and then did the same with the right boot.

"So Old Rossi's a friend of yours?" He set the boots together next to my feet.

Is he an enemy of yours?

"Friend of the family. Bertie picked him out for your replacement."

That got a small smile out of him. Light and shadow caught in the fine lines at the corners of his eyes. He was still looking down, his fingers slipping into the top of one of my socks and brushing it down my ankle, over my heel. His fingers drifted along the sensitive skin on the inside of my arc. It was almost soft enough to tickle.

"Bertie could take over the state in a week," he said.

I resisted the urge to run my fingers through his thick, dark hair. To grab hold and gently tip his face up to mine.

"She's the heart of Ordinary," I said. "Holds us together."

"Oh, I don't know." He tucked one wadded sock into my boot, then turned his attention to the other foot. "I can't imagine Ordinary being anything without Delaney Reed. I know I wouldn't be here."

I licked my bottom lip. Warmth from his touch was sending little soft electric flares up my skin, starting from my ankles and blooming up my legs.

Sleep was suddenly looking like a less appealing way to get rid of the day's stress.

"Where would you be instead?"

He finally tipped his head up, his eyes deep with shadow and glowing from candlelight. "Anywhere you were."

Now it wasn't just my breath that was caught. It was my heartbeat, and my entire body stilled at his words. His gaze.

How did you tell someone you had been in love with for almost all your life that you cared for them? How did you tell them you had fantasies about what life might be like with them?

How did you tell them you didn't want to screw this up, and that maybe being a day low on sleep and a lifetime high on rhubarb might be altering your decision-making skills?

And oh, yeah, how did you tell them an immortal vampire hippy thought they might be a dangerous threat?

"I'm going to be in bed," I heard myself say.

He blinked slowly, and the small smile on his lips told me he approved.

"Good," he said.

"Good," I replied. I stood.

He stood. We were so close, I could almost feel his heartbeat fluttering under his T-shirt and flannel.

This is where I say no. This is where I listen to the vampire and turn you away.

He leaned down, lips slightly parted, hand drifting to cup the side of my face with ridiculous tenderness, gaze searching mine.

This is where I listen to my heart.

I reached up and pulled his lips down to mine.

Heat kindled in that kiss, his mouth shifting gently to surround first my top, then my bottom lip, soft, slow, as if he had waited too long to taste me and wanted to make this last. He tasted of coffee and, slightly, oranges, and some other deep note that was wholly him. His tongue pressed gently at the seam of my mouth and I opened gratefully to him, and lost myself to the reality of my fantasy, of kissing him as I'd longed to for almost my entire life.

Eventually, he pulled back, rubbing one thumb over my swollen bottom lip.

"Delaney," he breathed. He lowered his mouth and kissed me again, longer, and so slowly it ached. I made a needful sound and rubbed my hands up his wide back. I tugged on his soft, short hair, then rubbed my hands back down to his lean hips.

I wanted this to last forever, this slow exploration, but I trembled with the need for more.

He was wearing too many layers. My fingers tugged at his T-shirt, slipped up beneath the soft cotton, and finally stroked the heat of his smooth skin along the edge of his low-slung jeans.

Ryder Bailey, I've been waiting for this. Waiting for you. I don't care what the vampire says.

I pulled away from the kiss so I could unbutton my shirt. Ryder's hands fell over mine, stilling my clumsy fingers over the line of buttons. He leaned forward and pressed a soft kiss on the tender skin beneath my ear.

"I have too many clothes on," I whispered.

"What should we do about that?" he growled against my ear, his breath soft and hot.

I shifted, twisted out of his hold, then scooted back on the bed.

"We should get naked."

He smiled and shucked out of his flannel shirt and T-shirt in one smooth over-the-head move. I tried to peel my gaze away from his bare chest.

Okay, no, I didn't.

I'd seen him naked. Recently, as a matter of fact. But here, in the butter-soft light of the candles, the hard muscles of his wide shoulders, thick chest with a dusting of dark hair, and flat stomach were even more defined.

He dropped his shirts to the floor. And crawled across the bed after me, then over the top of me, one hand braced on both sides of my shoulders.

We were so close, I could see the pulse of his heartbeat at his throat, but we weren't touching.

He was watching me, waiting.

I reached up, stroking his left shoulder where the tattoo of Leonardo da Vinci's hand capped it. I traced the bold lines of the words there and bit at my bottom lip. The art was stark in sepia brown against his tanned skin. Simple and beautiful on its own—on him, incredibly sexy.

I pressed my other hand—only my fingertips—on his other shoulder, and then dragged my fingers down the warmth of his hard chest, seeking the tight muscles of his stomach. His breathing hitched, and he held it as I explored. When he took his next breath, it shook a little.

I loved that I could make him feel that way. Loved that just a simple touch from me could make him tremble.

"Delaney," he said. I didn't know if it was question or request. I was focused on his other tattoo, the artist's compass and stars that spilled over the edge of his hipbone.

I wanted to put my mouth on it. I shivered a little, but not from the cool of the house. I felt like I was fevered, burning.

I watched Ryder's eyes as I slid my fingers into the waistband of his jeans.

He exhaled, almost a moan, and his eyes fluttered closed as his throat worked to swallow.

I unbuttoned his jeans and then pulled the zipper.

His eyes snapped back open as my fingers brushed softly over his boxers.

"Are you ready for this?" I asked him with a low burr in my voice.

He was firm and hard beneath my hand. I knew what his body wanted, but that wasn't what I was asking him.

"Are you?"

The moment stretched. Neither of us moved. The only motion in the room was the shifting of candlelight swaying in the shadows. I thought I saw something change in his gaze. Something that looked like worry or guilt. His mouth half opened, as if he were trying to decide if he should tell me something.

Then he smiled and that fleeting look was gone. His smile was soft, and honest, and said more than words ever could.

Don't make me regret this, Ryder Bailey. Please don't break my heart.

I draped my arms over his shoulders, holding the back of his neck with one hand, the other hand dragging up into his hair.

He closed the very short distance between us, his hands skating under my shirt and across my ribs and then around to my back and hip as he pulled me against him.

Then he eased me down and kissed me again, lips catching, teeth nibbling at the corner of my mouth, tongue dragging and licking. I bit his bottom lip gently but firmly to get his attention, and he grunted. "Yes?" he said against my mouth.

"Strip."

I felt his smile against my lips. He rose up on his knees above me.

"Is this a strip search, officer?" Mischief sparkled in his eyes. "Are you going to read me my rights?"

I laughed and covered my mouth with my hand, watching him with wide eyes. "Oh my God. You role-play?"

"Maybe."

"Maybe?"

He shrugged, a fluid roll of his shoulders, then shifted to the side so he could pull off his jeans and boxers, which he dropped down to the floor. "Maybe when there's a sexy lady cop in my bed."

I made quick work of my own clothes while he was occupied. I pushed under the covers, a chill washing over my skin, and held the blanket open for him.

"My bed."

He shouldered in under the covers, settling on his side, head propped on one hand, the other dragging over the curve of my breast, his thumb lingering sweetly over my nipple, then drifting down across my belly.

"Whichever bed," he murmured. "Only one sexy cop."

"Me?" I asked with all the feigned innocence I could muster with him looking at me like that, touching me like that.

He stilled. "Only you." The worry flickered in his eyes again, or maybe it was just the fluttering light of candles playing tricks.

His smile turned rakish. "Mother, may I?" His hand slipped down and down, curved at my hip, fingers gripping and releasing.

I groaned. "Maybe you should go back to the sexy cop game."

"Mmm. I don't know..." His fingers shifted to drift over my skin so softly, it was almost impossible to feel. "I might have some other games in mind."

"Do not pass go," I said as my hands slipped down his back and I drew one knee up to hook my ankle around the back of his leg, pulling him closer. "Do not collect two hundred dollars." I dragged my fingernails up his back and he inhaled noisily, arching his back up into my hands.

"Don't need two hundred dollars." He pressed his warm lips at the side of my throat, and a zing of pleasure rolled through my muscles, turning me into liquid heat. "How about a get out of jail free card?"

My stomach fluttered with desire and a tiny jolt of fear. What if I was making a terrible mistake?

I didn't care.

"Right now, let's just have us. No games." I combed my fingers through his hair, and lifted my other ankle to wrap around his leg, allowing him to settle more intimately against me, molding our bodies to each other.

He paused, his gaze searching mine with something I could not begin to understand.

"No games," he said softly.

He kissed me, and this time, this one moment, I knew there was nothing but truth between us.

CHAPTER 22

I WOKE slowly, the dreams of Ryder mingling with the memories of the last few hours.

Dreams couldn't hold a candle to the reality of him.

I smiled and shifted my hands, drawing my pillow under my head in a more comfortable position. Sex with Ryder had been fun. But after the joking and teasing, it had become something more. He'd held me with his gaze, his hands, his body, like he was trying to memorize me.

Like it would be his only, his last time to touch me.

By the time we were too tired to do more than hold each other, hands stroking gently, absently, the sleep I'd been putting off for over two days caught at me and tugged me down.

I just hoped I hadn't snored and drooled on him all night.

I opened my eyes. I was facing the west window, and from the soft blue-toned light seeping in through the curtains, it was just barely dawn.

It was silent in the room, dark.

And I knew without a doubt that I was alone.

I inhaled and let out my breath, calming the clatter of my thoughts all trying to crowd in past the roar of the unhoused power rolling through my head.

The swell of the power's song made me realize it had been quieter last night. Whether that was because of Ryder, my fatigue, or the various concoctions of rhubarb I'd imbibed, I wasn't sure.

I rolled over and pulled the covers tighter around my shoulders.

The other half of the bed was empty, the candles on the step ladder nightstand no longer burning.

A small piece of paper was folded into the shape of a little origami house, the door open to show writing on the inside, my name written above the lintel. I lifted the house and a tiny folded paper dog that somehow looked a lot like Spud sat in its place. So cute.

"I had no idea you were so clever with paper." There didn't appear to be any writing on Spud, so I unfolded the house. Inside, written in Ryder's square, clean style was a note.

"A dear John?" I sighed and rubbed my hand across my eyes. "Terrific." I sat, holding the covers against me in the cool of the room, and read.

DELANEY, I'M SORRY I COULDN'T STAY. WORK CAME UP. IF LAST NIGHT WERE RHUBARB, I'D GIVE YOU AN ELEVEN OUT OF TEN.
—RYDER

I didn't know if I should laugh or be offended. Had he really just left me a note comparing me to rhubarb?

I rubbed at my eyes again, a mix of emotions rolling out as laughter.

"You jerk," I groaned between snickers I couldn't stop. "This is no way to romance a woman."

The empty room had nothing to say about that, and I left the little unfolded house on the ladder and picked up Spud.

I took in a deep breath and let it out. Maybe it was better he wasn't here when I woke up. Maybe that would have been too intimate, too much of a promise neither of us were ready to keep.

Still, I would have like to have opened my eyes and felt him there next to me. Would have liked the chance to settle against him, wrapped in the scent that was spicy and rich and wholly his, mingled with the lavender of my sheets and the heavy vanilla perfume of the candles.

"Guess we don't always get what we want, eh, Spud?" I left Spud on the empty pillow and wandered off to the bathroom.

The scent of vanilla lingered in the smaller room. It had been sweet of him to fill the house full of candles. It had been romantic.

I smiled as I looked in the mirror.

"Well," I said to my happy reflection, my hair mussed, my eyes still soft and relaxed. "No matter where it goes from here, last night was worth it." I pulled out my toothbrush so I could get ready for the day.

I took a quick shower and had just finished pulling on my clothes and boots when my phone rang from the other room. I jogged out and picked up the phone, glancing at the screen.

"What's up, Jean?"

"Are you okay?" She sounded out of breath, her words sharpened with worry that wasn't quite panic yet.

"Yes? What's going on?"

"I woke up with a really bad feeling, Delaney."

"Woke up? You were supposed to be on night shift."

"I traded with Roy."

"Okay. When?"

"Last night. When else would I trade?"

"When did you get the bad feeling?"

"Just a few minutes ago. It hit me hard. It's about you."

"Are you sure?"

"It's about you," she said. "I'm headed your way."

I glanced out the window. Nothing but gray sky and wet trees and the low, quiet fog of morning. "Everything looks good here. Don't come to the house. I'll meet you at the station."

She hesitated, trying to make up her mind. "I don't know. I think you should hunker down. I'll come by."

"Jean."

"And lock your door."

"No need to be paranoid."

"I can be paranoid if I want to be. Lock your door."

"Sure," I said. I was so not going to lock my door.

"See you in ten."

I ended the call and stared at the phone for a minute. I knew Jean too well, trusted her small gift far too much to ignore her.

Something bad was possibly going to happen to me. Strangely, I wasn't all that worried about it. What was the advantage to being warned about possible trouble cropping up if that warning only made a person panic?

I calmly took off my flannel and strapped on my holster, then checked my gun and put it in the holster. I slipped back into my overshirt and walked to the door.

The doorbell rang with a two-tone lilt.

Trouble. Right on time. I drew my gun and approached the door from the side, then glanced out the small square window beside the door.

Death stood on my doorstep. He wore a bright red overshirt patterned with monkeys, bananas, and fancy little drink umbrellas. Under that was a T-shirt I couldn't quite read.

He was not the trouble I had expected.

"Killers don't usually ring the doorbell," I said through the glass.

"Indeed," he agreed.

"So I think you can just move along. I'm not planning on dying today."

"Very few plan to die any day."

"Seriously, Than, I know why you're here."

"Do you?" His flat black eyes glittered with something that might have been humor. Or anger.

"You're going to harm me."

His eyebrows lifted up into his cropped hair. "Am I?"

"Yes. Jean knew something bad was going to happen, and here you are."

He tutted and looked like he was having a hard time keeping a smile off his face. "Your sister may be correct in her gift, but she is incorrect in assuming I would cause you harm."

"You're not here to kill me?"

He pursed his lips as if considering his answer. "Dear Delaney. I am on vacation. Therefore, I am here to kill no one. If I intended to kill you, or do you *harm*"—he made the last word sound like a filthy insult—"I would first tell you so."

"Thanks?"

He nodded, as if promising to let someone know you were going to kill them was the height of propriety. "Would you open the door so that we could speak in a more civilized manner?"

I holstered my gun and put my hand on the doorknob. The door hadn't been locked during any of this exchange. He could have opened it any time he wanted to.

I opened the door. "What?"

"Good morning, Reed Daughter."

I leaned in the doorway. "Good morning, Than. What's up?"

"Although I have secured my business license, I have been informed that you will be among the persons of authority who must approve of my trade."

It wasn't usual for the chief of police to have a say in such things, but I'd found it was easier to head off the more disastrous career choices of new gods in town if I was in the loop from the beginning.

"Yes. I'll have a say in okaying your business. What kind of business do you intend to go into?"

"Aerials."

"Excuse me?"

"String and paper and wind."

I waited for him to continue. He didn't, instead just stood there looking at me expectantly.

"What are you going to do with string and paper and wind?"

He looked surprised that I hadn't guessed yet. "Kites, Reed Daughter. I will sail kites."

"Have you ever flown a kite?"

"No."

"You understand you'll have to make money from this. From selling kites. Pretty, bright, whimsical things for children and the young at heart."

"Yes."

"Do you really think a job in sales is playing to your strengths?"

"I thought the purpose of vacation was to relax. To be, for a time, not strong."

I couldn't help but smile at that a little. It was how the gods looked at it. Being a god meant a lot of responsibilities, a power constantly coursing through everything they did, everything they touched.

It could mean years and years of seeing that the one thing they had the power over was completely and thoroughly enacted.

For Death, I could see how getting a break from having to harvest souls might be seen as no longer being strong.

217

"Maybe," I said. "Okay. Yes. I approve of you running a kite shop. Have you chosen the location?" I grabbed my coat off the chair where it had landed last night, then stepped outside, shrugging into it.

He moved primly to one side so that I could walk past him onto the porch. It didn't matter that he was in a casual tropical shirt. He still moved like he was in a top hat and tails.

"I had expected to revive the current shop."

"The Tailwind?" It was a broken-down A-frame shack on the southern end of town that had once been a thriving kite business before the casinos, internet, and whale-watching trips became the normal for Ordinary. "Have you spoken to Bill Downing?"

"The owner from California? Yes."

"He agreed to sell it to you?"

"He agreed I could have the building and the name if I drew up a fair contract and paid him a portion of my profits for the next five years."

"Think you can follow through on that?"

"I assure you I am more than capable of sealing a contract for a dilapidated shack."

I had to grin a little. He sounded put out that I had doubted Death could close a deal. I started down the stairs and he followed behind me, his footsteps silent on the steep concrete steps.

"Good." A car was coming, tires grinding gravel at the lower end of the dead end road. Jean was here quicker than I'd expected. "I'd like to see more kites out in the sky."

I had reached the bottom of the staircase and turned to face him. That put the opening of the dead-end driveway and the sound of approaching tires at my back.

But it was the motion at the head of the driveway, a man stepping out from the bushes, that caught my eye.

"You were wrong," Dan Perkin said. He was in a dark gray coat, a silhouette in the deep of the early morning fog and darkness.

"Dan? What are you doing here?"

He raised his gun. "My root beer is a winner! I'm a winner!"

I raised my hands, palm forward. "It's okay, Dan. I agree. You're a winner."

"You should have given me ten out of ten!" His voice was high and ragged.

Sweat broke out on my lip, the cold of fog whisking it away. Dan was trembling with rage.

"We can fix this, Dan," I said. "I can fix this and you can win."

"Yeah, Delaney?" he scoffed. "Well, I can fix it too!"

The pain and force of the bullet ripping into my chest knocked me off my feet. I heard the gunshot a second after I fell, which seemed wrong to me. I landed on my ass in the sharp gravel, catching myself with one hand and trying to draw my gun with the other. I hoped to hell the car coming up the road wasn't Jean, and if it was, that she wouldn't put herself in the line of fire.

I was having a hard time getting a breath. My lungs burned as if someone had stuck a torch into them. Everything around me had gone freezing cold, my movements slow and stiff, the darkness shifting to an almost purple haze that was fuzzing up my eyesight.

I had to get on my feet. I had to get to my gun. I had to stop Dan before he shot anyone else—or before he shot me again. But I couldn't seem to get a grip on the world that was slipping, slipping. Someone had taken all the air along with the light.

Distantly, I heard Dan's yell of fury and anguish. "No! No! There are no bullets. There are no bullets!"

Then the screech of brakes and slide of blue and red lights bruised up the darkness.

I thought I heard Myra's voice, blinked hard to warn her, to tell her that Dan had a gun. But the only thing I could see was Death's face, hovering above me so close that I could see the shattering of silver lightning in his endless black eyes, the collar of his tacky Hawaiian shirt burning like a fire in the night.

"Reed Daughter," he said softly, an intimate voice that swept my fears away, even though I still couldn't breathe and I was thinking that was something I might want to be afraid of. "You cannot try to die. I am on vacation, after all."

That ridiculous statement and the amount of sincerity he delivered it with made me want to laugh, but I didn't have any air for that either.

Death put his cold hand on my chest, applying firm pressure to my wound as he shook his head disapprovingly. Then the world funneled down to a single speck of light that winked out.

CHAPTER 23

THE OCEAN was too loud. Waves rising and falling in a steady drone that filled my head.

I wished someone would just turn the darn thing off.

Rise, fall. Roar, roar, roar.

I didn't know how long it took, but I finally realized the ocean sound was my own breathing thrumming in my ears. I was lying down somewhere warm, maybe under a blanket? I couldn't feel most of my body, which seemed like a really good thing.

I wanted to slip back into sleep, or coma, or whatever soft oblivion I'd just accidentally slipped out of, but my breathing was way too loud.

"Time to wake up, Delaney," Myra said from next to me. "We're here. Come back to us."

Fingers brushed my cheek gently, then stroked back over my hair. Myra, I thought. Maybe Jean too—petting the top of my head like I was a nervous cat she was trying to comfort.

"Hey, Delaney." Jean sounded like she was trying to talk a cat out from under the car or refrigerator. "Wake up, sister."

I pushed at my eyelids. It took a lot of effort to crack them open. I thought I might be heavily medicated. Finally got my eyes to track.

A bright pink glob bounced somewhere near a white ceiling. Maybe a creature or ghost come to get a look at me?

I blinked a couple of times and the cheerful pink glob came into focus. It was a big bright balloon, swaying gently on a string. I rolled my eyes down, following the string that blurred in and out of focus. Myra and Jean were saying something. Maybe to me. I couldn't seem to follow their words. My head echoed.

The string ended with a pale, bony hand.

Death.

He wasn't smiling, but he didn't look angry, either. He had on a T-shirt that said: WE MIGHT BE ORDINARY, BUT AT LEAST WE'RE NOT BORING.

I snuffled a laugh. It was one of the T-shirts we printed up for tourists, much to the dismay of the little town of Boring, Oregon just southeast of Portland.

"There now," he said, and I wondered why I could hear his voice so well when everything else sounded like I had a metal bucket on my head. "It is about time you woke. I do have other matters to attend."

I was going to tell him I was so sorry to interrupt his busy schedule with my gunshot wound, but by the time I blinked, he stood next to me.

Death lifted my pinkie, which seemed like a really weird thing to do, and then patted my hand as if he were some kind of concerned uncle instead of the last face before the grave.

"Get well soon," he said slowly with just a little hint of delight, as if he were reading off a cue card. I had a feeling he'd never said those words before.

I wanted to respond, but I was tired and closed my eyes. When I opened them again, he was gone and Myra was sitting in the chair next to me. I thought maybe a little time had passed.

"How about a drink of water?" she suggested.

"Sure." The word came out breathy, but it felt good to be able to think again.

I was in a hospital room, the bed bent so I was almost sitting, a thin but warm blanket tucked around me from my chest to my feet. Both my arms were free, and there was an IV in the left one.

I took a sip of water through the straw Myra tipped my way. The water was cool and somehow tasted rich and clean. "What happened?"

"You got shot," Jean said from the other side of the bed.

I glanced over at her. She looked worried, her green and blue hair making her eyes dark and glittery. "I told you to lock your damn door."

Okay. Not worried. Angry. "He wasn't at my door."

She sighed. "I know, Delaney. You didn't stay inside."

"I didn't think…" I tried to come up with something more to say. "I didn't think."

"Damn right you didn't." She sat forward and caught my hand, turning it without messing up the IV line. "You were shot. When we drove up and saw you there on the ground…" Her eyes welled up and she shook her head, unable to speak. "Jesus, Delaney. Jesus."

"Here I thought the rhubarb would kill me."

"Not funny," she said, but at least she wasn't crying.

"What happened to Dan?"

"We arrested him," Myra said. "He's claiming he didn't know the gun was loaded. Says he's innocent."

"Horse shit," Jean said.

Everything in Myra's expression agreed with that statement. "His lawyer wants the trial moved out of Ordinary. Says he'd never get a fair trial here."

She was probably right. Dan had made a nuisance of himself to so many people that I didn't think we'd be able to scrape together an unbiased jury.

"Where are they thinking of transferring him?"

"Polk County."

That was east, in the valley. Far enough away from Ordinary no one could have heard of Dan, and a small enough town that he might be able to bargain down the charges.

"You put him up on assault with a deadly weapon?"

Myra's cool blue eyes held mine. "I put him up on everything I could think of."

I inhaled then stopped because it pulled somewhere deep in me, and I thought it might hurt a lot more if I weren't on meds.

"How long until I bribe my way out of here?"

"Uh, that would be never," Jean said.

"So a few hours?"

"You can't bribe your way out of here," Myra said.

"Why not? I did when I had to have my tonsils out. Everyone has a stack of parking tickets in their closet."

"No," Myra said. "I already told Alister I'd take care of his tickets and his library overdue fines if he promised me he wouldn't let you bribe your way out."

"Traitor," I grumbled.

She patted my upper arm, her clear eyes seeking out mine. "You were shot, Delaney. Shot. Through and through. Broke ribs. You were shot."

A weird chill ran down my spine at hearing those words. I was still pretty firmly in denial of the reality of the whole thing.

Dan Perkin had shot me.

Over rhubarb.

I giggled. Who got shot over a vegetable?

"Oh, great," Myra said. "Now you're going crazy."

I tried not to laugh, but laughter pushed up my chest and into my throat as if it were filled with helium. I snorted. It had to be the drugs. Getting shot wasn't funny, was it?

"No." I raised my hands to reason with her. A pink blob bobbed with that movement, making a little *tink-tink* sound. I looked up to see the balloon swaying gently on the string tied to my pinkie.

Death had brought me a pink balloon. I couldn't stop myself. I snickered then giggled again.

"Really?" Jean sounded exasperated.

"I'm fine," I insisted, trying to keep the laughter in. "It's the drugs. Just the drugs."

When I tried to think through what Dan had done, the whole thing just seemed so out of character. I mean, Dan was a blowhard and a pain in the butt, but he had never before shot anyone. Especially not a police officer in broad daylight in front of a witness. Even he wasn't that bold and stupid.

"Are we sure it was Dan?" I asked.

Jean swore softly and Myra patted my arm again. "He was standing there, the gun in his hand, and you hadn't even been on the ground long enough for the pool of blood to spread."

"Thanatos?" I asked.

"He was there too."

"No. I mean what did he see?"

"What did *you* see, Delaney?"

I didn't want to think about that. I'd never been shot before and I was finding the more I thought about it, the more the reality of it sank in, the less smoothly I was handling it. As it was,

I was already feeling like maybe whimpering like a baby might be about my speed.

"I, uh…saw Dan. He was angry."

"What did he say?" Myra used her cop voice. The one that calmly guided and soothed witnesses through remembering details of an event.

"He said his root beer should have won. That he should have won. I told him I'd fix it. That I could fix it for him."

"Did he say anything else?"

"Yeah. He said he could fix it too. Then he shot me."

Myra waited, and even Jean was silent.

"Do you remember anything else?" Myra asked, even more gently. It suddenly reminded me of Mom, whom I'd only known until I was twelve. Myra had that same soft comfort in her voice that Mom used when I had a fever or chicken pox.

I shook my head. "Thanatos was disappointed that I'd been shot. Other than that…" I searched my memories. "Wait. I thought I heard another gunshot. Did one of you shoot at Dan?"

"No," Myra said. "When we got there, Thanatos was standing behind Dan, his hand on his shoulder, keeping Dan from bolting. I thought you put Death's power away, Delaney."

I rolled my eyes. Okay, now she sounded like Dad. Doubting that I had carried out his orders and the job correctly, even though he had taught me, pretty much all my life, how to deal with all this.

Not that I was dealing with it well. He hadn't really covered the gunshot wounds over rhubarb ribbons in the job description.

"I did put it away. He doesn't have his power—except, you know, the little bit that lingers. All the gods have that."

"They do?" Myra asked.

I smiled. "Yes. It's what makes them so damn pretty."

Jean snorted. "What do they have you on? I might need to get some for when I want you to sign off on my vacation weeks."

"Week. Vacation week. I'm not that stoned."

"Was there anything else you noticed?" Myra said, back in cop mode. "Any sounds, any smells? Anyone else who could have been there?"

I bit down on a smart-mouth answer and instead took a few moments to breathe deeply and clear my mind.

I was a cop. Even drugged, I should be able to piece together what I'd seen firsthand less than twenty-four hours ago.

At least I thought it was still the same day.

"What day is it?" I asked with a jolt of panic that was quickly soothed away by all the happy chemicals floating through my veins.

"Friday evening," Myra said.

"Evening?"

Jean sighed. "Getting shot means surgery, Delaney. Surgery means recovery time. Recovery time means sleep. And sleep means it's Friday evening."

"How evening?" I had lost an entire day.

"Four thirty," Myra said. "You're awake in time for dinner. Think you can eat something?"

"Sandwich and coffee?"

She finally cracked a smile, though it looked like it was fueled by relief. "I'll see what I can do."

She stood and started toward the door. That was when I noticed she wasn't wearing her uniform. As a matter of fact, I was pretty sure those were jammie pants.

"Duckies?" I asked.

She turned. Gave me a tolerant look. "It has been a long day. Too long. And I like duckies. You have something to say about that?"

"I like duckies too. We should make it a part of the official uniform. Very intimidating."

She shook her head, but at least this time her smile was more than just relief. "I'm going to tell them to dial down your meds."

I scowled, but couldn't hold it for long. "Don't be a spoilsport. My boyfriend walked out on me and I got shot. I deserve a night up in the clouds."

"Walked out on you?" Jean perked up and slid her phone back into her pocket. "Is this Ryder we're talking about?"

"You mean that he left you at the judging?" Myra asked.

It took me an extended moment to try to think of what to say, which only made me sound guilty as hell.

"Oh-ho." Jean leaned her elbows on the bed's side bar thingy. "She does *not* mean the judging. Talk, drunkie. Tell all."

"There's nothing to tell."

"I'll be back," Myra said. "Don't hassle her, Jean."

Myra walked out. As soon as the door closed, Jean tapped my arm with a fingertip and wiggled her eyebrows. "Out with it. What happened with Ryder?"

"Nothing." I held her gaze. Must have done a pretty good job at it too, because she leaned back.

"Do I need to hunt him down and break a few fingers?"

"Wow. Way to go Mafia on me. What games have you and Hogan been playing?"

"The good ones." She narrowed her eyes. "Seriously, Del. What did he do?"

"It's…fine. He was— We were… It's all fine. I don't know why I even brought it up. Drugs."

And paranoid hippy vampires.

I lifted my arm again to show her the tubes, and the pink balloon made that *plinking* sound.

"He tied a balloon to my pinkie." I grinned up at it for a while.

Jean patted my arm. "He didn't hurt you?"

"Death?"

"Ryder."

"Oh." I frowned, thought about that, sort of prodding my heart to see if most of the pieces were still together. "He didn't hurt me. We're good. This is all just new. It's going to go how it goes."

"Yeah, totally new. You haven't been crazy in love with him for half your life."

"I think I've been in love with the idea of him."

"Oh, bull." She laughed. "You know him. You've seen him, been a part of his life. You are seriously in deep Xs and Os with the man. Not with the idea of who he is."

"Okay." I wasn't feeling up to an argument. "But being in love with him, or thinking I might be, doesn't mean I know how or what we're doing, you know?"

"It's called 'dating.' Part of the adventure is sort of figuring it out as you go."

Something else was on my mind. Rossi's warning. "Old Rossi—"

Her phone rang, and she pulled it out of her pocket and glanced at the screen. Whatever was there made her smile. She tapped the screen and quickly typed.

"Hogan?" I asked.

She glanced over at me. "No."

"Liar."

She grinned. "Maybe."

The phone rang again. She scanned the message and texted back. "Old Rossi? I heard he was baked at the judging."

Was he? I seemed to recall feeling like I'd gotten a contact high off him. Maybe all his warnings and doom were fueled by drugs. Jean was still texting, still smiling.

"Why don't to take some time off from hovering over me?"

"You sure?" she asked.

"Yeah. Myra's going to be back with my sandwich soon, and then I'll probably fall asleep."

She studied my face for a minute, then bent and kissed me on my forehead. "I'm so glad you're okay." Her face was still against my forehead.

"Me too," I whispered.

"Don't ever do that again."

"Promise."

She petted my head as she tipped her eyes down to give me a strong look. "I'm going to hold you to that."

"No problem. I'm good for it."

"Okay." She planted a quick kiss on the tip of my nose. "I'm going to step out for a minute. Get some coffee. I'll be right back."

"Say hi to Hogan for me."

"I will."

She left the room, and I closed my eyes in the silence that filled it. I really was a little hungry. But there was no way I was going to stay in this room overnight. I had a festival to take care of, a killer on the loose. And I wanted to have a little chat with Dan Perkin.

I was hovering on the edge of sleep when I heard the door click open. I jerked, my hand sliding to my hip where my gun should be and hitting the bar of the bed. I stared at the door, waiting for another gun pointed at me.

"Just me." Myra had a tray in her hands. "And food."

My heart pounded hard and fast, but I tried to wave at her. "Hey." The pink balloon bobbed and swayed. "Just caught me almost asleep."

She raised her eyebrows until they brushed her dark, straight bangs. "Sorry about that. How about a peanut butter and jelly sandwich?"

I smiled. "That's what they're calling dinner in this joint? No wonder nobody stays."

"That's what I asked them to make for you. Because it's what you always ask for when you're feeling bad."

"With strawberry jam?"

"With strawberry jam." She set the tray down on the rolling cart near the bed then set that up so the sandwich was easy for me to reach.

"Chocolate milk out of the carton?" I was still smiling. "I'm not six, you know."

"Look." She held up a straw. "It bends! Ooooh. Bendy." She bent it, then plunked it into the little square carton of chocolate milk.

I chuckled. "Thanks."

She pushed the tray around until it was over my lap. I took a bite of the soft white bread. Peanut butter and jam with chocolate milk was a pretty nice turn of events, considering.

"You're staying overnight, right?" Myra asked.

"Absolutely," I lied while I chewed.

She stood, watching me. "You know you still have enough time to find the right person."

"Which right person?"

"The one you need to give the power to in three days. Heim's power."

I picked up the chocolate milk and chased the straw for a moment before I got it in my mouth. Extra cold, just how Dad used to make it. It made me think of him, made me wish he were here. "That's not a lot of time, Myra."

"It's enough. And it means you can spend one night here in bed, resting from a bullet that clipped you across the ribs and the surgery to patch you up, right?"

"I already said yes."

"You were lying."

"Well, yes, but I understand how concerned you are now." I shrugged, and muscles pulled hot and stiff down my wrapped ribs. Ouch. Sudden movements were going to be a little out of my league.

"How bad is it?" I asked. I'd been ignoring that question, and my sisters had both waited until I was ready to know the answer.

"You're very lucky. It went all the way through, but broke a rib."

"Do I get to mummy up in one of those stretchy wraps?"

"They don't do that anymore."

"So I get shot and other than a broken rib and a bandage, I'm good to go?"

"I said you were lucky."

"Well, there's that at least." I shifted again and winced. I wanted the stretchy bandage, darn it. Even though the medication was keeping the pain at bay, it felt like my bones were rubbing together.

"Need more meds?"

"I think I need sleep." I gently pushed the tray away, and she reached over to drag it all the way to the side. "You don't have to stay here while I sleep, Myra. I have the cool little button thing." I lifted the call buttons in my right hand.

"I'll be here."

"Go home. Get out of your duckie pants—have you been in them all day?—and check in on all the things you need to. I'm here." I looked her straight in the eyes. "And I'll be here when you get back. Promise."

Her pale blue eyes misted just a bit. "You scared the crap out of me," she whispered hoarsely. "I wasn't there. I wasn't there in time. Me. Late." Then my cool, steady sister lunged forward and draped her arms over me, laying her head on my chest.

"Hey now." I patted her gently with my right hand. "It's going to be all right. I'm all right. We're still all together. We're still all here."

She held me for a long moment, and I settled into stroking her hair. She'd grown serious beyond her years when we'd lost Mom. I'd hoped that pain would pass for her and let a little light into her life, a little humor into her heart, but she kept her emotions closely guarded, even all these years later.

"I love you, My-my," I said softly.

She finally sniffed, then breathed in, pulling herself together. "I love you too," she said, straightening. "Get some sleep. And don't sneak out on me."

"Promise, and promise."

She watched me for a moment then bent to give me a kiss on my cheek. I stroked the back of her thick, smooth hair.

"See you in the morning," I said.

She nodded, wiped at one eye then straightened, and walked out of the room.

CHAPTER 24

I JERKED awake in the middle of the night. Someone was in the room with me. I thought it might be the night nurse, and tried to scrub an itch by my eye, but was too drowsy to lift my hand. They must have upped the dose on my medicines because even my tongue felt numb. I finally opened my eyes, rolled my head to one side.

A figure sat slumped in the chair by my bed, head bent into one hand with elbow propped on knee, other hand extended and resting on the back of my hand. I knew that silhouette.

"Ryder?" I whispered.

He stiffened slightly, raised his head. The only light in the room slipped pale and watery from under the door, just enough to see his face.

Had he been crying?

"Delaney." Spoken so softly, though there were only the two of us in the room. "I'm sorry."

"For what?" My heart picked up a beat.

Was there something else that had happened? Was someone else hurt?

"I shouldn't have left you. I should have stayed. This is my fault. Us. This. All this."

He wasn't making any sense. He looked angry.

"I got shot. That doesn't have anything to do with you. Part of the job. My job."

He shook his head once, his eyes going hard, lips pressed in a frown. He was pulling away, even though he hadn't shifted an inch. He was leaving me. Ending us. Even as he sat right there, his hand on mine.

"I'm sorry." His voice was low, soft, and so very, very cold. "Last night was a mistake."

"No," I breathed.

He went on as if I hadn't spoken, his words even, almost recited. "I left this morning because I realized you got the wrong idea. That it might be something more than one night. I was just up for a good time. Curious, after all this time of knowing you, what it would be like."

He shrugged, patted my hand, and pulled back. "But you wanted something more, right?" He lifted one eyebrow and gave me a smirk I wanted to smack off his face. "I'll still help out with the rally. If you want me to work a different shift, there's no hard feelings."

He sat there. As if it were nothing. As if last night were nothing. As if I were nothing.

Jerk.

"You are not breaking up with me in a hospital, Ryder Bailey."

"I am."

Silence stretched out around that statement, a hungry blackness growing between us.

"We can still be friends," he said.

"Can we?" My heart was screaming, my stomach sick. The power song roared and raged in my head and my body hurt. But for Ryder Bailey, I smiled. "I think that's over now too," I said calmly. "No hard feelings."

He glanced away from my gaze, swallowed once, then met my eyes again. There was nothing to read in his expression. Nothing in his body language that matched the pain in me.

Bastard.

"All right, then." He stood. "I'll be going. Maybe I should check in with Myra about my hours?"

"Maybe you should leave. Now." I hated that my voice shook.

He didn't move. For a moment, his mouth tugged down at the corners. His hands, loose at his side, clenched into fists, and then let go. "Goodbye, Delaney. Get well soon."

I turned my head and closed my eyes. The sound of his footsteps grew quieter and quieter. I heard the door open, letting in the softer sounds from the hall, and then he was gone.

The room was silent, but nothing inside me was. I felt the hot slip of tears down the curve of my cheek and gritted my teeth against a sob.

I would not let that man make me cry. I would not let him break my heart. I wiped angrily at my face and breathed until I was under control. I was done with this place. With this pain. But even though I was angry, every muscle in my body was heavy, tired, and begging me to surrender to the medications flowing through my veins.

I closed my eyes, slipping, losing my grip on wakefulness. The medicine dragged at me, tucking me breath by breath down into sleep.

I didn't know how much time passed, but when the nurse gently touched my arm, I woke.

"How are you feeling, chief?" she asked.

"Uh, good. Better. I'm ready to leave."

My heart lurched with the memory of Ryder, but I shoved it aside. I had more important things to deal with.

Dan Perkin had shot me in broad daylight. He'd shouted something when he'd done it. Even through the haze of pain, he'd sounded panicked more than victorious. Almost like he hadn't expected the bullet to actually hit.

He might have finally come to his senses after pulling the trigger. That happened often enough with crimes of passion.

But Myra said Dan hadn't thought the gun was loaded. He was claiming complete innocence.

What if he really was innocent?

I took a deep breath, stuttered to a stop as my left side caught fire, waited out the pain, and carefully exhaled. Bad, but not bad enough to keep me in bed. I'd gotten enough sleep. What I needed now were answers.

"I want to be released," I told the nurse. "Can you bring me the forms?"

"Your doctor wants to check on you before you're released."

"I'm leaving." I pushed the covers away and slipped my legs over the edge of the bed. "Take out the IV, please. And get me the forms to sign." Then, in my best chief of police voice. "Now."

It took more than that to convince her, but I was determined. She finally gave in.

Someone, probably Jean, had brought in a pair of black sweatpants and another one of Dad's old Grateful Dead T-shirts. Good enough. I took some time getting into my clothes and zipped up the black hoodie with FIGHTING BARNACLES across the back of it.

I was out of breath, a little woozy. But I got my shoes on and rested for a couple minutes until my head and hands stopped shaking.

Walking wasn't great, but not impossible if I just took it a little slower than my normal pace. I kept my arm across my ribs to keep them from jostling too much.

The nurse shook her head at me as I passed the front counter. She handed me a bag of medicines with instructions on how many to take and when.

I thanked her, set my sights on the front door, and, with my pink balloon bobbing above me, headed into the night.

CHAPTER 25

HERRI'S BAR, Mom's, had three things going for it tonight: it stayed open late, served damn fine coffee, and was right around the corner from the hospital.

I walked in and took a table in the corner where I could keep an eye on the door, since I expected one or both of my sisters would track me down before long.

It was just past midnight on the Friday night of the festival. The place was loud with drinkers and the clash of music against televisions, which were tuned to a live rugby match going on in some other part of the world.

Herri worked the bar, her long hair striped with red catching fire as she moved and laughed and hassled the clients and employees alike beneath the spotlights hanging above her. She looked natural here. Comfortable.

She had six wait staff on tonight, an even mix of men and women who all wore red T-shirts with the Mom's logo across the chest.

I knew she'd seen me come in, but she hadn't made eye contact since I'd taken the table and ordered a ginger ale.

Walking out of the hospital had seemed like a good idea at the time. I wanted to leave my pain—body and heart—behind me. The cold night air only served to remind me that I was not exactly in top form. Still, I wanted to keep my mind off things.

Ryder.

The way I saw it, I had three important things to deal with: Heim's murder, Dan shooting me, and finding someone to take on the god power. First things first. I nursed the soda while scanning through files on my phone—notes about Heim's murder I had pulled together what felt like weeks ago, but was only days ago. I scrolled through the list of suspects.

It was still a small list: Dan Perkin, Chris, Margot Lapointe, and Lila Carson. Herri, Walt the deck hand.

Jean and I had already talked to everyone on that list except for Heim's missing deck hand, Walt. I didn't know if Myra had gotten any hits on his location and I wasn't going to go into the station to check up on that now.

I read through Myra's report. She had searched the boat, talked to the harbor master. There was nothing there to indicate if anyone unusual had been aboard. No murder weapon, not even a drop of blood to mark the crime.

Coroner was convinced someone had hit Heim on the back of the head. Pushed him overboard. He could narrow the time of death down by a variety of factors, including the state of the corpse and the turn of the tides. Heim had been murdered Sunday evening and everyone we'd spoken with had an alibi.

Someone was lying.

"Where's your boyfriend, Delaney?"

I glanced up. Cooper looked like he'd had plenty to drink. He stood with his feet wide, a beer in one hand. He had on a tight white T-shirt that was thin and snug across his lean muscles and showed just how trim he was at the waist and hips, faded jeans, and boots. His brown eyes were storm-dark as he stared at my lips then snapped up to my eyes.

My stomach flipped and blood rushed hard across my chest and face, and the song, the noise, the clamoring of the power in my head rose like someone had just cranked the volume to one hundred.

Cooper looked like sex. Even shot and bruised and tired and on meds, I could remember what sex with him had been like.

Ryder didn't want me. Cooper did. But did I want Cooper?

No. I knew the answer to that a year ago. Cooper and I were done.

I shook my head at myself and tried to lean back in my chair in a way that didn't make half my body throb.

"You're drunk, Cooper."

"I'm in a bar, Del," he said a little too loudly, drawing the attention of the people nearest us. "Why the hell else would I be here?"

I stared at him, trying to decide how to defuse this situation. "You done yelling? Or do I have to sit through the whole show?"

"You think you're fooling me? Acting calm. Acting…" He waved his beer at me like it was a brush he could paint me with.

"All right. Get it out."

"Don't tell me what to do. You think you can just tell everyone what to do in this town? I know you, Delaney. Standing in your daddy's shoes and acting like you know something. You're just a scared little girl who wants someone to hold her hand, and when someone comes back to offer you that, you slap it away. You got a badge, you got a reputation, but you don't have anything under control."

"Done?" I asked, low, calm.

He scowled. Pretty much everyone in the place was watching. These sorts of shows were big news on the gossip circuit in a small town.

I didn't care. I'd known Cooper for a long time. I knew he struck out at other people when he was in pain, even if they had nothing to do with his pain. He was hurting and drunk and I was a handy target.

"You want to know why I came back to this piss hole, Delaney?" he shouted. "I came back for you!"

And there it was, right on cue: our unfinished business.

Out of the corner of my eye, I saw Herri walking our way.

"Did you hear me?" he cried. "I stopped everything and came back here. To this…to this place! For you. I need you, Delaney. I need you to need me too."

About half the bar was silent, staring our way. The other half was too drunk to care. Someone shouted at him to shut up.

I kept my expression calm. I'd seen Cooper like this before. He was feeling lost and flailing for something to hold on to. He'd been lost for most of his life, eyes on a horizon that never led to home. He had told me he had come back to town looking for something. Hoping to find something here.

The easiest thing to think he was looking for was the one thing he knew he couldn't have. Me.

He'd been the one to push us away, to push me away. And in our time apart I'd done a lot of honest and painful looking around in my own heart.

I liked Cooper. Could even love him as a friend who had once been more than a friend when he wasn't being an ass.

But I knew with all my heart that we weren't the horizon the other was searching for. We'd been a safe port for a time, but even if Cooper had stayed in town, even if he'd wanted to stay with me, it never would have lasted.

He deserved something real. He deserved what he was looking for, not some ghost of the past he was willing to settle on having.

"We should talk about this later," I said gently. "When you're sober."

He made a sound low in his throat and lunged forward. Maybe it was the medicine, or the fact that I was still in pain, but I didn't think fast enough to move away. He grabbed my arm and jerked, forcing me onto my feet.

I gasped in pain as everything in my body caught on fire, and then I punched him in the face with everything I had.

The screaming of the song in my head went to white noise, and for a moment, I was lost, floating on pain and an unhoused god power that seemed intent on getting free of me.

No, no, no! I couldn't lose grip on it now.

A part of me knew I was standing in a bar. But the rest of me was somewhere else, somewhere in my mind, fighting against a power that would not be denied.

The wave of power and song dragged me under, and the bar faded from my sight. All around me was song and thrum and a need to possess, to control.

I had to contain the power. Had to shovel it back into me, somehow, hold it in the imperfect vessel of my body. A vessel it would no longer tolerate.

And if I lost? This power, Heim's power, would devour my body and pour free like a wave over jetty walls, roaring into Ordinary to tear it apart.

How was I supposed to fight it?

Delaney. My father's voice, near, urgent. Was I dying? *Fight.*

239

That was the plan. I just didn't know how. I pushed upward with imaginary fists, pushed out with imaginary arms, scrabbling and kicking to find purchase against the song that swallowed me whole and sent me spinning. Power slammed me around, churned until I couldn't find the way up. I couldn't breathe, couldn't think.

A memory flashed:

The kitchen light shone in my eyes through the crack of my bedroom door. I couldn't sleep, even though Mom had tucked me in hours ago. It wasn't Myra's soft snores from the other side of the room that kept me awake.

It was the music.

A shadow crossed the light, throwing me into darkness, then light shone on me again. Dad was pacing in the kitchen. He did that sometimes.

I tucked my stuffed crab, Polly, under my arm. I was probably too old for a stuffed toy—I was almost nine, after all—but tonight I clutched her close.

Dad leaned both hands on the edge of the kitchen table, arms locked, back toward me, his head hanging down. He was still except for muscles in his forearms that flexed and flexed, bunching and lengthening as he squeezed the table's edge like he was trying to hang on to something for dear life.

A bunch of papers were scattered across the table and the floor. Dad had been furiously drawing again. Drawing a lot. He did that sometimes too.

One paper by my foot held an image of a woman's face I'd never seen before, but it was scribbled out with big, looping lines, like the pencil had traced her face so many times it had completely lost the details it was trying to define. As if he were looking for that person and had no way to find her.

These pictures scared me, even though I didn't know why.

"Daddy?"

He turned. It was not my father standing there. It was his body, his Grateful Dead T-shirt, his sweatpants. But everything inside him wasn't him. It was the song in my head. Too loud. Consuming me. Consuming my dad.

I cried out and pressed my hands over my ears, smashing Polly against one side of my face.

And then something broke and washed away. The song was gone.

It was just my daddy standing there. Just my daddy, who blinked hard, as if struggling to see me in the bright light of the kitchen lamp.

"Delaney?" he said. "Baby?"

I nodded, crying, scared of what had just happened, even though the song was gone now.

"Oh, baby," he breathed. He was across the room in two strides, gathering me up into his strong arms and holding me tight as he carried me out of the room. "It's okay. It's okay." I had one arm wrapped around his neck, Polly still smooshed on my other ear.

Pretty soon we were sitting in the living room in his big chair that rocked.

His arms around me felt safe. We rocked for a long time. Long enough I stopped crying.

"What did you see?" he finally asked, his cheek tipped against the top of my head. "Did you see lights and colors?"

I shook my head, the scratch of his unshaved chin rubbing in my hair. "It was the music," I whispered. "I heard all the music. All the voices. And the music was inside you and it was too loud and you weren't you anymore."

Daddy's body had gone a little stiff. He'd stopped rocking, and then started again, exhaling.

"You hear it." He nodded. "Okay, honey. It's okay. Is it loud? The voices and music. Did it hurt you?"

"No." I thought I might be acting like a baby, so I leaned back enough to show him I was okay. I was brave. "What was it?"

His blue eyes were sad, but when he smiled, laugh lines crinkled at the corners. "It's a very special thing. A treasure that our family has the honor to protect. It's power. God power."

"Like Mr. Odin and Mr. Crow sometimes have?"

"Yes. And looking after it is an important duty, but sometimes it can be hard too."

"Like being a police officer."

"Yes."

"I'm going to be a police officer," I said, snuggling back down against his wide chest.

"What happened to firefighter?"

I rolled my eyes. "I'm not a vampire, Dad."

"It's not just vampires who can fight fires," he said with a chuckle.

I pulled back again. "I want to be a police officer." I was very, very serious. "And I want to help you protect the god power song."

He swallowed and nodded, his hand on my back warm and wide. "I think you will have to, Delaney. And I think you'll be very good at it."

"I will?"

"Yes. Because you always know what is right, and what is wrong, no matter how hard or sad that can be. And when something is scary or stronger than you, you face it. You will stand strong like a tree that buries its roots under stone and mountains, and nothing will stop you from sheltering others from the storm."

"I want to do that," I whispered. "I want to be the tree."

"You will," he whispered back, leaning his forehead against mine.

Fight, Delaney.

I shoved every ounce of my energy against the power. Strained to break through that wave of sound, to find the surface, the air, the real world again.

I stretched for solid ground. Roots into mountain. My blood, my family, stood against the powers of this world. I'd be damned if I let one god power hissy fit take me down.

I dug deep and braced myself, spreading my arms wide, and did exactly what my father had told me to do: I faced into the storm.

That's it. That's good.

"Delaney!" Herri's voice.

Herri's arms around me. Herri's bar slammed into focus.

I blinked, trying to figure out where I was. I scanned the room for Dad, sure that he must be there, that he must be beside me, close. Telling me to fight. Telling me I had done the right thing.

Face the storm.

I thought I caught a haze of light at the corner of my eye, but when I looked, all I saw was the bar, filled with people staring at me.

"What happened?" My mouth was dry, throat hot. I thought I was going to barf.

"You're all right," Herri said. "I got you. Let's sit down over here, okay?" She kept her arm around my waist and started leading me to a table. "Watch your step."

I glanced down.

Cooper lay unconscious, crumpled on his side, his nose bleeding. Sven Rossi, Herri's vampire bouncer, crouched beside him, tapping him on the cheek.

"What happened?" Details were spotty, but some of the fog was clearing.

"Something beautiful," Herri said. "And a long time coming."

Was she talking about Cooper on the floor or the power that was now quiet and still?

I didn't know how that worked, but I felt that for maybe the first time since Heim's death, I actually had a handle on the power. I had made it shut up and sit down and think about its actions.

Chalk one up for the Reed family.

"My hand hurts."

Herri chuckled and helped me sit in the booth.

The crowd gave up on whatever show they'd thought was going to unfold and went back to their drinks, conversations, and screens.

"You feeling okay?" Herri's hand was solid on my shoulder as she bent to get a better look at my face. "You are very pale."

"I got shot."

Her eyes narrowed and she lifted her head, looking around the bar. "When?"

"This morning, early."

"Who?"

I shook my head. "I'm not so sure."

"You didn't see them?"

"No, I did. I'm just not sure that he did it."

She released my shoulder and sat across the table from me. "Why aren't you in the hospital?"

I lifted my eyes and studied her heart-shaped face. She was pretty in the way all deities were, her power shining in her like a quiet, single chord of sound humming. Dad had once told me she was the colors of peacock feathers, all blues and greens and indigo. I wondered if her power would sound like the blues too, or something soft and lilting.

"I'm the chief of police and I know my rights. I have the right to leave the hospital if I want."

She raised an eyebrow, disapproving. "All right. Tell me who might not have shot you."

"Dan Perkin."

She didn't look surprised. "Why do you think he didn't?"

"It just doesn't line up. He's angry, but he's not violent. If Dan Perkin shot someone every time he was mad about something, there wouldn't be anyone left alive in Ordinary."

"Granted," she agreed. "So who in town wants you dead, Delaney? Who else could have held a gun and squeezed the trigger? And do they want Dan to take the fall for it?"

I chewed on my bottom lip and thought it over. Those were good questions. I wish I had good answers. "Could be someone who doesn't want me to rehouse Heim's power. Maybe the same person who killed him?"

"Which would be deities and creatures, since they are the only ones who know about god power."

"Have you heard of anyone who might want to settle their problem with me via bullet?"

"Other than maybe the guy you just decked—nice hit, by the way—no."

"Do you think it could have been Cooper?"

She held my gaze. "Do you?"

He had come back into town right when this entire mess had begun. Was probably even in town when Dan's rhubarb patch had blown sky high. I pushed aside my personal feelings and focused on Cooper's personality, his actions in the past, his behavior.

"No," I finally admitted. "Cooper's more of the get-drunk-and-yell-at-your-ex-girlfriend kind of guy."

"Well, I don't know what to tell you, Delaney," she said. "Someone killed Heim. Someone shot at you, possibly intending to kill you. Maybe what you have on your hands is a mortal serial killer."

"Terrific. That's so much better."

Cooper groaned, and then cussed while Sven asked how many fingers he was waving around much too quickly for the mortal eye to track. "Sorry about that."

She patted my hand gently. "Don't you let it bother you. Any time you feel like laying someone out, you come on down. Beer's on me."

"I'll remember that."

"Good. Now do you need a ride home?"

I felt eyes on me and turned to look at the door.

Myra was striding my way, her hair a little mussed and her sweat jacket pulled over what was clearly a pajama top. She did not look happy.

"No need. I think the cavalry just arrived."

"What the hell are you doing out of the hospital?" Myra demanded when she was close enough.

"Getting a drink?" I said.

She narrowed her eyes. "I'm taking you back."

"I already checked out."

"You can't check out of a hospital to go to a bar. What were you thinking?"

"I was thinking I needed to figure some things out."

"In a bar?"

"Why not in a bar?"

She snapped her mouth shut and glared. "We're leaving. Now."

I was surprised she wasn't yelling. "Thanks, Herri."

"Like I said, anytime, Delaney." She slid out from behind the table and started back through the crowd.

"Sit down," I said.

245

Myra glared.

"Please. I need to say this while it's all fresh in my head. It's about the cases."

She gave in. Sat. "You have ten minutes."

"What if the two crimes are connected? Heim's murder and Dan maybe shooting me?"

"Definitely shooting you."

I ignored that. "What connects those two crimes?"

"The Rhubarb Rally is the only thing Heim and Dan had in common," Myra said.

"And if the exploding rhubarb really was someone trying to kill Dan, like he said?"

She frowned. "So if this is about Dan, then someone has blown up his garden, and is now framing him for shooting you—which he did—and now you think someone is framing him for killing Heim? But he has an alibi for Heim's time of death."

I rubbed at my bruising knuckles. Cooper had a hard head. "People lie. Someone is lying. We need to double-check the alibis. Any word on the deck hand?"

"No. The rally is taking up everyone's time. The APB is out, but nothing yet. What happened there?" She tipped her chin toward Sven, who was dragging Cooper up onto his feet and marching him off to the door.

"I hit him."

"You *what*?"

"He was pushing me around. Drunk," I added. "Thinks I owe him something since I'm his ex-girlfriend."

"Jackass," she muttered.

"Huh. Ex-girlfriend."

Her eyebrows drew down. "What about it?"

"Dan doesn't have any."

"For obvious reasons. And?"

"And Heim did."

"Lila."

I nodded. Something was tickling at me. A memory just beyond my reach. It felt important. And it had something to do with Lila.

"How long has Lila been back in town?"

"Just this week."

"So why did she come back?" I asked.

"I think she and Margot were tying down loose ends with their property here."

"During the week the town shuts down for the Rhubarb Rally? During the week Dan's garden blows up, and Lila's ex-boyfriend drowns? Coincidence?"

"I hate that word."

I braced my hand on the table to help me push to my feet. "Me too. We need to talk to them again."

"I'll talk to them in the morning. You need to sleep." She moved to wrap her arm around my back. I was afraid she might squeeze me too hard, but she was careful to support me without jostling my sore places. Walking sucked. I should have taken my pills.

"Do you know what I heard on the way over here?" she asked as we headed to the door.

"No." I had a pretty good idea, actually. Ham radios were still a thing here in Ordinary, keeping a running commentary on the weather, our high school baseball team the Barnacles, and, on slow nights, bar fights.

"Someone said you punched Cooper in the face and knocked him out. I asked myself, would my sister check herself out of a hospital hours after being shot, and get in a bar brawl with her ex-boyfriend?"

"No?" I said.

We were at the cruiser now. The night was starless and so dark that even the bar's neon sign couldn't seem to pierce it.

At least it wasn't raining.

She opened the door and helped me into the front seat. I was not looking forward to the seatbelt, but she pulled it out before I could even start to twist toward it, and buckled me in, making sure the shoulder strap wasn't too tight.

I closed my eyes and worked on breathing through the pain from that short walk.

Myra got in the car, started the engine, and headed down the street. It was late enough—or really, early enough—that there was no other traffic on the road.

"Are you taking me home?"

"You can't walk up that many stairs."

"Please don't take me back to the hospital." I couldn't help it—I sounded pitiful.

She hesitated, then pressed her lips together. "I should."

"I'll just make them release me again."

"What do you have against hospitals, Delaney?" she asked, exasperated.

The image of Mom hooked up to machines that had done her no good flashed behind my eyes. Myra had been too young to remember. Not me.

I wiped my hand over my eyes, and it was shaking. "Nothing."

She exhaled. "Fine. You can stay with me tonight."

"Really?"

"Really."

She flicked on the blinker and I closed my eyes. I opened them when the car stopped. We were parked in her garage. She helped me out of the car, through the utility room and kitchen, then into the spare bedroom.

I really needed those pain pills.

I sat on the edge of the bed and tried to help take off my boots, but she pushed my hands out of the way and took care of my shoes and my jeans. Ryder had just been doing the same thing a day ago.

Don't think about Ryder. Ryder's gone.

Melancholy swept through me and I was too tired to fight it.

"You okay?" Myra asked as she unzipped my hoodie and eased it off my arms, then pulled a soft cotton nightgown over my head. It smelled like her perfume—something on the sweet side of gardenia.

"Delaney," she said softly, this time drawing her fingers across my forehead and then pressing the back of her hand there, checking for fever.

I wanted to tell her that I'd slept with Ryder, even though Old Rossi had warned me he was trouble. Old Rossi was right. Ryder had walked out on me.

I wanted to tell her about almost drowning in the power song, and how Dad had been there to help me.

But the pain in my side had stretched out and locked into my muscles. My stomach hurt and my head ached.

"Somebody shot me," I mumbled.

Myra's hand returned to feel my forehead. "I know," she said. "Have you taken any medicine?"

"Not since the hospital. Dan doesn't hate me that much."

"Did they send you away with pills? Delaney? Look at me."

I raised my eyes. Or opened them. I wasn't sure which.

"Where are your pills?"

"Coat." Then she was gone, which was too bad, because I was hoping she'd stay and help me crawl under the mattress so I could suffocate my pain away.

I worked on pushing myself back a bit. Whimpered as I lifted my legs up onto the bed, but didn't barf. I was calling that a win.

I was trying to get under the covers when Myra appeared again. She pushed the covers clear, baring sheets that were light blue with tiny pink flowers on them. Myra might come across as stern or unemotional to most people, but I was pretty sure she was the softest heart out of all of us Reeds.

Especially in private. I wouldn't be surprised if the nightgown I was wearing was frilly with lace and bows.

"Delaney? Are you listening? Come on, honey. If you don't take these pills, I'm going to drive you back to the hospital."

"No," I said. "No hospital. I can take the pills."

She handed me a cup of water. "Open your mouth."

I did, not even complaining that she was treating me like a child.

She dropped two pills in my mouth and I drank enough water to wash them down and then drank a little more, hoping that it would settle my stomach.

"Just lean back. Easy." She guided me down to the cool sheets and soft pillow, and the relief of being horizontal was immense. I shut my eyes, listening to her move around the small room.

"My?" I asked.

She hummed from the far corner of the room. There wasn't a bathroom attached to this room, so I wasn't sure what she was doing there.

"I think Dan was angry."

She sniffed. "Yeah?"

"I've seen him that angry before. Red face. Shaky hands. Yelling."

The bed dipped as she sat down beside me. "Yeah. So have I." Her hand was at my forehead again, even though I was pretty sure I didn't have a fever.

"He's never shot anyone when he was that angry. Not once."

"I know."

"Why did he do it this time?"

"I don't know, Delaney. You said he was mad about the contest." Her fingers stroked my head, smoothed my hair.

The pain meds crept out over my muscles, easing. The soft sheets, soft bed, and soft blankets worked their own unique magic on me.

"Sleep." She sounded a hundred miles away. "And no sneaking out this time."

I finally figured out the noise she had been making. She was booby-trapping the room so she'd hear me if I got up. The window was over in that corner. She was probably setting it up so I'd have to push a wind chime out of the way if I tried to open it.

"Paranoid," I mumbled.

"Druggy. Sneaky. Prone to bar fights."

"I don't think Dan shot me."

"It looked like Dan shot you."

I thought that over for a while, my brain slowing and slowing.

"Yeah, but this is Ordinary."

When I didn't continue, she said, "And?"

"And nothing in Ordinary is ever how it really looks."

CHAPTER 26

I REMEMBERED Myra waking me up for more pills. I told her to leave me alone, but most of my words got stuck in the pillow I'd dragged over half of my face.

When I finally woke enough to push the pillow away, it was hours later, and I decided a trip to the bathroom was a really good idea. A wide strip of bubble wrap was stapled outside the bedroom door, long enough I couldn't just hop over it.

"Really?" I stepped on it, and half a dozen air chambers popped. I smiled at Myra's alarm system. Took another step and set off another round of popping.

"Delaney, dear?" Pearl appeared in the hallway with a cup of tea. "I was just going to try to wake you up."

"Hey, Pearl." I shuffled toward the bathroom. "Did Myra make you babysit?"

"You know I'm always happy to help. I thought my medical background might be useful. I'll change your bandage when you're ready."

"Hold on a sec. I'll be right out."

I made use of the facilities then stared at my reflection in the mirror while I washed my hands in warm water.

I tended to freckle, but my job kept me outdoors enough that I maintained a tan under all my spots. Right now I was sheet-white against medium brown hair that seemed too dark, my blue-green eyes gone almost gray.

If I had met me on the street, I'd say I'd had a couple of bad days. I'd also sit myself down and insist I eat a solid meal and get some sleep.

My stomach was twitchy at the very idea of food, but I'd probably have to take my meds again soon anyway, and I hadn't eaten anything since the half peanut butter sandwich at the hospital.

I wanted a shower more than food, but I couldn't remember if bathing was approved with the hole in my side.

There was a soft knock on the door. "Delaney?"

I opened the door. "Sorry. Moving kind of slow. What time is it?"

"Twelve thirty."

"In the afternoon?" I asked, shocked.

"Yes."

"Is it Friday?"

"Saturday." She held a cup out for me and I took it.

The inviting fragrance of tea with sugar and cream wafted up to me, and I wondered why I never drank tea. I took a sip, then another, as warmth spread out from my chest and my fingers soaked in the cup's heat.

Pearl walked away, leaving me there to lean on the sink with my tea. When she came back, she was carrying a kitchen chair.

"Sit there. I'm going to get a blanket, then take a look at your wound."

Pearl was kind and efficient and impossible to say no to. She checked my ribs, gave me my pills, then sent me into the shower, promising to re-bandage my wound when I was done.

The combination of hot water, pain pills, and tea cleared my head.

It was Saturday. I'd missed the sunrise blessing of the regatta that signaled the beginning of the Rhubarb Rally. I'd missed the first day, and now half of Saturday. The rally would be in full swing, with rides, food, entertainment, and local businesses representing their wares.

Myra and Jean would be busy policing the crowd, probably with Ryder and Roy. No one would be at the station, except for Dan Perkin, who should still be in the holding cell.

I got out of the shower and into the clothes I'd worn from the hospital. I wandered into the kitchen, where Pearl had a bowl of oatmeal waiting for me. She'd arranged the raisins in the bowl to make a smiley face.

"I hope you like it that way." She handed me a spoon as a not-so-subtle hint that I should eat.

The buttery-smooth porridge was just the right amount of sweet and nutty. My appetite that had been missing in action suddenly roared back to life. "I need to fill out some paperwork on the shooting," I lied as I finished the last bit, standing at the kitchen counter.

Pearl walked toward me, her hands folded neatly in front of her. "Is that what you want me to tell Myra when she calls?"

"Would you just tell her I'm on the couch sleeping?"

"Delaney. I don't think you are...steady enough to be on your own today. Are you doing something you don't want your sister to know about?"

"Maybe a little. I want to go talk to Dan. I think... I don't think he's really the kind of guy who would shoot someone."

Pearl looked down at her hands, and a frown tugged her mouth.

"Do you know something about this, Pearl?"

She shook her head, her eyes finally drawing back up to mine.

"He's... I know he's a trouble maker. Too angry at...everything. But I've never seen him resort to violence before."

"Okay. That's good to hear. Is there anything else?"

"I don't think Chris Lagon was responsible for blowing up Dan's rhubarb patch."

It seemed like an odd jump in the conversation, but I followed along. "Do you know who might be?"

She nodded, an almost imperceptible movement.

I waited.

"Dan," she said.

"Dan what?"

"I believe he blew up his own rhubarb."

"He... Okay. Why would Dan do that?"

"By accident. I think..." She seemed to make up her mind, and all hesitancy disappeared. "I think he had bought the dynamite and planned to blow up something else but changed his mind."

"What something else?"

"Chris's tanks. Not all of them, but the ones containing his rhubarb beer. I think he was experimenting with how much dynamite he'd need to take out his competition. Not Chris—just the beer. And it backfired."

It made a certain sense. Dan had jumped on the chance to lay the explosion blame on Chris—an easier and less violent way to take out his competition, which suited Dan's style. But Chris had his alibi for not being available to set the dynamite in Dan's yard. Chris was with Margot Lapointe.

"Did Dan tell you that?"

"No. But he mutters to himself when he's angry. And he's always angry." She smiled almost fondly, and I found myself amazed at her capacity for patience. "I heard him while I was working in my flowerbeds. At first, I thought he was arguing with someone, but when I looked over in his yard, he was arguing with himself."

"About blowing up Chris's beer?"

"About if he should test it on his own rhubarb."

"Did he actually mention the dynamite?"

"No. But very early the next morning, he was out in his backyard, and that was when the explosion happened. I hadn't put together that he might have blown up his own garden. I mean, who does that sort of thing?"

"Dan." I sighed. "That's the sort of thing I'd expect from him."

She nodded. "That's what I'd been thinking. But I didn't have proof. But if you're doubting that he shot you, I thought you should know I'm doubting his story about the explosion."

"I'll keep it in mind. Thank you, Pearl. It helps."

She folded her hands in front of her again. "You're still going, aren't you?"

The song of Heim's power was filling my head again. Not to the point of pain, but it was a pressure I couldn't duck. I had two days to find the mortal the power belonged to and still had no idea how to do that. If I wanted any time alone with Dan, it would have to be now.

Dan was the beginning of all this, and I'd just have to start with him and see if I could unravel the week's events.

I tucked my hair back behind one ear, wishing I had a rubber band. "Dan will be transferred to the valley on Monday. Now would be best. Plus there really is paperwork I need to work on. If I get tired, I'll nap on the cot."

"I don't like it, but it's not like I can tie you up. Let me get your medicines."

"Thanks," I said, getting into my coat. "Um, can I ask a favor?"

She raised her eyebrows. "I won't lie to your sisters."

"I know. Would you mind driving me home? I'm going to need my car."

CHAPTER 27

IT TOOK three times as long as normal to drive the short distance to my house. The day had turned out pleasant and sunny. Good weather on a weekend meant people were pouring into Ordinary for the festival.

That made for a nice spring kickoff for local businesses. But for the regulars who lived here, it meant suddenly living in an overpopulated town that wasn't quite big enough to handle the influx.

Pearl dropped me off in my driveway, and I ducked out of her car repeating that I was fine and I was going to be fine, and if I wasn't fine, I'd call her.

She drove off and I walked over toward my parked Jeep.

Two steps across the crunch of gravel and a wave of nausea hit me.

Dan screaming, holding the gun at arm's length as if it were a stick he could stab me with. Death looming behind me, an oddly comforting shadow.

Then Dan squeezed the trigger.

I planted one hand on the hood of the Jeep and opened my mouth for air, pushing that visceral memory away. The scent of pine and salt tasted like blood on my tongue.

Hold it together, I told myself. *Take this one step at a time.*

I breathed until my hands stopped shaking, then crouched to pull the spare keys out from the magnetic holder in the wheel well. Once inside the car, I studied the area from a cop's perspective. Dan had been standing in the middle of the cul-de-sac. Than and I had been near the stairs leading up to my house.

There was a dark stain on the gravel that must be my blood.

A sick chill washed over me, and I leaned my head against the steering wheel until the nausea passed. I was fine now. Everything was fine.

I looked back up and wiped sweat from my forehead.

Think. If Dan's gun wasn't loaded, where did the bullet come from?

The end of the cul-de-sac was hemmed by coastal pines, Oregon grape, and salal bushes. Far below that was the beach and ocean.

The house across the street was an empty vacation home built far enough off the road that several trees and bushes obscured the face of it.

Someone could have hidden there on the walk, or porch, or behind the bushes. What were the chances someone with a loaded gun was lurking behind Dan?

Out here in the light of day, it seemed like a far-fetched idea. But then, this was Ordinary. Far-fetched was sort of our middle name.

"Dammit." I dug a clean plastic sandwich bag out of my glove box and got out of the Jeep. I walked to the neighbor's house, scanning the ground. The gravel didn't seem disturbed. The bushes weren't broken. I paced a grid of the cul-de-sac, slowly covering the area. Any evidence from the shooting would have been found by Myra, Jean, and the crime scene techs.

The road was churned from the vehicles that had come and gone since I'd been shot, obscuring tire tracks and footprints.

Maybe Dan did it. Maybe he was angry enough about not winning the contest that he shot me.

The wind stirred and a flash of color under the glossy leaves of a salal bush caught my eye. I bent, groaned at the pressure in my side, and picked up the item with the baggy.

It was a thin purple feather. Weird.

I dropped the feather into the bag and tucked it in my coat. I scanned the area one more time, but didn't find anything else. Time to go talk to Dan.

Traffic was stop and go all the way down Highway 101, the frequent pedestrian crossings adding to the mess. Businesses lining the street had put goods on the sidewalk with big "sale" signs to lure shoppers. It was a town-wide festival and rummage sale.

My heart lurched. Was that Ryder's truck turning out of traffic and down a side road? The light changed before I could get a better look, but my heart still raced.

Ryder Bailey was the last thing I wanted to deal with today, or ever. My plan was to ignore our night together, ignore our

257

friendship, and ignore he existed until it no longer hurt to think about him.

You dumped me while I was recovering from a gunshot wound. Jerk.

What was it with men dumping me when I was at my lowest?

I turned into the station and strode to the door. The sign on the door said: Closed. We kept the office locked up on festival days, since we usually pulled double shifts with crowd control. I keyed in the code and flipped on the office lights. The door *snicked* shut behind me. I didn't lock it. I was in. If someone came by looking for the police, I'd be here.

But first, Dan.

I walked down the other hallway and keyed in the code for that locked door, which opened into our two-cell holding area.

Dan sat on the edge of a small cot behind bars, his arms resting on his legs, his head hanging, fingers worrying at a hangnail. He was muttering quietly to himself—Pearl was right, he really did talk a lot—but stopped when he heard the door open.

"Delaney!" He jumped up to his feet and grabbed the bars.

My hand shot instinctively down to where my gun would be if I were carrying.

Maybe Pearl was right. I wasn't steady yet, still too jumpy from the last few days. I took a deep breath and tucked my hand into my pocket to hide how much it was shaking.

"Hey, Dan." I leaned against the wall farthest from him, my other arm across my ribs protectively. "We need to talk."

"I'm so sorry, Delaney," he blurted. "I didn't know! I don't know how the bullets got there. I just wanted to scare you. That's all. I didn't know. I didn't know."

He was babbling. I watched him plead with me. He might be faking it, his panic nothing more than realization that he had made a mistake and he was going to pay for it for a very long time.

I didn't want to believe him. Dan Perkin was a pain in the neck on pretty much all levels. He had no real friends in town, and I didn't think anyone would feel the least bit of remorse if he were locked up for life.

But my job was to look at the facts objectively.

And I was damn good at my job.

"I need you to calm down," I said in the tone of voice I used when trying to talk Kressler and Wallery out of their garbage barrel battle. "Can you do that for me?"

He scowled like he was about to go off on a rant, but then he looked me up and down and slumped, pressing his forehead against the bars.

"Yeah," he said. "I can be calm. Am I gonna need my lawyer here? Because I think she's running the tie-dye booth."

"No, you won't need your lawyer. I'm not trying to trap you. I just want to ask you a couple things."

He nodded, his forehead rubbing on the bar.

"Did you buy dynamite and blow up your garden?"

"I…" He licked his lips, his gaze skittering. "Yes," he whispered.

"Were you having thoughts about blowing up Chris's beer vats?"

He nodded.

Okay, two for two. Pearl had been right.

"Did you try to blow up Chris's beer vats?"

He shook his head, miserable, though I didn't know if it was because he hadn't had a chance to blow up the beer or because I'd asked him about it.

"Did you kill Heim?"

He jerked away from the bars. "What? No! Why would I do that?"

"He was a judge in the contest, Dan."

"I'd never!" he sputtered. "Never! Kill someone? I wouldn't. I can't believe you would accuse me."

"You pointed a gun at me, Dan," I said quietly. "And you pulled the trigger."

"I…I didn't know it was loaded. I don't know how that happened, Delaney. You have to believe me. I didn't load that gun."

"If you didn't, who did? Who had access to it? Who have you let handle it?"

"No one. No one." He shook his head and gripped the bars again.

I waited, trying to decide if I believed him. I sighed. Even though I didn't like it, I thought he was telling the truth.

"Okay, so you were waving around an empty gun—not the smartest move, Dan."

He opened his mouth to argue, then, to my surprise, nodded. "I wasn't thinking. I just wanted…wanted you to pay attention to me."

"You have my full attention. I need you to really think about this: who do you know that hates you enough to frame you for shooting me?"

"I told you no one touched my gun."

"I believe you."

He was halfway into a syllable before he snapped his mouth shut. "You do?" He narrowed his eyes suspiciously.

I nodded. "So if you didn't put bullets in your gun, and if no one else did, then there had to be another gun with bullets on the scene. Who knew you were angry at me? Who knew you would go to my house with a gun? Who would want you blamed for shooting a police officer?"

He shook his head, his eyes open with a kind of wonder. "I don't know. So many people hate me, it's hard to say."

I smiled sadly. He wasn't wrong.

"Have you seen anyone around your place who isn't usually there? Someone in the vacation home down the street? A car you're not used to seeing around parking near your house?"

He lowered his eyebrows, thinking. "No. I don't think so, no. Well, those sisters are renting down the street."

"Sisters?"

"Lila Carson and the blonde, Margie or Maggie, or—"

"Margot." I swallowed as a chill washed over me. "Margot Lapointe. How long have they been there?"

"How should I know? I don't keep track of every little thing in my neighborhood."

I just stared at him. Waited.

He blushed. "Maybe a couple weeks? The blonde moved in first, I think. Then the other one. See them around everywhere. Well, the blonde. I think she was following me. Spying on me for that Chris Lagon. I have rights, you know. Rights to privacy."

I was listening with half an ear. I hadn't even checked to see where the sisters were staying while they settled their business in town. I'd assumed they rented a hotel room.

Still, renting a house near Dan didn't exactly make them culpable in the shooting. It was a small town. Everyone lived near everyone.

I rubbed at my forehead. "Okay. That might be helpful. I'm glad we had this talk."

"Wait," he said. "Are you leaving me? You're not leaving me here, are you? You can't leave me."

"I can't drop the charges yet, so yes, you are staying here until I can check your gun and see if a bullet was fired from it recently and whether or not that does anything to clear your name."

"You'd do that for me?" He sounded genuinely surprised.

"If you're innocent, I'll do everything I can to make sure that you're released. That's how the law works."

I punched in the code and gripped the door handle to pull it open.

"Delaney?"

I paused, but didn't twist back to look at him, since I was pretty sure that would make my wound bleed.

"I saw Walt, Heim's deck hand, the night before Heim drowned. He...he was drunk. He'd been at Jump off Jack's and was talking about making money that had nothing to do with fishing. I don't know what he was talking about. Didn't care. Still don't care. But...well, he left town the next day and Heim shows up dead. Think that's anything?"

I let go of the door and turned all the way to face him again. "Was he with anyone?"

"Who?"

"Walt. Did you see him talking to anyone else in the bar that night?"

"Chris was there."

"Chris is always there. Someone else?"

"Yes!" he said triumphantly, as if it had just occurred to him. "The blonde. She was there. Sat at the table with Walt. I know she did. Left before he got chatty. Is that helpful? Does that help?"

Margot was in Dan's neighborhood. She would have been aware of his comings and goings. She might have seen the gun he kept in his car. But how would she know he intended to shoot at me?

"Delaney," he repeated. "Does it help?"

"Not yet. But if it does, I'll let you know." I left the room and walked back to my desk. I picked up the desk phone and called Myra's cell.

"Officer Reed," Myra answered crisply.

"Hey, Myra. Don't be mad at Pearl."

"Where are you?" she growled.

"At the station. I'm fine. She made me happy-face oatmeal and gave me my meds."

"Delaney…" She reined her voice in to keep the anger down. She was really frustrated. "You need to turn around and drive back to my place and park yourself on my couch. Now."

"Wow. You sounded a little like Dad right then. So I talked to Dan and Pearl. Turns out Dan blew up his own rhubarb patch."

"Okay. Why do I care about this?"

"He says he didn't have any bullets in his gun."

"Yeah, I heard him yelling that all day yesterday."

"I believe him."

Myra paused and the crowd noise around her grew louder. Children laughing and squealing, people talking, and in the background, a voice I recognized as Thor crooning out a rock-n-roll ballad. He had a good voice.

"You believe Dan Perkin—who was standing right in front of you and pulled the trigger—didn't shoot you," she said. "Have you lost your mind?"

"Did you find the bullet casings?"

"Yes."

"Did you check to make sure they were the correct bullets for Dan's gun?"

"We're processing the evidence."

I waited.

"Not yet," she said. "You were shot, Delaney. In surgery. Jean and I stayed with you after we locked up Dan. Then you ran away to a *bar*. That morning I'd had to run dawn crowd control for the regatta blessing. We haven't had time to do anything else, and as far as I care, Dan can sit and stew."

"How was the blessing?" I asked, realizing Myra probably hadn't gotten any sleep in the last twenty-four hours.

"Poseidon almost drowned himself."

Of course he did.

"So, pretty much like normal?" I couldn't keep the smile out of my voice.

"It's not funny, Del."

"It's kind of funny."

"All right." She huffed out a breath. "Let's say Dan is innocent. Then who the hell shot you? That wound was not made by an imaginary bullet."

"I think there was someone else out there."

"I hate that idea."

"Me too."

"Do you have a lead on who might want you shot and Dan in jail?"

"Not really. But Dan said he talked to Walt, the night before Heim washed up."

"Not following you on this."

"Heim's drowning."

"Yes?"

"Dan makes a great fall guy. No one likes him. No one would miss him if he were locked away for murder. No one would argue that he was capable of being angry enough to pull a trigger on a judge over a rhubarb contest."

"No one would have to argue that because he did pull the trigger."

"Yeah," I said. "I know. But if he's telling the truth and there were no bullets in his gun, then he should be up on aggravated menacing charges of pointing a gun at a police officer instead of attempted murder."

She sighed.

"How does Walt fit in with all this?"

"Dan saw him drinking at Chris's bar the night before Heim died. He was bragging about making money. Earlier that night, Walt had been sitting with Margot Lapointe."

"So?"

"Margot and Lila recently moved into a rental in Dan's neighborhood."

"Hold on." The phone was muffled as she pulled it away. I heard her sharp whistle, then: "Down from there. Don't lick the jellyfish!"

I grinned and wandered over to start a pot of coffee.

"Okay," she said a couple seconds later. "Walt was talking to Margot. No crime in that. How does that link her or Dan to Heim's death?"

"I don't know yet. But outside my house I found something."

"You went back to your house? Alone?"

"To get my car. Pearl dropped me off."

"Why did I think you'd actually listen to her and stay put?"

"I have no idea. You know how I hate being sick on the couch."

"Since when?"

"So I was looking through the bushes."

"Delaney."

"I found a feather."

"That's important because?"

"Lila and Margot have feathers in their hair."

"Birds shed feathers all the time."

"Not purple feathers."

"You think Lila and Margot were in your driveway, with a gun, at the same time as Dan, waiting for him to pretend-shoot you, so they could for real shoot you and frame him for the crime? That's a complicated and unlikely plan."

"But not impossible."

"Almost impossible. Which you'd realize if you weren't high on Percocet."

"I'm not high. Just…floaty."

"One feather doesn't implicate Lila or Margot."

"I know. We need to talk to Walt. See if he let anyone get on that boat with Heim."

"We will handle that tomorrow," she said firmly. "Not today. And by we, I mean Jean and me. You are going to go home and sleep before that wound gets infected."

"Sleeping won't stop an infection."

"Delaney. This is me, telling you that if you don't drop this murder case for at least one day, I am personally going to drive over there and tie you down to a cot."

"Sounds kinky."

"Well, if you want kinky, I can send Ryder your way. Jean told me about you two."

What did Jean know? That we were dating? Well, that wasn't even remotely true now.

"Hey," I said, avoiding that conversation. "Have you seen him?" There was maybe a little too much worry in my voice.

"Ryder?" She paused. "Earlier today. Why?"

"No reason."

Because he broke up with me in the hospital. Because no matter how sad I feel, I'm starting to feel something else: angry.

"What happened with Ryder?" she asked. "Did he hurt you?"

"No. We...he...uh...we're done."

"Done?"

"We tried a date. It didn't go well. He ended it."

I could hear her quiet breathing and the sound of the festival filtering through her phone.

"When did he end it?"

I did not need an angry sister going after my boyfriend.

"Just, if you see him, let him know we need to talk, okay? Now: how's the rally going?" I asked in boss mode, ready to change the subject.

"Good. Busy. Weather's cooperating. Go home, okay, Delaney? Jean's still worried about you."

"Roger that. Eat a deep-fried rhubarb dog for me."

She snorted and cut off the call. I hung up and rubbed at the headache starting behind my eyes. The power was singing along, spreading out in my head like it was testing the boundaries of my control. It was looking for a way out.

I would love to give it one.

A sound at the back of the office stilled me.

I hadn't locked the front door. Someone was in the building with me. Someone who had gotten past me while I was questioning Dan.

DEVON MONK

I quietly opened my drawer, looking for my spare gun there. Nothing. I hadn't been wearing my gun since I'd been shot, didn't even know where it was.

Shit.

I moved quietly down the hall to the door to the cells, wondering if Dan had anyone in his life who would be trying to break him out. I peered through the small window in the door.

Dan was lying on his cot, his back to the door. He didn't look like he was waiting for someone.

If it wasn't to spring Dan, why would someone break into a police station?

I turned and stopped.

Margot Lapointe stepped out of the records room at the far end of the hall looking as startled as I felt. Her blonde hair was loose around her shoulders, the curve of lavender-feathered hair extensions drifting near her jaw. "Chief." Her eyes darted side to side, checking the shadows for movement. "I was looking for the bathroom. What are you doing here?"

"Well, I work here." I smiled. "Bathrooms are this way." I motioned toward the office behind us.

She turned and walked out into the office area. But before I could reach my desk, she turned again.

She had a gun pointed at me.

"Easy." Training and painkillers rushed to keep me calm. "You don't have to do this, Margot. We can talk."

"He had to take his revolver," she muttered, eyes never straying from my face. "After I went through all the trouble of knowing which guns he owns. Which guns he keeps handy. He used the damn revolver."

I could tackle her, probably get shot again in the process. If she landed a decent blow to my ribs, I'd black out.

No cell phone.

Landline too far away.

No one coming to work today.

"I watched him for *weeks*!" she said, her face twisted in disgust. "He loved his new Glock. Couldn't wait to try it out. But then he uses that piece of crap Colt on you."

I glanced at the gun in her hand. Glock.

266

And suddenly it made sense, even though it was almost impossible.

"You were in the bushes," I said. "You fired the gun at the same time Dan did. It was your bullet that hit me."

"The bullet they took from the scene doesn't match his gun," she said. "But I've got that covered now." She patted her free hand over her pocket.

"Margot, we can work this out."

"Oh, this works out perfectly. You're here alone. Just. Perfect."

A shadow briefly crossed the window in the door behind her. It was probably a tourist looking for directions and leaving, since the Closed sign was posted.

Good. I didn't need any more people getting hurt.

"What about Dan?" I asked. "Is he in on this with you? You and Lila?"

"That idiot? The only thing he's good for is to blame everything on. And Lila has nothing to do with this!" Her hand shook, her knuckles going white.

I wondered if I could pull on the power inside me and use it to stop her.

But the power was nothing but useless noise in my head. I was not the mortal allowed to wield it.

"He broke my sister's heart!" she yelled. "He ruined her life, ruined her business. She gave up everything for him, and he took and he took. Took her life away. She's never been the same. He took her away from me. He deserved to die. He deserved it!"

"Heim?" I said, wishing the threat of a gun in my face would clear the drugs out of my brain. I was thinking too slowly. Still a step behind her. "Lila didn't kill Heim."

"No," Margot said, shaking her head with little jerks. "She didn't have to. I love her. I *love* her," she snarled. "Nobody hurts her again." She raised the gun.

My head suddenly cleared. Nothing like a bucket of fear to get the brain working.

"If you shoot me, they'll know you did it. My sisters are police officers. They won't stop until they find you."

DEVON MONK

"They won't even look for me," she sneered. "They'll think you let Dan Perkin out of his cell and he shot you before he committed suicide."

This was it. No more time for talking.

The front door swung open with a bang.

I lunged for her.

Margot pivoted, gun swinging with her, leveled at the man who strode into the room.

Ryder Bailey.

No, no, no! He will not be shot before I get a chance to be mad at him for dumping me.

"Down!" I yelled. I jammed a shoulder into Margot's back. We crashed to the floor. I landed hard on my bad side and yelled. I grappled with her, scrabbling for the gun.

She twisted under me, threw an elbow at my ribs. I didn't have room to break away, didn't want that gun in her control, and took the hit. It felt like half my body was on fire. Silver lights bashed and broke in front of my eyes. I slammed her hand down and the gun skittered away.

"Do *not* move!" I growled and yanked her arm back. I used my weight and leverage and straddled her as a bloom of fresh blood poured down my side.

It had all happened in a second.

"Freeze!" Ryder barked. "Now!" The slide and clack of a gun was louder than the roaring in my ears, louder than my own heavy breathing, louder than Margot's swearing.

I stilled instinctively, and so did Margot.

"Delaney? Are you hurt?" Ryder asked.

Other than that knife you buried in my heart?

"Get the handcuffs in the desk drawer next to you." I shoved up onto my knees and dragged Margot's arm behind her until she hissed. I rested one knee in the middle of her back.

"You have the right to remain silent, Margot," I said between hard breaths. My entire left side felt like a beast was sinking teeth into me, chewing and chewing. Hot blood trickled down and soaked the waistband of my pants. My vision was still star-studded.

Power, which had been of zero use to me, rolled and screamed through my headache.

The combination of new pain, old power, and Ryder's voice—"Are you hurt?"—made me want to barf.

I swallowed until I got my nausea under control and patted Margot down one-handed, making sure she didn't have any other weapons on her.

She struggled a second, and I was more than happy to lean a little harder on her. "Just settle down and let me finish. Then you can call your lawyer."

I glanced up as Ryder gave me the handcuffs.

He had a Sig Sauer in his other hand, held down and to his side like he was comfortable holding a firearm. I frowned up at him, at his calm confidence in a situation any normal person would consider highly charged and should maybe be nervous about.

He was as cool as a trained veteran.

"Thanks for the assist." I clamped the handcuffs over her wrists.

"Was she alone?"

I looked up at him again. His head was raised, eyes narrowed as he searched the shadows of the office.

That question, his stance, were not meshing with his architect civilian vibe. Most people in town carried a gun. But there was something more than just "hunter" in his stance.

"I think so," I said. "I'll put her in lockup and we'll make sure."

I pushed up to my feet, keeping my arm pressed against my side and doing my best not to wince or whimper, my other hand on Margot's wrist so I could haul her up.

I didn't know if it was from the lack of a weapon or the cold cuffs around her wrist, but all the fight seemed to have drained out of her.

"Where was I?" I asked conversationally as I frog-marched her down the hall to the cells. "Oh, right. You have the right to remain silent."

Margot hung her head and walked quietly. Ryder followed behind, and stood in the door as I got Margot settled in the other cell next to Dan, whose shouting just added to the hammering in my skull.

I ignored Dan and walked over to Ryder, favoring my side with a slight limp. I stopped right in front of him. "You ass."

He frowned. "Excuse me?"

I walked past him and he stepped into the hall with me, letting the door close and lock behind him.

"Myra sent you over, right? That's the only reason you're here, right? Because you made it pretty clear you didn't want to be anywhere near me."

He winced and dropped his gaze to the floor. "I saw your Jeep in the parking lot. Thought maybe I should see how you were...after I..."

"Dumped me in the hospital while I was still bleeding from a bullet?" I supplied.

His jaw locked and I saw the lightning flash of anger in his eyes before he got it under control. He gave me a hard smile. "Would it have been any better if I went on pretending I wanted to date you?"

Oh, that was low. All the sweet words from our one night together, all the gentle caresses, the pleasure, the need, the laughter, the feeling of pure *rightness* of being with him, thinking of him as mine, swirled away down the drain of the hole he'd just punched in my heart.

He watched me, eyes growing wary.

In the next heartbeat my heart galvanized. And then there was nothing in me but iron-hot anger.

"You had your chance, Ryder Bailey," I whispered, low and fierce. "Old Rossi was right. And I will never forget what you really are."

He jerked slightly, as if something I'd said shocked him. Then there were too many things in his shifting eyes to decipher. "Good," he whispered.

I lifted a hand to rub at the pain behind my eye. My fingers trembled. They were covered with blood.

"You're bleeding." Ryder reached for my hand, something that looked like real worry crossing his face.

No. You don't get to care for me when it's convenient for you.

I turned and stalked over to my desk before he could touch me. "Just do your job, reserve officer." I picked up the phone and blinked until I could see the numbers. If there were tears in my eyes, they were angry tears. I dialed. "Stand in the hall in front of the door to the cells and make sure no one gets in or out."

He locked his jaw on whatever he'd been about to say. Then he squared his shoulders and walked back to position himself in front of the cell door.

Sorrow sat in my chest like dark coals, but anger was the flame that kept me warm. And it was also the only thing that was keeping me on my feet.

"Myra?" I said as soon as she answered her phone, the room going a little dark and fuzzy at the edges. "I could use some help over here."

CHAPTER 28

T<small>URNED</small> O<small>UT</small> both Myra and Jean rode to my rescue.

Also turned out I couldn't argue my way out of going to the hospital when my sisters double-teamed me and I was blackout dizzy from blood loss.

I plucked at the thin blanket that covered me, ignoring the tubes taped down to my arm. It was past dinnertime and I was an odd mix of restless and exhausted. Jean lounged in the recliner chair thing on one side of my room, doing something on her phone.

My sisters refused to let me out of their sight, even though that meant we'd had to call up to Tillamook and borrow a couple of their officers to help out with the rally. Which meant I owed the police chief up there a favor.

Again.

I shifted my feet and scooted up a bit, trying to get comfortable.

"Need anything?" Jean asked distractedly.

"No, I'm good." I picked up the tablet Myra had given me after I'd begged her to leave me something to do. I pulled up the report I'd been writing.

Margot had confessed to shooting me, which cleared Dan of some of his charges. I thought he might be able to get his remaining charges lowered if he listened to his lawyer's advice.

Margot had also confessed to bribing Walt to let her stow away on the boat and to hitting Heim on the back of the head. She said him falling overboard was an accident. I wasn't sure the jury would see it that way. Once Margot started talking, she hadn't stopped, droning through all her plans, all her hurt and anger, like she was in a trance.

They found Walt working a ship down in Bandon. He was en route and should hit town in a couple hours to corroborate her story. Then their fate would be up to the judge.

Myra was off finding Lila to let her know her sister was in holding. I was stuck in a hospital bed.

Again.

I sighed and closed the report. There was nothing more to add.

"Are you sure you don't need anything?" Jean asked again.

"A new brain?"

"You haven't hardly used your old one yet."

I glanced over at her. Her fingers moved across her screen as she concentrated on a game.

"It's almost Sunday," I said.

"Yep."

"If I don't find someone to give Heim's power to by Monday night, things...will get interesting."

She chewed on the inside of her cheek then stabbed at the screen a few times.

"Jean. Are you okay?"

She finally looked over at me. "I can't believe what he did."

"Dan?"

"Ryder. I can't believe he did that to you." It was hard to see the betrayal in her eyes. She'd always thought Ryder and I were a match made in heaven. That he was some kind of quiet hero who would one day realize the love of his life had been in his life, forever. Real life didn't work that way. Not even in Ordinary.

"I couldn't believe it either," I said with a smile I didn't feel. All I wanted to do was have a good cry, but all the tears in the world wouldn't change a single word that he'd said.

"Can we forget about Ryder right now?" I asked. "I really need to figure out who I should give this power to."

She took a drink out of her travel mug, which was probably full of Mountain Dew and Red Bull. "Have you narrowed it down at all?"

"Not you and not Myra. That's about it."

She made a face at me, then crossed her legs and leaned sideways in the chair. "The power calls to its own, right?"

"I don't know."

"You hear the power, right? Dad used to see them, but you hear them?"

I nodded.

"Does the sound of it ever change?"

I thought about it. "It shifts. It gets louder sometimes."

Hurts more sometimes.

"Does it get louder every time you've been around one person in particular?"

I shrugged and wished I hadn't. My shoulder ached. Everything ached. "I haven't been paying attention to that."

"Wow, you really suck at this." She smiled to soften her words.

"It's not like I haven't had other things on my mind this week. Bullets, blood. Rhubarb."

"And don't forget a fistfight in a bar with Cooper. Seriously, what were you thinking?"

"That he was a jerk and annoying the crap out of me."

"Funny how you used to date that."

"He didn't used to be that annoying."

She took another drink and made a so-so motion with her hand. "He did sort of roll into town out of the blue and mess up your life."

"Apparently men like to do that to me."

She was quiet for a minute. "Do you still love him?"

"Cooper?"

She just shook her head, her eyes holding mine.

"Ryder?" I asked.

Yes. I shoved that faint thought firmly away. "No. That's done."

Liar, my heart whispered.

"What about Cooper?"

"Cooper is different. He's..." *Not Ryder.* "Different."

"Okay," she said after a long moment of silence. "So let's narrow it down. Cooper came back right before Heim died. If the power calls to its own, maybe it was calling him."

"Lots of people come and go in town..." My voice faded as I remembered a conversation I'd had with Cooper. "Cooper said he thought he'd left something here. Left something in Ordinary even though he doesn't like this town. He came back looking for it. I thought he meant me, us, what we had..."

"But what if it was the power?" Jean sounded excited. "The power inside you, calling him."

Everything in me went cold and still. Even my brain. Even the song of power in my head.

Yes.

"Delaney?" Jean uncrossed her legs and pushed up out of the chair. "Are you hurting? Are you breathing?" She cupped my cheek, her dark blue eyes wide and worried. "Breathe."

"Cooper." I exhaled.

"Keep breathing," she said.

"What if it is Cooper? What if he is the mortal I'm looking for?"

"I just asked you that." She paused, studying my face. "Do you think he is?"

"Check me out of the hospital. We'll find Cooper and I'll talk to him about it. See if he wants it. God power has to be accepted. You can't force anyone to take up that kind of burden. Things go really wrong really fast if you try to."

"Has someone tried to force it on someone in the past?"

"Didn't you ever listen to anything Dad told us?"

She crinkled her nose. "You were going to take over his job, and Myra's serious enough about this stuff for all three of us. I figured if there was something I should know, you'd fill me in on it."

"Yes. Someone tried forcing a god power on a mortal who had refused it, and it went very, very bad, very, very fast."

"How bad?"

"Bubonic plague bad. As in, it started the plague."

She sucked air in through her teeth. "Well, let's not do that. So you need to talk to Cooper, right?"

"First I need out of the hospital. Then I need to talk to Cooper."

"You're staying here overnight."

I whined.

"Delaney," she said sternly. "You were shot. Then you got in a bar fight. Then you wrestled a suspect who ripped your stitches and added bruises to your bruises. You're staying in the hospital until tomorrow morning. And it will only be Sunday. Plenty of time to find Cooper and give him the god power."

"Unless it's not his."

"It will be a good place to start, and you'll still have two days left if it isn't."

"Or maybe it is his and he'll turn it down anyway."

"You really think Cooper Clark, a man with an ego the size of Jupiter, would turn down the chance to be a god?"

"It's not just a power. It's a commitment. Heimdall was the god who was supposed to sound the alarm on Ragnarok. He is the ever-vigilant, eyes-on-the-horizon, doing-good-for-his-brethren kind of god. His power is about waiting patiently, and being there when someone needs him. Cooper's more of a cut-and-run kind of guy."

She frowned. I wasn't wrong.

"If anyone could talk him into it, it would be you."

"I'm not so sure about that. I did hit him in the face."

"You should be ashamed of yourself. Not calling me first so I could watch."

I shook my head and smiled. "Did anyone tell Chris about Margot?"

Her smile slipped and she glanced at the floor then back at me. "You don't need to worry about that right now, Delaney."

"I'll take that as a 'no,' then? You should tell him, or have Myra do it. He needs to know. Heim was his friend and he was dating Margot, or really, she was using him to get access to Heim. He'll need someone to tell him it's not his fault."

"We'll make sure he knows." She patted my arm. "Stop working, would you? Get some sleep."

I didn't want to. But it had been a long day and I'd used up my reserves. "You don't have to stay."

She chuckled. "We tried that once, remember? You're a flight risk." She arranged my blanket to cover my feet more evenly then patted my leg. "I'll be over here if you need anything."

I lowered the bed and shifted around until I got comfortable.

Jean picked up her phone and grinned at the screen before she tapped at it with her thumbs.

I knew what had put that look on her face. "Say hi to Hogan for me."

She just snorted and curled up around her phone, her back toward me as if I were going to spy on her texts.

I watched her for a minute, a wash of melancholy filling me. I loved seeing her happy and excited in the beginning stages of a relationship. But seeing her so happy and relaxed just made me wonder how it had all gone wrong with Ryder.

The sex had been good.

No, it had been great. Fun and easy. My fantasy of what it might be like to be with Ryder had been thoroughly exceeded.

It was the after-sex part where things had fallen apart.

Old Rossi had warned me he was trouble. Old Rossi had been right.

I closed my watery eyes.

I'd been hoping for more. For a chance to explore…him, explore us. Explore what we could be together.

But that wasn't in the cards. That wasn't what he wanted. Ryder Bailey wasn't the man I thought he was.

The image of him busting into the station, armed and ready to throw down, was hot, yes. Undeniably hot. And the worry in his eyes when I'd been bleeding. The anger that had quickly looked like regret until he stowed it away. All that added up to…what?

Confusion. Ryder Bailey confused me.

Ryder Bailey didn't want me.

And I didn't want him.

Liar.

I ignored my heart and let the painkillers take me gently into sleep.

CHAPTER 29

IT HAD taken until Sunday afternoon for me to be discharged from the hospital. I couldn't prove that they were dragging their feet to make me pay for checking myself out early before. But after repeated reminders that I was injured, and should not be left on my own because I was likely to just re-injure myself, I got the hint.

Myra strolled into the lobby just as I was finally holding my release papers and trying to decide who I was going to call for a ride.

"Home?" she asked.

"I want a shower and a change of clothes."

She was quiet as we walked out to the cruiser. After we were both inside her car, I asked, "What's wrong?"

She started the engine and maneuvered out into traffic. "We can't find Cooper."

A chill ran through me as the power twisted. "What?"

"Jean told me you thought Cooper would be the right fit for Heimdall's power. So I went to find him. He's gone."

"What do you mean, gone? How gone?"

"We think he left town yesterday. The last person who saw him said he had his backpack over his shoulder and was walking north."

"Hell," I breathed.

"We'll figure it out," she said. "I put out an APB. If he's hitching, we'll find him once he hits a town."

I knew we'd find him. Eventually. But I only had two days left before this god power would no longer remain on hold. I had to find someone to give it to by tomorrow. After that, the power would tear Ordinary and all of its inhabitants apart.

"Okay. I think we need a plan B."

"What do you have in mind?"

"I need to be around as many people as possible. Maybe there's someone else the power will respond to. But first I want clean clothes."

THE RALLY was busy even though it was early evening by the time Myra and I made it to the festival. The weather was mild and clear, and the strings of lights hung off wooden arches and booths created a canopy of glowing color, lending an irresistible magic to the place.

Rides roared and hissed and burbled with music on the south end of the rally. We made our way slowly past those, in between the even-noisier carnival games where a few folks called out and waved to Myra and me.

I'd taken the time to shower at home and changed into comfortable jeans, Converse, and a sweater. I'd wasted a few extra minutes in my bedroom, staring at the blankets still messy from the night with Ryder, his cologne lingering on my sheets. The little origami Spud still rested on his pillow. I should've just thrown it away.

Instead, I'd picked up the tiny dog and tucked it into my purse.

Memories of the night flowed through me. Honesty in the darkness, need and release and pleasure. We had both wanted that. Wanted each other. How had the daylight turned it into lies? "Good a place as any. Let's rest." Myra's voice pulled me out of my reverie. We had wandered past the food stalls, which were centrally located along the main pathway. Picnic tables, chairs, and benches gathered in the area.

"I'm not hurt that bad," I grumbled.

She gave me a look and pointed at the bench. "I'll believe that when you aren't the color of paste."

"Sparkly paste?" I eased down onto the bench, trying not to favor my side.

She snorted. "Want something to eat?"

I drummed my fingers on the table and grinned at her. "You always try to feed people to make them feel better."

"Please." She rolled her eyes.

"No, it's kind of sweet. Mom used to do that."

Her eyes drifted over my shoulder. "I remember that."

Mom had been gone for fifteen years. Myra had been ten years old when she died. I'd been thirteen, and as the oldest, probably had the most memories of her. Still, as time went on, more and more details of her had faded and blurred.

"You remind me of her sometimes," I said gently.

Myra finally shifted her gaze to me. "I miss her." Her normally guarded eyes swam with emotion.

I nodded, not knowing what to say to make it better. I settled on the truth. "Me too."

She swallowed, then pulled her composed, cool mask back on. I watched as her eyes reverted to their icy blue. It made me realize I hadn't seen a lot of my sister—the sister behind the cool mask of her job and duty—lately. "She always made me think there was nothing I couldn't tackle. She never gave up. On anything."

I nodded.

"You remind me of her sometimes too," she said quietly.

A crowd of teen boys barreled through the picnic area, arms over each other's shoulders, pointing at the sky and chanting, "We're number one!" then yelling the Barnacle cheer.

Myra and I both gave them a quick look. All noise, no real trouble. They climbed over and on top of a picnic table and starting arguing about who was going to buy the corn dogs and chili fries.

"Could be one of them," Myra suggested.

I chuckled. "I hope not. I'd hate to ruin their lives."

She finally sat next to me, her shoulder brushing mine. "Are you kidding? What teenager wouldn't want to be a god?"

"True. In that case, I hope not, because I'd hate to ruin our lives."

She grinned. "Amen, sister."

We sat there crowd-watching, me listening for any change in the power as hundreds of people strolled past. Other than a runaway puppy Myra helped catch, it was a pretty easy way to spend four hours.

But by the end of it, I hadn't felt an unusual attraction or volume change in the power. Just to make sure, we'd walked all the way north to the crafting and selling booths to check out the behind-the-counter venders, strolled through the main hall, and then loitered at the exit to parking. I'd been near every person in attendance.

Nothing.

MYRA TURNED off the engine of the cruiser in the drive below my house.

"I still think you should come home with me instead."

It was midnight, and I had my elbow propped on the edge of the window, my fingers over my eyebrows, as if even the moonlight was too much.

It wasn't the moonlight. I was tired, aching, and the song in my head was grating at me so much that I thought bamboo spears under my fingernails would be more pleasant.

"I really want my bed tonight. Yes, I promise to take my pills," I said before she could remind me. "And yes, I'll call before I come into the station tomorrow." I opened the door and got out of the car without groaning too loudly.

She shifted her left hand on the steering wheel and dipped her head so she could see me through the passenger door. "We'll find Cooper. I promise."

I gave her a thumbs-up and a smile I didn't really feel. "Call me as soon as you do, okay?"

She nodded and I shut the door. I stood there a moment watching her drive away, then my gaze tracked to the bushes where Margot had recently hidden to shoot me.

A chill ran over my skin along with that memory. It was going to take a while for me to feel secure here again. But I knew I'd manage. One step at a time.

"If this stupid power doesn't kill me first," I muttered.

The power seemed to rouse at that thought, filling up all the spaces in my brain where my own thoughts should be.

I pushed back, tired, but determined. Then started up the stairs to my house, one step at a time.

CHAPTER 30

I MADE an appointment with Death. We met early Monday morning at a little coffee shop called the Perky Perch that had once been a tiny, out-of-place Victorian cottage overlooking the ocean.

Yesterday's good weather seemed to be holding, although there was a heavy fog shrouding the horizon where the gray of the ocean met the blue of the sky.

Today, in less than twenty-four hours, Heimdall's power would break out of me and tear the town apart. And while I would love to say we'd find Cooper in time, I knew Cooper. When he wanted to disappear, he did exactly that.

Thanatos strolled into the small space and seemed amused by the cozy interior and oceanfront views. He was wearing a slim black T-shirt with sedate gray letters that said, ORDINARY MAN. Instead of the Hawaiian shirts he'd seemed so fond of, he was wearing a knit forest-green cardigan with a subtle repeating pattern that looked like rows of bunnies engaged in butt sex.

I stifled a grin and wondered where he was finding these things. Better yet, I wondered who was taking advantage of his newly mortal self and was selling him these things.

He saw me at the table and crossed the small room to sit in the chair across from me.

"Good morning, Delaney Reed," he said in his smooth and cultured voice. "Have you ordered my drink?"

"I did. They serve a hot chocolate that will make you sing."

He glanced down his nose at the mug on the table in front of him. "I see."

I sipped my coffee and waited to see if he would try it. He drew the mug across the table, cradling the warmth in his palm. "Are we here to discuss the merits of chocolate, or my singing voice, Reed Daughter?"

"Well, neither," I said. "I have a favor to ask you."

He lifted the mug and took a sip. He blinked, his black gaze riveted to mine, his stare incredibly intense.

I waited. "Feel a song coming on, Than?"

His lips twitched at one corner. "Not in the least."

I pointed at him. "That's what we mortals call a lie."

He blinked again and rested the mug against his palm. "I am curious as to this favor."

I wiped my hands on my jeans, slicking away the sweat there. It wasn't particularly warm in the shop, but I felt like everything inside me was vibrating with the rhythm of the song in my head. It was like having the worst case of nerves, while also running a marathon. I felt shaky, a little nauseated, and overstimulated.

"I want to know the repercussions of my death."

He held still in a way I'd seen very few people manage. Then he drew the mug back to his mouth and took another sip.

I felt the silence stretch out, and decided I didn't have enough time left to wait for anything. Not even Death.

"Specifically, I want to know what happens if you kill me while I'm containing a god power."

"Specifically," he said.

"Specifically."

"It would be a great disappointment to me, Reed Daughter. I would miss you. Specifically."

"Oh," I said softly. I swallowed against the mix of emotions. It was kind of him to say that. But kindness—if that was what that was—wouldn't solve my problem.

"I...I need to know if my death would somehow keep the god power from tearing apart the town. If I die holding it, containing it, will it slow it down? Stop it?"

"I am not the guardian of power. That burden your family alone must bear."

I laced my fingers on the tabletop and nodded. "I know. I know you're not an expert in guarding powers. But you know your power like no other being. I want to know if Death can kill a power."

He sat back, his face almost serene with wonder as his dark eyes studied me like I were something he had never seen before.

"Such a thing..." he whispered with hollow longing.

"Is that a yes?"

He shook his head slightly, bemused wonder still relaxing his features. "I do not know."

"Crap." I slumped against the back of my chair. "There goes my nuclear option."

He sat up straight again, his fingertips stroking the curve of the mug before he slipped his fingers through the handle. It seemed to be an unconscious motion, but the way he did it made me think he was petting a cat.

Or a bunny.

I tipped my head a bit to get a better look at the repeating pattern in his sweater.

Yep. That was one hundred percent bunny loving going on.

"What I can assume from your question is that you are no longer confident that you can bridge the power to its mortal vessel. Is that correct?"

"Confidence in my ability isn't really the problem," I said, even though, yes, I was worried that I wouldn't do that part right too. "The problem is I think the mortal vessel has skipped town before I could give him the power."

"And why would he do that?"

"I kind of punched him in the face."

Than tipped his chin and blinked quickly. "That is... I see," he said. "And who do you believe is to take on the mantle of Heimdall?"

"Cooper Clark."

"What actions have you taken to find him?"

"We put out an all-points bulletin. Every cop on the West Coast is looking for him."

"Yes. Of course." He lifted his mug again, drank. This time he hummed just a little after he swallowed.

"Was that a happy hum?" I said. "It sounded musical."

He ignored me. "Which non-mortal actions have you taken to find him?"

I blinked. "What?"

His eyes hardened with something that looked an awful lot like glee. "You have a town of vacationing gods who could easily regain their powers for a brief time. At least one among them must be a hunter. And then there are the vampires who seem quite capable in scenting familiar blood, the werewolves who are quite possibly even better hunters than the gods or vampires, and any number of far-seeing and divining creatures and deities who may offer some small amount of use."

I stood so quickly that the table shook. Than lifted his hot cocoa to safety before it spilled.

"I can't believe I didn't think of that." Yes, the gods had offered to help, but I'd assumed they meant something with lightning bolts and locus curses. It never crossed my mind to drag them into the very mundane action of tracking down a runaway.

"You are a beautiful genius!" I stopped beside him and impulsively planted a kiss on his cheek.

He grunted, but his mouth curved up what might, almost, in the right light, pass for a smile.

"Yes," he said, smoothing his features until he appeared uninterested and irritated. "I am."

I waved over my shoulder and hurried out of the Perky Perch.

Just as I hit the parking lot and was trying to get my keys out of my pocket, Myra pulled up in her cruiser. She rolled down the window. "I thought you were going to call this morning and come in to work."

I held up my hand to tell her to hold on, and walked over to the passenger side of the cruiser. She popped the lock so I could get in.

"What's wrong?" she asked.

"Nope. What's right. I need you to get me to Bertie. Fast."

Myra had the car in gear and the lights on before I even had my seatbelt buckled.

And for the first time in a week, I thought we might actually be one step ahead of this disaster.

WE CAUGHT up with Bertie in front of her house just as she was walking out to her car. Having a sister who always showed up at the right time really came in handy.

Bertie hadn't wanted to take any time out of her very tight schedule to deal with us, but we promised we would let her get back to the final wind-down of the Rhubarb Rally, which seemed to involve an awful lot of costume judging, dancing, and something with eggs I didn't quite catch.

"And the breakdown will last until at least nine tonight..." Bertie said.

"All I need is a basic schedule of some of deits and creats," I said.

She paused in her rambling list of complaints. "What did you just call us, Delaney Reed?"

"It's just cop talk... Look. I know you're busy. But if I don't find Cooper *very* soon, there will be no town left for the next Rhubarb Rally."

She frowned. "Is the power giving you that much trouble? Your father always seemed to handle his duties without interrupting the festivals."

"He had a little more experience. I'm sure there were a few times, maybe when he was new to this, that things went less than smoothly."

She stared at me with those hawk eyes, like I'd just said the last wrong thing.

"Did he speak to you of those things?"

The way she said it, so measured and calm, was more frightening than if she'd yelled at me.

"No. I was just guessing."

She shook her head, and some of the stiffness melted out of her body. "Let's not waste time. Come inside. I can draw up the information you need."

She strode up her carefully tended walkway, the rolling stone river garden on either side flickering with shiny glass orbs, clever little stone structures, and just the right amount of herbs and tough succulents mimicking waterside plants and flowers.

"Shut the door," Bertie said when we'd entered the foyer. "Come back to my office."

We did as we were told and were standing next to her tidy wooden desk in her tidy, but thoroughly modern, office.

"What do you need to know?" she asked.

"The schedules of anyone who would be willing to help me hunt down Cooper. I'm thinking some of the Rossis, the Wolfes, maybe Crow or Odin, or someone who has some kind of tracking skill."

"With or without their power?" she asked.

"Easiest without. That's where the vamps and weres come in. But if I can talk a god into taking on their power for a limited time, and talk Crow into releasing it for them, that would work too."

"And you expect me to know each of these individuals' current schedules and predilections?" she asked archly.

"Don't you?" Myra drawled.

She sniffed. "Yes," she said. "I do."

Her golden-tipped fingers flew across the keyboard, and she'd plucked information out of a variety of folders, compiled it all into one document, and pressed "print" in less than a minute.

"Now, ladies," she said, as she stood and smoothed her hand down her tailored suit jacket. "I wish you both good fortune in finding your prey." She held the single sheet of paper out to me. It was a list of over two dozen people in Ordinary, ranked from most willing and able to assist to the least. "If you still haven't found Cooper by this evening, do come see me again."

She gestured to the doorway, and Myra and I startled back into motion and made our way to the front door.

"Thank you for this," I said, pausing on the porch while she locked the door. "It will really help."

"I know it will, dear," she said, patting my arm. "Everything is going to be just fine."

She brushed past us, and was in her car and headed off to the rally before we'd even made it down her front path.

"Remind me never to let her run for political office," I said.

Myra chuckled. "Oh, I don't know. She'd clean up the town in a week and be ruling the world in a month flat. Now that you have the list, what's the plan?"

"We go to the station, get Jean in on this, and raise ourselves a posse."

CHAPTER 31

"YOU WANT us to hunt down your ex-boyfriend," Odin said matter-of-factly. "And kill him."

"No!" I said for the third time. "Not kill him. Yes, find him."

We had gathered at the station. Roy was here to hold down the fort, and Ryder had been given the day off. Until further notice. I was surprised Myra had been that gentle on him.

We'd gone down the list, crossed out a few people we knew weren't really "team players," and had settled on calling in an even ten.

Out of those ten, eight people had showed up: Ben Rossi and Jame Wolfe, who both still looked like firefighters even though they were in jeans and T-shirts, the twins Senta and Page Rossi, and the gods Odin, Thorne, Crow, and Herri.

The fact that the gods were there meant a lot to me. What I was asking of them—to pick up their god powers and help me—didn't come at a small price.

Once a god picked up their power, they were off vacation and had to leave Ordinary for a year, just enough time for this old world to circle the sun from point A to point A. It wasn't a part of the contract the gods signed to get into Ordinary; it was just the way god power worked.

I'd asked Dad about it once and he'd shrugged. There were things about god power even we Reeds couldn't understand.

Crow had agreed to unlock the three gods' powers, and his, as soon as we made a plan for how to find Cooper. I didn't think any god had ever given up their vacation time for a Reed. Or at least Dad had never spoken of it.

Which meant this was a really, really big favor. One I didn't know how I'd repay.

"No killing," I repeated.

"You don't have to worry about them, Delaney," Jame said with a predatory flash of his teeth. "The day a god can out-hunt a Wolfe is the day I give it up and move to Cabo."

"Better tell your boyfriend to pack his sunscreen, then," Thorne said.

Thorne wasn't actually Odin's son, or maybe in a way he actually was. Thorne had picked up Thor's god power about eighty years ago, and he and Odin had come rumbling into town and taken their first vacation together. Thorne had taken to Thor's power with an instant delight, as happened with most people newly godded. He even looked every inch the tall, powerful, yellow-haired Norse warrior, and always called Odin father.

His day job was owning and running the music and record store in town.

Ben sucked on the back of one fang, staring at Thorne like he was considering a Merlot to go with dinner. "Want to put some money on who's going to bring Cooper down?"

"Nobody's going to bring Cooper down," I said. "He comes back alive."

"Yes," Thorne said, "of course. We shall bring the quarry in without a scratch. How much money do you have, Firefang? Enough to make this interesting?"

"No," I said, "we will not make anything interesting while we hunt for my ex-boyfriend."

"Make what interesting?" Crow, who could sense a bad bet going down a mile away, had to join in.

"Just a friendly little bet," Ben said with a smile that would freeze a mortal in place. Unfortunately, neither Crow nor Thorne were mortal.

"Between friends," Thorne agreed. "My father and I against you and your boyfriend."

"Gentlemen, please," Crow scolded. "Money makes for a boring bet."

"Shoulder devil." I scowled at Crow.

Crow winked and gave me a big grin.

"Doesn't have to be money." Ben licked his lips, his eyes flicking to the side of Thorne's neck as if he were imagining sinking his fangs in all the way to bone. The other Rossis in the room chuckled and Jame shifted to press his wide hand on Ben's lower back, maybe reminding him that if there was going to be someone getting bit, it was going to be his lover, not some random thunder god.

"You don't have the stomach for it, bloodboy," Thorne scoffed.

Jame growled. Ben glowered.

Crow snickered.

"You're the one who needs daddy at his side," Ben said.

Odin snorted and shook his head, his arms crossed over his chest. "Thorne doesn't need me to win his fights."

"If we don't believe you?" Crow mocked.

"Boys," Herri said, sighing, "reel it in. You can cheat each other blind or bite each other bloody, or beat each other boneless after we find Cooper."

"No biting," Jame growled, his hand fisting in the back of Ben's shirt. "That's off the table."

Both Ben and Thorne huffed like little kids who'd just been told to clean their rooms.

"Name your price—" Thorne started.

"What's the plan, Delaney?" Herri asked.

I threw her a grateful look.

Myra spoke up. "The last person who saw Cooper said he was hitching north out of town. That was a day ago. He could be in Canada by now."

"How long have you got before *boom*?" Sage tipped her blonde head my way.

I didn't point out that she made it sound like it was a death sentence. I didn't point it out because she was not wrong.

"Today. The power needs to be in a new vessel by midnight tonight."

"Plenty of time," she said. "We'll find him, Delaney." She smiled, showing a lot less fang than Ben, a dimple popping in her cheek.

"Do you have a successor in place?" Odin asked casually.

That was the other big consequence I'd been avoiding. I hadn't trained anyone else in how to be a bridge for god power. Myra and Jean hadn't shown any signs of being someone who could pick up those duties. Though the ability always passed down the Reed bloodline, we were the only Reeds in Ordinary.

That didn't mean we were the only Reeds in the world, though.

"If I go down, someone will show up on Ordinary's doorstep, confused, and needing some guidance for how to re-vessel a power gone rogue. I expect you all to be very helpful to him or her."

"Not gonna happen," Crow said. "We might gain a new Reed—maybe even one with a sense of humor—but we'd lose our police chief. Then who would we make pity-judge the rhubarb contest?"

I reached out and slapped him on the back of the head.

He laughed and rubbed at his head, backing out of my reach.

"Do we split up?" Jame asked.

"Yes," everyone in the room answered almost simultaneously.

"Except for Thorne and his daddy, of course," Jame added.

Odin sighed.

"Okay," I said, trying to head off a fistfight. "Stay in contact. Use cell phones." I nodded to the gods. "And thank you all for giving up your final day at the Rhubarb Rally to help me with this."

That was met by a room full of confused looks.

"Why would we stay for the rally?" Odin grumbled. "Someone already won the sculpture contest with that ridiculous Rhu-ban the Barb-barian atrocity."

Jame and Ben laughed. "Yes, we did, didn't we?" Ben's grin was smug. "You're getting old, god."

Odin glared at him, storm and fury and wrath—every inch the god he was. Then a very small smile curved the corner of his lips. "You have no idea. Are you sure there's no killing?" he said to me.

"No killing at all."

Odin shook his head, then slapped Thorne on his beefy shoulder. "Not hardly worth my time if there isn't going to be blood. Delaney, I'll sit this one out."

He gave Thorne a pointed look, which he then turned on Jame and Ben. "I'm sure you can handle this just fine without me."

Great. I'd already lost one god to a petty squabble.

"All right," I said.

"You go on without me, son," Odin said to Thorne.

Thorne grinned, his eyes glinting with some kind of shared joke between them. "I'll see you in a year, Father."

Odin grinned back. "Say hello to the old world for me."

Crow flattened his hand over his chest. "Such a touching farewell. Can we just get on with it already?"

MYRA REFUSED to let me go alone anywhere, much less north toward Tillamook, and it would have been a waste of time to argue with her, since she was driving. The gods and creatures had scattered, promising to be thorough and non-deadly in their search.

"Think Odin really only wanted to come if there was bloodshed?" Myra asked.

I stared out through the Douglas fir, hemlock, and sword ferns that crowded the side of the road.

"I think he and Thorne had some agreement about who gave up their vacation first. Probably some bet he won."

"Poker?"

"Or that croquet game they started up a couple months ago."

"Croquet." Her voice held a level of disbelief we Reeds really should be done with by now. "Thor and Odin. Wickets and tiny mallets?"

"Tiny hammers," I corrected with mock gravity. "They play it on the beach over at the cove. Apparently you can hear the swearing and insults for miles. A few of the other gods have joined in. I heard rumblings about starting a league. It's serious business."

"As long as no one dies," she said.

That brought on a heavy silence.

"If we don't find Cooper in time…" I said as Myra kept her eyes on the twisting road that rolled through cow farms and forested hills.

"We'll find him."

"If we don't," I said, a little more firmly, "I don't want you or Jean trying to pick up the power."

She was quiet. After another mile or so, she took in a short breath. "Do you really think Jean and I could stand on the sidelines while our home and the people we care for are being eaten by a god power that our family has vowed to guard?"

"No," I said quietly. "But I think you could leave. Get out of the blast zone."

"You aren't paying attention, Delaney. You know we'd never walk away in a disaster."

"I know." I rubbed my eyes. The headache had gotten much worse with the song of power and exhausting pressure.

"We would never walk away from you," she said.

The truth of that made my chest tight.

"Idiot. We love you. We are not going to lose you."

The pressure in my chest eased, and I closed my eyes against the overwhelming prickling of tears I refused to give in to. I sniffed and nodded. I was pretty sure I was the worst keeper of power in the history of the keepers of powers, but having Myra and Jean—my sisters, my family—at my back meant everything to me.

I rubbed at my eyes again, drawing away the wetness, and leaned my head against the window, hand propped over my eyebrows to shield the bright light. "Thanks."

"You hurting?" she asked after another mile of silence.

"Some. Headache."

"Sunglasses in the glove box."

I reached forward and pulled out a spare pair of Aviators. I slipped them on, sighing a little at the relief. It wasn't a lot, but any little bit helped.

"Take your pills?"

"I did. I think this is more Heimdall's power being pissy than my injury being sore."

"Too bad we don't have something for that," she said.

"Power Vicodin?"

She shrugged. "Or someone in the family who can ease pain."

"Like that's a real thing."

"There have been people in the Reed line who were healers."

"Dad tell you that?"

She nodded. "He left me a lot of family history books."

I chewed on the inside of my cheek, thinking about how that made me feel. Good, I decided. Out of the three of us girls, Myra was serious and patient enough to actually sift through old records. "I'm glad," I finally said.

"I know it's usually passed down to the eldest…"

"I'm glad," I said again, patting her leg. "Dad had good instincts. He knew when to break the rules."

"Good news," Crow said from the back seat.

Myra swerved. I yelped and half turned, while I grabbed for a gun I didn't have on me.

"What the hell, Crow?"

He sat in the back seat where he'd just appeared, a canary-eating grin on his face. "God power. You should try it sometime, Delaney. It's just all sorts of fun."

Myra cussed quietly through clenched teeth. She had gotten the car back into our lane, which was good, because there were only two lanes on this part of the old highway.

"If you ever do that again," Myra said, "I will kill you, Crow."

He chuckled. "Don't you want to hear my good news?"

I planted my hand over my side. I was pretty sure I'd ripped a stitch or two. It was bleeding again.

"It better be that you found Cooper and he's waiting for us in a nice, quiet room, ready to take on the god power," I said.

He threw his hands up in the air. "Yes! That's it exactly. How did you guess?"

"Really?" I searched his face.

Crow smiled, and some of the mischief faded under a warmth I'd seen many times since I was a kid. "Really."

A dizzy wash of relief rolled through me, and I grinned. "Holy shit. You're amazing! Where is he?"

"The casino."

"Which casino?" Myra asked.

"Our casino. Just outside of town."

Myra immediately flicked on the blinker, pulled onto the narrow shoulder, and did a U-turn to get us heading south.

"Is someone there with him? Someone who can make sure he won't run?" I asked.

"Hera, Jame, and Ben all stayed."

"Good. Have you told Jean?"

"Thor said he'd mention it to her."

I glanced at the clock in the console. "So we're, what? About an hour away?"

"Or a second," Crow said.

I glanced at him again. He had his arms crossed over his chest, looking entirely too pleased with himself.

"You'd do that for us?"

He nodded. "It's been a while since I've stretched my wings and used power, you know." He somehow made it sound dirty. "It feels real good. Makes me want to do all sorts of things to you innocent mortals."

He winked at me, and the light that flickered in his eyes was not the warmth and humor I usually saw from my friend. The man in the back seat of the cruiser wasn't Crow. Or at least he wasn't just Crow. This was Raven, the trickster, the god.

And if there was one thing I knew, it was that gods in the wild were dangerous, temperamental creatures.

"Do I need to draw up a contract with you first?" I asked. "To make sure that you will only do the things that I actually want you to do?"

He rolled his eyes toward the ceiling of the car and sighed. When his gaze ticked back down to me, the odd god power light was a little dimmer and the eyes of my friend were brighter.

"While it's very, *very* tempting to say yes and spend some time bargaining you into a contract, I think you should just trust me on this one."

"Like a stupid, innocent mortal?"

He leaned forward, fighting back a smirk. "Or a brave one. Trust me, Delaney. You know you want to."

I glanced at Myra. She studied Raven in the rearview mirror, then looked away to catch my gaze. "Go."

"Okay. Take me to Cooper."

"My pleasure." He winked.

We were standing in a carpeted hallway of the casino, the sound of piped music and games rattling in the background.

I'd never been manhandled by god power before. It wasn't settling well.

"Delaney?" Raven tipped his head to make eye contact.

I leaned against the wall, one palm flat against it to keep me standing, the other cupped around my ribs. "Don't come any closer. I might yark on you."

He sucked in a breath. "Right. The Reed family immunity. I forgot. Probably shouldn't let a god power do anything drastic with you for the next few hours."

I straightened and took better stock of my surroundings. No one else was in the hall, and there was a closed door right next to me. "No problem. It's going to take me that long to talk Cooper into this."

I reached for the door just as it swung inward.

Jame Wolfe stood in front of me, his head tipped to the side like a puppy that had heard a strange noise. His warm eyes flicked over to Raven, and he tipped his head the other way.

"Hey, Jame," I said. "Gonna let me in there?"

"Sure." He stood aside, his eyes following Raven, his shoulder hunched up like he was ready to fight. I thought this might be the first time he'd ever seen Crow carrying power.

The conference room had a bank of windows with the blinds closed, a dark wood table down the center of it, and a vampire, a goddess, and my ex-boyfriend seated in the comfortable swivel chairs around it.

The power in me rang out with a shout, a chorus, reaching.

Hera nodded as I walked in. She looked different carrying her power too. A sort of regal air clung to her, even though she was still wearing her jeans and leather jacket. Ben stared at Raven and licked his bottom lip, a quick flash of fang pressing there, his eyes flickering with a hungry glow before he looked away.

Okay, we were all a little tense. A little off our normal footing.

Especially Cooper, who not only had a hell of a black eye, but was also glowering at me.

"What the hell is this all about, Delaney?" he demanded. "You send out your...your hitmen to kidnap me? This is taking crazy ex-girlfriend to the next level, don't you think?"

"Kidnap? Where did Crow find you?"

"*We* found him," Ben corrected. "Here, at the casino, rehearsing for the show."

"Escorting you down to a conference room isn't kidnapping," Jame rumbled.

"Keeping me here is," Cooper said. "There's a band. For me to be in that band, I have to rehearse with it, not sit in a conference room with people who won't answer my questions."

"Give me a minute with him alone, please," I said.

Hera's voice was smooth and alluring. "I would rather we stay with you."

I held open the door, not falling for the bedazzlement she was oozing. The Reed family immunity was good for that. "I'll call you all back after we talk, and he has a chance to make his decision."

They all filed out past me. I pointed at Raven. "No eavesdropping."

He pressed his fingertips to his chest and made an offended sound.

I shut the door in his face and heard his muffled cackle.

The song of power was louder, a chorus of voices clashing and shattering into breathtaking harmonies.

If Cooper wasn't the right person to take Heim's power, he sure did have a way of stirring it up. I could barely hear myself think through it.

"What is going on, Delaney?" Cooper asked again.

I sat in the chair next to him, swiveling it to face him.

"Okay, I need you to hear me out on this, Coop."

He shut his mouth and blinked hard a couple times. It had been a long time since I'd called him by his nickname.

"There are things about Ordinary that you don't know. You might have suspected them when you were little, or in those odd moments when there wasn't an easy logical explanation for weird things that you saw or heard."

This was the speech my Dad had given more than once. But my nerves were wired so tight, I thought maybe Cooper

297

could hear the blood rushing through my head, the song leaking out my ears. I'd never had to explain this to other people.

I'd never had the lives of all the people in town hanging on if I was able to convince someone of the impossible.

"Ordinary was founded many hundreds of years ago. Before America was called by that name. This little stretch of beach was chosen as a vacation place for people, for beings, who carry power. Those people set aside their powers while they vacationed here. Their idea of a vacation was to be mortal and live a normal, ordinary life.

"Some of those people have come back every year, or just stayed on in Ordinary and lived a long...very long time. You know them. You grew up with them. Crow, Herri, Odin, Frigg. They carry great power, except for when they're inside Ordinary's boundaries. Outside of Ordinary, they are gods."

I swallowed and wiped my hands on my jeans, waiting to see how he would react to that.

"That's...impossible," he said quietly.

"Almost impossible." I patted the air in front of me, begging for his patience. "These people—these gods—are vulnerable when they vacation in Ordinary. They not only live a mortal life, they are also actually mortal. Which means they can catch colds, break legs, fall in love. And they can be killed.

"But their power cannot be killed. When a god dies, that power must be picked up by a new person. A mortal person. Someone with the strength, endurance, and dedication to carry that power and all the burdens and joys that come with it."

His lips were pressed together in a tight line. He was scowling, his eyes intense. "It can't be true."

"It is."

Time ticked out between us.

"Remember junior year?" I said. "Spring? The Barnacles were playing the Smelts and weather was supposed to be a downpour?"

He nodded. He played second base for the Barnacles. I knew he'd remember.

"We got three inches of rain that day. The entire town flooded. But not the baseball field. It hardly sprinkled there."

"Wha—"

"Thor. He had a bet riding on the outcome, picked up his power, and influenced the weather."

"That was just a freak storm."

"That was a god. The bus crash?" I said before he could argue. "Elementary school kids going on a field trip to the zoo. That eighteen-wheeler smashed head-on into the bus at sixty miles an hour. Should have killed them all. Everyone walked away without a scratch, including both drivers."

"Who?" he asked.

"Bast. She was driving to a hair appointment and saw it coming. Drew on her power. Saved those children."

"But... Jesus."

"Hasn't come by as far as I know. The mudslide that should have wiped out half the town, but somehow missed every house, did no damage to the roads, and instead left behind a rather nice waterfall and hiking trail? Nilus wanted a new park. The lighthouse—"

"Okay. There's been some weird stuff."

I nodded.

"But gods? In Ordinary? In this crummy town?"

"In this crummy town."

"Crow and Herri?" he asked.

"And others. Aaron, Kim. Um...Zeus and Odin, obviously." I rolled my eyes. "Heim," I added, a little more softly.

"But Heim's dead."

"I know. His power isn't. That's why I'm here. It's my job to make sure his power is picked up by a mortal worthy of it. A mortal who will become a god."

"That comes with the badge?" he asked.

"Nope. That comes with being a Reed. I think you came back to this crummy town for this. For power."

"I came back because I thought I left something behind."

"I think you're right."

He rocked back in his chair and rubbed his hands over his face. When he dropped his palms, his smile was still confused. "I'd be crazy to believe you."

My stomach dropped and all the butterflies turned into razor blades. There wasn't much time left. What could I say to make him believe me? I opened my mouth, not ready to give up. He spoke before I could.

"But I've always been a little crazy, right?" He grinned.

I exhaled a shaky breath. "Yeah, you have, Coop. It's one of the things I like about you." My hand trembled as I dragged it back through my hair. "So what do you think about becoming a god?"

I could practically see the gears in his head working through hope, fear, lust, doubt, and a chaos of other emotions.

"Me?" he finally said.

"You."

"What...what kind of god?"

"Heimdall's power is one of protection. He is the watcher of the gods, the sentinel with his eyes on the horizon, the one who will warn the other gods of war, of the end of times, of Ragnarok."

"He's the amber alert god?"

I grinned. "He's whatever it is you make the power become. He has a magical horn. And he was in that superhero movie."

"I haven't seen it."

"You should. Heimdall was badass. Hot."

"Yeah?" His grin was back.

I resisted rolling my eyes at him again. "You know this isn't a movie, though. You will have responsibilities you can't ignore. For all of your life, which might be very, very long. It's a big commitment and one you have to step into willingly. It will change everything."

He shifted in his chair, fingers gripping his knees as he leaned forward. "Tell me honestly that you're not bullshitting me, Delaney."

"God power is real. I think you're strong enough to take one on. I think...I think that's what you came back into town for. What you were really looking for. Not me. You were looking for the power that belongs to you. I am not bullshitting you. All you have to do is say yes, and the power will be yours and then you'll know I'm telling the truth."

He held his breath, his eyes searching my gaze, no longer lingering on my mouth.

I tipped my head. "Breathe, Cooper," I said gently, reaching over toward him. "You've still got a little time to decide. To think this through."

I pressed my palm against his hand on his knees, and the shock of that connection rocked through me.

A small moan escaped his lips, and I had to catch my breath at what that sound stirred in me. Not an emotional need—or not *my* emotional need. That sound, that desire I could feel rolling off Cooper stirred the power.

And the power was hungry, singing, calling.

For him.

"Do you feel that, Cooper?"

His eyes were glazed with heat. With desire.

"That's the power. Your power, if you'll take it." I kept my hand firmly over his, the contact of our hands strengthening the connection.

All the worries, all the butterflies, all the tension in me was wiped away. Just asking that question, offering the power to someone as my family had done throughout the generations, seemed to settle something in me. It was like climbing a rope and finally reaching a knot I hadn't ever made it to before.

"If I say yes?"

The power's song shifted again. Harmony and trill.

"If you say yes, then you'll need to come back with me to Ordinary. I'll give you the power, and then…" I shrugged.

"And then?" He leaned forward, rolling his hand beneath mine to slot our fingers together.

"And then you're a god," I said.

He stared at my mouth a moment before his gaze lifted to my eyes. "Yes."

The song roared to a stunning single note that swelled with joy. It was so loud I didn't know how everyone in a three-mile radius wasn't hearing it.

I grinned. "Good choice."

CHAPTER 32

DESPITE RAVEN offering to just "snap" us back to Ordinary, I insisted we wait for Myra to arrive. It gave Cooper enough time to quit the band gig, and for me to change the bandage on my side.

Myra showed up just when we'd finished.

Of course.

"Don't forget the housewarming," Ben reminded me as we walked out of the casino and stopped on the sidewalk in front of it. "Saturday."

"I'll be there," I said.

"We'll have beer." Jame threw his arm over Ben, who wore what passed for vampire casual: a beanie, sunglasses, long-sleeved shirt, fingerless gloves, jeans, boots, and a lot of sunscreen. "But bring your own rhubarb."

I grinned and shook my head. Ben slipped his arm around Jame's wider hips, hooking long, pale fingers into his belt loop as they turned and strolled off to Jame's truck. They paused beside it for a quick rock-paper-scissors. I didn't know who won, but Jame opened the passenger door and shoved the slighter man into the cab with a laugh.

"I will be leaving, Delaney," Hera said.

"Who's going to look after the bar?"

"I arranged for my absence." Her eyes hitched up on the horizon. All I saw there were hills thick with trees and a gray sky. I thought she must see a lot more.

"With who?" I figured the least I could do was make sure her bar was cared for while she was gone.

"Chris Lagon. The gill-man."

It was weird for her to talk to me as if I didn't know the people in my town. But then, the god power thrumming through her must be all kinds of distracting.

"Good travels to you," I said, as my father had said many times before. "And when you need a little time off, Ordinary will be waiting."

Her eyes flicked back down to me and the chorus of song flowing around her was enough to stop my breath.

"Thank you, Delaney. If I can, I'll be home soon."

Then Hera simply wasn't there anymore. She was gone. The space she'd been occupying felt strangely hollow and cold.

"Need a ride?" Raven asked.

I glanced over my shoulder. He waved at the motion-sensor camera over the casino doors. The doors refused to open.

"I'll catch a ride with Myra."

"Right, then. See you soon." He took a few steps back from the door, lowered his shoulder, and sprinted toward the big glass doors.

"Don't!" I yelped.

Half a second before he would hit those doors, he disappeared.

His bright laughter drifted away over the ramming beat of my heart.

"Jerk." I didn't know how they were going to explain that on the security tape. Hoped they'd just write it off as a glitch. Or maybe Raven had made sure he wouldn't show up on the tape.

"Let's go." Myra took my arm and guided me over to the cruiser, where Cooper was already waiting.

I got into the front seat, Myra behind the wheel. "Is it settled?"

Cooper nodded in the back seat. "I said yes. I don't know what happens next, but I'm looking forward to it."

I glanced at him in the rearview mirror as Myra took us out to the highway. Power pushed and tumbled in my mind, a thousand songs in one, all of them belonging to Cooper. "So am I."

HEIMDALL'S GOD power wasn't stored in the kiln with the other god powers, since it hadn't been willingly surrendered. But the heavy concentration of god powers in one place would act as a good grounding rod.

And so we were going to do the transfer at Crow's shop.

Jean's truck was in the parking lot, and so was Mykal Rossi's SUV. Mykal was an EMT, and I thought that was a good bit of foresight on Jean's part in case things didn't go as smoothly as we hoped it would.

The neon CLOSED sign glowed in the front window, but Raven opened the door and waved us in. "Long time no see! Come on back to the fire."

Jean pushed past Cooper to give me a big hug. "Good job," she whispered against my cheek as she clung to me.

I rubbed her back. "Save it for when I get this power settled, okay?"

I walked through the main room and back to the old kiln. Mykal stood off to one side, his hard case of medical supplies, a stretcher, and a defibrillator all resting next to his feet.

I gave him a nod and tried not to worry that he, and all his equipment, were here.

He smiled, showing his sharp canines.

Raven stood next to the furnace and Cooper waited in the middle of the room, arms crossed over his chest, looking lost.

I positioned myself in front of him, Myra and Jean standing behind me.

My heart raced so hard I had to do some deep breathing to stay calm.

"Okay. I need to ask you for your agreement officially. Are you ready?"

Cooper unwound his arms and shook his hands out, like getting ready for a wrestling match.

I waited until he nodded.

"Cooper Clark. Will you accept this power, ancient, magnificent, and pure?" It was a short question. I'd memorized it when I was just a kid. But standing here as the bridge for the power in front of the man who would become the vessel for the power gave the words an authority and weight that I'd never imagined.

"Yes," he said. "I accept the power."

I knew there was something else I was supposed to say, but at his agreement, the power leaped.

Leaped out of me, slipped from my hold, and hit Cooper like a lightning bolt out of the sky.

Voices filled the shop, thrumming, shouting, joy and passion. The song, the power, demanded entrance, demanded release. Distantly, I heard my own voice. Small, faint. A whisper among so many others.

I was the connection, the road, the string over which the song of power was plucked. The single point in this world where power and vessel could meet. Join.

I was, for one infinite moment, harmony.

Then silence swallowed me, so dark and soft and deep, I wondered if I'd been wrapped in thick velvet.

"Holy shit," Cooper said in a trembling whisper. "Holy shit."

I blinked and the world returned.

Cooper was gripping me by my upper arms, gazing down at me, his eyes filled with a light, a power, an otherness I'd never seen in him. It was alien and strange to see him as not quite the man I knew. But then his lips curved in a very Cooper smile. "Well, that is a hell of a thing."

"Are you okay?" I asked.

He nodded and stepped back until his arms were at full length. He gently released his hold on me.

"I'm good," he said. "Really, really good. Delaney, it's…" He shook his head, all out of words.

Heimdall's power surrounded him in a low, happy chord. It was where it belonged. In safe hands.

"Good," I said. "Maybe we can all get some rest."

"Not yet," Raven said. "I still have some vacationing to do." He stepped forward and clapped Cooper on the shoulder, then shoved the other man out of the way. "Help me stash my power in the furnace, chief?"

"I don't think it works that way."

"Maybe not with the other gods." He grinned. "But, hello? Trickster?"

I glanced at Myra and Jean. They both shrugged. "All right," I said. "Let's see if you're right about that."

Turned out he was.

By Tuesday, the tourists had left. The residents of Ordinary seemed to release a collective exhale. The Rhubarb Rally lights, whistles, and bells were officially packed away and recorded in the history books.

I'd even seen Death, in his pressed slacks, shiny shoes, and bright Hawaiian shirt, standing on the edge of the glittering blue ocean, a bright yellow kite in his hand.

If I were the kind of woman who prayed, I'd pray I'd never have to carry another god power again. It had changed me, left marks somewhere deep inside me, lingering behind my thoughts, my sanity, like scars pulled too tight. I hadn't told my sisters about that yet. They were worrying enough about me. But the marks the power had left behind scared me if I thought about it too much. I didn't even know what kind of damage it might have done, didn't know if it would heal.

I felt ten years older. I ached everywhere.

Reeds had acted as bridges for god powers for centuries. I hoped this was just a part of the job, and the wounds left from the power would heal as quickly as my physical injuries so I could get back to my real job.

Myra was at her desk finishing with the deck hand's statement. He had corroborated Dan's story. Walt had indeed been drunk when Margot approached him. She'd offered him a lot of money to take her to Heim's boat and show her around. He was fuzzy about if she'd stayed on the boat or not. When he woke the next morning and heard Heim had been killed, he'd bolted.

He had a couple misdemeanor priors he was hoping wouldn't catch up to him.

Dan was still on the hook for waving a deadly weapon at a police officer. I figured the local judge would remove all firearms and explosives from his home, give him a few months of jail time, then move him on to community service.

I was hoping the community service might actually go some distance in changing his petulant attitude. If not that, maybe cooling his heels for a while in jail would.

Lila had come in to see her sister before Margot had been transferred down to the Lincoln County jail. They'd cried while hugging each other.

It didn't matter how long I was a cop—it was still hard to see people screw up their lives. But Margot had killed Heim, and I couldn't find any forgiveness for that, even if she'd done it out of a twisted sense of love for her sister.

With her confession, Margot would remain in jail until her trial. After that, it would be up to a jury and judge to decide her fate. I suspected her lawyer would angle for an insanity plea.

Cooper had left town again. But this time he'd left with a big ol' grin on his face and a cheeky promise that he'd be back when he needed a rest.

He'd finally found his horizon to chase. And Ordinary would always be a home when he needed one. It was still weird that Crow's power had transferred back to the kiln. I guessed every rule had an exception.

And Ryder...I tried not to think about Ryder.

I thought about him constantly.

The door to the office opened and Jean sauntered in with a gust of cool air. "Guess who got her box filled with free hot donuts this morning?"

"Please tell me that's not a euphemism," Myra drawled.

Jean snorted and placed a pastry box down on the coffee station. "Maybe."

"Why are you here?" I asked.

"I switched shifts with Roy for the week. Why are you here? Aren't you still shot?"

"I'm healing. Might as well be sitting here doing paperwork instead of sitting at home being bored."

She worked the lid off the box, her eyes dancing at the contents. "You're setting a ridiculous standard that I hope you know I refuse to follow. If I get shot, I'm gone for a month, at least. Huckleberry twist?"

"Yes, please."

She brought me the donut and took a bite out of a maple bar.

I took the knot of glazed huckleberry pastry. It was still warm. "You aren't kidding. These are fresh."

She grinned with her mouth full and held up one finger. She picked up my coffee cup and took a gulp, washing the donut down.

"Hey," I said. "Sick person. Germs."

"I'm not going to catch a bullet wound. I've been thinking about Ryder."

My stomach flipped but I took a big bite so I couldn't talk.

"About how he broke up with you in the hospital," she added.

I had too much donut in my mouth to say anything, so I just glared at her.

Myra was still frowning, a piece of paper in one hand, her pen rocking between the fingers of her other hand.

"Did he say why?" Jean asked.

I stole back my coffee cup and drank. The donut had gone dry in my mouth and my appetite was gone. I didn't want to talk about this with my sisters. I didn't want to think about Ryder ever again.

Liar.

"Except that my sisters are suspicious and nosey?"

"He's different," Myra said.

"What?"

"Ever since he came back to town a year ago. It didn't really hit me for a couple months, but there's something different about him."

"He's eight years older?" I suggested.

Why are we talking about Ryder?

She shook her head. "Have you ever asked him about his college training?"

"Some. He got a degree in business and architecture. Why?"

Can we stop talking about Ryder?

"It's hard to put my finger on it, but if you hadn't told me what he majored in, I'd guess he'd gone into the military."

I just sat there staring at her as the chill clenched my chest and stomach. She had just nailed the thing that had been niggling the back of my mind. How he'd come into the station when Margot was holding me at gunpoint. How he'd been calm, demanding, in control.

That wasn't a small-town boy who had spent his autumns elk hunting. That was a man who knew how to handle firearms and people in life-threatening situations.

Jean hung up the phone. I hadn't even heard it ring. "Mrs. Yates' penguin is strapped to a surfboard tied to the jetty. And the tide is rolling in."

I pressed my finger to my nose.

Jean did too, and Myra, who was seconds too late, swore. "Fine. I'll go rescue the penguin while you two stay inside where it's warm and eat donuts."

"You told me to get some rest," I said.

She stood and swung her coat on. "I told you to go home."

"Well, maybe I will."

I didn't want to stay here and talk about Ryder any more, and I was pretty sure that was all Jean would want to do.

"What about me?" Jean asked.

"You get to stay and cover Roy's shift just like you wanted to," I said.

"Fine. But the donuts stay."

CHAPTER 33

MY HOUSE was north of the station. I drove that way through the neighborhoods instead of the main street, weaving between yards peppered with tiny bungalows, rough-hewn cabins, and shiny new condominiums.

It would be easy to go home. It would be easy to rest, to take a few days off.

I had certainly earned it.

But I soon found myself driving out of town, north, just north, the road twisting against hills and fields, the ocean rolling deep and endless to my left. Towns even smaller than Ordinary huddled along the edges of the road, frequent and then fewer as more and more road stretched between them.

I found solace in the road, in the drive, the sound of the engine, the light and shadow of sunlight through trees soothing all my raw edges, inside and out. I tried not to think of Ryder.

All I thought about was Ryder.

Soon buildings were replaced by signs that pointed to rivers, trailheads, and campgrounds.

When the sign to Netarts came into view, I turned left toward the tiny community pressed up against the bay.

Curly's was a chocolate-colored cedar shake one-story beach house with frothy white trim that perched at the highest end of a wide parking lot ending on a narrow beach and a couple boat ramps. The ice cream store had expanded by adding a barbecue smoker on the side porch, and the painted wooden sign declared desserts, espressos, and sandwiches were now served.

I smiled and got out of the Jeep. It was almost noon, and the day looked like it was going to warm up nicely.

Perfect day for ice cream.

I walked up the wooden stairs and across the covered porch. I stepped into the shop and the cheerful server, a young woman who didn't know me, my job, my town, or my crazy life, guided me over to a table by the window.

I took the chair that put my back to the door and let me stare out over the bay and the ocean and blue sky beyond.

I ordered ice cream first because life is unpredictable. After that, I settled in for a sandwich. Since the shop wasn't too busy, I ordered a coffee and let time drift as I stared out at the sand and sky and ocean and didn't think about Ryder.

Much.

"Mind if I join you?"

I hadn't expected anyone to find me here. My heart tumbled hard against my ribs, pumping out a flood of feelings too tangled to name.

"Ryder," I said, my voice almost a whisper. "I don't think I can do this here."

"Do what?" he asked quietly. "Have dessert with me?"

I looked up at him. He wore a soft T-shirt and worn jeans, his work boots traded in for a pair of running shoes. His dark hair was mussed from the wind, hazel eyes almost gold in this light. He stood with his weight on one foot, as if uncertain that I would tell him to stay or to go.

He held a caramel sundae in one hand, his other hand tucked in his back pocket, leaving his elbow out at an awkward angle. He used to stand that way in high school when he had to read in front of the class.

"Did you follow me?"

"No. I just thought…" He glanced out the window, and something like sadness passed over his features. "I just thought you might be here. You told me you missed it. Missed this. I saw you leave town. So maybe. Maybe yes, I followed you. I almost didn't, but then… Maybe I should go."

Yes.

No.

"You're here," I said. "Sit down before your ice cream melts."

He took the chair across from me, the blue sky and sand framing him as he stole their beauty.

I was still angry. But I'd known him all my life. It wasn't like we hadn't argued before. Gotten into fights. We both knew how to apologize, how to keep our friendship a friendship.

I wasn't sure if that was what we had anymore, if we even had anything to keep.

"So Myra fired you," I said over the top of my coffee as I held the cup to my lips. I didn't drink, but I needed the illusion of a barrier between us.

He dug his spoon into the ice cream, mashing and mixing it beneath the caramel, gaze fixed on it, but not eating. "We knew this was a temporary thing."

I wondered if he meant the job or us.

I took a sip of my coffee. It was cold. I set the cup down and we both stared carefully at the table between us.

"You said Old Rossi was right." Ryder stuck his spoon in the melting mess of sundae and picked up the paper napkin, wiping his fingers on it. His gaze lifted to catch mine. "Right about what?"

"I don't think that matters now."

Gold. His eyes were pools of mossy gold ringed by deep green. I'd been looking into those eyes for so many years. Looking for the man I thought I could love.

"Please, Delaney."

Myra said he had come home a different man than when he had left. But this man in front of me was the man I'd always known. My once-friend. My always-and-never love, Ryder Bailey.

"He wasn't happy we hired you. Thought you would be trouble."

"He said that?"

"Yes."

"I wasn't trouble."

I raised my eyebrows. He winced and looked down.

"I wasn't trouble at *work*," he clarified. "I was good at the job. Would still work there if you need—if the department needs more hands."

"I'll keep it in mind. But for now I need some space, Ryder. It's been a shitty week."

"Not all of it." His eyes on mine again. Soft. Warm with the kindness I knew, and aching with something I'd only glimpsed.

Desire.

He couldn't still want me. Not after he broke up with me. Did he only want the things he couldn't have?

Nope. I would not play that game. I was taking my heart and going home.

"It's getting late," I said.

He reached across the table, his calloused fingertips brushing the back of my hand. "Old Rossi isn't what he seems to be."

That stopped me cold. Did he know that Old Rossi was a vampire? A very old and powerful one. Or did he know the secrets of Ordinary? Was that why Old Rossi thought Ryder would be trouble?

"What do you mean?"

Ryder bit his bottom lip, looking angry at himself for having said that much.

"He's…involved in some business. I don't know the details. Nothing I can prove. But I've heard enough to know he isn't what he seems to be, Delaney. He has the attention of some people who do not appreciate his way of doing things. Stay away from him. I don't want you—anyone getting hurt."

Okay. So both the vampire and the architect thought the other was dangerous. Which one was right?

"You're doing business with Old Rossi?" I asked.

His jaw locked. "No."

"I am a police officer. You can tell me what you think is going on, and I might be able to help."

"No. It's… No." He swore under his breath and looked over his shoulder out the window, away from me.

"What are you afraid of, Ryder Bailey?"

He dragged his palm over his face, then back over his hair. When he met my gaze, he seemed in control, gave me an easy smile that did not reach his eyes.

"You were shot, Delaney." His gaze searched mine, seeking understanding there.

I waited. He didn't say anything else.

"I know," I finally said. "I was there when it happened. Lots of crappy things happened that day."

That, apparently, wasn't the response he wanted. He shook his head and glanced back out the window, frowning, then returned to me with a sigh.

"I could have handled that better," he admitted. He wasn't apologizing, nor was he asking for forgiveness. This was just a statement of facts.

It was always our first step in trying to rebuild our friendship. Facts.

"I'm angry," I said.

That was a fact too. But what I didn't tell him, what I would never tell him, was how much he had hurt me and how hard it would be for me to trust him again.

"Is that why you followed me here today?" I asked.

"I just…I need you to know Old Rossi might not have your best interests in mind," he said.

"And you do?"

I clamped my mouth shut. I hadn't meant to ask that. Hadn't meant to let the hurt out where he could see it.

My heart was pounding.

Don't answer that, don't answer that.

His voice was low, intimate. "I always have."

Then don't leave me.

"I need to go," I said in a rush, all the air in my lungs used up, all the space in my chest pounding, pounding.

All I had wanted was ice cream. How had this gotten so complicated?

I stood and pulled my wallet out of my purse.

Ryder stood too, reaching for my hand. "Wait, let me—"

"No, that's fine, I got—"

Our hands collided, and I dropped a few bills on the table.

"Sorry." He quickly scooped up the bills. "Let me pay…"

Lying on top of a twenty-dollar bill was Spud, the little origami dog Ryder had folded and left beside my pillow. He held it in his palm for a long moment, staring at it.

"Oh," he said, the word holding far too many emotions. "Delaney, I—"

Not now. Not here. No.

I plucked the little dog out of his hand. His eyes followed it, watched as I carefully tucked Spud back inside my wallet, but in a safer place behind my driver's license.

He opened his mouth, shut it, words lost to what seemed like regret.

Join the club.

I leaned forward and kissed him. It was fleeting, just a brush of my lips against his. I felt the surprise in his inhalation, the tightening of his body, his mouth opening on the shared breath that stuttered between us before I pulled away.

"Goodbye, Ryder."

His hand, just his fingertips, stretched as if to reach me, as if to hold on to a quickly fading ghost.

But I kept moving, turning, walking. Until sunlight surrounded me and the breeze dried tears I refused to let fall.

I got in the Jeep and started the engine.

"You can do this, Delaney," I told myself. "You can move forward without him."

Liar, my heart whispered.

"He is sorry, you know."

I jerked at the voice. Herri—or rather, the goddess Hera—sat in the passenger side of my Jeep. She still looked much like her mortal self. But instead of wearing a tank top and jeans, she wore a beautiful flowing gown that seemed to catch whole galaxies in the folds, like peacock feathers glittering.

"Who's sorry?"

"Ryder."

"Is that why you're here? To tell me he feels bad about breaking up with me while I was lying in a hospital bed? I wasn't the one who wanted to end this."

She smiled, and it was filled with both sorrow and warmth. "And now what is it that you want?"

I rubbed at my forehead, trying to corral ragged thoughts. "He's made it clear where he stands. I just need some time to get over it."

"The heart never abandons its desire."

Really not helpful, since my heart's desire doesn't desire me back.

She gently placed her hand on my hand. I could feel the warmth of her skin, but also a sort of electric vibration, her power poised and vibrant beneath her touch.

"There is more to Ryder than you know, Delaney." Her bronze gaze burned and held me captive. Even with the Reed immunity, I felt pinned beneath the presence of her power.

I wanted to ask her what she knew. Wanted to ask her why Ryder had left me before we'd had a chance to find each other.

Wanted to ask her if maybe there was still something there, in his heart that echoed my need for him. But I could not speak.

"There is more to the push and pull of power amongst the hungry. Ordinary will play its role in the days to come. You will play your role. I do not wish to see you or your family falter."

"Falter?"

"There is a war coming. Rising on the winds, lapping at the shores of Ordinary."

"War?" Everything inside me went tight with panic, my broken heart momentarily set aside. War was way above my pay grade. I was trained to transfer god powers and keep the peace. I wasn't trained to fight any kind of battle.

"What am I supposed to do about it?"

"Choose your allies carefully," she said, as she released my hand, her eyes still holding me in place. "And fight."

Then she was gone, leaving the faint scent of pomegranate perfume behind.

My heart was pounding too fast, the echo of her touch on my hand tingled with heat. There was no doubting that she had been here, in my car, warning me.

War.

"Great. As if the last week wasn't crazy enough." I lowered my head onto the steering wheel and just sat there for a minute, the warm afternoon sunlight pooling heat on my shoulders.

It reminded me of my dad's wide, warm palm, comforting, steady.

I could do this. No, *we* could do this. My carefully chosen allies and I. All I had to do was figure out who those allies might be.

I took a deep breath, let it out slowly, and straightened. "I got this. Whatever is coming toward Ordinary, will have to get through me first."

And then I put the car in gear and followed the road home to face the storm.

READY FOR MORE ORDINARY MAGIC?

POLICE CHIEF Delaney Reed loves the busy days of summer, even though the small town of Ordinary Oregon is overrun with mortal, and not-quite-so mortal tourists. Staying busy keeps her mind off Ryder Bailey, the man she is desperately trying to fall out of love with.

But when a god power goes missing, and the creatures in town gear up for war, she finds herself forced into a difficult decision: trust the devil with a dark past, or trust the man with an even darker future that might kill them all.

DEVILS AND DETAILS:
ORDINARY MAGIC - BOOK TWO

Coming July 2016

ACKNOWLEDGMENT

I FIRST stumbled upon the idea of Ordinary, Oregon in a short story I never published. As often happens with my short stories, this world grew bigger than I could easily squeeze into a few words. So I finally sat down and gave Delaney, Ryder, Myra, Jean, Than, Crow and the rest of the town a novel.

Is there a real Ordinary, Oregon? Well, yes and no. Ordinary Oregon is sort of a happy mishmash of Lincoln City, Depot Bay, and Newport, Oregon. When I needed a place for vacationing gods and unusual creatures, my mind instantly went back to my childhood visits to Lincoln City, Oregon. I'd always expected magic to be hidden in the sandy nooks and crannies of that sleepy little beach town.

There is, however, a real city of Boring, Oregon. I think if Ordinary were real, Boring and Ordinary might have quite the friendly little rivalry.

I want to thank my beta readers, Dejsha Knight, for listening to my wild ideas and being willing to read all of the really rough drafts and Dean Woods, who stuck with me and always had great and patient advice. Thank you to Sharon Thompson, who not only has heard about this story for years, but also agreed to read the book when it was still full of errors. Crazy and brave, all of you.

Thank you, Deanne Hicks, for telling me to stop messing around and bake the cakes, Eileen Hicks, for loaning me her sharp eyes, and Arran at 720 Editing for a quick and thorough read through. That beautiful cover is all Lou Harper who didn't give up on the project when we were trying to nail down the tone. Thank you Lou for being awesome!

Thanks to the Deadline Dames for being supportive and amazing—your friendship means the world to me. Thanks and love to my biggest fan, husband Russ Monk who is shamelessly proud of this writing thing I do. I'm shamelessly proud of you too. Thanks and love to my sons, Kameron and Konner for that ridiculous weekend where you tried to name my characters by combining street signs we drove past, for helping me pick decent titles, and for so much more. You Monk men are the very best part of my life.

But the biggest thank you goes to you, dear reader. I am so happy that you gave this story a whirl. I hope you enjoyed the people and world of Ordinary, Oregon and that you'll come back soon to see the not-so-ordinary surprises Ordinary has in store for us all.

ABOUT THE AUTHOR

DEVON MONK is a national best selling writer of urban fantasy. Her series include Ordinary Magic, House Immortal, Allie Beckstrom, Broken Magic, and Shame and Terric. She also writes the Age of Steam steampunk series, and the occasional short story which can be found in her collection: A Cup of Normal, and in various anthologies. She has one husband, two sons, and lives in Oregon. When not writing, Devon is either drinking too much coffee or knitting silly things.

Want to read more from Devon?
Follow her online or sign up for her newsletter at:
http://www.devonmonk.com.

CPSIA information can be obtained
at www.ICGtesting.com
Printed in the USA
FSOW01n1553190916
25184FS